Becoming Finnigan

Karen and Tony Muldoon

High Tide Publications
Hardyville, Virginia

High Tide Publications
Post Office Box 183
Hardyville, Virginia 23070
www.HighTidePublications.com

Publisher's Note: This is a work of fiction. Names, characters, places, and incidents are a product of the author's imagination. Locales and public names are sometimes used for atmospheric purposes. Any resemblance to actual people, living or dead, or to businesses, companies, events, institutions, or locales is completely coincidental.

Cover Design: Matthew Archambault and Carl Johansen

Ordering Information:
Quantity sales. Special discounts are available on quantity purchases by corporations, associations, and others. For details, contact the "Special Sales Department" at the address above.

Book Title/ Author Name. -- 1st ed.

ISBN 978-0-9884637-9-0

Published in the United States of America

Dedicated to our mothers

two very special women

Marion DeFeo

and

Ruth Muldoon

CHAPTER ONE

SPRING 1998

I never wanted to be mediocre. But with a name like Althea Burnside, I suppose it was to be expected.

A nurse named Althea was especially kind to my mother during the last hours of a long and excruciating labor. Mom was so grateful that she named me after her. Just my luck! If the nurse had been named something exotic, like Francesca or Ariel, my whole life might have been different.

Francesca would have been seductive, mysterious; Ariel, lighthearted and ethereal. Althea is just a somber lump.

And none of my nicknames was any better.

Pumpkin, when I was a baby. Because I was born in the middle of October — round and orange. Yuk!

Butch when I went to school. Because I was a tomboy. If I'd wanted to be a sportswriter, I guess I could have kept that name. Butch Burnside does have a ring to it.

Holly was the one that stuck. The guy who sat behind me when I worked at the *Cherry Hill Record* said I reminded him of Holly Golightly from *Breakfast at Tiffanys*. I don't look a bit like Audrey Hepburn; so it must have been my kooky personality. Kooky, I can live with, but most people my age don't get the connection. They think of Holly as a tree or a Christmas decoration. Some people still call me Holly — especially in my lighthearted moments. But to most people, I'm Althea.

I don't know why I'm rambling about that. Maybe it's just because I'm in such a funk. I spent the last three years of my life slaving over a novel based on the life of Dolley Madison. A President's wife who had an ice cream named after her. It had to happen sooner or later.

Anyway, Dolley's uncle ran the Indian King Tavern in Haddonfield, New Jersey, where I grew up and still live; so I thought I'd take what's known about her and weave a racy tale. Three years, every spare minute. Research about the period. Long nights massaging the keys on my laptop when I should have been out looking for Mr. Right.

I finally finished *Queen of the Indian King* Friday night, celebrated with a split of champagne and slept till noon on Saturday.

This morning, a glorious May Sunday, I walked up King's Highway to our local Starbucks and snuggled into one of their lurid purple, overstuffed easy chairs with a latte, a croissant, and the *New York Times Book Review*, where I hoped to see my picture and my book someday.

The *Times Book Review* isn't very big, maybe twenty pages on an average Sunday… but this time it hit me right in the head — like a club. Right there, headlined on the front page, was *The Belle of Haddonfield*, a fact-based novel about Dolley Madison by some guy named Joel Finnigan.

It got a rave review. They loved it. God damn their evil souls!

I wanted to scream, but I didn't dare. Our Starbucks is right on the corner of Kings Highway and Haddon Avenue, the crossroads of the known world. A real honest to God, paper tearing, chair throwing, screaming conniption would be certain to draw a crowd.

"You'll never have a latte in this town again, young lady," I imagined them snarling.

Besides, Haddonfield isn't zoned for conniptions… hell, a girl can't even enjoy a good scream here.

Three fucking years! Do you believe it?

I left my paper and the latte. The croissant I stuffed in my mouth. After all, at a time like this a girl needs comfort food. Then I stalked out. I do really great stalking.

The sun was still high, but the day seemed darker and colder on the walk back home.

So, what now? How could this happen? Dolley was a part of me. I'd researched her endlessly. When I wrote her story, I knew she was speaking through me. And now this Finnigan character — whoever he is — had beaten me. He'd pulverized my soul, and I'd never even heard of him until what was becoming, for me, Black Sunday.

So what are you going to do now, Althea?

Buy the damn book. See what Finnigan did with my story. *My* story. Was it really my story to begin with? What about all those long, philosophical talks in my writers group about the nature of art, of tapping into the universal soul where the story already exists, about simply being the vehicle through which the tale is told? I'd bought into all that. I really believed it. So why was the universe playing such a cruel joke on me? Why couldn't Finnigan's book have come out three years ago, before I'd invested so much of my life in *Queen of the Indian King*?

Or even better, why couldn't he still have a year's work to go on it? My book would be on the bestseller list before he even shipped his off to the copyright office.

On the walk home, down Kings Highway, past the damn Indian King Tavern, I decided I couldn't bear to read his book yet. So, I loaded up on old classics from Netflix: *Sleepless in Seattle*, *Bridget Jones's Diary*, and of course, *Breakfast at Tiffanys*.

For two days I watched old movies and ate junk food. I gained five pounds in the process. Damn Finnigan! Not only had he ruined my writing career, he was making me fat, too.

Finally, on Tuesday morning, I said, "Enough. Stop wallowing, Althea. It doesn't become you."

I turned on the radio. Vivaldi's "Spring" was playing on WRTI. Spring signifies renewal. It was a good omen. So, how should I use this omen? I wasn't sure I had the energy to start something new. Besides, Finnigan's book still haunted me. I really should buy it. Then I'll be able to see that it's crap — which it probably is — and I'll feel better about what I wrote.

But, what if it really is wonderful? The *Times* wouldn't have raved about it if it wasn't.

Maybe I'll learn something.

I threw on a pair of jeans and an old sweatshirt and marched up King's Highway to our local book store, Cabbages and Kings, where I forked over $23.99 plus tax for *The Belle of Haddonfield*.

When I got home, I took a deep breath and poured myself a glass of cabernet to bolster my courage.

Then, I filled the tub with hot water and a relaxing aroma-therapy bubble bath. I stripped naked, eased myself into the fragrant water, and allowed the scents to work their magic. When I felt sufficiently composed, I took a sip of wine and turned to the back jacket flap to get a look at my competition. Joel Finnigan's face stared back at me and I nearly dropped the book into the bath water.

CHAPTER TWO

MIRACLE CHILD

T hings were finally going right for Joel Finnigan.

For years, he'd felt like Joe Btfsplk, the guy in the Li'l Abner comic strip who walks around with a cloud over his head. Life had not been kind to Finnigan. Yet no matter what came his way, he always picked himself up and faced the future with the hope that next time, things would be different.

Connie, his ex-wife, once told him that if there were a nuclear war, he'd look at the mushroom cloud and say, "Oh, what beautiful colors."

Finnigan was more than a glass-half-full kind of guy. He saw the empty glass just waiting for even more good wine. If you had to use one word to describe Joel Finnigan, it would be 'irrepressible'. He had been through World War II, the nasty politics of academe, and one or two other sorrows buried so deeply even he couldn't find them anymore. But he took satisfaction from regarding himself as a tough old buzzard who could still make a difference.

The Belle of Haddonfield was proving a success; though nowhere near the scale of Stephen King or Mary Higgins Clark, but his was not a horror story or a mystery. And, as historical novels go, *Belle* was right out in front. It was well regarded, and bringing in enough to make Finnigan's life a little more comfortable — or at least less uncomfortable.

"If these are what they call my declining years, it ain't such a bad decline," he muttered as he rolled out of bed, looking forward to another fine Sunday in Philadelphia.

He was the only one in the bed, and had been for many years. There was a sadness to that, but Joel had had his moments and at seventy-four there wasn't much he could do about it now anyway. He was generally satisfied with what was turning into a long life.

Finnigan's optimistic view of life was formed almost from the moment of his conception. He was a very well-loved baby who came to Mick and Ruth Finnigan late in life. They'd wanted a child desperately. Finally, just before Ruth's fortieth birthday, Finnigan was born. He was their miracle child, and they doted on him. Everything Finnigan did was a source of wonder to them. No other child was as precocious or as cute or as funny. Mick and Ruth took him everywhere they went. If little Joel wasn't welcome, they left. If friends didn't want a baby at their adult dinner party, the Finnigans stayed home.

Mick and Ruth made sure he knew the world was a joyous place — safe and awe-inspiring and full of love.

Then it all, literally, came crashing down.

When Finnigan was four, Mick and Ruth were killed in a freak accident. It was seared into his memory.

He didn't think much of it when he saw his father climbing a ladder to fix some shingles on a warm summer Saturday, or maybe it was a gutter on the roof of their rambling house in Ambler, Pennsylvania. Ruth was holding the ladder to steady it while Mick climbed laboriously up to the roof.

Suddenly, he heard Ruth cry out:

"No, Dan, no!"

Dan, the big black Lab that lived next door, had vaulted over the hedge between the Finnigan and the Stokowski yards and dashed toward Ruth, hell bent on leaping up and giving her an affectionate big, slobbery face lick. He was close to seventy-five pounds, and he knocked Ruth off balance. Down she went, gripping the ladder in panic.

"Ruth, what the hell!" Joel remembered Mick shouting as the ladder went out from under him.

Those were the last words Joel heard from either of his parents. All 200 pounds of Mick came crashing down on Ruth, and that was the end of them both.

Joel Finnigan had become an orphan.

Mick's sister Kate took Finnigan home with her to their big old farmhouse in Delaware County, just about a mile from the west bank of the Delaware River.

Kate and her husband, Tim O'Brian, had six kids of their own, but Tim made a good living and had done quite well for himself in the stock market. Besides, their only nephew had no other relatives. So it was the O'Brian farm or an orphanage.

Life went well enough the first few months. Then came the crash of '29 and Tim O'Brian lost everything.

At first, the Great Depression was something that seemed to be happening far outside Joel's well ordered life. Sure, the O'Brian tribe had moved into a smaller, somewhat shabbier house in Essington. Dinners were a little less sumptuous than before and Tim came home from work — when he could find work — in tattered blue overalls and muddy work boots instead of a crisp suit and tie, but things didn't seem too bad to Joel until one grim night when he lay in bed, listening to Tim and Kate arguing.

Their voices were all too loud and clear through the cheap, thin walls.

"There's no more money left, Kate! We can't afford to keep him; not when we have to feed our own six as well."

"What's to be done with the boy then?" Joel's aunt responded.

"How the hell do I know? The Diocese runs an orphanage… and there's the State Home for Boys."

"St. Michael's Orphanage! The State Home; over my dead body, Timothy O'Brian! Mick's only son is not going to one of those… those Goddamned… warehouses!"

Aunt Kate's taking God's name in vain was even more of a shock to the shivering, frightened Joel than the prospect of being shipped off to an orphanage. He already knew of at least three kids who had been shipped off to Saint Mike's or the gruesomely named State Home, never to be heard from again.

What became of them? Were they chained to a wall in some sort of dungeon, or worked to death in a factory or deep in a coal mine? He didn't know, but the very thought was enough for him to soak his pillow with tears of sheer terror.

But Aunt Kate's fierce determination, or maybe Uncle Tim's better angel, prevailed and Joel Finnigan stayed right there in Essington and soon came to agree with President Roosevelt: the only thing he had to fear was fear itself.

Finnigan's parents had loved him dearly, as did his Aunt Kate. She was the only champion he needed.

And if they were poor now, surely things would improve in the future. He was his mother's miracle child. Fate must have something good in store for him.

Then he met Susanna Winslow.

CHAPTER THREE

GOOD-BYE DOLLEY

I don't believe it. I don't fucking believe it. Finnigan's an old man for crying out loud. He must be seventy at least — maybe even eighty.

If he was so intent on writing about Dolley, why didn't he do it years ago? And it's his first novel. He's a history professor — a retired history professor who wrote books about war and politics.

So here I am struggling to make my mark as a writer, and this old fart retires, tries his hand at a novel, and screws me out of my big chance. What makes it even worse is the *Times* was right. It is good. No. It's not just good. It's brilliant. I hate him.

I thought maybe I'd still have a chance to do something with *Queen of the Indian King*, but after reading *The Belle of Haddonfield*, I just can't. In fact, it makes me wonder whether I'm really a writer after all. Maybe I should go sell shoes or learn to bake bread. At least that would be something useful, not to mention profitable.

Get a grip Althea; if you weren't really a writer, you wouldn't be so driven. There must be a lesson in all of this.

That's how I manage to get through times like these. I tell myself there has to be a lesson in it. But I sure as hell can't see what it is this time. Suppose I start another project and somebody else has the same idea? I guess the only way to protect myself is to write about my own life. But I'm not even thirty, and I haven't really had a very exciting life.

I suppose I could invent something. After all, that is what writers do. I must have used up a boatload of whole cloth on *Queen of the Indian King*, but we already know where that got me.

I could make it a BOATS — Based On A True Story. BOATS are hot right now.

The dramatic opening chords of Beethoven's Fifth disrupted my orgy of self pity.

Why had I chosen such a triumphant ring tone?

"Hi, Mom."

"I was worried about you, Althea. You seemed so down the last time we talked."

"I'm okay," I told her. "I just need a new writing project to get my mind off the Dolley Madison fiasco."

"Do you have anything in mind?"

"I was thinking about your life in the commune. You could tell me what it was like, and I could write a memoir of a hippie childhood. It would be a good story about mid-20th century life — in California anyway. I mean, hell, the 19th century didn't do much for me."

"Where would you start?"

"At the beginning, I guess. 1968 was a significant year. Jules Witcover even wrote a book about it: *The Year the Dream Died*."

"Jules Witcover?"

"The *Baltimore Sun* columnist."

"Right," Mom said. "And 1968 was the year Martin Luther King and Bobby Kennedy were assassinated. There were riots and protests."

"Doesn't it seem perversely appropriate?" I asked. "1968: The Dream Dies and Althea Burnside is born. It would be a great scene setter. Then we could talk about you being a nude dancer…"

"Althea! Don't you dare!"

"But it's just a novel."

"Althea! We do live in Haddonfield, you know."

"Okay, Mom. Okay.

"Other than that, I'll help you any way I can. Your father…"

"Mom, I… let's talk about it later. Someone's on the other line. I've got to go."

"Okay, honey. Whenever you want. Love you."

"Love you too."

I didn't like putting Mom off so brusquely, but I just couldn't bear hearing about my dad — that flaky, self-indulgent artist who didn't care enough about me to try to stop Mom when she packed me and our few meager belongings in her clapped out old VW and started heading back East.

The reporter in me wants to know all about it, but if he could forget I ever existed, why should I want to know about him?

Sid Burnside has been the only father I've ever known.

True, he's the dullest man in the universe. He'd be the first to admit it. But as I grow older, I've come to realize what a rock he is. You can always depend on him. He and Mom have a great relationship. I guess one part of me wanted — wants — the steady kind of love they have. But the other part has always been hell-bent on getting love from a man like the one who abandoned me before he had a chance to know me. Dear Old Dad.

How else can I explain dropping out of school at the age of twenty to marry that jerk Tommy Corcoran? It was the old story about the starry-eyed girl and the bad-boy jock who can't keep their hands off each other. Then they get married and he turns into somebody she never guessed was hiding behind that sexy veneer. Or maybe she knew it all along and just didn't want to see it.

At least I was smart enough to get out of it without a kid. Someday, but not with that buttwad. It didn't last a year.

The more I thought, the more depressed I became. I had to get out of the house. I walked aimlessly down Kings Highway, but my dark cloud followed me. I started thinking about fathers again.

After my break-up, Sid talked me into going back to Temple to get my degree. I think he hoped that I'd follow in his footsteps and go to law school and maybe, eventually, into the firm. But finding things out and writing stories must have worked their way into my blood somewhere along the line, and I found myself drawn to the cold, hard bosom of journalism. I went to work at the *Cherry Hill Record* the same summer I graduated from Temple. I was not quite twenty-three, and I had visions of moving on to the *New York Times* or the *Washington Post* in a year or two. But three years went by in the proverbial flash and I still wasn't a superstar.

I've had my moments. But who hasn't? So what if I broke the story about Councilman Rancini taking kickbacks and won a bunch of awards for it. Who cares? Well, I guess I do. I was rather proud of that story, and the one I did on the homeless people in Camden, and the one on property confiscated in drug arrests. Actually, Harry Rutledge and I collaborated on that one. I didn't want to work with him at first. Not after the welfare story that jerk Tim Morrissey and I did together. Some collaboration, I worked and he paraded around like a prima donna and got half the credit. But Harry and I came up with the same idea at the same time; so I had no choice. Besides, I had a bit of a crush on him. Too bad he's married. All of the good ones are taken, and there are rules about messing around with married men, damnit!

Working with Harry was the 180 degree opposite of that fiasco with Morrissey. Harry and I complemented each other. I'm good at organizing and interviewing and he was great at finding the details I missed and smoothing out the rough edges in my copy. We won the Best Interpretive Reporting Award from the New Jersey Press Association for that one.

I really was a pretty good reporter if I say so myself, but when I turned twenty-six, I knew I had to do something. I was in my mid-twenties and time was ticking away. The big three-oh would be here before I knew it.

Then Dolley Madison got her hooks into me, just as she had done to half the swains in Haddonfield, before moving up to the President of the United States (you go girl!).

I was reminded of her every time I passed the Indian King. I started out by reading everything I could find on her, and from there it was just a short step to filling one yellow legal pad after another. Her life would make a great historical novel. Soon Dolley and I couldn't let go of each other and the pages started flowing from the legal pads into the dark, digital depths of my computer.

It wasn't long before the *Record* started to become a nuisance. It was too hard to write newspaper copy all day and then shift into the novelist mode at night. But what choice did I have? I couldn't ask Sid to invest in my flying leap of faith. Finally, when the end was so close I could smell it, I calculated that I could make the little money I had saved up last for a few months while I gave Dolley my full attention and she led me to fame and fortune.

But how was I to know that Dolley was two-timing me with Joel Finnigan?

Would it have mattered if I did?

Probably not. A writer and a character can become very close. Losing Dolley Madison was like losing a lover.

I'm totally lost now. It feels as if somebody has turned off all the lights and I can't find the switch to turn them back on again.

Maybe I'd have been better off if I stayed at the *Record*. At least I'd be able to pay my rent on time.

Without even realizing how I got there, I found myself sipping a mocha latte at Starbucks — the same place I'd read about *The Belle of Haddonfield*. That didn't help my mood any. I sunk even deeper into the pit my life had become. Then I heard a familiar voice.

"Hey, Althea. Mind if I join you?"

If it had been anybody but Harry Rutledge, I'd either have told him to go to hell or politely said I was in the middle of plotting a sensitive scene for my novel and needed to be alone.

But Harry was different.

I looked up at the tall, handsome man who could have played the lead in a James Bond movie, stared directly into his sexy brown eyes, and pointed to the empty chair across from me.

"How's the book coming?" he inquired.

"Don't ask. I was just getting ready to send out pitch letters when I read a review of a similar novel."

"You mean *The Belle of Haddonfield*? I saw it in the *Times*. But I don't see why that should stop you. There can be more than one novel on the same subject. *Belle* is probably nothing like your book. You're a damned good writer, Althea. Look at all the awards you've won."

"I read *Belle*," I told him. "It was brilliant. I can't compete with that."

"Want me to take a look at your manuscript? We were always a pretty good team. Maybe I can help."

"Thanks, Harry," I said. "I'm just too depressed right now. How are things at the *Record*?"

"Same old, same old."

Harry checked his watch.

"Gotta go. Gotta interview the mayor."

"See ya," I said.

I felt myself smiling after he left. Harry could do that to me. Damn. If only he weren't taken.

Becoming Finnigan   19

CHAPTER FOUR

SUSANNA

If irrepressible was the only word to describe Joel Finnigan, then 'proper' would be the only word to describe Susanna Winslow.

She was the product of a good Catholic education and might have become a nun if it hadn't been for Justin Welch.

Justin lived next door. Her parents and his were the best of friends, and it was clear since they were toddlers that both the Winslows and the Welches hoped the kids would end up together one day.

Of course Justin teased Susanna, and made her cry. But that was when they were very little. As they grew, they plotted innocent mischief together. Later, they told each other their deepest secrets and became the best of friends.

Eventually, they fancied themselves in love and just before Justin shipped out to the Pacific to singlehandedly win World War II, he asked Susanna to marry him.

Of course, she said yes.

Justin thought they should seal the bargain in a nearby motel. After all, they loved each other and would be married as soon as he came back — that is, if he came back.

Susanna was sure going to that motel would send them both straight to hell.

Instead she sent Justin to war with the promise that their love would be all the sweeter because they had waited.

In reality, it was more than just the fear of hell that held Susanna back — although that, in itself, would have been quite enough.

The truth was, she wasn't all that anxious to go to bed with Justin. Oh, they had done their share of necking like most kids their age. It always left Justin panting and pleading for more, but, although Susanna enjoyed the kissing, she never felt the gnawing longing in the pit of her stomach that some of her girl-friends described. She loved Justin, but it just wasn't all that hard to remain a 'good girl.' She sometimes wondered if something was wrong with her.

All that would change in a heartbeat the day she met Joel Finnigan.

CHAPTER FIVE

LOVE AT FIRST SIGHT

A ll Joel wanted was to find a Christmas present for Aunt Kate. The last thing he needed now that he was almost on his way to World War II was to have his entire life turned upside down, but love, like so many other things, works in mysterious ways.

It had been a busy six months. He had graduated from high school in June of 1942, and the next month, he was off to Camp Toccoa, Georgia, to join the newly-formed 506th Parachute Infantry Regiment. They were training for a new kind of warfare, pouncing on the enemy before he even knew they were there. Joel — like everyone else in the 506th — took particular pride in creating a new style of soldiering: perfect uniforms, gleaming jump boots, blue paratrooper patch on the rakish overseas caps and, above all, the 'Silver Wings'. The 506th was swept up by the idea of leading the way for the whole damned Army.

After a hard summer of basic training, Finnigan and the rest of the 506th moved on to Jump School at Fort Benning, Georgia.

His Christmas present was a powerful slap on his left shoulder by Sergeant Thomas Begley, and the harshly simple command "Go!" which cracked like a rifle shot and sent him springing from the aluminum-framed doorway of a U.S. Army Air Corps C-47. It had all happened so fast. He'd watched the men in front of him step out of the plane and told himself he must have been crazy to join the 506th. But he wasn't about to back out now.

Joel's exit from the C-47 was perfect. Everyone was perfect on their first five or ten jumps. They followed the book to the letter and remembered every word that their Jump School instructors had bellowed into their ears. It was after those first perfect jumps that that they started feeling overconfident and got all busted up.

Joel kept his head back and his eyes fixed firmly on the horizon. This was definitely not the time to look down. A big step forward, assisted by a hard push with both arms against the door frame, took him clear of the noisy, echoing fuselage into the blast of air thrust back from the propeller.

Then automatically and, again, perfectly, he clamped his hands over the reserve parachute pack on his chest, brought his legs together, bent slightly at the waist and lowered his chin to his chest so the abrasive shroud lines would not peel the hair, and skin, from the back of his head as the parachute streamed from its back pack.

The strangest sensation of all, and one that Joel never tired of, came as his legs were swept upward by the prop wash and he watched the tail of the airplane passing overhead, above the soles of his glistening jump boots. It lasted only until the parachute filled with air, brought him up hard against the straps of his harness and began drifting down toward the earth.

Joel never, throughout the rest of his life, experienced anything quite like those few seconds between leaving the airplane and the opening of his parachute. During that time, he was completely subservient to the laws of gravity and aerodynamics. If it weren't for his thoughts, he might not even have been aware of his own existence.

"I think, therefore I am."

He recalled reading that somewhere and, floating down from the sky, he made up his mind to read it again, and pay it more attention. Perhaps old Descartes had it right.

Those first five jumps at Fort Benning had earned him the silver wings he now proudly wore, and the ten day furlough that would allow him to see Aunt Kate again after all these months.

Joel had no idea what to get for Aunt Kate as he walked into Lit Brothers at 8th and Market in Philadelphia, but he was sure that he could charm some salesgirl into pointing him in the right direction.

He decided to start at the ladies' jewelry counter.

Susanna Winslow stood behind the counter rearranging the display cases. She was a shade over 5' 6" with long, sandy hair that hung halfway down her back, a figure that could stop traffic and calm, steady blue eyes that he imagined could see right into his soul. Joel had never seen a girl like Susanna and well before that cold December afternoon was over, he knew he never would again.

"Can I help you, sir?" she said in a warm, level voice.

"Uhhh… yeah… yes. I'm going home for a late Christmas celebration, and I want to get something nice for my Aunt… Kate."

"She must be a special aunt."

"She is. She raised me since I was four… ever since my parents died."

Jesus, I'm tripping over my own tongue. She'll think I'm an idiot.

"I'm so sorry about your parents. Did you have anything special in mind for your aunt?"

The supreme confidence of the eighteen-year-old paratrooper drained right out of Joel Finnigan.

"Ahhh…. a bracelet… a necklace… I don't know."

"How old is your aunt?"

"Oh, God…. sixty, about… I guess."

Susanna reached into the glass display case and, without a moment's hesitation, reached for a cameo locket. Joel thought her hands, long, graceful and delicate, were as beautiful as the rest of her. She held the locket out for his inspection. His confidence hadn't even begun to recover but, having the presence of mind to recognize a definitive now or never moment, he cupped her left hand in his right and drew it closer… the better to see the locket, of course.

He was amazed at how easily and naturally Susanna's hand slipped into his. Ignoring the locket and looking up at her, he was pleased to see her eyes flutter with the barest hint of nervousness and her smile change from professional friendliness into something deeper.

He gave the locket a cursory glance, and then looked back at Susanna's face.

"That's the one," he said. "The lady on the front even looks a little bit like you… like Aunt Kate, I mean."

"She'll love it. That'll be seven fifty. Would you like me to wrap it?"

"Sure."

Susanna turned her back to ring up the sale and find a little box for the locket. Joel hoped that she wasn't too good at arithmetic and would be a little slow with the sales slip. That way he'd have a few more seconds to admire her long, slender legs, her perfectly molded hips and her sensuously contoured shoulders.

She took a piece of gift wrap, then hesitated.

"I have an idea," she said as she turned back to Joel.

"Why don't you go to one of those automatic photograph booths, have your picture taken and put it in the locket? Then you can bring it back and I'll wrap it, and you can give it to Aunt Kate that way."

"That's great," Joel exclaimed. He looked at his watch. It was nearly noon.

"Do you get a lunch break?"

"Yes." Susanna looked at her own watch. "Right about now, in fact."

"Good. You show me where there's a photo booth, and I'll take you to lunch… a thanks-for-the-help lunch."

"Sure," Susanna replied, without hesitation.

She turned toward a thickening lady of middle years who was at the cash register ringing up a diamond necklace sale.

"Do you mind if I take lunch now, Denise?"

"Sure, Suz," Denise said, with a smile that showed she knew that there would be more than just a sandwich on the menu.

"Don't rush it, either. It's slow today, and old Harper isn't in."

Joel tried not to make his smile too obvious. He may not have known just where this was headed, but he knew that Susanna Winslow was the girl of a lifetime and that he'd be a damned fool to let her go by.

*****

The sun on Market Street seemed to be shining a lot brighter than it had when Joel walked into Lits a half hour earlier. He and Susanna walked west on Market for about a block, until they came to a Horn and Hardardt automat practically in the shadow of Philadelphia's immense ornate City Hall. It was bright even in the shadow of that grotesque pile of masonry, and they each sensed that it was because the world had been turned upside down and that everything had changed in the simple process of picking out a locket for Aunt Kate.

"I always get a kick out of this place," Susanna said as they took their places in the line before the wall of tiny, chromium-framed compartments where the day's soups, salads, and sandwiches teased the customers from behind their glass doors.

"Everybody dashes over from City Hall and inhales their lunches in a single gulp so they can race back to something terribly, terribly important."

"There is a war on," Joel replied. It wasn't the most original response, he knew, but everyone had been using it as the universal answer for everything since December 7, and it leapt readily to minds that were focused on other things.

"Yes, there is a war on," Susanna said, sadly, as she fished a corned beef on rye from its chrome-lined hole in the wall.

"I like these the best," she said.

Joel took a corned beef on rye too, and followed her to an empty table.

"How much time will you have at home?" Susanna asked.

"I'm on a ten day furlough. I'm due back on the fourth."

"So soon?" she said, disappointment evident in her voice. "I guess you have to. Will you be going overseas soon?"

"The 506th is a special unit. We've got lots more training before we go parachuting into… into… wherever they tell us to jump."

As Susanna picked up her sandwich, Joel noticed her ring.

"Damn," he thought. "I should have known someone like her would be taken."

"Is that an engagement ring?" he asked.

"Uh… yes," Susanna replied awkwardly.

"Is he in the service?"

"Yes. He's a marine. He's been fighting at Guadalcanal since August. They even made him an officer, after the ones above him got killed." There was a slight pause as she twirled the straw in her soda glass. "I just wonder if there are German girls or Japanese girls as worried as I am."

"Probably not. They're the ones who started this war, remember."

"Not the girls, I'll bet."

She threw the last quarter of her sandwich back on its plate and polished off her Coke.

"Let's get out of here," he said.

He reached for her hand as they strolled through the great City Hall arches into its central courtyard. She didn't resist.

Joel already hated that God damned jarhead, but it was clear that civility would be the best policy.

"You've known your marine for a while, I guess."

"Since I was a baby. Justin lived two houses down from me. We grew up together. Everyone expected us to get married someday.

"He asked me before he went away. I didn't even think about it. But now…" She hesitated, then shyly went on.

"Now I wonder if I…"

"If you made a mistake?"

"I just don't know," she told Joel.

"I've known Justin my whole life, but in some ways I feel that I know you better, even though we just met."

"Yeah, I feel like that too. Is this what they call love at first sight?"

"I don't know," she said with a shy smile.

"Well, something is happening. That's for sure. And if you're having doubts about Justin, I think we ought to see where this is going."

The big City Hall clock chimed out 1:30.

"Don't you have to get back to work?"

Susanna looked at her watch and giggled.

"Half an hour ago. Denise is a sweetie, but I really ought to get back."

"We forgot the picture!" he said.

"I know where there's a photo booth," she said. "Let's go."

The booth was small and incredibly cramped. But it was not so small that Joel couldn't pull Susanna down on his lap just before he dropped his quarters into the slot. The photo machine clicked, snapped, and groaned and then spit out a strip of four tiny photographs of a young man and woman who were obviously smitten with each other.

When they got back to Lits, Joel folded the photo strip back and forth until it was neatly creased. Tearing the strip precisely in half, he tucked two of the photographs into his shirt pocket and gave the other two to Susanna.

"No, wait," he said. "Give me the locket."

Susanna reached into her handbag and took out the locket. She held it while Joel took one of her photos and carefully tore their images out. She took the fragment and, with a little more careful trimming, tucked it into the locket, so that when it was opened, they were looking right into each other's eyes.

Joel hardly fumbled at all as he undid the clasp and placed the chain around Susanna's neck. He watched approvingly, and with great admiration, as it dropped into its place between her perfect breasts.

"I thought that was for Aunt Kate," she said.

"I want you to have it. I'll get something else for Aunt Kate," Joel said.

He lifted her face toward him and kissed her, warmly and fully on her expectant mouth.

She threw her arms around his neck and prolonged the kiss.

They stayed that way for a long time; their lips together, their arms around each other and the firm contours of their young bodies offering erotic promises.

They were oblivious to their surroundings until Denise's voice intruded. "I hope your lunch was as good as dessert, Susanna."

Embarrassed, they staggered slightly from the dizzying kiss and jumped apart.

"Gotta get back to work," Susanna said with a dreamy smile.

"Susanna," Joel whispered too softly to be heard. "I'm going to marry you."

CHAPTER SIX

YEARNING

I wish I'd meet someone and fall madly in love at first sight. Of course, he'd have to fall for me, too.

We'd look into each other's eyes and everyone else would disappear — just like in 'West Side Story' or 'Romeo and Juliet'. Only, it wouldn't end in tragedy. We really would live happily ever after.

I've always loved that story about men and women really being one soul that was split apart, and each half searches until it finds the lost piece of itself.

Oh God, I'm turning into a dreamy-eyed romantic. Well, so what! It would be nice to believe there's one special person meant just for me.

Althea, get real. That kind of thing only happens in romance novels. Hey, maybe I should write one. At least I could live it vicariously.

CHAPTER SEVEN

JUNE 5, 1944

J oel was always on Susanna's mind. Or maybe it would be more precise to say he was always in her heart and even when her conscious mind wasn't thinking about him, he was there with her.

But on this particular day — June 5, 1944 — she was acutely aware of Joel. And for the first time since they'd said good-bye nine months before, she was worried about him. She always had a low-level sense of anxiety. But this was different. She could feel danger around him. She had no idea where he was or what he was about to do, but she felt it all the same.

It made no sense, but there it was. She wanted to grab a pen and a piece of her pretty flowered stationery and write to him. But she thought better of it. She knew her feelings would be transparent. She didn't want him to worry about her worry-ing about him. She would wait. It would pass, and she would tell him only how much she loved him and wished he were sharing the ordinary day-to-day pleasures that mean so much more when done with one you love — simple things like eating dinner, or taking a walk in the park on a sunny summer day.

She never felt that way about Justin Welch, even though he had already been in combat. She owed Justin a letter, but it was becoming increasingly more difficult to write to him. She and Joel planned to marry when Joel came back, but she couldn't bring herself to break off her engagement to Justin. Not until after the war. She'd heard too many stories about men becom-ing reckless and taking foolish risks after they received a Dear John letter.

Joel understood.

"As long as I'm not the one who finally gets the Dear John," he told her.

"That will never happen, my love," she said.

So she poured her heart out to Joel in her letters. She told him about the apartment she had rented and the life she was planning for them when he returned. She told him how much she missed him and loved him.

And she wrote to Justin. Cheery letters about day to day things that really didn't matter.

But today, she would write to neither. Today was different — although she still didn't understand why.

CHAPTER EIGHT

POOR OLD SERGEANT FINNIGAN

There was an old paratrooper named Sergeant Finnigan,
And he had a beard growin' down from his chin agin,
He jumped from a plane and it blew right in agin,
Poor old Sergeant Finnigan,
Begin agin.

The "Poor Old Sergeant Finnigan" ditty had been composed back at Fort Benning after Finnigan's first jump. Homer Barstow, a gangly hillbilly from as deep in the Ozarks as you could get, cobbled it up as a more or less affectionate jibe at the kid from Pennsylvania who was, if such a thing really existed, a natural paratrooper.

They hadn't a clue what he'd been thinking during that first jump, but he landed so perfectly and with such a big grin that Homer said if you didn't know better, you'd have thought he was the jumpmaster himself. Barstow and the rest of the 506th swore Finnigan had been born to jump out of airplanes.

Finnigan wasn't so sure about that. The first jump was long past and he knew damned well there was going to be a big difference between jumping into the secure, sometimes softly plowed, fields of Georgia and jumping into occupied France with thousands of indignant Germans doing their damnedest to shoot him dead before he hit the ground.

The first line of Homer's ditty was accurate; he really was Sergeant Finnigan. In the rotation of duties aimed at finding the best candidates for the stripes, Joel had been made acting squad leader of the 1st Squad of the 1st Platoon of Company B. By the time he said good-bye to Susanna and sailed to Liverpool on the troopship *Samaria* the previous September, the stripes had been sewn permanently on his shirtsleeves.

He and Susanna hadn't had much time together since that late December day a year and a half ago when they first met. Susanna had taken the train to Fayetteville twice after the 506th was absorbed into the 101st Airborne Division and transferred to Fort Bragg, North Carolina. She also met him in New York just before he shipped out to Liverpool. Because there were so few opportunities to be together, the time they shared was precious. They talked for hours and they kissed and held each other very close. They never fully gave in to their passions. It was a struggle, but they knew it would be even harder to say good-bye if they did. They would wait until the war was over and they didn't have to part.

The vibration inside the C-47, only one of the many planes carrying the 101st to France, smoothed out just a little as it lifted off the bumpy runway at Upottery, England on the dark cold night of June 5, 1944.

Now he, and everybody else, would find out if he really was a natural paratrooper.

*****

The thirty men of 1st Platoon stood next to one another, jammed in fifteen to a side in the long, aluminum, pipe and wire lined fuselage. Second Lieutenant Dave McNamee, a high school history teacher from New Milford, Connecticut, was in the rear of the plane, the better to lead the way through the door into the black and deadly sky.

Joel was all the way forward on the left side of the plane, right behind the cockpit where he could check everyone's weapons and equipment, insuring that all of the 1st Platoon kept what the 101st's proud new march called their 'Rendezvous With Destiny.' As Platoon Sergeant and second in command of the 1st Platoon — a position to which he had been promoted in the weeks before D-Day — he would be the last man out of the plane.

The paratroopers wished for the relative comfort of the canvas bucket seats along the sides. But standing would make it easier to get out, either when they reached the drop zone or were shot down in flames. There were more than a few cynical bastards who insisted that Major General Maxwell Taylor, commander of the 101st, said that paratroopers should die on their feet and not sitting on their asses.

Joel reached into the pocket of his field jacket and took out the photo booth picture of him and Susanna in the first glowing moments of their love, and stared at it during the last, frightening moments before his descent into hell.

The white line of surf breaking on the French coast passed beneath the plane. Joel slid the picture back into his pocket, checked his watch, and exchanged glances with Lieutenant McNamee.

"Okay, troopers," Joel shouted over the engines' roar.

"Check your weapons — loaded, a round in the chamber and, for Christ's sake, the safety on."

"Aw, Sarge, we checked 'em five times already," came a plaintive voice from near the center of the C-47.

"Check 'em a sixth time, dammit," Joel snapped back. "I don't want you tanglefeet shooting each other by accident on the way down."

"Yeah, the fuckin' Krauts'll do that for us," someone cracked.

1st Platoon grumbled, but they checked their weapons. They were as locked, loaded, and ready as they had been on the ground back at Upottery.

The last man had just shouted out his readiness when they were grotesquely illuminated by the warning light flashing ominously on the forward bulkhead.

They were approaching Drop Zone D, near the town of Carentan.

McNamee, laden down with his main and reserve parachutes, his field pack, and his Thompson submachine gun with enough ammunition to satisfy its ravenous appetite, waddled to the door. He shivered in the cold air as the jumpmaster, a burly sergeant, opened the door and began leading the 1st Platoon through the paratroopers' final liturgy.

"Hook up!"

A clicking metallic chorus rippled through the C-47 as thirty nervous men snapped their ripcords onto the steel static lines that ran down each side of the plane.

"Check your equipment!"

Fingers that had stopped shaking only when the warning light flashed on skipped nimbly and expertly over the parachute packs and harnesses of the man in front.

Everyone was as terrified as they had been before the light came on, but this was not the time to forget the lessons drummed into their heads from Fort Benning to the final training jumps at Slapton Sands on the Devonshire coast of southern England, a place that was just a little more than an hour behind, but now seemed so very far.

"Stand in the door," the jumpmaster commanded. McNamee turned smartly to his left, edged his booted toes over the sill, gripped each side of the door frame, and stared rigidly ahead into the night.

The light flashed green.

"Go!" the jumpmaster roared. He reached out to tap McNamee's left shoulder, but it wasn't there. The lieutenant had jumped, and a long drink of water from Montana was shuffling into his place.

"Go!"

And the cowboy was gone too.

One by one, the men of the 1st Platoon shuffled out the door until only Joel and the jumpmaster were left in the plane.

"Go!" he shouted, and Joel went.

*****

Joel's rapid fall from the C-47 was broken by the sharp, joint-straining jolt of his opening parachute. His ride to earth was actually peaceful. It would last only a few more seconds, until the Germans realized what was happening. He saw flashes and heard the rattle of small-arms fire several miles away, near the town of St. Mere Eglise where other troopers from the 101st had jumped. Many of them were shot dead in their harnesses before they even reached the ground.

Drop Zone D was rushing up at him as if he had no parachute at all. He was barely out of his harness and hadn't even thought about his part in the 3rd Battalion's mission of capturing a pair of bridges over the Douve River near Brevard when he came upon the first German soldiers he had ever seen. They were running straight toward him, shooting at anything that looked remotely like an American paratrooper; dropping toward the killing ground, tangled in their parachute harnesses or already dead in the muddy, shell-torn field.

Joel wondered if they were as frightened as he was, but they were too close for him to spend much time thinking about it. He flipped his M1 off his right shoulder, snapped the safety off and brought them down with four quick shots — two for each.

"Good ol' Sergeant Finnigan," a weak voice croaked from the dark.

It was Homer Barstow, the first man of the 1st Platoon Joel had seen since he jumped. Homer had broken his right leg as he landed on the rough, rocky field, but he was at least out of his harness and picking off Germans as best he could with his M1. He wouldn't be going on to Brevard and would soon be on a landing craft back to England, but only if he survived the next few minutes.

"You all right, Homer?" Joel shouted over the roar of a battle that had degenerated into more of a deadly brawl than any of the neatly organized campaigns displayed on the maps back at Eisenhower's headquarters.

"Shee-it, no, I ain't all right, Sarge! My leg's all busted up to hell.

"Look out, Sarge!" Homer cried as he unleashed five rounds from his M1.

Joel spun around to see what Homer had shot.

Two Germans were down, knocked off their feet and flung backwards by Homer's .30 caliber hailstorm. But the third kept coming. Joel only had an instant to swing his rifle butt up and out, straight into the man's face.

The German went down, his face bloody and his jaw smashed. Joel snapped his rifle into position and fired off his remaining four rounds to make sure he stayed down.

"Where's Lieutenant McNamee, Homer?"

"Hell, Sarge, I don't even know where the fuck I am. I think most of the guys are right close by, though."

The firing seemed to slacken, particularly the sharp, rapid bursts of the German submachine guns. The paratroopers were obviously up against a fairly small unit responding to the American surprise. But they'd be back, a whole hell of a lot more of them with even more deadly weaponry, and the 506th had damn well better be ready.

"First Platoon! On me," Joel bellowed.

One by one the men of the 1st Platoon emerged from the smoky darkness. Of the thirty men who had jumped onto Drop Zone D, twenty-two gathered around their Platoon Sergeant.

Lieutenant McNamee was not among them.

Joel fished a tightly folded map from the side pocket of his muddy field jacket.

"Where we goin', Sarge?" asked Tony Fabrizi.

"Shut up for a second," Joel snapped as he studied the map.

"Don't worry, Tony. We'll find Krauts whichever way we go."

He found what he was looking for on the map; a narrow road at the edge of the drop zone which he estimated was about half a mile from their position. The small compass in his pocket gave him an approximate direction.

"Let's go, troopers. Spread out and stay ready. We're not alone here tonight."

"Fuckin' A," Fabrizi growled.

Joel spread the men out in a rough skirmish line and led them across the field. They stepped over the dead of both sides as they moved toward the ditch and narrow wood line alongside the Brevard Road. They encountered more and more of their fellow paratroopers as they moved toward the 506th's assembly point.

Of the 680 men who had jumped with the 3rd Battalion, 500 assembled at their designated point, the ruined farm of some poor Frenchman who had once tended Drop Zone D with skill and loving care. Company B, with 100 of its original 150 jumpers, was gathering around its commander, Captain Paul Arnold.

"First Platoon reporting, sir," said Joel. "Twenty-two men, sir."

"Jesus Christ," the captain muttered.

"What the hell would they have done if they knew we were coming?"

"Yes, sir. We had a hell of a fight for the first few minutes."

Arnold's dirty face was creased by the hint of a smile.

"It looks like you did all right, Sergeant Finnigan. I want you to take over First Platoon when we move out to Brevard."

"Me, sir? Where's Lieutenant McNamee?"

"At the aid station. He won't make it tonight... not this attack anyway."

"I'd like to go and see him, if we have time, sir."

"Yeah. Grab his map case, too. Get right back here. We're moving out in about thirty minutes."

Dave McNamee was propped up under a cruelly shattered tree. His face was pale, drawn tight in pain, but he looked as good as anyone could whose left arm had been broken in the landing and whose right leg had been shot almost completely away in the fight on the drop zone.

"The Krauts really dropped a load on you this time, Joel," McNamee said with a weak grin.

"Me, Lieutenant? It looks like you came out second best."

Joel knelt beside McNamee.

"Yeah, but they left you in charge of First Platoon."

"Captain Arnold just told me. It's an honor I could do without."

"Bullshit, Sergeant. You'll be a good platoon leader, better than me, probably. If this army was smart they'd make you an officer."

"Shit," Joel growled.

McNamee struggled painfully to pick up some equipment lying on the ground beside him. The pain made him give up after just a few seconds.

"Take my map case, Joel. It's got everything you'll need. Take my binoculars too, the better to see the bastards with."

Joel slung the map case over his right shoulder and the binoculars around his neck.

"You might as well have my Thompson, too."

"I think I'll stick with my M1, sir. It's been damned useful tonight, and I'd feel like I'm walking out on my wife… if I had a wife."

McNamee, who knew a little bit about Susanna, smiled up at Joel.

"You will, Joel, if you get the First Platoon through this."

Joel rose to his feet and adjusted his gear to make it ride more easily.

"I'd best be getting back, Lieutenant. We'll be going after those bridges pretty soon."

"Yeah, those goddamned bridges."

McNamee looked up at Joel with a thoughtful, ironic look in his eyes.

"You know, Joel, I'm supposed to be teaching history, not getting my ass shot off in it."

"Yes, sir. It looks like they missed your ass, but you're right, none of us should be living this."

Joel saluted and left his lieutenant under the tree, waiting for the medics to carry him back to Utah Beach and a ship bound for England on the first leg of his long return to New Milford. On his brisk walk back to the 1st Platoon, Joel couldn't chase Homer Barstow's satire from his mind:

"Poor Old Sergeant Finnigan."

*****

Joel had guessed wrong about German reinforcements dashing helter-skelter to the drop zone. They knew exactly what the 506th was up to and fell back to fight for every inch of the Brevard Road until they came to their fixed defensive machine gun nests and mortar emplacements on the banks of the Douve River, right in front of the bridges. If they could hold the bridges long enough, they would be able to send their tanks and infantry across them to attack the American forces struggling ashore on Utah Beach and drive them back into the English Channel.

The Army liked to call it the Big Picture, but neither Joel, nor anybody else on the ground in those terrible pre-dawn hours of June 6, had a thought to spare for anything but his own small ride on this particular hinge of fate. They saw only what was right in front of them, which for Joel, and his 1st Platoon, whittled down now to just fifteen men, was to take out the German defensive position guarding the end of the bridge assigned to Company B.

God, how Joel hated the motto 'Follow Me' he had seen all over the Army's Infantry School at Fort Benning. It was such an easy thing to say on the training fields of Georgia, where all the guns fired blank rounds.

And it was the only thing to say in the short, sharp battle at the Douve River. The 1st Platoon lay hunkered down in the ruins of a small farmhouse about fifty yards from the bridge. As

Joel's eyes flashed over the scene, he prayed to God that someone else would charge the bridge, or that the Germans behind the rifles and two machine guns would have the good sense to beat feet all the way back to Germany and their plump fraus.

No such luck, of course, but 1st Platoon did get a break when the sergeant in charge of the defending Germans suddenly stood up and directed his men's fire off to the left. The target turned out to be three French cows blundering around in the noise and confusion, but they made just enough of a ruckus to distract the Germans and give Joel the opening he was looking for.

The German sergeant went down in a hail of rifle fire from Tony Fabrizi. Joel jumped to his feet, his M1 clutched in his right hand and his left fumbling on his belt for a hand grenade.

"First Platoon! Follow me!"

Joel took ten quick steps and stopped. He pulled the safety pin from his hand grenade and threw it in a long, graceful arc into the German position. It was one of four delivered by the good throwing arms of the 1st Platoon.

The Germans had spotted the paratroopers' assault and were just swinging their guns around to meet it when the grenades went off right in their midst. It was over in a few seconds. Tony Fabrizi was the first over the stacked sandbags that encircled the German position, with Joel right behind him.

The pit was awash in blood and littered with bodies in various states of dismemberment. One man rose from the carnage and pointed a machine pistol right at Joel.

It was the last thing he ever did.

1st Platoon suddenly found itself engulfed in a mass of paratroopers as the rest of Company B dashed onto the bridge. Joel jumped as a heavy hand came down on his right shoulder.

"Good work, Sergeant," Captain Arnold said, and then galloped onto the bridge.

Nobody had been lost in that final, desperate attack on the German defenses. That was something, anyway, and since the firing from the other end faded out as the enemy fled or died, he gave his men a quick smoke break before they gathered up their gear and followed him across the bridge.

Joel found Captain Arnold at the far end. He was the only officer in sight and he was taking in a constant stream of reports from his radio operator and exhausted messengers who stumbled in from the dark with the morning's butcher's bill.

"First Platoon reporting, sir," Joel said with as snappy a salute as he could muster.

"It looks like we got our bridges, Captain. The tankers will be happy."

"Yeah, but I won't be happy until I see their tanks on this side of the bridge. The battalion's down to 170 men, Sergeant."

"Jesus," Joel whispered in a soft, horrified tone. "We jumped with 680."

His stomach felt nauseous and his knees weak.

"The whole battalion; 170 out of 680?"

"You've got it, Sergeant Finnigan," Arnold replied grimly. "Colonel Wolverton and Major Grant were both killed back at the drop zone, and I don't know where the hell the rest of the regimental staff is — scattered all over."

"It sounds like you've got the battalion, sir."

"I guess so, here at the bridges anyway. Shit, I've got second lieutenants commanding companies no bigger than platoons and sergeants leading platoons cut down to squads."

"That's us, sir. The First Platoon's down to fifteen men."

"And you'll stay in command, Sergeant. I want you to set up a defensive perimeter around this end of the bridge. Have your men get whatever sleep they can, but I want half of them on alert at all times."

Arnold cast an exasperated eye over the battlefield.

"I hope that armor gets up here from the beach in one hell of a hurry," he said. "I expect to see the Germans as soon as the sun comes up, and right now, they could flick us off like a fly off a horse's ass."

"They haven't had much luck so far, Captain."

"No, Sergeant, they haven't. Let's keep it that way until the Second Armored Division gets here."

*****

The next morning, after a mere twenty-four hours in France, the tattered, bone weary remnants of the 506th moved south toward the grimly, but aptly named Dead Man's Corner. Combat Command A of the 2nd Armored Division was moving up from Utah Beach as fast as it could for the assault on Carentan. But Dead Man's Corner had to be taken to stop the 17th SS Panzergrenadier Division from digging in at that key point to meet the oncoming American threat.

The fanatical SS men mounted a strong defense of Dead Man's Corner. The 1st Platoon of Company B lost three men, and was down to only twelve by the time the 506th withdrew to Beaumont for the night

The equally battered 3rd Battalion of the 501st joined them during the night and the American paratroopers finally took Dead Man's Corner on June 8.

Joel managed to adopt, or inherit, enough strays to rebuild the 1st Platoon to all of twenty men by the time he received orders to leave Dead Man's Corner in the care of the 2nd Armored Division and move into Carentan. Since the 2nd Battalion of the 506th, the 3rd of the 501st and the 401st Glider Infantry Regiment had already run the Germans out of Carentan, Joel Finnigan and the 1st Platoon rode into town atop the two tanks from Combat Command A with hardly a shot fired.

The Germans made one more attempt on the morning of June 13, but were beaten back by the steadily increasing American strength. Joel felt, with great relief, that he was fading back into the forest of olive drab fatigues as the 506th rejoined the rest of the 101st Airborne Division, first for guard duties around the crucial port of Cherbourg and finally, more than a month after D-Day, onto the landing ships headed back across the English Channel.

CHAPTER NINE

LETTER FROM HOME

August 21, 1944

My Dearest Joel,

I can't believe it's been nearly a year since we said good-bye and you sailed off to war.
You have been in my heart every minute, but then I've told you that so many times before. Do you ever get tired of hearing how much I love you? I know I never get tired of you telling me you love me. How I long for the day we can do it in person.
I read every word I can find about the war in Europe. And when I do, I wonder where you are and whether you are jumping into another battle. I wish you could be somewhere safe behind a desk. But then, I realize you would never settle for that. It is your courage, your idealism, your willingness to risk everything for all of us back home that is part of the love I feel for you. You are my own personal hero, Joel Finnigan. But how I long for your return, my love. Please be safe. Win this awful war and come home to me so we can begin our life together.
I look forward to the day when I will be Mrs. Joel Finnigan, pushing a baby carriage with your beautiful son lying peacefully asleep inside, hurrying home to make a special dinner for a very special husband.

Yours always,
Susanna

CHAPTER TEN

LIEUTENANT FINNIGAN

Joel took out the well-worn photo booth picture of him and Susanna. He lay back on his cot and let the memory of that day carry him to a far better place.

That memory evolved into a daydream about returning to her after the war. He drifted to sleep and the daydream became an erotic dream with him gently unbuttoning her blouse as they moved toward finally fulfilling the promise of their love. But the dream was shattered by the noise of a truck engine outside on the company street.

Susanna's delectable beauty was once more out of his reach and it was back to the business of war for 2nd Lieutenant Joel Finnigan.

2nd Lieutenant Joel Finnigan; it was still hard for him to believe that he rated a salute from men old enough to be his father, not because he was such a splendid guy but because the U.S. Army, in its infinite wisdom, said he did.

It had to happen, of course. By the time the 506th was withdrawn from Normandy it had less than a quarter of the men who had jumped on D-Day. Survivors of that terrible year since their first meeting back at Camp Toccoca were promoted and spread throughout the 506th, both to replace the missing men and to lead the flood of youngsters constantly coming over from the states, or turned out by the jump schools the Army had established in England. Joel was one of ten battle-tested platoon sergeants who were summoned to regimental headquarters and handed orders proclaiming them officers and gentlemen by Act of Congress and by order of General Taylor.

Instead of being transferred to a new outfit, which was normally the case, Joel was made the official leader of the 1st Platoon of Company B. Most of the men he had jumped with in Normandy were gone, either dead, in the hospital, or assigned elsewhere in the division. He wanted all the old hands he could get, however, and he asked Captain Arnold if he could make Tony Fabrizi Platoon Sergeant and make four others buck sergeants, or at least corporals, so they could become squad leaders.

"You can have Fabrizi, Joel, but we need to send the others around the division. You've got some good men coming in with the replacements. Get 'em, quick, Lieutenant. There's something big coming up."

"Any idea what, sir?"

"Not a clue, so far, but General Taylor has all the regimental commanders up at division headquarters, and I doubt they're talking about the softball tournament."

There had been at least the start of a 101st Airborne Division softball tournament during that all too brief summer of 1944. It was supposed to help keep everyone in good physical condition and take their minds off the real reason they had come to Europe in the first place. But now, as the summer moved into early August, more and more games were getting cancelled, the tempo of training jumps had increased, and the march back to the war picked up its ominous pace.

Years later, Joel was to laugh scornfully at the historians and journalists who, without ever having heard them themselves, wrote about the thundering drums and blaring trumpets of the 506th's return to the European continent. Nevertheless, on September 17, well before the summer of 1944 cooled down, Joel found himself once more in the back of a C-47. He was flying northeast from England, this time across the North Sea.

He sat back near the door — General Taylor had finally let them sit down — while Tony Fabrizi, the sergeant's stripes still new and stiff on his sleeves, sat forward in Joel's old Platoon

Sergeant's position beneath the dreaded jump lights on the forward bulkhead. Between them sat the thirty paratroopers that made up the 1st Platoon of Company B. Only four of the men in that C-47 had jumped on D-Day, just over three months earlier. The rest were new and impossibly young looking, compared with the twenty and twenty-one year old grizzled, battle-scarred veterans of the Douve River bridges and Carentan.

An ironic grin creased Joel's face as he looked down the length of the C-47. Having heard all the war stories from Normandy, the new men were serious, and no doubt some of them were even scared to death, but nearly all of them seemed glad to finally be getting into action.

My God, I must have looked just like that myself on June 6 — before I jumped out of the airplane.

Let's see how they feel at the end of the day — if they see the end of the day.

"There is a pleasure to being mad that only madmen know," Joel recalled having read somewhere. Samuel Johnson wrote that back in the 18th century, he recalled, and damned if old Sam wasn't right.

"Check your weapons," he ordered, "locked and loaded."

"Aww, for Christ's sake…" moaned a voice from the middle of the plane. Joel succeeded in hiding his grin.

"You heard the Lieutenant," barked Tony Fabrizi, "check your damned weapons, troopers."

Yes, things sure were different now. He didn't have to yell at paratroopers anymore. He had Tony to do it for him.

*****

Joel and his platoon were about to kick off Operation Market-Garden, British Field Marshal Montgomery's bold stroke that, if everything went as planned, would bring the war to an end, perhaps by winter. The 101st and 82nd Airborne Divisions and the 1st Polish Parachute Brigade — bloody-minded men eager to exact a terrible revenge on the despoilers of their homeland — were to jump into Holland and secure a series of bridges between Eindhoven and the Rhine River. British armor driving up from the south was to cross the bridges and then plunge into the Ruhr River valley, the heart of German heavy industry.

The idea was that if it was deprived of its tanks, artillery pieces, and bullets, the German army would collapse. It was an idea that made sense to Joel. The sooner the war was over, the sooner he could get back to Susanna.

For one of the first times in his paratrooping career, Joel was anxious to hit the ground. There were not even the few seconds of relative quiet that he had savored all too briefly during the Normandy jump. The sky over Holland was bright and clear, but it was defaced by the sinister black clouds of exploding anti-aircraft shells and streaked by tracer rounds from German rifles and machine guns.

He was amazed to find that the 1st Platoon made it down intact; nobody landed with so much as a sprained ankle. He left Tony Fabrizi to assemble the platoon while he went to find the Company Commander and prepare for the attack on the bridge at Zon, just a couple of miles to the northwest.

But there would be no attack on the Zon bridge and Joel found Captain Arnold flashing a broad, ironic grin at his rapidly assembling platoon leaders.

"I'll be damned," he said. "It looks like the Krauts are on our side this time."

A powerful German 88 crashed into a stand of trees near the edge of the drop zone, sending Arnold and the platoon leaders diving for cover,

"It sure as hell doesn't look like it, Captain," Joel replied with more than a hint of sarcasm.

"Well, probably not," said Arnold, "but at least the bastards blew up the Zon bridge for us and got the hell out of town."

"That was good of them," said 1st Lieutenant Mark Doulton, Executive Officer of Company B.

"I guess we can go home now."

"Not a chance," Arnold replied. "We've got to head back down the road, link up with the British armor, and then come back to take Eindhoven. Company B will lead the regiment, and Joel, I want your First Platoon to take the point."

The Germans, who Monty's staff insisted weren't supposed to be there, lined both sides of the road and gave it the grim name 'Hell's Highway'. Joel's M1 more than earned its keep as 1st Platoon was invariably the first to meet the enemy and then hold him down with rifle and machine gun fire while the rest of Company B, followed by the full strength of the 506th, came up to clear out the opposition and re-open the road.

"Jesus, they're fighting like sons of bitches," an exhausted Tony Fabrizi said as he and Joel rode back north atop a British tank.

"They should be. We're headed right for their border," Joel replied. "How would you feel if they landed at Atlantic City and were headed toward Philadelphia?"

"I guess I'd fight like a son of a bitch too," he mused.

Tony cast Joel a slight grin.

"I've heard all about those Philly cheese steaks, Lieutenant."

"Pat's are the best."

"Okay. I can't let the Krauts have Philly until I've been to Pat's; so, yeah, I really would fight like a son of a bitch."

"It's the same for us, Tony. We're going to have to fight like sons of bitches if we ever want to try some really good Wiener Schnitzle."

*****

The paratroopers fought hard, harder even than at Normandy, but by the middle of October it was becoming obvious that Operation Market-Garden was going nowhere. The end finally came on a chilly night as the first hint of winter began to torment northern Europe. Company B had just fended off yet another German attack when Danny Syzmanski, Joel's radio operator, tapped him on the right shoulder.

"The Old Man wants to see you at the CP, sir."

"Just me?"

"No, sir. He's calling for all the officers."

"Okay. Contact the Platoon Sergeant. Tell him to get the men ready to move and then get whatever rest they can. I'll go see what Captain Arnold wants."

"Do they have another dirty job for us, Lieutenant Finnigan?"

"Don't they always, Danny?"

Company B's command post was set up in the one intact room of what had once been the Opheusden police station. Paul Arnold stood at a long desk in the middle of the room studying a map. First Sergeant Ed Ruth oversaw the ebb and flow of messages and issued a series of routine orders while the Company Commander spoke in quiet tones with his officers — all but the Exec.

"We're getting out of here, Joel," he said as the 1st Platoon Leader joined the conference. "We're no closer to Germany than we were two weeks ago, and General Taylor says we're about to be clobbered by a coordinated attack from the east and the west."

Joel stepped forward for a look at the map, which told a grim story.

"It looks like Max is right," he said. "They have us by the balls. It's no great surprise though, sir. My Platoon Sergeant's getting the guys ready to move out."

The three other Second Lieutenants nodded their agreement. Their platoons were also ready to go, or soon would be.

"Good," the Company Commander said. "Get back to your platoons, then. We'll move as soon as I get some orders.

"All but you, Joel. You too, Clark."

The 2nd and 3rd Platoon leaders left. Joel and 2nd Lieutenant Clark Westfield drew closer to Arnold for the dirty job that Danny Syzmanski thought he was only kidding about.

"Lieutenant Doulton is dead, gentlemen," Arnold said simply. "That last attack got him."

He turned toward Joel.

"You're my new Executive Officer, Lieutenant Finnigan. I want you to take your First Platoon and Westfield's Fourth Platoon back toward Arnhem to find about 120 British paratroopers. They've been cut off and shot up. They still have some ammo, but you'll have to hurry before the Germans get to them.

"Then, start moving south down Hell's Highway. With any kind of luck, we'll all get out of here."

*****

Joel and his two platoons from Company B didn't encounter the stranded British until after the starved, exhausted paratroopers had been brought safely into Arnhem. They fought off one more German attack and helped shepherd their charges back down Hell's Highway until they met the trucks that had been sent up to transport them back to France, far from the fiasco into which Operation Market-Garden had degenerated.

"You sure earned your nickel on this trip, Lieutenant," Tony Fabrizi wheezed from the floor of the two and a half ton truck. He was in pain, aggravated by the bone-jarring ride, but in no real danger from a leg wound suffered during the retreat from Arnhem.

"Hell, we all did, Tony. And stop calling me 'Lieutenant' all the time, at least till we get out of this damned truck."

"Yeah, but look at it this way, Lieutenant — Joel — you jumped as a Platoon Leader and you're coming out as the company exec."

"We're lucky to be coming out alive," Joel replied. "I had your job when we jumped at Normandy. That was a lot easier. I just had to make sure everyone kept his weapon clean and let someone else make the decisions."

"Somebody else is always making the decisions. If you were General Taylor, Eisenhower would make 'em. If you were Ike, Roosevelt and Churchill would call the shots for you.

"The way you're going, Joel," Tony said with a weak, ironic chuckle, "you could be a general yourself before this is all over."

"Right, Tony. Then I could invent cock-ups like this."

Joel found himself thinking during that long, uncomfortable, and frustrating retreat about who had invented the cock-up that was Market-Garden, and how it earned the GI's definition SNAFU: Situation Normal All Fucked Up. Lieutenant McNamee, lying wounded beneath a tree on the Brevard Road had planted something in Joel's mind.

"I should be teaching history, Joel, not living it," he remembered McNamee saying.

Maybe, just maybe, if he followed the direction that McNamee had pointed out, he'd be able to make sense of all this lunacy, and keep the goddamned fools from doing it again.

*****

In the way of armies everywhere, the 506th held a regimental parade a week after they arrived at Camp Mourmelon le Grand. General Taylor himself was there to dispense the honors and awards that the 506th had been accumulating since D-Day. For Joel Finnigan, the general had a Silver Star, second only to the Congressional Medal of Honor, for his actions in France, a Bronze Star for Market-Garden and the silver bars of a First Lieutenant.

CHAPTER ELEVEN

CHRISTMAS IN BASTOGNE

December 16, 1944

My Dearest Susanna:

Well, here I am in Paris looking at that silly photo we took the day we met. It's a ritual every time I sit down to write to you. Not that I need a picture to remind me of you. Your beautiful eyes, your lovely smile — and all the rest of you — are etched in my memory.

Still, I like to look at that photo and remember the day we met, then think ahead to the day we can finally be together again. The thought of you and the life we will share keeps me going.

The outfit is in pretty good shape; so I've been able to get away for a couple of days.

I just finished dinner in a little place called Felix's just off the Place de la Concorde. It's a lot different from that Horn and Hardardt near Lits, but the company isn't nearly as good.

We'll have to make it a point to come here for dinner, just the two of us, someday. You've probably been reading about the war in the Inquirer or the Bulletin; so I won't bore you with a lot of details of what turned out to be a very busy Fall. We were forced to retreat. None of us likes retreating, but I do think we moved the ball a little closer to the goal line. I have to believe that, otherwise all the guys we left behind, Americans, Brits, Poles and God knows who else, will have died for nothing.

I'm still amazed that I've made it through since June 6 without a scratch. I'm even more amazed that the Army was insane enough to give me a pair of silver bars.

Can you believe it, 1ˢᵗ Lieutenant Joel Finnigan?

If that's not enough, I'm also the Acting Company Commander, at least until we get a fresh captain to take the job. Captain Arnold, my Company Commander since D-Day, has been promoted to Major and is now the 506ᵗʰ staff operations officer. I'm just keeping his seat warm.

The Germans are steadily falling back and a lot of people around here think the war will be over by springtime. But believe me, from what I've seen so far, they have plenty of fight left in them and they might have a couple of surprises for us. Springtime would be fine with me, though. I'm responsible for more than 300 guys now and all I really want to do is get them back home. That's really all that keeps any of us going.
There's a lot of work to do before I can go home, but…
Gotta go. There's a big MP sergeant headed right for my table and that can't mean anything good.

All my love,

Joel

*****

"Everyone's been ordered back to camp, Lieutenant," the big sergeant said.

Joel stuffed the letter into his pocket and threw what he hoped was the correct number of francs on the table.

"What's up, Sergeant?"

"Dunno for sure, sir. I think the shit's done hit the fan somewhere up north."

*****

Thus did 1st Lieutenant Joel Finnigan, still not old enough to vote or even buy a drink back in the United States, come to be standing before the officers and sergeants of Company B, 3rd Battalion, 506th Parachute Infantry Regiment of the 101st Airborne Division, asking them if they had ever heard of a town called Bastogne.

Hardly anybody had heard of the place until December 16, when German tanks and infantry plunged into the southern portion of the Ardennes forest in Belgium, intent on capturing the network of roads that would take them to the port of Antwerp where allied troops and equipment were coming ashore in an unstoppable tide.

"Bastogne is the key to this whole thing," said Joel.

"It's the key to the road network up there, and if the Germans take it they can run wild all the way to Antwerp and stop all our reinforcements and supplies. If we don't hold Bastogne, we're screwed, gentleman, and this war can go on until 1946 or even '47.

"As you know, General Taylor is back in the states, so Brigadier General McAuliffe will command the division.

"Let's go."

Since nothing even remotely like a fresh, new captain had materialized at Camp Mourmelon le Grand, the newly minted Major Arnold brusquely told Joel that he could erase the word 'acting' from his title as commander of Company B. Maybe there would be time to promote him to captain when this Bastogne business was finished.

For soldiers who had always taken great pride in parachuting boldly into combat, it seemed ironic the 101st Airborne Division went into the most desperate, crucial battle in its history in the back of ugly, trusty old two and a half ton trucks.

As Company Commander, Joel rated a jeep and driver for the headlong dash through the winter night from France into Belgium. His ride was somewhat more comfortable than the hard wooden benches of the trucks, but Joel found himself missing the physical and spiritual warmth of having his buddies packed tightly around him. He had no buddies now. He was the old man, and came sadly to the conclusion that the storied loneliness of command also meant freezing his ass off.

*****

The Screaming Eagles rolled into Bastogne during the night of December 18. There they found the shot-up remnants of the 9th and 12th Armored Divisions, the 705th Tank Destroyer Battalion, and several hundred unattached soldiers who had been separated from their units in the initial German attack. They were the only ones who could hold Bastogne until Lieutenant General George Patton's Third Army, more than one hundred miles to the south, could come over frozen, snow-covered roads to their rescue.

"Old Blood and Guts is out of his fuckin' mind," a paratrooper grumbled as he slithered over the snow and ice on the march to meet the Germans.

"Hell, we can't even walk on this shit, and Georgie thinks he can get a bunch of tanks and dogfaces up here before the Krauts wipe us out? Shee-it! He's out of his fuckin' mind."

Joel heard the man and was tempted to tell him to shut the hell up. But he didn't. Not only was it a soldier's inalienable right to bitch without mercy, but bitching about Patton, Eisenhower, Montgomery, and everybody else above the rank of Private First Class was fine as long as it kept the men's minds off the winter misery surrounding them.

"I hope you're saving some of that for the Germans, Kelly," Joel said to the complainer.

"You bet your ass, Lieutenant. I want some Kraut balls for Christmas tree ornaments."

The 506th passed through Bastogne itself, and was about halfway between the little villages of Foy and Bizory when a cluster of jeeps appeared ahead at a railroad crossing. The various commanders were breaking their units out of the line of march into positions chosen to best stop the German advance, at least until Georgie got there. Joel's Company B anchored the 3rd Battalion's north facing defensive line near the railroad crossing. The rest of the battalion extended the line to the left where the 2nd Battalion carried it further west to Recogne and the 3rd Battalion of the 502nd.

The 506th dug in on the east side of the road.

And there they waited, cooking up what hot chow they could, keeping their weapons from freezing up, and alternating their woolen socks to ward off the dreaded trench foot. But before he did any of that himself, Joel peered through his binoculars at the white, fog-shrouded field before him. Nothing moved in the approximately half-mile of open ground between him and the woods opposite the 506th's defensive line. But he knew there would be a lot of movement, and sooner than anyone would like.

Back at Company B headquarters, next to a rough hut of canvas and a few planks over the remains of an old chicken co-op, Joel poured himself the first palatable cup of coffee he'd had since he left Camp Mourmelon le Grand.

"Excellent coffee, Top," he said to Ed Ruth.

"It's all Jaworski's doing, sir," the 1st Sergeant replied with a nod in the direction of the company clerk who was bent over a small stack of official forms.

"Thank you, sir," Jaworski said. "It's some local stuff I managed to… liberate when we were going through Bastogne."

"Liberated, is it? But, tell me, Paulie, how come you're working on company paperwork while half the German army's beating down our door?"

Jaworski smiled and affectionately caressed the Thompson submachine gun propped up against the wall beside him.

"Lucille's all ready for the big dance, Lieutenant. Don't you worry about that."

Paulie took his hand off his beloved Lucille and slapped it down atop his pile of army forms.

"But if I don't have these reports up to Battalion in the morning, I'll be in awful trouble. You too, sir. The Colonel would be really pissed."

Joel was lucky to swallow his mouthful of stolen coffee before he burst out laughing and sprayed it all over his headquarters. "Okay, Paulie. You're right; an army travels on its stomach and fights with its ammo, but it would damn sure collapse without its daily reports."

Joel walked over to Ruth, who was taking the reports from Company B's four platoons as they dug in along their half-mile section of the line.

"Paulie's got a great future in the Army, Top, once we're…"

A joke about the Army's and Paulie's shared devotion to paperwork was supposed to have followed next; Joel's attempt at the sardonic humor that kept soldiers putting one foot ahead of the other since the time of Alexander the Great. But he never got to finish it. He was cut short by a storm of mortar and machine gun fire that plunged into the 1st and 2nd Platoons, just about fifty yards from the Company B command post.

Joel dropped his coffee, grabbed his M1, and leapt for the entrance. He had a full eight-round clip in the rifle and the safety off before he got there. Damn lucky he did, too, because the first thing he saw was a squad of German infantrymen — at least twelve of them — charging through the bloody gap that had been blasted open by the mortars and machine guns.

He felt strangely calm, with none of the blood lust that had fueled him in Normandy and Holland. Dropping to his left knee, he slapped the M1's stock against his right shoulder, and picked out a target, a tall shadow wrapped in a long, flapping greatcoat nearly hidden by the smoke and swirling snow.

The M1 recoiled against Joel's shoulder and the tall German wasn't there anymore. He swung his rifle to the right and brought down two more Germans before the thunderous chatter of Ruth's and Jaworski's Thompsons joined the deadly chorus.

First Sergeant Ruth moved steadily forward with a hard, expressionless look on his face, cutting down attacking Germans as he went. Joel expected that of Ed Ruth, a professional soldier when he was still a schoolboy, but Paulie Jaworski really amazed him. The little, bespectacled company clerk was wading into the Germans with a look of joyous savagery on his smooth, unlined face. Five of them went down before Paulie's Thompson.

Joel picked off one more German who was lunging toward Paulie while he was reloading Lucille. Paulie gave Joel a wave of thanks and went back to killing Germans as though it was the most natural thing he had ever done in his life.

Ruth and Jaworski moved forward with Joel into the gap briefly opened up by the Germans. There was fire from the right and left as the 1st and 2nd Platoons recovered, sidestepping to close the nearly exploited opening.

The Germans were in full retreat, with helmeted, great coated figures slogging back across the open ground toward the tree line. 2nd Lieutenant Clark Westfield materialized in front of his company commander.

"I want you to stay right here, Clark. Send the wounded and the dead back to the CP, then seal up this hole. They'll be back, the bastards."

"Yes, sir," Westfield replied. "Just when I thought we had 'em beat."

"Didn't we all, Clark? Didn't we all?"

Joel couldn't resist smiling at Paulie Jaworski on the walk back to the command post.

"Lucille really was ready for the dance, Paulie."

"Yes, sir. She's a good old thing… never let me down."

"You were terrific, Paulie. You must've gotten half the Germans who managed to get through our line. There's got to be at least a Bronze Star in this for you."

"Hell, Lieutenant Finnigan, I'm not huntin' medals. But after all my work, if those Kraut bastards had screwed up my reports, I would've really gone after the fuckers."

*****

'And so it continued both day and night.'

The words from "The First Noel" left a bitter taste as the German attacks kept coming, one after the other. If the bad weather continued to make a parachute resupply of ammunition and food a cruel pipedream, Joel was certain that the Germans would prevail.

Georgie Patton was pushing his Third Army northward as hard as he could, but Joel knew damned good and well that he would be dead before the Third Army ever got to Bastogne. The only real question in Joel's mind was whether he would be dead of exposure before the Germans got close enough to shoot him.

He found he was able to keep warm, more or less, by staying constantly on the move. He had been out among his men on the morning of December 20, and returned to the chicken coop command post to find Major Paul Arnold waiting for him and warming himself with a cup of Paulie Jaworski's coffee.

"Jaworski here deserves a medal, or something," the Major said with a nod toward the company clerk.

"He does that, Major," Joel said as he poured himself a cup and sat on a wooden crate that once held C-Rations.

"Did you come all the way up here just for a cup of Paulie's coffee, sir?"

"I wish that was the only reason," Arnold said. "We're pulling back into Bastogne. First Battalion and Tenth Armored can't hold Norville any longer, and the 105th Infantry Division is being pushed out of St. Vith. We're going to form a ring around Bastogne and hold on."

"Can we hold on, sir? I'm out of nearly everything."

"Believe it or not, Joel, you're in better shape than most. It really doesn't matter, though. There's no getting out of Bastogne anyway." Arnold swallowed the rest of his coffee before vanishing back into the cold and snow.

Joel knew he only had to nod in First Sergeant Ruth's direction to have the retreat orders sent out on the Company B radio net. But this retreat, to the eastern suburbs of Bastogne, was a far different thing than the retreat from Holland two months earlier. Company B was not retreating to safety, but only to a new position from which to face the steadily encroaching danger.

The Germans' attacks kept coming and the paratroopers kept beating them back. Penetrating cold and weariness that went straight to the soul had become the natural state of being, and as he forced his aching body and tired mind into keeping Company B a cohesive part of the defense of the crossroad city, Joel forgot about Susanna's waiting arms.

He caught a nap dreaming not of Susanna but of what he would do when the Germans came again.

It was not a very long dream.

"Hey, Lieutenant! Wake up!" Paulie Jaworski shouted in his ear. "You've been out for an hour, sir."

"Thanks, Paulie. Anything going on?"

"Yes, sir. We're getting reports of something moving around on our front."

Joel clapped his steel helmet on his head and reached for his M1. "Another attack," he said. "Pass the word."

"Already done, sir."

He arose to the sound of rifles and machine guns, but was surprised when it faded away more quickly than he expected. The guns had barely gone quiet when Clark Westfield was on the radio reporting that it was not a major attack. It was just a probing action, or maybe some unfortunate German infantrymen, as cold, tired and confused as everybody else in Bastogne, had just stumbled into the field of American fire by mistake.

"Don't be such an optimist, Lieutenant," Joel barked into his microphone with unusual annoyance. "...count on the Krauts to make any kind of mistake and they'll kill you dead. Keep everyone on their toes. I'll be around in a few minutes."

"Yes, sir," Westfield replied.

Clark Westfield was still puzzling over Joel's unusual testiness which is why he was so pleasantly surprised when his Company Commander arrived at the 1st Platoon's CP with an easy, amused grin on his face.

"Everything seems fairly quiet, sir... for the moment, anyway."

"They'll be back, count on it," Joel replied. "But we'll kick their asses out of here soon enough."

"You sound like the optimist now, sir."

"Gotta be, Clark. Did you hear what General McAuliffe told the Germans?"

"I didn't know he was on speaking terms with them."

"Those Krauts sent four guys into the 327th's line under a flag of truce, asking McAuliffe if he wanted to surrender."

"What?"

"Yeah… surrender. Know what he said?"

"No."

"Nuts, he told 'em… nuts."

"Do you think the Germans know what that means?"

"Damned if I know, Clark. They'll figure it out soon enough though, and when they do, they'll be really pissed. So let's all stay ready."

"Yes, sir," Westfield replied with a surge of fierce pride.

On December 22 the weather finally broke, which allowed clouds of C-47s to darken the crystalline cerulean sky and drop the tons of food and, most importantly, ammunition for which the defenders of Bastogne had prayed so fervently. As he joined with his men in gleefully cracking open the crates and refilling their bellies and ammunition belts, he couldn't help thinking of the classic Christmas scenes of children ripping open their presents.

The lethal Christmas gifts had barely been distributed when it came time to put them to use. On Christmas Day a strong German force flung itself at the village of Hermroulle.

*****

It was, Joel learned later, the enemy's last attempt to break through the cordon around Bastogne. Most of the German strength had been shifted slightly to the west for the attack on Hermroulle, where they were met by the 1st Battalion of the 506th, the 705th Tank Destroyer Battalion and a battered, but still fighting, task force of tanks from the 10th Armored Division.

Joel kept his attention on his front, beating back the attacks that kept popping up along the line. But he was also studying his map and trying to think ahead. He called Clark Westfield, who was now functioning as his Executive Officer, to the Company B Command Post.

"They're raising a lot of hell over near Hermroulle, Clark. I want you to go around to each platoon, personally, and warn them to get ready to move on over there."

"Why not use the radio, sir?"

"Because we have no orders to move, or even get ready to move. I just want to make sure everybody's ready to go, just in case. Let's be ready for whatever they tell us."

Constantly riding his men to stay sharp and ready was always good. But as Joel and First Sergeant Ruth listened to the regimental radio net and plotted the course of the battle on their map, it gradually became clear that they would not be needed at Hermroulle. The 1ˢᵗ Battalion and the tankers were successful in stopping the Germans' two attacking columns of tanks and infantry.

Those they didn't kill, they captured and the rest melted away back east, toward Germany.

"Look at those bastards, Lieutenant Finnigan," Ed Ruth said as the first column of unarmed, defeated German soldiers were marched through Bastogne into captivity. "Some of them look downright happy. You'd think they won the goddamned war."

"In a way they have, Top; their own personal wars anyway. They're still alive and the Russians won't get them."

The rest of the afternoon of the day after Christmas passed in relative quiet; quiet for the midst of a truly desperate battle, anyway. Joel was enjoying his first hot meal in days, even if it was from a GI mess kit, when Paulie Jaworski burst into the Command Post in a state approaching panic.

"Tanks," he yelped, "we've got tanks coming up from the rear… I can hear 'em! The fuckers got around behind us!"

"Shit," Joel growled as he threw his mess kit on an ammunition box, grabbed his M1, and headed out to face another attack.

Instead, he confronted an American Jeep with a 4th Armored Division colonel in the right front seat and a major from the 3rd Army staff hanging on in the rear. Behind them rattled a long line of M4 Sherman tanks, all snow-splotched and mud-covered from long, hard days on the road.

Joel slung his rifle on his right shoulder, reached across his chest for the sling with his left hand, and saluted as smartly as he had ever done as a private in Georgia.

"Relax, Lieutenant," the colonel said before Joel could report formally.

"Third Army's here, young man."

"Welcome to Bastogne, Colonel. We've been keeping the fire warm for you."

"Sorry we're late. We didn't miss the party, did we?"

"Hell no, Colonel," Joel said, with a dramatic gesture toward the east.

"They went that-a-way."

"Okay. We'll take 'em now. It looks like your guys could use a break."

The colonel motioned for Joel to step closer to his Jeep.

"Tell me, Lieutenant; did your general really tell the Germans 'nuts' when they asked if he wanted to surrender?"

"He sure as hell did, Colonel.

"We all did."

*****

Thus ended the Battle of the Bulge. It did not really end as much as it bulged in the opposite direction.

It was the middle of January, 1945 when Joel was able to have Ed Ruth assemble Company B, now down to 200 men from the 300 who had ridden into Bastogne with him just a month before, to read them the order they had all been waiting for.

"We're leaving, men," Joel said without preamble.

"We'll march back to Bastogne to trucks that will take us up to the Alsace-Lorraine country."

"Aw, shit," someone groaned from the rear ranks. Joel let it pass.

"I know," he said with a grin, "but intelligence says the enemy is falling back. We may see some more action, but nothing like we had here."

Not being a professional soldier looking forward to pinning ever more impressive hardware onto his shoulders, Joel always hated the pompous speeches that officers liked to give at moments like this. But this one time, knowing they had more than held their end up in one of the most crucial battles of the entire war, he felt he had to say something.

"What you guys have done here this month has been heroic. It'll go down in the history books and people will be talking about it 100 years from now.

"But only you — we — will remember how it really was. Like everyone, I wish I could have been someplace else, but since I had to be here, I'm thankful it was with you.

"You're the best soldiers and the best people I've ever met. The greatest honor any of us will ever have will be to have had one another for friends."

Generals Eisenhower, Matthew Ridgeway, and Lewis Brereton, commanding general of all the American and British airborne troops in Europe, said much the same thing a few weeks later at Camp Mourmelon le Petit. The entire 101st Airborne Division was paraded before the three generals to receive the Presidential Unit Citation for their defense of Bastogne.

It was the first time the citation had been presented to an entire division.

CHAPTER TWELVE

SANSOM STREET

August 15, 1945

Susanna, my love,

It's over. I'm coming home — to you. I leave Obersalzburg sometime tomorrow. I'll go to France by train. Then it's a ship from Cherbourg, unless I cross the English Channel and sail from Southampton.

That's the Army for you — hurry up and wait, except for last December, of course, when we had to hurry up and get to Belgium without a moment to wait for winter gear.

God, there were times during that terrible Christmas in Bastogne when I thought I'd never see you again.

After fighting so hard to get here, and losing so many friends along the way, I never thought Germany could be so beautiful. But it is, at least the part we're in. There wasn't much fighting in Bavaria; so the towns and villages are still in good shape and it's almost like being home.

The strangest thing of all is that the people, except for a few die-hard Nazis, seemed really glad to see us. I've been staying in a lovely home, with a few other officers from Company B. The old couple who own the house have been wonderful — always a pot of coffee on the kitchen stove and a nice, comfortable easy chair to fall into after a day on patrol.

I guess some of the locals are as glad to be rid of Hitler as we are.

I can't even begin to tell you how much I'm longing to see you.

Things have changed so much since I left you and sailed off to Liverpool. It's hard to believe that I'm a 1ˢᵗ Lieutenant and Company Commander. I must have done fairly well at it because I was offered a promotion to Captain and even a West Point appointment if I'd stay in the Army.

It's no great credit to me; guys just kept getting killed off.

I don't think any of it happened because I was such a great soldier. I just wanted to get back to you as soon as I could. It seemed the best way was to get the war over with as soon as possible. I did my best to help make that happen and I guess that's what they noticed.

Don't worry, though. I've had enough soldiering to last me a lifetime.

As I meet more and more Germans, including the soldiers, I find it hard to believe that we were all trying to kill one another just a few months ago.

I didn't feel nearly so kind-hearted when the 506ᵗʰ liberated the concentration camp near Landsburg in April. It wasn't one of those big extermination camps, but more of a camp for slave laborers, rounded up from all over Europe to work in the war factories.

Still, it was the worst thing I've ever seen in my life. There were men, women, and even little kids, half starved to death, staggering around like walking skeletons. The ones who weren't that fortunate were stacked like cord wood waiting to be tossed into mass graves as quickly as possible before they became a public health problem.

It made me realize, in a way that our own propaganda couldn't, the monstrousness we fought against. It made it all worth it. I want to spend the rest of my life trying to understand how this could have happened.

Until just a few days ago, we were training and staying in shape so we could go out to the Pacific and help finish off Japan. Thank God, that won't be necessary now, but I do have to wonder if that terrible bomb we used hasn't cost us a lot of the moral superiority that kept us all going through the war.

Of course, based on what I saw here in Europe and what I've learned about the Japanese, if I were President Truman I'd almost certainly have done the same thing.

Not even the winner, no matter how noble his cause, can come out of a war with completely clean hands.

Good Lord! I've just realized what a Gloomy Gus this letter makes me seem like. But I'm not, my darling Susanna; I swear I'm really not. I feel a sense of mission though, one that we'll go through together, and I feel very confident and happy about it.

I'll call you when I get to New York.

You call the preacher.

All my Love,

Joel

*****

S usanna's hands trembled and her eyes filled with tears as she read Joel's last letter from Germany for at least the tenth time.

The time for reading letters was over, at last. Her para-trooper had already called her and was waiting in the lobby of the Curtis Publishing Company building on Washington Square, where she had taken a job as a secretary shortly after Joel sailed away.

What would she find?

What would he find?

Were they ready for the reunion — this, of all reunions?

They had waited for so long.

She tidied her desk, put Joel's letter back into her bag and joined the crowd, most of whom were women, for the elevator ride down toward the sunshine of the midsummer afternoon. The elevator was a capsule of all the hopes and dreams of America, newly plunged into peace and trying to find its way back to normal living.

"Is yours back yet, Flo?" one of the girls from accounting asked a receptionist.

"Another month, I think. He wrote me his ship just got in to San Diego."

"… planning a big homecoming?"

"You bet," the receptionist purred with a lascivious smile.

"How 'bout you, Suz?" Flo inquired. "I'll bet you have a nice see-through nightie all ready for action."

Susanna had exactly that, but before she could open her mouth to reply, the elevator clanked to a stop on the sixth floor. Mr. Gordon from ad sales got on and an awkward hush settled over the car.

Mr. Gordon's son Rob had taken off from Lakenheath, England just about a year ago to deliver a load of 500-pound bombs to Germany. He had been incinerated when his B-17 was jumped by German fighters over Dusseldorf, which made the women on the elevator not want to talk about happy home-comings.

"Dear God," Susanna wondered, "will we ever get over this universal sadness?"

The elevator reached the lobby. The door slid open and she found the answer. Her answer, anyway.

Joel looked so fine in his perfectly pressed uniform, complete with his mirror-shined jump boots, his paratrooper wings with stars that denoted his combat jumps in Normandy and Holland, his Silver and Bronze Star ribbons and, above them all, the blue rectangle of his Combat Infantry Badge.

He looked good, even beyond the uniform. He was tall, fit, and tanned.

Susanna and Joel did not rush into each other's arms and fall into the passionate embrace that the news photographers had already turned into a stereotype. They simply joined hands, stayed at arm's length, and looked at each other.

"God, you're beautiful," he said.

"That's a cliché, isn't it?" he added with a degree of embarrassment. "But not if it's true, I guess."

"Let's get out of here, Lieutenant Finnigan."

Their kiss waited until they got outside into the warm sun that shone down on Washington Square. They wrapped their arms around each other, and the day grew warmer still.

Susanna's nipples hardened as she pressed her body against him. She felt the wetness between her legs, and the steadily increasing size and hardness beneath Joel's Army issue trousers told her she was having the same effect on him.

She damned, double and triple damned, the layers of clothing that lay between their hungry bodies.

"Let's get out of here before we become the talk of Washington Square," she whispered.

They didn't talk much as they walked through the narrow streets of Old City Philadelphia toward the small walk-up apartment on Sansom Street that Susanna had rented in anticipation of Joel's homecoming. There was some idle chatter about Joel's Atlantic crossing and the train ride from New York, but nothing of any real substance. There was only the deep communication of lovers who didn't need to say anything, and the silent, burning ecstasy at the end of their walk.

Susanna led the way up the stairs, warmly happy in the knowledge that Joel was just a few steps behind, admiring her long legs and the gentle sway of her exquisitely rounded hips. She unlocked the door, stood aside, and let Joel go in first, to see the place she had prepared for them.

He took off his overseas cap and stood quietly in the middle of the living room. He said nothing, but Susanna could see the approval in his eyes.

"You like...?"

"It's exactly what I thought it would be. All through Europe... Bastogne... even Bavaria... this was always the place."

"Sit. Get those jump boots off... they look uncomfortable."

Joel shrugged off his Army jacket and sat on the sofa to unlace his boots while Susanna disappeared into the kitchen. She returned bearing two long-stemmed glasses, filled more than halfway with a wine of the deepest red.

"I had to search all over Philadelphia for this. It's French, from before the war."

She handed Joel his glass. "Welcome home, Joel. Welcome home, my love."

They each took a sip of wine, without once looking anywhere but into each other's eyes. They put the glasses down and fell into a long embrace that raised their emotional and physical desires to heights they had only imagined since 1943.

The wetness and the hardness returned as they ground their hips together. Tenderly, very gently, they explored one another's mouths with active, probing tongues. Joel cradled Susanna's face while tears of happiness were brimming in her eyes.

"Undress me, Joel," she whispered. "Please undress me, my love."

Their hands fell eagerly to the joyful work of unfastening belts, buttons and snaps. Shirts, trousers, skirts, blouses, bra and underwear were tossed carelessly aside until they stood naked in the middle of the living room.

They came together again. Their hands ranged freely over their bodies. They explored, ever more eagerly, and stoked their fires to an ever higher intensity.

Susanna slipped her left hand between Joel's legs and held him gently.

"You're so big," she said, looking up at him with widening eyes filled with amazement and longing.

"You do have that effect, lady," he replied.

He put his arm around her slender shoulders and guided her toward the bedroom.

She grasped him again as they sank onto the bed. Now Joel was able to reach down between Susanna's legs to begin the slow, gentle massage that carried them both to the edge of sanity.

"You're so open," he said in amazement.

"I'm open for you, Joel," she said, "only for you… forever."

He continued the massage, until Susanna gasped, quivered, yelped, and finally exploded in a paroxysm of her ecstasy.

"Now, Joel," she demanded.

"Please."

The first time was frantic, almost a little clumsy. It was the desperate coupling of two lovers driven nearly mad by more than a year of anticipation. After that, their love making grew more languorous and gentle as they developed into lovers in the truest sense. Susanna marveled at the knowledge that her greatest pleasure lay in bringing pleasure to Joel.

Joel rose, took Susanna's ankles in his hands and held her legs as far apart as they could go while her delicate feet reached toward the ceiling. She wasn't just opening her body to let him inside, but reaching out and drawing him into her as voraciously as he was thrusting into her, going right up through her until she felt he was touching her heart from the inside.

Each time it ended with a shattering, noisy eruption, as they cried out the joy they found in giving each other the best of themselves.

They were joined together, basking in the afterglow as Susanna caught her breath and regained her composure.

"Thank you," she said, savoring not just the moment but the miracle that Joel entrusted to her keeping.

"You could turn out to be habit forming," Joel said.

"I'd better be," Susanna replied.

*****

It had all happened exactly the way Joel knew it would, through his long trek through Europe and Susanna's equally long wait in Philadelphia.

And it kept right on happening as Saturday bloomed into the fullness of the summer sunshine.

"Are you hungry?" Susanna asked from deep within the crook of Joel's right arm.

"Damn right," he replied as he lifted her face toward him for another penetrating kiss and cupped his left hand over her right breast.

"No, silly... for breakfast."

She pulled herself from him and jumped playfully out of bed.

"You put on some coffee. I'll throw some bacon and eggs together," she said, skipping happily toward the bedroom door.

Joel followed and started making coffee, unsure if he was making it too strong, or too weak, because he concentrated too much on the glory of the naked Susanna to keep very close track of just how many scoops he put into the percolator basket.

Susanna put bacon and eggs on the counter and reached into one of the upper cabinets for a frying pan, offering Joel a spectacularly unobstructed view of her firm, perfectly rounded breasts. He could still feel their warmth and vitality.

"What a morning," Susanna said contentedly as she laid the bacon strips out in the pan.

"... every day, for the rest of our lives," he replied.

"That sounds about right to me," she said as the bacon began to crackle.

"Jez - uz, lady," Joel cried in mock alarm. "You ought to throw a top on before you burn something important."

"Watch the bacon," she replied. "I'll be right back."

Joel watched the bacon, and a good deal more besides.

True to her word, Susanna came right back, clad only in Joel's khaki GI shirt. His jump wings, ribbons, Combat Infantry Badge, and lieutenant's bars had never been displayed quite so well.

"Would I make a good paratrooper?"

"The whole German army would have surrendered without a shot."

"Even in Bastogne?"

"You'd have been really cold in that outfit."

"But you would have kept me nice and warm."

She took out the bacon, placed it on a paper towel to drain and then turned to the eggs.

"Scrambled… fried… sunny side up?"

"Scrambled, please."

"That's how I like them too. I guess we really are compatible."

The eggs exceeded, by far, the very best of the powdered variety that the U.S. Army ever had to offer — except at Camp Toccoa, where they came from a local farmer. Susanna finished hers first and poured them each a second cup of coffee.

"I want to make your breakfast for the rest of our lives, Joel."

She said it simply, directly, and without any ringing declarations of love or passion. That was just the way it was going to be. It was what the chance meeting at Lit Brothers and the long wartime letters had all been leading toward; and now they had arrived.

"How soon?" he asked. "How soon can we get married?"

"We already are, really."

"Oh, yeah. But I was thinking about the long white dress, flowers, bridesmaids, and all that."

"And a big wedding cake?"

"The biggest."

"Chocolate?"

"Chocolate."

"In that case we'll go up to City Hall Monday morning and take out a license. Denise, my old boss from Lits, will be the witness."

"What church?"

"How about St. Tom's in Chester? Aunt Kate started taking me there when I was five."

"Well, since you promised chocolate... St. Tom's it is."

They drained off the remains of their coffee, looking at one another over the rims of their cups.

"We can't do any more until City Hall opens Monday morning," he said.

Joel took the dishes to the sink and turned on the water. Susanna followed and began rinsing them.

"What shall we do with the rest of the day," he mused.

Susanna shut off the water and turned to face him. Her fingers ran quickly down the buttons of his GI shirt.

"There must be something," she purred as she shrugged the shirt off her shoulders and let it drop to the kitchen floor.

*****

The rest of Saturday, on into Saturday night and Sunday morning they made love, dozed peacefully in each others' arms and then awoke to make love again.

*****

"I ought to get going pretty soon," Joel said as their second glorious night together gave way to daylight.

"Ha! So that's the kind of girl you think I am. Slam, bam, thank you ma'am, and then out the door."

"Aunt Kate and Uncle Tim don't know I'm back yet. I've got to officially come home — especially since I'll be leaving them first thing tomorrow so we can get to City Hall as soon as it opens."

"Well... in that case, you'd better get going, soldier."

CHAPTER THIRTEEN

ALTHEA'S PARTY

I'm so unhappy. I'd run away and become a nun, but I'm not Catholic. I wonder if they take Methodists. I'd love to hide away in one of those tiny convent cells where I could contemplate my life and how it got so screwed up.

Don't be so melodramatic, Althea. You can always go back to journalism.

Yeah, right. I've written all the daily newspaper stories. If you've covered one axe murder or election, or something that puts the Mayor in the sack with the Town Clerk, you've covered them all.

If only the Mayor would get into the sack with the Chief of Police.

No, thank you. I've already done newspapers.

I've got to stop talking to myself. I'm turning into one of those dotty old ladies with ten cats and I'm not even thirty.

God, I'm horny. What I really need is to get laid. Relieve all the tension. But with my luck, I'd probably hook up with a guy with AIDS. Things sure were easier in my mom's day. There's always the trusty old vibrator. But I'd sure love to have a man's arms around me. Well, not just any man. Certainly not another Tommy Corcoran.

He sure was a jerk. But he was hot. No, hot didn't even begin to describe him. Dark, curly hair, sexy deep brown eyes… and what a bod! All that weight-lifting really paid off. I still get wet just thinking about him. The way he'd…. I'd better stop.

Why didn't I listen to myself when I began to wonder about him? Right, I already figured that one out. He was irresponsible and self-centered like my father. Besides, he was going to rescue me from my dreary life. It was exciting to be with somebody who had his own set of rules. I liked that. With him, I'd be speeding through life on a Harley with the wind in my hair, not sitting in the passenger seat of a Mercedes like my mom.

I wonder what it would have been like if Mom had stayed in California. My whole life would have been different. I can just see myself. Little Pumpkin surrounded by all those hippies. Growing up a free spirit in a world full of free spirits.

Would I still have become a writer?

Probably. It's in my soul.

Would I have written about Dolley?

Probably not. I never would have heard of the Indian King Tavern. I wouldn't have been drawn to colonial history. I might have done something on the California Gold Rush instead, or maybe on the clipper ships that stopped in San Francisco on their way to the Orient. Or maybe I'd write some weird experimental kind of thing. Yeah, that's probably more likely.

But then I never would have had Sid Burnside for a step-dad, and he's a rock. I really love him.

He's just so boring.

If I'm destined to marry my father, maybe it should be someone like Sid. I should settle down and have kids with a responsible man. Mark Steinfeld's been after me for years. Maybe I should give him a chance. He's not bad looking. Actually, he's rather handsome — in a bland sort of way.

And he's steady. Responsible. He has a good job at some insurance company… I can't think of which one. He doesn't really turn me on, but maybe if I gave him a chance it could be different. He's not repulsive or anything.

But I can't just call him. I wouldn't want him to think I'm too anxious. He might not want me.

Maybe I can have a party. Invite all the people I've been meaning to call. If Mark comes and he's still available, I'll give him a chance. If not, well who knows who might show up?

*****

When you come up the stairs into my apartment in the Kingsway Manor on Kings Highway, you come right into the living room. You'd be facing a large, white wall that, because I have yet to hang any pictures, could make a really good back-drop.

I have to confess, and modestly too, that I can look damned good when I put my mind to it. Don't forget, Tommy Corcoran got pretty turned on himself. I've got a nice tush and boobs that have stood me in good stead for a few years now, thank you very much.

I spent the day positioning furniture and adjusting the lighting so it would throw a really good silhouette. I established my best position between the lights and the wall, like a stage director setting up his actors' marks, and then hit the shower.

I was hot and a little sweaty after a day of moving furniture and floor lamps into position, but as I toweled myself dry, I felt satisfied with what I saw in the full-length bathroom door mirror. Mark Steinfeld would never be able to get enough.

I only hope he wants more — a lot more.

*****

Mark was the first to arrive. I knew he would be. He's always punctual. And, he definitely liked what he saw. He handed me a bottle of wine, gave me a kiss on the cheek and an appreciative glance.

Jim Dowd, the business reporter, was right behind him, and Mark, in his perfectly pressed khakis, burgundy V-neck sweater and white shirt, couldn't wait to talk to Jim about the latest news on actuarial tables. He was every inch the up and coming insurance executive.

He'll do, I thought.

Harry Rutledge, my partner in award-winning and would-be partner in romance if he didn't already have a wife, arrived next with the woman who had kept me from pursuing my romantic fantasies with him — broad bottomed, balloon chested, loud mouthed Marissa Rutledge.

I had to wonder:

What in God's name does he see in her?

CHAPTER FOURTEEN

JUSTIN'S LEGS

The drive up Route 1 toward the Snyder Avenue Bridge over the Schuylkill River took forever. Uncle Tim had lent Joel his old '37 Ford convertible. He'd kept it in pretty good condition during the war years and it ran perfectly. Monday morning traffic wasn't all that bad either.

Joel couldn't get to Susanna fast enough. In time, he might be able to afford one of those big Mercedes he had liberated at Obersalzburg, but it still wouldn't be fast enough.

"You get to that girl, hold onto her and don't ever let her go, Joel Finnigan," Aunt Kate admonished him at his welcome home dinner on Sunday night.

"I won't, Aunt Kate, believe me, I won't. She's drawn a life sentence."

"Good! And she has the same thing in mind for you?"

Joel nodded.

Did she ever! If Aunt Kate had only known about the Friday and Saturday nights he had shared with Susanna… but he would never tell dear old Aunt Kate about the passions that he and Susanna had unleashed on Sansom Street.

She took both of his hands and looked into his eyes.

"I saw what your father and mother, God rest their souls, had together and I'm so happy it's come to you."

Aunt Kate smiled and Joel realized that she knew all about Friday and Saturday nights, or at least had made a pretty good guess.

"Now, you be at City Hall the minute it opens and get that wedding license. Then, bring that girl back here for a big engagement dinner. I want to meet my niece-in-law, daughter-in-law, whatever she'll be, and welcome her to our family."

*****

Joel inched through the Center City traffic, found a parking spot on Eighth Street, and raced up Sansom Street.

Susanna met him at the door. Later he would realize that something had seemed a little bit off but, just then, with her standing before him, he was not inclined to see it. She wore the same dress he had so frantically torn off her on Friday night.

It was clean and pressed, in contrast to Susanna's dark, troubled face.

He took her in her arms and kissed her. Their tongues joined and he started fumbling at the row of buttons running down her back. She drew him to her, her firm breasts pushed against him, and then she pushed him away.

"Joel, we can't," she said in a quiet, tremulous voice.

He looked and saw the tears running down her face.

"Nervous? Don't worry, love. All we have to do is fill out a couple of forms and then go for a blood test."

"I love you, Joel," she sobbed.

"And I love you, Susanna. So what's to cry about?"

"We can't get married."

"Okay. Living in sin is fine with me."

"No. We can't see each other again… ever."

Joel had read many literary descriptions of moments like this and he had seen more than a few of his 506th brothers driven half mad by Dear John letters from stateside, but it didn't prepare him for this. He felt as though he'd been kicked in the gut.

"Susanna, what's the matter? Yesterday you couldn't wait to be Mrs. Finnigan."

"I love you, Joel. But we can't get married."

"Why?"

"Justin Welch," she replied.

"The Marine?"

"He lost both of his legs on Peleliu. His sister called me this morning. He's coming to the Navy hospital here in Philadelphia. He doesn't want me to see him like he is."

Joel had seen enough legs, arms, and horribly truncated torsos in the snow of Bastogne and too many other battlefields to know that he wouldn't want anybody to see him either.

"Didn't you tell him… write to him?"

"Remember I told you I couldn't do it until he came home?"

"But he must have guessed. You couldn't have written him letters like you wrote me."

"No. Of course not."

"But now you have to go to him? How can you give up what we have?"

"I don't have a choice, Joel. Ever since we were children…"

"Children! Children my ass!" he exploded in unexpected rage.

Justin Welch, United States Marine Corps, had wounded him more grievously than any German could have ever done.

"Are we children? Were we children… in there?" he said, pointing at the bedroom door, now closed.

"No, Joel, we're not children. Children don't have such a thing as duty. That's why it has to be this way."

She collapsed onto the sofa and sobbed uncontrollably. When she was finally able to look up at Joel, her tear-stained face and lost, waif-like eyes almost made him want to start crying too.

"It's a trust. It's expected. And now that he's lost so much… it would be a betrayal. Could you ever want me if I did that?"

"Yes, yes I would," he replied softly. "I'd want you no matter what."

He wanted to sweep her up, kick open the bedroom door, and love her as tenderly and deeply and fiercely as he had done just two nights before.

But he saw instantly that it would be no good. It would have been a sad lovemaking that, after what they had known and felt, would have been a cold, joyless business. If all he was to have were memories of Susanna Winslow, he wanted them to be of her laughing, wildly passionate and hungry to draw him into the very depths of her.

Her mind was made up, and no matter how he felt, to try and go back would hurt too much.

He bent down and kissed her on the forehead. Each of them wanted to say something, but the words just wouldn't come, and they would have been the wrong ones in any case.

So he turned and left his love sitting on the sofa in the place that had filled their dreams throughout the dreary war years. He walked down the front steps into an emotional desert in which he knew he would wander for a very long time.

CHAPTER FIFTEEN

THE INSURANCE MAN

I can't believe it. I'm in love... with Mark Steinfeld, of all people.

Mark offered to stay after the party and help me clean up. He even washed the dishes, and that alone made him a real keeper. While he was drying, I poured us a couple of drinks... some Courvoisier I keep for when Mom and Dad come to dinner. We took them to the sofa. I lit a vanilla candle and we stared at the flame and sipped our drinks.

He reached over and began stroking my hair and the back of my head, which always gets my motor running. The next thing I knew, I was naked and we were heading for the bedroom.

I was really glad I'd thought to wash the sheets.

The sex was... good... really. I was surprised. It wasn't falling off the edge of a cliff wild like with Tommy. But then, look how that turned out.

It was... well, nice... with Mark — sort of like a cup of chamomile tea, and God knows I need some calming influences in my life.

And he is kind of cute when he talks about his work. I can't imagine getting all that excited about investigating insurance claims. But if it makes him happy, that's fine with me. It's what makes him so steady.

Anyway, it's time I was a bit more practical about men. After all, what did lust ever get me... besides great sex, of course? But what about afterwards? Tommy always kept me on edge. I never knew what he was going to do next.

There was a lot of anger in Tommy. We'd have a good night in bed and the next morning he'd explode if I made his breakfast toast too dark, or not dark enough. Tearing up my books and drafts of articles was one thing. But when he took to bouncing me off the walls... well, it was time for this girl to hit the trail.

Mark, on the other hand, is so predictable. We've been seeing each other twice a week for the past three weeks. I wanted things to move faster than that; so I didn't answer the phone when he called on Thursday. I knew it was him because he always calls two days before we're going out... and always at eight thirty. I didn't call him back until Saturday morning. It drove him crazy.

I haven't done any serious writing since I read Finnigan's book. I've started a couple of magazine pieces and done some odd reporting jobs for the *Philadelphia Inquirer*, but nothing of any substance. This Finnigan business has knocked the creative wind right out of me and I'm totally uninspired.

I'm always reading, or writing something in my notebook, but it's nothing like mining the life of Dolley Madison.

I did take a job at the Breadman here in Haddonfield, just a few steps from the Starbucks where this all began. 'Doctor Dough,' a Canadian biochemist who can't seem to get his visa problems sorted out, whips up some really wonderful bread, and I have a great time keeping the shelves organized and taking care of the customers.

I've even learned to say "Shabot Shalom" when I sell the challah bread every Friday morning. It always gets a smile from the Jewish ladies and that makes me feel very good.

Best of all, there's no heavy lifting and I get to take home some really great bread.

CHAPTER SIXTEEN

CONNIE

A fter Finnigan left Susanna, he started walking aimlessly. He was shell shocked. He'd gone through the entire war without experiencing this, but he'd seen it in others. The dazed look after seeing the guy next to you blown apart, or watching someone's body parts land next to you. Now he had that same disbelief and loss.

The lighted sign on O'Flynn's Bar on Walnut Street drew him like a bowl of milk draws a stray cat. He went inside and got shitfaced.

He woke up the next morning with Connie Fiorenzi's tongue in his ear. Before he could open his mouth to ask who she was, where they were or how they got there, her tongue was outlining the contours of his lips and her hands were working their way down his body where her tongue soon followed. It was clear she wanted more of what they'd been doing the night before, and Finnigan's body was quite willing to accommodate her.

He just wished he knew who the hell she was.

She couldn't be a hooker. She wouldn't have stayed all night. And she certainly wouldn't be so eager for an encore.

Whoever she was, it wasn't the time to think about it. It wasn't the time for thinking about anything. It was the time for reveling in Connie's erotic charms and blotting out the memory of Susanna Winslow.

An hour later, when Finnigan was physically exhausted and peacefully drifting between sleep and wakefulness, he remembered what had happened.

He'd met Connie at the bar. He was struck by her because she was so different from Susanna. She was short and slightly overweight with the biggest tits he'd ever seen. Her jet black hair was short, and her vacuous eyes were deep brown. She exuded sex. And Finnigan needed any opiate he could find to block the pain of losing Susanna.

He was vulnerable. So was Connie, or so she had said, and now here they were.

Connie raised her head and smiled wickedly at Joel.

"Five times," she said. "Five times! Can you believe it?" She gave him a squeeze with her right hand. "I think you're all ready for Number Six."

"Yeah," he groaned as he rolled over toward her.

Connie pushed him gently back on the pillow.

"I'm sore, from overuse, so…"

She shifted her body, bent over Joel, and did things with her mouth that he never thought possible.

"I oughta write a book on giving blow jobs," she said afterwards. "The regular way, with the guy on top, is great, and it's the only way to make babies, but to really keep a man, there's nothing like a great blow job."

"You're the best," Joel replied.

If only she, or he, had known how much more there was to it…. but Joel wasn't thinking very much then. He was a young man and a romantic, and the thing that romantic young men use to think with too often dangled between their legs instead of between their ears.

It was easy for Joel to give himself over to Connie's erotic inventiveness. True, she was heavier and coarser than he might have liked, but she didn't really look bad, and no woman on earth possessed the regal presence and gentle grace that was Susanna Winslow's.

Finnigan and Connie spent the next two days in the motel room where they had awakened. In between erotic romps, they ate deli sandwiches and pizza and drank champagne. When they talked, it was about food and sex and how glad they both were that the war was finally over. If the conversation started to get too personal, Finnigan reached for Connie and shut her up with a kiss. By the end of the second day, he knew that being with Connie was the only thing that would keep him sane after Susanna.

They drove to Elkton, Maryland that night and were married by a justice of the peace. It was the beginning of one of the darkest chapters in Joel Finnigan's life.

CHAPTER SEVENTEEN

GIOVANNI FINNIGAN

E lkton appeared very romantic in the movies. Whenever boy and girl found themselves so desperately in love that they could wait no longer, they would elope to Elkton where there was no waiting period, drag a kindly old Justice of the Peace out of bed in the middle of the night and, as the music rose just before the final credits, go on to live happily ever after.

Did the sweet old JP know, or want to know, how many of the marriages he officiated were desperate affairs of convenience from which the sheepishly grinning couple drove away, back up Route 40 into lives of unremitting sadness?

He'd have no reason to know, nor would Joel. It wasn't until a month later when they had driven west across the newly opened Pennsylvania Turnpike to visit Connie's family in Franklin that it came to him that, in her world, marriage vows were a declaration of war between men and women.

"Did you hear about Tony Gravano?" her mother Maria asked at dinner.

"No, what, Ma?" Connie replied.

"He's in the hospital; a stroke."

Their eyes lit up at that news — Connie's and her sisters: Anna, Joan and Louetta.

"It's about time," Joe Fiorenzi," growled from the end of the table. "That big house, the goddamned Cadillac… are you gonna pass the spaghetti sauce or not, Maria?"

"Angie loved that Cadillac," Maria said sweetly, as she passed the sauce.

"And she really knew how to break Tony's stones until she got it," Anna giggled.

"I heard her a couple of times when Tony came home from the factory on payday. She'd jam her finger on the table-cloth and say 'Put it right there, stupido, put it right there.'"

"Don't talk like that, Anna. You'll scare poor Joel away."

"Scare Joel," Joe snorted. "That Irishman ain't ascared of nothin'. He was a goddamned general, for the Christ's sake."

"I wasn't a general, Joe, and, believe me, I was scared all the time."

Joe stiffened and sat back in his chair. The Fiorenzi girls looked at Joel as though he'd exposed himself right there at dinner.

"We don't talk to my father like that, Finney," Connie sniffed coldly.

As the ritualistic "meet the family" evening continued, Joel began to realize that he had fallen into a society in which the woman who really knew how to break her husband's stones was the most admired of their sex; and if she could put him in the hospital with a heart attack or a stroke, like poor Tony Gravano, then she was a real heroine.

It was no wonder so many of the men, after leaving their life's blood in the factories or coal mines of western Pennsylvania, took to drink or had girlfriends on the side, which unquestionably drove the women to a greater and more lethal rage.

Joel thought he had left war behind. Now he was in a place where it was the natural state of being.

"So, Joely, when you gettin' a Cadillac?" Joe asked querulously from the head of the table.

"A Cadillac? I don't think so, Joe. I'm working at a newspaper and I'm planning to go to school at night to study history."

"History? Shit! Nobody cares about history no more."

"You're a big goddamn war hero. You gotta make somethin' offa it."

*****

Joe unknowingly, or very much so, had set the tone for Joel and Connie's life together, with Connie at the very center of it.

"And why not?" she thought. She deserved it, and her family had always expected her to be the one who lived in the big house on the hill.

And, of course, there was the baby to consider. Joel didn't know yet. But once she told him, he'd have to move them somewhere better. She had only agreed to that tiny apartment because they needed someplace to live. She certainly wasn't going to move in with his Aunt Kate.

Joel wanted to live with Aunt Kate and go to college full time, but Connie insisted that he get a job. After all, he did have responsibilities. She figured he'd give up the ridiculous idea of school sooner or later, and get to the business of their real life.

*****

It wasn't long before the Finnigans found a bigger apartment, a little farther west on Spring Garden not too far from the Philadelphia Museum of Art. It still had only one bedroom, but there was a little alcove off the living room where Joel could set up a desk and typewriter, the tools he needed to pursue the life of a student and writer.

It was also the classroom in which he learned one of life's fundamental and most painful truths; being alone is bad enough when you're by yourself. It was a life that could be lived in reasonable contentment, if not happiness.

But to be alone with somebody else living in the house was the worst by far. It was an emotional and spiritual desert from which no escape seemed possible.

Not that he minded, at first. The larger Connie grew, the lazier and more argumentative she became. She ignored him, except when she wanted him to fetch something for her, and she was completely indifferent to his work, except for when she was actively hostile to it.

Many a night he came home, tired from a hectic shift on the rewrite desk, to find her snoring loudly on the sofa with the dishes and leftover food from dinner still sitting on the table.

He would invariably clear the table, throw the spoiled food into the garbage can and then start doing the dishes. Try as he might to be quiet, Connie always awoke and came bustling into the kitchen.

"Jesus Christ! Can't you do anything right?" she'd snarl as she elbowed him away from the sink.

"I'm sorry. I didn't mean to wake you."

"Well, you did. It's bad enough you're out all night. You don't have to stagger home and raise hell all over the house."

"There was a bad accident on Delaware Avenue."

"Yeah, yeah. You were out having a hell of a good time."

"Six people were killed. That wasn't a good time."

"Right. I'll get the dishes, stupido."

It was aggravating, to say the least, but Connie was carrying his child, after all. Pregnant women were... strange... from time to time, and Joel knew that he had to be patient.

The coming baby meant more to Joel than he thought it would. He would much rather have been going through the pregnancy with Susanna, but he was looking forward to it and found, deep within himself, a determination to be as good a husband and father as he could be.

"What will we call him?" Connie asked sweetly one evening as they sipped their after dinner coffee.

"Him? What makes you think it's a boy?"

"He's big enough," she said as she caressed her enormous belly. "...and the way he kicks! Besides, my father would hate me if I didn't give him a grandson first."

"I think that has more to do with me than you," replied Joel.

"You can't tell him that, Finney. He's from the old school."

"Well, that's not the way I read it."

"The way you read it! You've always got your nose in some goddamn book or other… as if the doctors who write them know anything."

"They are the experts."

"Yeah. And if the book told you to jump off a bridge, would you do that too?"

"What about a name, Finney?"

"I've always liked Liam, or how about Timothy, after my Uncle Tim?"

"Liam. Li… am Finnigan? That's a name for an Irish potato farmer."

"Well, Tim Finnigan was one of James Joyce's heroes — *Finnigan's Wake*."

"Is that something else you found in one of those books? You want my kid to be named after some goddamned drunk? Forget it, Mister Finnigan's Wake."

"What do you have in mind, then?"

"Oh, forget it! I'll think of something. I always have to think of something. God, Finney, do you always have to be a clod hopper from the Old Country?"

Ultimately, when he first saw his son, Joel did have to admit that a boy named Giovanni Finnigan was certain to go far.

"Nice kid," Joe Fiorenzi said, as if he was appraising a new car.

*****

Giovanni Finnigan grew up straight and strong and smart. Joel loved that boy. No matter how hard the day had been at either the *Inquirer* or the night classes at Temple, Joel was never too tired to take the little guy up in his arms and hear his excited account of the day just past.

Connie wasn't the least bit interested in getting up in the middle of the night to feed him, or walk endlessly through the apartment when he couldn't sleep or just needed comforting; so Joel gladly took that duty.

Giovanni was a trophy for Connie, a gold star that she used to verify her womanhood and her place ahead of her un-married sisters. She loved to strike what became known as her Madonna pose in her living room easy chair, with Giovanni at her copious breast and a look of infinite superiority on her face.

"You like that better than daddy's old books, don't you?" she'd say softly, while at the same time looking scornfully at Joel.

"I'll bet you can't wait 'til daddy finds a real job."

"I have a real job, Concetta," Joel would reply in a calm, icy tone that drove Connie mad.

"Yeah, right; you've got a job sitting on your ass all day. You could be working construction with my father out in Franklin instead of fiddle-fartin' around with those books."

They had had this conversation before, and Joel was tired of it. Working construction in western Pennsylvania with Big Joe Fiorenzi was not going to happen and there was not going to be another argument about it.

Joel got up from his chair and headed toward his small study.

"Where do you think you're going, professor?"

"It's time to get started on my senior thesis."

"Thesis-phesis. You're going to stay right here."

"I can't, Connie. This is important. I've got to get to work."

"Work! Your daddy doesn't know what work is, does he sweet-ums?"

Joel bent over, kissed his son on the forehead, and went to bury himself in the records of the British Navy's operations in the Chesapeake Bay during the War of 1812.

Connie countered by becoming, or at least acting, more loving and displaying her robust sexuality. Joel could not fail to respond to that and he readily jumped in between Connie's legs, or wherever she wanted him at any particular moment.

She also developed another form of her campaign of marital warfare. She had plenty of games designed to wear Joel down, or provoke him to rage, but her favorite was to sneak into the bathroom while Joel was finding refuge in the shower, fill a glass with cold water, and dump it over him.

It was a godawful shock. Joel would be lost in the solace of the pulsing hot water, alone, at peace with his thoughts of 1812, and yes, of the lost Susanna, when Connie would thunder into his reverie to remind him that she, and only she, was at the center of his universe.

Later, years later, Joel would be amazed that he had put up with Connie's cold water torture for as long as he did. He must have been a coward, or at least an idiot, he thought. He hated it, almost to the point of violence, but Giovanni Finnigan would not be allowed to see his parents fighting; so he stretched the bound of reasonableness.

"Connie," he said one morning after she had wrecked his morning shower. "I don't like it when you pour cold water over me in the shower."

"Oh, I don't like it when you pour cold water over me in the shower," she trilled in her sing-song, mimicking voice.

"And I don't want you to do it again."

"And I don't want you to do it again. Who the hell died and left you boss anyway, professor?"

But Connie was great in bed, and her blow jobs truly had charms to soothe the savage breast; plus there was Giovanni. So, the cold water treatment continued… until May, 1950.

Things were going generally good for Joel. His paper on the War of 1812 had been a winner, and he was being encouraged to develop it into a broader study for one of the history journals. He was graduating from Temple with honors and had been accepted into graduate school, but better, far better than any of that, Giovanni loved to crawl into his arms at every opportunity.

"I love you, Daddy," the boy would say as his eyes grew heavier.

"And I love you too, Tiger."

Yes, the world was bright when he climbed into the shower on the night of May 17; at least until he heard Connie come into the bathroom and start running the water in the sink.

"I really hope you're not going to dump a glass of cold water over my head," he said in an emphatically calm tone.

"I really hope you're not going to dump a glass of cold water over my head," she mimicked.

Joel's muscles tensed and his anger rose.

"I… really… do… advise… against it," he seethed.

Of course the cold water came, and when it did Joel exploded in a killing rage he hadn't felt since 1945.

"Goddamn it!" he roared as he thrust back the shower curtain and burst from the shower, naked, dripping wet and fit to commit murder.

Connie turned and tried to make a break for the bathroom door, but it was too late. Joel seized her by the throat and slammed her against the wall. His left fist was raised, cocked and on the verge of driving right through the center of her face.

"For five years," he said, "I have asked you not to do that, and for five years that is exactly what you have done."

"Aw, Finney," she whined. "Can't you take a joke?"

"It is not a joke, Concetta. This is not a drill, goddamn it!"

"Go ahead and hit me, you son of a bitch," she snarled. "I always knew it would come to this."

Joel's reply was interrupted by a whimper from Giovanni's room, and he was ashamed of his outburst. He relaxed his grip on Connie's throat and lowered his left arm.

She wrenched herself free and dashed from the bathroom. Joel shut off the shower, took a large towel, and went into the bedroom.

Connie followed a few minutes later. Giovanni was calmed and fast asleep, but Connie wasn't finished with Joel.

"What'll they say at Temple when they find out you're a wife beater? Do you think you'll ever get into your goddamned graduate school?"

"When they meet you, they'll understand completely," he replied.

"You know, Finney, I'm sorry I ever got involved with you."

Me too.

"I never would have married you if I hadn't been knocked up."

"What!"

Finnigan stared at her in disbelief.

Connie covered her mouth. "I...I'm sorry, Finney," she said. It was the first expression of remorse in the five years they'd been married.

"Finney, I didn't know what to do. My family would have disowned me."

"You used me, Connie," he said quietly.

"Oh, Finney," she replied as she stepped toward him. "I didn't know what else to do."

He stepped away from her.

"You could have told me. You could have been honest. If you'd told me the truth, I could have forgiven you. But all these years, we've lived a lie. Get out of here. Go away."

"Finney, please..."

Finnigan took her arm, walked her out of the bedroom, then went in and shut the door behind him. He put on a pair of jeans and a Temple sweatshirt, then laced on a pair of gym shoes and headed for the front door.

"Are you walking out on us, Finney?" she asked in a voice that, for the first time, sounded frightened.

He didn't answer.

CHAPTER EIGHTEEN

ALTHEA'S MINUET

I want to marry Mark and have a baby. He says he loves me, but he acts so cold and distant sometimes. I think he's afraid to make a commitment. But my biological clock *is* ticking and even I can't wait forever.

I've toyed with the idea of forgetting to take my birth control pills, but that would be a shabby trick. I mean, if he suggested it, they'd be in the trash can in an instant, but I just can't do it on my own.

Every time we seem to be getting really close, he backs off. Then I get annoyed and act cool to him, and he brings me flowers and tries to endear himself to me — until I start acting lovey. Then he backs off again. It's a strange dance we do. I can't get close to him unless I act like I don't want to. I suppose I could find somebody else, but I really feel invested in him. If only he'd suggest living together, that would be a start.

Maybe if he thought I was interested in someone else, or that I'm thinking of moving away... my lease will be up soon. I could tell him I'm going to California. I have nothing to keep me in South Jersey. That will get him going. I can hear him now.

"Nothing? Am I nothing? Don't you care at all about me?"

"Of course, I do, but we're getting too involved and we really have no future. You're not ready for a commitment. I'm not sure I am either. We both love our freedom too much. If I stayed here, we'd probably end up doing something stupid — like moving in together. I'm tired of this silly damn courtship game. It would be nice to share my life with someone I love who loves me, but you'd probably expect me to spend every minute of my time with you. No, it just wouldn't work."

"Why wouldn't it? You said we both love our freedom?"

"I don't know."

I can see it all now. He will be begging me to stay and move in with him or get a place together. From there, it's only a few short steps to the altar. Althea, you really are brilliant, you know.

CHAPTER NINETEEN

MIDNIGHT WALK

T he stone steps leading up to the Philadelphia Museum of Art went on forever. Finnigan had been up
them before, of course, and there was a time when
he could have run up carrying a full field pack and an M1 rifle,
but now, as an emerging academic in his late twenties, the steps
seemed harder.

He could have run up if he really had to, but he could feel
his heart rate increasing and his breath coming harder as he
neared the top.

He paused when he reached the broad courtyard leading to
the front entrance, locked now as the clock neared midnight,
and looked back down the Benjamin Franklin Parkway toward
City Hall — his destination on the morning of the day his life
fell apart.

As his heartbeat and breathing returned to normal, the anger drained out of him as well. He was glad to be rid of it. He
did not like the way rage affected him.

Aside from that nonsense with the cold water, tonight's
blow-up really wasn't all Connie's fault. They had both been
vulnerable and easy targets for each other's sadness and sexuality that night at O'Flynn's and, anyway, he was a firm believer
that when all the forces that drive the human heart were in
alignment, there was nothing to be done to change the outcome.

He was fated to be with Connie. Not like he had been with
Susanna Winslow. Nothing could ever be like that, of course,
but he had turned his back on it five years ago and now his life
was with Connie.

If she had told him she was pregnant, what would he have done?

Nothing, probably — considering his frame of mind at the time.

Sure, Connie was hard to live with at times, but he always felt that was to be his punishment for failing to stand up to Susanna's misguided sense of duty and his infantile reaction to her ultimate rejection. He could have fought for her and led her to see what great gifts had been set before them.

But he didn't.

Where was it written that he had to get shitfaced drunk and marry the first woman who opened her legs for him?

No, Connie wasn't the girl of his dreams. The girl of his dreams had gone off with the legless Justin Welch. Now he was with Connie. She was great in bed, or had been until tonight; she made terrific lasagna and she had presented him with a wonderful son.

Little Giovanni Finnigan was the center of Joel's life now. He was a good looking four year old and a completely wild savage, as four year olds are supposed to be, and Joel loved him.

Giovanni would have to be told of his parentage someday, but not just now. Joel didn't need to wrestle with that problem at the moment. It was a good many years off; so he started back down the steps, purged of his anger.

*****

Joel had been gone less than an hour before Connie began to realize how empty the apartment was without him in it. As the time went by, she became more and more certain that it would remain empty. He'd probably come back for his clothes and those goddamned dust catching books, but he was gone.

He might even try to take Giovanni, but she'd put up a hell of a fight about that.

She knew she had gone too far this time. She had been trying to get a rise out of him for the whole five years of their marriage, but he was always so pleasant, so reasonable, and so easygoing.

Men weren't supposed to be easy going, goddamnit! They were supposed to stomp around the house, bellow like mad elephants, and bang the waitresses at the truck stop.

Would Big Joe Fiorenzi sit on his ass reading a goddamned book while some big-tittied haridan ran the show?

Like hell he would! "Honor and obey" were the core of the marriage vows and, by God, it was up to men like Big Joe to see that they were enforced to the letter. It was his duty, especially to his fellow males.

Of course the women of Big Joe's world had to give as good as they got if they were to survive. How else were they to get their Cadillacs, their yearly trips to Florida and, most of all, their houses on the hill?

These things were the spoils of the eternal war between men and women, just as the truck stop waitresses were for the men. And war is a violent thing. Attack and defend but never surrender.

But Joel… Jesus H. Christ! He didn't rant, stomp, or bang waitresses. He never drank much, and he didn't bet on the ponies or the ball games, which really made him suspect out there in Franklin.

"Be sure and marry a gambling man," her mother had always preached to Connie and her sisters. "That way you'll always have money."

There were times when Connie felt she had been a failure as a woman. She had borne a fine son but she never got a rise out of Joel, except in bed, and couldn't make him aware that she was supposed to be the center of his universe. Until tonight, that is.

When Joel came storming out of the shower and took her by the throat, Connie didn't know whether to be frightened or thrilled that she had finally succeeded in getting him to act like a real man.

She wondered what would happen when, and if, Joel came back from his midnight hike. He was, after all, a man who had killed some of Germany's toughest soldiers with rifle, knife and, for all she knew, his bare hands.

What was he capable of now that she had succeeded in hurting him far worse than the Germans ever could have done?

She jumped as she heard his key turn in the lock.

Joel walked into the apartment with the same calm demeanor that had always thrown Connie into a rage.

She stood up to face him. She opened her mouth to speak, but the words wouldn't come.

Joel looked at her with clear, steady eyes. It was, she imagined, the same look that many a German infantryman saw in the instant before Joel killed him. He continued across the living room to his study, and closed the door behind him.

CHAPTER TWENTY

MOVING IN

Mark and I are moving in together. We found a great apartment in an old Victorian house at the other end of town. It's just the kind of place I've always dreamed of living in. It has character... oddly shaped rooms painted in bright colors, and a real fireplace. Of course, we only have the first floor, but how much space do we need for just the two of us? And, there's a sunny little room in the back that will make a perfect office.

Finally, my life is becoming settled. I'll be able to give up the bread store and write full time — that is, if I ever get out of this slump. Ever since Finnigan's book came out, I haven't been able to write anything worthwhile. I've had some great starts, but I can't keep anything going.

Actually, I'm really too busy now anyway — getting everything ready for the move. I'm happier than I ever remember being. I can't understand why people think I'm sullen.

I was going to Philly yesterday and the toll taker on the Ben Franklin Bridge really pissed me off. Here I was thinking about the big move and he says, "Come on; smile. It can't be that bad." I felt like shutting the window on his hand. I hate people like that. For all he knew, I could have just found out that I have cancer and I only have three months to live.

Did I really look that miserable? How could it be when things are finally going right for me?

CHAPTER TWENTY-ONE

TRUCE

When Finnigan finally came out of his study, he acted as though nothing had happened. Connie was uncharacteristically quiet.

Finally, she yelled at him.

"Say something, will you! Scream at me if you want to! I can't take this God damned silence."

"Forget it," he replied.

"Forget it! You can really forget it?"

He put his hand over her lips.

"What do you want me to do, Connie? Leave you? Get a divorce? Hit you?"

He took his hand away.

Her mouth opened, but no words came out. "I...I...," she started. Then she ran from the room and locked herself in the bathroom where he could hear her sobbing uncontrollably.

Finnigan was in bed when she finally opened the door an hour later. She crept in beside him while he pretended to sleep. She put her hand on his back, but she said nothing.

Joel barely noticed her. He had taken refuge in a compartment deep in his soul that was closed to everything but the warm, soothing, erotic essence of Susanna Winslow.

Connie tossed and turned, as she usually did when she wanted Joel to pay attention to her. The more she did, the more Joel retreated into his fantasies about Susanna. He could feel her against him, with not a stitch of clothing between their young, questing bodies. Her breasts were firm and her nipples hard. Her arms and legs opened to draw him inside and her voice, tremulous with unrestrained desire, spoke quietly and urgently of their love and all that she wanted him to give her.

Susanna had been given a new role in the life of Joel Finnigan. He recalled a sermon in which the preacher spoke of the cool, refreshing water that God provided for parched wanderers in the scorched, unforgiving wilderness of the soul.

That was the role Joel reserved for the newly ephemeral Susanna — the bringer of divine sustenance in an otherwise barren emotional landscape.

Joel knew he and Connie both wanted to turn back the clock; he to 1945 and Susanna; Connie, to the time before that last glass of cold water and her untimely revelation about Giovanni's parentage.

They could do no such thing, of course, and so they came to an unspoken agreement, not to forget it — they never could do that — but to act as though it had never happened.

The next day started just like all the days before it. The apartment was unchanged. So too were the streets of Center City and the Temple campus. Joel and Connie were uncommonly civil, but nothing would ever be the same again.

CHAPTER TWENTY-TWO

SECOND THOUGHTS

I think I made a mistake, but I don't know what to do about it.

Moving in with Mark was supposed to be the answer to my dreams. I love the old house. I really want to be settled, and I do love him. Really I do. It's just that something doesn't seem right. I felt an indefinable reluctance when the moving truck pulled up outside my apartment. This was something I'd wanted, something I'd had to work to make happen. Now that it really was happening, I wanted to yell, "Stop! Maybe we should wait."

But I couldn't. Mark and I both had given up our apartments. I had to be out the next day, and he only had a couple of more days. Besides, we gave the new landlord two months' rent and a security deposit. I wanted a commitment. Now I was committed, and I wasn't sure if I wanted to be.

I told myself it was probably perfectly normal jitters. Once we're moved in and settled, things will be different. But it's been a month now and I feel a vague emptiness.

Mark is thriving. It's as though moving in with me allowed him to take off a mask he'd been wearing. Not that he's changed so dramatically, mind you. He's still the same, solid — spelled boring — wait, I didn't mean that. Or maybe I did. But boring can be good. Right? It's safe and secure. That's what I need. It's like eating a well-balanced meal instead of junk food, even though junk food tastes so good.

It's time I grew up. I really want a baby and if I'm going to be a mother, I have to be responsible. Things will get better. I know they will. Or maybe I'll learn to be content. After all,

Mark really is a good man, and you know how hard they are to find.

CHAPTER TWENTY-THREE

CONNIE'S BIG MOUTH

C onnie just couldn't help prancing around in time with the rollicking, galloping tempo of the *Light Cavalry Overture* on the front lawn of the president's house at Washington College. Her beaming smile and wildly bouncing fore and aft quarters created quite a spectacle as she cavorted before the faculty and their wives.

Joel cringed and most of his colleagues could only marvel at what was unquestionably the highlight of the concert and lawn party welcoming the new teachers to the cozy liberal arts college in Chestertown, Maryland on the Eastern Shore of the Chesapeake Bay.

"It's certainly time somebody brought a little fun to this old place, Doctor Finnigan," said Greg Leone, chairman of the American History department and the man who now held the power of life and death over Joel Finnigan.

"She certainly is a lot of laughs, Doctor Leone," Joel replied.

"Greg, Joel, Greg. We're much too small a school for all that."

A small school was exactly what Joel had been looking for as he neared the end of the long march toward his Ph.D. and began searching for the place to begin his teaching career, fulfilling the promise inspired by the wounded Lieutenant Dave McNamee back on that bloody, shell-blasted battlefield in Normandy. At a bigger school, such as Temple or Penn, he'd most likely have found himself as just another dogsbody, catching all the freshman classes or whatever else the departmental grandees felt was beneath them.

But Washington College, in the soft, green Eastern Shore countryside, was just the place. Joel caught some of the introductory freshman classes of course, even chairman Greg Leone did that, but he'd have the more interested, and interesting, upper classmen as well. Best of all, he would have the time and encouragement to develop his doctoral dissertation, a detailed study of Operation Market-Garden, into a full length book.

It was the perfect situation for Joel, but not for Connie and she never stopped telling him about it.

"Just how the hell long do you expect me to live in this godforsaken wilderness?" she snarled on the drive back to their rented house in Rock Hall after that memorable faculty lawn party.

"Not very long, if you keep prancing around like that."

"Prancing around! You listen here, *Doctor* Finnigan; everyone knows us now..."

"They certainly do, Connie."

"... which is a hell of a lot more than they would if I left it to you."

"Look Connie," Joel said, controlling his anger, "Washington is a well respected college and we're off to a pretty good start — or we were."

"A good start! A good start in the asshole of the world, you mean! What's the point in my being Mrs. College Professor in a shit hole like Chestertown?"

"Connie, I swear you're like an overgrown two-year-old."

"So, now I'm fat too."

Truth to tell, Connie was headed in that direction. Her tush was broadening markedly, her breasts were headed toward her knees, and she had a little pot that didn't quite make her look pregnant.

*****

"Joel's a doctor now, honey," her mother said at the graduation party out in Franklin.

"Maybe he can put you on some kind of a diet."

"He's not that kind of a doctor, Ma."

"Jesus, I'll say he's not," Big Joe said as he came in from the yard.

"I asked him what I should do about my piles. He didn't have a clue; can you believe that? What the hell kind of doctor doesn't know shit about my piles?"

Big Joe made it clear that he had been well and truly embarrassed by his son-in-law. He had invited what seemed like half of Franklin to come out to the house to meet the newly minted Doctor Finnigan. They did, and each one found a moment to sidle up beside Joel to ask him about their backaches, toothaches, diabetes, and chronic flatulence.

"Nobody even believes you're a real doctor," Connie snapped as they neared Rock Hall.

"Yeah," Joel replied with a wicked grin. "I don't know shit about piles."

"Well you don't have to admit it, for Christ's sake."

*****

And so, Connie stomped and pouted. She never got to like the Eastern Shore and driving around to Baltimore or Annapolis for a day's shopping was her idea of nothing to do. Sure, Joel — Mister Goddamned Professor — was doing well enough, for Chestertown, but she was nowhere.

The other faculty wives found her too coarse and barely literate; she was never invited to any of their social functions.

"All they want to do is sit around on their fat asses and talk about goddamned books."

"It is a college, Connie."

"My ass! What the hell do you get from books anyway? Here I am, stuck in God knows where and your advice is to read a goddamned book."

"You gain knowledge, Connie," Joel ventured warily.

"Knowledge, shit! How the hell smart do you want to be anyway?

"All you really need in life is a good line of bullshit."

*****

Connie, ever her father's daughter, certainly had a good line of bullshit, not that it was doing her much good.

Well, at least I can get laid on a regular basis, she consoled herself.

Maybe she couldn't pull her legs back as far as she used to but, what the hell. She might not be able to get a rise out of Joel in one way, but in the sack... oh boy!

But even that seemed different. Lately, when Joel was on top of her and driving hard toward the finish, Connie would look into his eyes and get the distinct feeling that he was looking at someone else.

He didn't look like he was making love to her; just plunging a knife into her, again and again, as though he was trying to kill her with it.

Then there was the matter of the rubbers. She longed for the days when he went off inside her like a fire hose, filling her with his essence and making her yell for more. But now he always made sure to roll one of Trenton's finest over himself before sliding in between her legs.

"Why are you using those things?" she asked one night. "Don't you like me anymore?"

"Of course I do, Connie," he replied dully.

"No more babies?"

"Not now, Connie. It isn't the right time."

"When will it be the right time?"

"Oh, I don't know. There's the Holland book and, well... now's not the time. Besides, you hate it here. Would you really want to go through a pregnancy on the Eastern Shore?"

Connie sat bolt upright in bed and glared down at Joel.

"That's right! You're getting enough from the girls up at the college. What the hell do you want a new baby for when all those nineteen-year-olds are just dying to get their legs around you?"

"Jesus, Connie. You're being ridiculous," he said as he rolled over and pretended to go to sleep.

*****

Joel was always pretending to fall asleep. Sometimes he really was. He knew Connie wondered how any man could fail to be driven into a libidinous frenzy by her newly emerging persona as a Silvana Magnani-style Italian sex goddess, complete with a low cut, boob-flashing slip.

The truth was that Connie was becoming a slob. She cleaned up well enough for brief appearances at the mandatory college functions but she remained a slob, in her ill-fitting, wine and spaghetti sauce stained slip even as she insisted to Joel that she was the sexiest, most desirable woman that ever walked.

She had no idea how far she was moving from the center of Joel's life. Emotionally he was still sustained, perhaps even kept sane, by his memories of Susanna Winslow. She was his cool water in a dry land. Not a day, and often not an hour, went by when he didn't curse himself for letting her go. But, even as he damned himself, he offered thanks that Susanna had passed through his life, no matter how briefly, and hoped that she was enjoying a good life with Justin Welch.

Locking Connie out of his mind also helped Joel focus more tightly on his professional life. He was proving a gifted teacher and, because he had been there himself, his two-semester course on the war in Europe was always oversubscribed, even by callow youths to whom history meant the week before last.

Away from the classroom Joel worked on his Market-Garden book. His journals, access to the original documents and thoughts of the key commanders and politicians of the time and, most of all, his own vivid memories of those terrible days and nights along Hell's Highway, yielded a fine mixture of historical scholarship and heartfelt personal narrative.

Market-Garden: The Allied Gamble insured Joel's place as a major historian of the campaigns of World War II. The book didn't even come close to making the *New York Times* bestseller list, but it was snapped up by students of the war, history departments at several universities around the country and it did, over the years, earn Joel somewhere around $50,000, which wasn't half bad.

"So, now you're like Mickey Spillane, or maybe Norman Mailer," Connie exulted, her house on the hill almost in view.

"It's about time you made something off playing soldier."

"We weren't playing, Connie, believe me. This book isn't going to make millions…"

"It's not? Jesus…."

"…and you and I aren't going to see much of it, either."

"What? You mean I don't get anything for putting up with all this bullshit?"

"Well, I do think we should use some of it for a down payment on the house in Rock Hall…"

"Oh, Christ!"

"…but most of it is going to Giovanni. I'm putting it in a trust fund, at least until he's twenty-one. It'll get him through college and maybe even give him a fairly decent start in life. I don't know enough to handle the money myself, and…"

"You don't know enough to handle shit! I'll take care of the kid's money."

"…if you had any control over it, it would be gone in a year."

*****

Neither was Greg Leone all that happy with the modest success of *Market-Garden: The Allied Gamble*. It wasn't the money. The Caspar Leone Foundation back home in Boston sent him enough every month to keep him from becoming too dependent on his Washington College paycheck. It even financed a couple of his research trips.

But the foundation that was started with his grandfather's somewhat questionably acquired money couldn't pay for what drove Greg Leone. He was the biggest dog in the Washington College History Department, and he was becoming increasingly worried that Joel Finnigan might steal his bone right out from under his nose.

"He's a damned popularizer," Greg fumed at President Houghton Mills. "His book is displayed in the front window of the Chestertown Book Mart. A Washington College history professor's book in a store window, for God's sake!"

President Mills took a long moment to light his pipe, and then offered his reply in a slow, thoughtful tone that was even more maddening.

"I don't know, Doctor Leone. Joel's book doesn't seem to be driving Michener's *Hawaii* off any best seller lists... even in Chestertown."

"It's going to make sure his son goes to college," Leone replied indignantly.

"And there's something wrong with that?"

"But it's too vivid, too... too... exciting! History books aren't supposed to be exciting."

"Oh, nonsense! It was a hell of a good book, Greg. It kept me up for two nights straight. Joel's research was impeccable; and he was there, at Arnhem and Nijmegen — his account ought to be vivid."

"But it was all about Privates and Sergeants. Where was Montgomery or Eisenhower in this so-called great historical document?"

"Privates and Sergeants fought the war, Greg. They fight all the wars."

President Mills leaned back in his chair.

"Doctor Finnigan is writing history in a new way; with a new voice if you will. That young man is the future, Doctor Leone."

"The future, right, and I'm the past as far as old Mills is concerned," Greg fumed as he stalked out of the administration building. You can't do anything about the future but meet it head on, and it was up to him to figure out how to do it.

*****

The spring of 1959 was a busy one for Joel. He had been invited to speak and present papers at several universities and history seminars around the United States. He was even invited over to The Netherlands for a celebration of Arnhem's liberation from the Germans and it was when he returned home after the long, trans-Atlantic flight to Baltimore that he found the cross he had carried for nearly fifteen years had finally been lifted from his shoulders.

He turned off Main Street at Durding's drug store and drove sedately down Sharp Street toward Rock Hall Harbor. He was about two hours ahead of schedule and he didn't want to surprise Giovanni or Connie too badly.

But he did. The living room light was on, not turned all the way up, but just brightly enough for Joel to make out Greg Leone leaning back comfortably in his favorite easy chair and Connie on her knees before him, her face buried deeply into his unzipped trousers.

Joel had evidently walked in at a crucial moment, or immediately after the crucial moment. Greg was still gasping for breath and was capable only of offering an indolent wave of his hand by way of greeting.

Connie lifted her head. Her cheeks were puffed out and her eyes wide with astonishment and fear.

She took a deep swallow and wiped off her chin.

"Hi Joel. Can I get you a beer?"

"How civilized," Joel replied, "how very damned civilized."
There was a dangerous pause.

"A man comes home, finds his wife with his learned colleague's cock in her mouth and all she can say is 'Hi Joel. Can I get you a beer?' As a matter of fact, you can. It's been a long drive over from Baltimore."

Connie levered herself back to her feet and scurried into the kitchen for the beer.

"Oh boy, this is awkward," Greg said, recovering his equanimity and zipping up his fly.

"Just a little bit," Joel replied.

Connie returned from the kitchen carrying three mugs of beer.

"I think we can all use one," she said. "This isn't what it looks like, Joel."

"It isn't? It looked like quite a bit to me."

"Greg and I love each other."

"That's good, Connie. I'd have hated to find you sucking on the cock of a complete stranger."

"I'm afraid it's true, Joel," Greg interjected. "We intend to get married."

"Yeah," Connie said defiantly. "You've been running all over the country this spring, and sampling those Dutch girls, too."

"And Greg just stepped into the gap, as a favor to a colleague, of course. Very good of you, Greg," he said with a nod in Leone's direction.

Connie stepped up to Joel. She dropped her defiant pose and lowered her eyes like an embarrassed school girl.

"We're in love — me and Greg. We're going to move in together right away."

"Here? In Chestertown? That sounds a little clumsy to me."

"No, not here, old man," said Greg. "In Boston. I'm going to be the Executive Director of the Caspar Leone Foundation."

"At a hundred thousand a year," Connie said proudly.

"It looks like you'll finally get your house on the hill."

"On Beacon Hill, Joel, on Beacon Hill."

"Are you leaving for Boston right away, then?" Joel asked.

"Goddamn," said Connie. "You're still as calm and reasonable as ever. You catch me with someone else's cock in my mouth, and you haven't even raised your voice."

Joel retreated to his study and began organizing the papers and books he had brought back from Arnhem. He could hear Connie and Greg going here and there about the house as she packed her things and prepared to move out to Greg's place in Edesville that very night.

They'd be seeing enough of each other over the next few months as the divorce, property settlement and, most important of all, custody of Giovanni, moved through the courts. But for now, it was enough just to be rid of her.

"I'm going now, Finney," Connie called from the front door. Greg waited nervously, half afraid she might be offering Joel one last chance.

Hearing no response, Connie opened the door and left. Joel watched through the window as they went down the walk to Greg's car. Connie led, her anger evident in every brisk, resolute step. She carried one small overnight case, while Greg struggled along behind, laden down with her three overstuffed suitcases.

"That poor son of a bitch," Joel said with a sympathetic smile.

CHAPTER TWENTY-FOUR

LOST IN A DREAM

I'm suffocating. I want to scream but no words will come. I feel trapped. I have no right to feel this way. I'm living with a good man who loves me. But I feel so alone; more alone than I ever felt when I really was alone.

Mark has no sense of who I am.

Last night I woke up puzzling over a bizarre dream I had. I was lost in Camden and trying to get home, but I had to walk through a really bad neighborhood. Threatening looking teenagers were hanging out on the corner and I was afraid to walk past them. I turned around and tried to find another way. All of a sudden I was walking along the railroad tracks. I realized I could take the train, but I didn't have the right change and I was on the wrong side of the tracks anyway. I felt lost and afraid. Then this little old man with a cane came up to me and said, "Honey, can I help you across the tracks?"

I woke up confused and started trying to figure out the dream. I wanted to wake Mark and talk to him about it, but I knew he wouldn't understand. He doesn't look at life the way I do. It's funny, though… I wasn't really sure how I looked at life before, but now that I'm with Mark, I know what I am not.

I want to be somewhere else, but I don't know how to get there. Maybe that's what the dream was about.

Anyway, if I left, Mark would be devastated.

I just don't know what to do.

I think I'll buy some chocolate.

CHAPTER TWENTY-FIVE

FAULT LINE

Years later, Robin Williams would say that whoever could remember the 1960s hadn't really been there. Joel really had been there, and he remembered all too well.

The 1960s were the years in which Joel, and the others of his generation, passed from the stressful demands of World War II and rebuilding their lives in the 1950s into the realization of their hard won power. They had passed their teenage years at the tail end of the Great Depression, came brutally of age in the white hot forge of bloody combat, and sharpened their intellectual swords courtesy of the GI Bill. Now, they were poised to take control of a world that had control of them for far too long.

Joel had faced, and accepted, responsibility before: when he joined the 506th Parachute Infantry Regiment, when he assumed command of Company B, when he stood before his students and, most of all, when he made certain that his writings had assured Giovanni's future.

Now it was time for Joel, and the rest of his cohorts, to take up the lead, the point as they called it back in Normandy.

January 20, 1961 was cold, and Washington, D.C. was paralyzed by the previous evening's snowfall. But Joel was warm, the heat of an impending great adventure racing through his veins as the new President, only a few years older than himself, laid his task before him.

"Let the word go forth from this time and place," the young President said, "to friend and foe alike, that the torch has been passed to a new generation of Americans — born in this century, tempered by war, disciplined by a hard and bitter peace, proud of our ancient heritage and unwilling to witness or permit the slow undoing of those human rights to which this nation has always been committed today, at home and around the world.

"Let every nation know, whether it wishes us well or ill, that we shall pay any price, bear any burden, meet any hardship, support any friend, oppose any foe to assure the survival and the success of liberty."

God knows, the challenges were there. New winds, generated by men like Martin Luther King, Jr., and thousands who might forever go unnamed, were certain to change the face of the American South. The White Citizens Councils, the Ku Klux Klan, the depraved sheriffs and voting registrars would have their last paroxysm of hate-fueled rage, but they too would change or be flushed away by the flooding tide of history.

History had always been subject to the readings and interpretations of constantly evolving ages, but if Joel had learned one absolute truth on his journey to professorship, it was that while history might falter or even adjust itself, it could never be reversed.

Abroad, the communists had to be contained until their bizarre system collapsed of its own weight. Joel was as worried as anyone else about the massive nuclear build up on both sides of the Iron Curtain, but his view of history told him those fearsome devices would never be used and that the battle, if it came to that, would be fought with rifles and bayonets.

Everything was going to change. It had to. It should have changed long since.

The war had been a profound distraction, of course, but the essential truth didn't fully come to Joel until later that night at Freya Schultz's apartment in Baltimore. Their lovemaking had drained them of all the day's tensions — Freya from a long and unusually complicated heart operation, and Joel from his long day of traveling from Philadelphia, to Washington and finally into the warm bed and inviting body of this particularly talented surgeon.

"What was it we were withholding?" Joel said sleepily as he stroked Freya's long, ash blonde hair and her graceful, naked shoulders.

"You didn't withhold anything, Joel," she said quietly.

She squeezed his chest even tighter.

"I'm sorry, Freya. I've been trying to sort out my thoughts from today and there was one piece missing."

"After Jack Kennedy's speech? He said it all."

"He did, but I think Robert Frost really put the cap on it. He recited "The Gift Outright" from memory. I don't remember the exact words, but it had to do with finding salvation within ourselves."

Freya lay silent for a long while, thinking and tracing the outlines of his face with her long, sensitive fingers.

"I think Frost was right," she said at last. "We have all the knowledge and all the equipment, but it's nothing without our souls?"

"That's it. You give it to your patients every day and I try, every day, to give it to my students."

"A very concise diagnosis, Doctor Finnigan. Now, how about you putting your soul into your equipment and giving it to me?"

"Again! Doctor Schultz, I'm astonished."

"We can't withhold treatment now, Doctor," she said as she gently guided him on top of her. And once more, Joel withheld nothing.

*****

Joel, and so many of his comrades — alive and dead — had given so much of themselves during the war. It was time now for Joel to give once more, not just to tell the story of the two-year history of the 506th, but the story of the men — boys, really — of the regiment, how they lived, how they died, and just what their gift meant.

Joel sat before his yellow legal pads and a carefully arranged row of Number 2 pencils. He had learned in his days on the *Inquirer* rewrite desk to bang out breaking stories on a typewriter, but for serious, thoughtful composition, legal pads and Number 2 pencils were the only thing.

Freya, despite her precise German manner, had awakened Joel's interest in the art and craftsmanship of the Italian Renaissance. There were times, when he was working on a major piece, that he came to flatter himself by feeling very much how he imagined Michelangelo Buonoratti felt when he was carving works of great beauty from blocks of carrara marble. Joel took a great deal of satisfaction in his work as he crafted each letter by hand and filled his stacks of legal pads.

Also, by lining up his pencils according to their length, he was able to postpone the actual start of writing until the dreadful moment when he could put it off no longer.

Silver Wings: A Paratrooper's Story began during the early days of the 506th at Camp Toccoca, and vividly traced the story to the final, boring summer at Obersalzburg.

"We thought we were going to die. We were more certain of that than of anything else in the universe," were his opening lines. They were the truest, most honest lines he had ever written, and once Joel opened up his soul and unleashed the ghosts of 1944, the words flowed non-stop.

*****

Joel was a little bit afraid of what he might find within himself as he began writing *Silver Wings*. He had, throughout most of the 1950s, been able to read through the stacks of operations orders, statements, letters, journals and interviews with the key commanders and strategic planners involved in the allied airborne operations of World War II. The fact that he had been there himself couldn't help but find its way into his schol-

arship and, indeed, gave his work a extra element of hard worn
verisimilitude, but he did not know what he would find as he
recreated, first in his mind and finally on his legal pads, his own
recollections of jumping into Normandy, of the machine gun
rounds kicking up the dust at his feet during the mad charge to
the Douve River bridge, the cold, rainy running battles along
Hell's Highway in Holland and finally — the most horrific of
his memories — the savage cold and endless attacks in the
smothering snows of Bastogne.

A research grant, easily obtained for a professor of his
standing, would have allowed him to return to Europe and
spend the summers of 1961 and 1962 revisiting the old battlefields. But he turned it down. They were etched in his mind and
would never fade and, except for Normandy in the late spring,
none of the old places would look or feel the same. Bastogne in
the soft, warm greenness of an Ardennes summer could never
call to mind the misery and fear that ruled the place in that terrible Christmas season of 1944.

New apartment buildings, downtowns, highways and resi-
dential developments every bit as bland as America's "little
houses made of ticky-tack" had changed the old, terrible places
as Europe strove mightily to put the war behind it.

No, what really troubled Joel as he moved through his wartime memoir were things that would never, could never, appear
in *Silver Wings*, or anywhere else. The letters he had received
from Susanna were more emotionally difficult to revisit than
any battle or campaign.

Susanna, the memory of her, had never really left the secret
compartment deep in his heart since 1942. It was the memory
of Susanna and her love that helped him hang onto his sanity
during the hellish years with Connie.

There had never really been anyone else for Joel Finnigan.

And Dr. Freya Schultz — as fine as she was — was not
Susanna.

It was not fair but it made it easier when the time came, as
it had to, to end his affair with the doctor. They had made love

with particular gentleness and sensitivity just before she told him.

"I'm going back home to Germany, Joel," she whispered.

"Oh?"

"I've been offered a full professorship at Heidelberg..."

"Heidelberg... I'm impressed."

"My parents don't live far away, in Nellingen, near Stuttgart. They're getting on and I ought to be near them. Would you come with me?"

"To Germany?"

"They'll be happy to see you this time. I promise," she said with a chuckle.

Freya and her damned sense of duty! It almost felt like Susanna and Justin Welch all over again.

Still, it wasn't a bad idea. He had spent a long weekend in Heidelberg in the early summer of 1945 and found it one of the most beautiful cities he had ever seen. It had suffered only minor damage during the war and retained most of its ancient charm.

He could think of few things finer than sitting on the banks of the Neckar as it flowed through the old city with a stein of Dinkelacker in one hand and the hand of a beautiful, brilliant surgeon in the other.

"Fraulein Doktor Schultz," he said thoughtfully.

"I think Frau Doktor Finnigan sounds better," she replied truthfully.

"I have to stay here, Freya. I'm writing the story of my people."

"My people too," she replied. "Who do you think you were fighting against? I had two uncles at Bastogne, you know. It was a world war, Joel. Your work could be even finer and more meaningful if you came to know the people on the other side."

"I have to stay here, Freya. This is my place."

"I know," she said sadly, as she tightened her grip on him.

"Germany is my place — the Neckar Valley. I have to go."

"I know that too, Freya."

"Joel? Make love to me one last time."

And so they did. Two days later Freya was on a Lufthansa flight to Frankfurt. They promised to see each other during summer vacations, but they each knew they never would.

*****

Joel missed Freya, but the end had to come and he was happy that he had not hurt her. She didn't deserve that. She was a warm, passionate woman, one of the truly good people he would ever know and a fine surgeon destined for greatness. She would have been a fine wife, but she was not Susanna. She looked a little bit like her, tall, blond, and graceful, but the feeling just wasn't there.

Each time they had made love during their year of commuting between Philadelphia and Baltimore, when he held her face between his hands in the last frenzied seconds before he exploded deep within her, he could see only Susanna as she looked during that life-changing weekend on Sansom Street.

And that was not a fair thing to do to a woman as fine as Doctor Freya Schultz.

A couple of girls followed Freya. But they were just that, girls, in almost idle affairs on summer weekends at Cape May or down on the Eastern Shore. And none of them were anywhere in his consciousness on a bright, pleasantly warm Friday in late November of 1963 as he sat in his faculty office at Temple reading the publisher's proofs of *Silver Wings*.

The book had turned out well and Joel was happy with it. The publisher liked it too, and while it was too late to be out in time for Christmas, it would be ready for the 1964 spring list — if he got the proofs back in time.

Joel was nearing the end of the final section, the long march from Bastogne eastward into Germany to the summer days at Obersalzburg, when Jenny Keith appeared in his open doorway with a stricken look on her face.

"Kennedy has been shot," she said simply.

Her words struck Joel deep in the pit of his stomach. "What?"

"Turn on the radio. Kennedy's been shot."

Jenny was a brilliant young cellist and graduate music student. At 5'11", she was nearly as tall as Joel. She was slim, with smooth flawless skin of the deepest mahogany, and spoke with the musical lilt of her Caribbean ancestry.

"God, she's beautiful," Joel thought as he reached out to turn on the radio on the window sill behind him.

And here I am, the gray on my head already prominent and me on the verge of becoming the kindly old professor. But any carnal impulses were banished by the announcer's voice reporting that young John Kennedy had indeed been shot in Dealey Plaza on the way from Love Field to the Dallas Trade Mart.

"Those goddamned Ku Kluxers," Jenny seethed, verging on tears.

"Let's find out first," said Joel. "It could be the Klan. They were mad enough after he opened up the University of Mississippi last year. Right wing Cubans are mad at him for blowing the Bay of Pigs operation. Castro's people are mad at him for even trying it and God knows what the Russians are capable of after the Cuban Missile Crisis last October."

"Don't forget the Mafia," Jenny added.

"Of course not. And then there are the ordinary nut cases."

"I'm scared, Doctor Finnigan. What if it's a coup or something?"

"Jenny, the only thing we know is that he's been shot. I know it's hard but we have to stay calm."

Jenny shivered, wrapping her arms around herself to ward off the chill of fear.

"I don't want to be alone," she said.

The stentorian voice of the announcer filled the room, telling Joel and Jenny that the presidential motorcade had arrived at Parkland Hospital and that a Catholic priest had been hustled into the emergency room.

Joel flipped off the radio. He took Jenny's elbow and guided the shaken black girl into the crisp late autumn sunlight.

The coffee shop was not big. A lunch counter ran along one side and a juke box, unplugged now, dominated the far wall. Nearly twenty round tables were packed into the room, each one ringed with shocked, wan students and teachers who were sucking up more coffee than Joel had ever seen consumed at one time since he left the 506th.

And over it all lay the voice of Walter Cronkite. There was some talk about the killing of a Dallas policeman named J.D. Tippit, and the arrest in a movie theater of someone named Oswald. But as to President John F. Kennedy himself, the news was so unrelentingly grim that it was hardly a surprise when Cronkite announced:

"Ladies and gentlemen, the President of the United States is dead. He died at 12:03 p. m.... Dallas time."

Everyone knew it was coming. Each successive report made it plain that Kennedy could not possibly live with such a ghastly head wound. But, even so, a stunned silence descended over the coffee shop. It was broken, finally, when a tall, blond, exquisitely beautiful girl named Maggie looked up from the notebook in which she had been writing furiously.

"So much for humanity," she said.

"She's right, Doctor Finigan," Jenny whispered. "What's to become of us now?"

"We'll go on," Joel replied. "There's still so much for us to do."

*****

Silver Wings came out shortly before Memorial Day, and the onset of summer found Joel wondering what to do next. There would be another book, of course. He was a compulsive writer and there would have to be another book but, at the moment, he hadn't the faintest idea what it would be.

It would come to him, of course. The history of the United States was too rich and his mind too fertile for his creative processes to lie dormant for very long. The trick was not to force it. Ideas came in their own good time and it was best not to rush into something just for the sake of doing something that would almost certainly turn out wrong. Joel decided, therefore, to immerse himself in life and wait.

As the summer of 1964 drew near, the world was rich, yeasty and full of promise, particularly in the South where people long repressed were appealing to the goodness of their neighbors to right their region's historic wrongs, and in the North where thousands of college students, still filled with the idealism of the Kennedy years, mobilized their campaign to help them do it.

It was a force that excited Joel and reminded him of his own youth. This newly developing battle for the soul of America inspired the same idealism that drew him to the 506th and, later, to his new life as an historian and professor. The stakes were as high in 1964 as they had been in 1942, and it was a battle that Joel knew he had to join.

The recruiting station was a card table in the lobby of the student center. The Student Nonviolent Coordinating Committee — SNCC, or "Snick" as they liked to call themselves — was signing up volunteers to go to Mississippi and register black voters for the 1964 election.

Jenny Keith was the recruiter. She sat behind the table, tall and gracious, handing out literature, taking down the names, addresses and telephone numbers of young men and women ready to endure a summer of heat, humidity, and the new type of southern hospitality conveyed by snarling German shepherds, billy clubs and fire hoses.

"Hello, Jenny."

"Doctor Finnigan! Are you here to sign up for Freedom Summer?"

"I am, as a matter of fact."

Jenny held her notebook out to him. He filled in all the spaces and gave it back.

"What inspired this?" she asked. "I always saw you as an observer, studying and writing about things without really getting involved."

"Do I really seem like that?"

"Sometimes."

"Maybe, sometimes, but this is not one of those times, Jenny. Remember the day President Kennedy was shot?"

"God, yes," she replied. "I remember everything about that day; even what I had for lunch and what I wore. It must be like the old folks remembering everything about Pearl Harbor Day."

"Hey!" Joel replied with a laugh. "I remember everything about that day and I'm only forty. Besides, you're...how old?"

"Twenty-three."

"Pearl Harbor was attacked the same year you were born... Granny."

Now it was Jenny's turn to laugh and Joel was charmed.

"Touché, Doctor Finnigan. I apologize."

Joel leaned across the table and put on his best solemn face and grave voice.

"Go and sin no more, my child. For your penance, join me for lunch when you're finished here."

*****

Jenny Keith came for lunch, and she stayed. He knew that something was happening between them. Perhaps it had started as far back as November 22, 1963, but as she approached the table, Joel stood and felt an old familiar feeling rising from deep within him.

It looked like Jenny was feeling it too. She slipped gracefully into the chair opposite Joel. Her smile radiated then dimmed ever so slightly as she took in the surroundings.

"I remember the last time we were here," she said, "listening to Walter Cronkite."

"That was a bad day," Joel replied.

"Today will be better, Doctor Finnigan."

"You've graduated, Jenny?"

"In January. I passed my audition and I'm to join the Philadelphia Orchestra in the Fall."

"Good. Now, please stop calling me Doctor Finnigan."

Jenny's smile resumed its former brilliance and her eyes danced happily in her smooth mahogany face.

"Yes, Joel. I've wanted that for a while now."

Casually, almost absently, Joel slid a salt shaker across the table toward her. Jenny looked at him. Her smile grew wiser than he had ever seen before. She placed the pepper shaker beside the salt and pushed them a few inches back toward him.

Black and white. Side by side. The gesture was enough to tie the tongue even of Joel Finnigan.

"Your soup is going to get cold," she said by way of breaking the tension.

Joel smiled and took a spoonful of his chicken pastina soup, and Jenny started on her fruit salad.

"What made you sign up for Freedom Summer?" she asked between the pineapple and the cantaloupe.

"It's something that has to be done," he replied simply. "In a way it's like 1942 all over again."

"I know about those years, Joel. I just finished reading *Silver Wings*. I tried the *Market-Garden* book, but got lost in all those official orders and analysis." She was silent for a moment. "It must have been awful, Joel."

"It was, but it was twenty years ago and it was all worth it. So, what I helped do for the French, the Dutch, and the Germans — most of them, anyway — I thought I should do for my own people."

"Your own people?" Jenny asked skeptically.

"Americans," he said. "It's one of the missions Kennedy left for us to accomplish."

Jenny reached across the table, pushing the salt and pepper shakers aside, and took his right hand.

"You're a good man, Joel Finnigan. I like idealists."

"Oh, Jenny. It's just another job. We're all works in progress."

"Right," she said decisively. "Let's get out of here."

Their hands sought each other as they began walking down Broad Street together in the warm late spring afternoon. More than a few people looked askance, but they didn't give a damn. Before they realized it, they had walked all the way to Spring Garden Street and Joel's apartment.

"Would you like to come up for a drink?" he asked.

"Good grief! Did you make that one up all by yourself, Professor? Yes, I would Joel. I would like it very much."

They went upstairs and drank more deeply of themselves than they thought possible.

*****

The sun was setting and they still hadn't had enough of each other. They lay together in the bed, without covers because it was too warm, admiring each other's recumbent bodies.

"I'm glad we had plenty of light," he whispered in her ear.

"You like seeing black and white together?" she asked.

"God, yes, especially white me sliding into black you."

"Me too," said Jenny. "I wish I could have seen all that too."

"There's a hand mirror around here somewhere," he said.

"Let's find it. Please Joel."

Finding the mirror set off a new wave of eroticism. They rode the wave, over and over, and it was completely dark when they lay exhausted in each other's arms, perspiration glistening on their bare skin, looking into the new world that had opened before them.

"God, I wish I had a movie of that," Jenny said in a playful, tired voice.

"It would probably land us both in jail," replied Joel, "especially where we're going."

"To Mississippi," she said. "Hell, they put everybody in jail there."

Jenny propped herself up on her left elbow and looked down at Joel.

"Are you hungry?" she asked.

"For you? Yes, insatiably."

"Me too. Let's eat something so we can get back to this."

They rolled out of bed and walked naked into the kitchen. Jenny looked into the refrigerator and turned to look back at Joel with wry amusement.

"Ham and eggs? Honestly, Joel, that's all there is."

"I usually only eat breakfast at home. I eat out the rest of the time."

"Ham and eggs it is, then," she said as she took them out of the refrigerator and moved toward the stove.

"I have a tolerable burgundy around here somewhere," he said.

"Ah! You are civilized then, Doctor Finnigan. Set the table and pour the wine. The ham and eggs will be ready in a minute."

*****

The burgundy went down uncommonly well with the ham and eggs. So much so, in fact, that Joel recharged their glasses and took them out to the living room. Jenny was waiting, her back to him as she studied the photographs on the side table.

Joel stopped in the doorway and drank in the sight of her; her long black hair hanging past her broad, perfectly rounded shoulders and her narrow waist as it curved gracefully toward her slender hips, masterfully sculpted buttocks and her long legs.

She sensed him admiring her. She picked up a framed photograph and turned to face him, holding it between her firm, proud breasts.

"Who's this?" she asked.

The picture was of a tall, strong looking young man in a high school football uniform.

"That's my son. Giovanni."

"Giovanni Finnigan? And I thought we were a strange combination."

"It was his mother's idea. The kid turned into a terrific tight end. He got a football scholarship to UMass."

"What's he going to say about us?"

"What's to say about us?"

"About his father's coaly tootsie. What's your family going to say?"

"You know, Jenny," Joel said thoughtfully, "on the tombstone of every Irish mother are engraved the words 'What'll the neighbors say?'"

"Do you care, Joel?"

"No. I had enough of that when I was a kid."

"Good. Now, take me back to bed."

*****

Shortly after Joel and Jenny discovered each other, a tall, graceful woman with the first traces of silver just beginning to show in her light hair sat on the deck of her mountainside home in Marin County, California and read the last few pages of *Silver Wings*. She came to the end, closed the book and laid it on the redwood table beside her. Then she wiped the tears from her eyes and went inside to make dinner.

*****

Tears ran from Joel's eyes as well, the result of smoke irritation rather than emotion. The storefront that he and Jenny were using for an office and one room apartment was going up in flames, and he was certain that they were about to die a horrible, painful death.

They had barely heard the sound of the plate glass window breaking as a brick, then a classic Molotov cocktail, were hurled into what had been Cyrus Bottom's hardware store on the outskirts of the little delta town of Hoskins, Mississippi.

Cyrus himself was dead. His face had been blown off by a shotgun on a dusty back road as he returned from a day of registering voters. His wife Merrilee and their three children had already fled for the relative safety of her sister's home in Milwaukee.

Thus did Bottom's Hardware become available for use as a local headquarters for voter registration in the Mississippi River delta region. Jenny ran the office, signing up people who walked in to exercise their rights, while Joel roamed the back country roads taking registration forms to those who couldn't get into town. Their Sundays were spent speaking at black churches all over the delta, and their nights in the back room that once housed the Cyrus Bottoms family.

The difference between the summer of 1964 and the winter of 1944 was that in 1944, Joel knew the German enemy was always out there, when they were coming to kill him, and how he could defend himself. In Mississippi, however, it was impossible to tell which smiling insurance man, feed salesman, or Bible thumping preacher had a little white pointed hat and roamed the night looking for someone to kill.

He never did discover which night rider tossed the firebomb into the storefront office. He and Jenny were lying on, rather than in, the bed, too tired after a long day under the fierce Mississippi July sun to make love. They were jolted into wakefulness by the fireball bursting out front and the splintering of wood as three men — two big and one scrawny, who smelled as evil as he looked — crashed through the back door into the bedroom.

"Joel!" Jenny screamed in terror. Her scream was cut short by a resounding slap across her face.

"Shut up, nigger bitch!" one of the fat ones bellowed.

Joel's wartime reflexes were intact, and he leapt from the bed, ready to fight, only to be met by a knee driven up hard between his legs. He doubled over and dropped to the floor, gasping for breath through the smoke and the pain, conscious only of the building heat and the savage glee of his attackers.

"Shee-it, lookee here. We got us a real nigger-lover this time."

Jenny sat up in the bed and pulled her knees to her chest. Her eyes widened in horror at the scene before her.

As Joel's head cleared, he was able to make out the thin, scarred, weasel face of the smallest of the night riders as he stepped forward and tore Jenny's T-shirt over her shoulders.

Joel struggled to his feet but four fat, strong arms held him fast. He watched the mean little one, Hootie by name, punch Jenny full in the face. She flew backwards in the bed and as her hips rolled upwards, he reached under her and tore off her panties.

"Oooh, ain't that some sweet dark meat," he sneered as he grabbed her hair with his right hand and unzipped his jeans with his left.

"Jee-zuz, boy! What the hell you doin'?" cried one of the fatties.

"I gotta get me some of that," Hootie said as he guided his penis, swollen more by blood lust than anything sexual, toward Jenny's mouth.

"Come on, boy! This here place is on fire."

"Don't you worry none. I get off real quick."

Then it was Jenny's turn.

"You try it, cracker, and I'll bite it off real quick," she snarled through bared teeth.

"She means it, boy. Now let's take this white nigger-lover and get out of here."

The two fat ones dragged Joel outside. Hootie knocked Jenny unconscious and dragged her naked body to a plain wooden chair. He took a length of old rope from his hip pocket and tied her to the chair, then dashed out into the back yard.

"Now, let's make sure she has a black ass," Hootie snarled in Joel's face.

Hootie had dragged the chair into the center of the room so they could stand in the yard and watch Jenny burn in the flames as they steadily advanced.

"Just think," he said sorrowfully. "That poor girl could have died with the memory of me coming right down her throat."

And that, by God, was enough for Joel Finnigan. His head had cleared just enough to be filled with a murderous rage he had not felt since 1945. He wrenched his right arm free and jammed it into the fat, rolling gut of one of his captors. When the man let go and doubled over, Joel grabbed him by the neck, flipped him onto his back and bolted back toward the burning building.

Jenny wasn't hard to find. The fire hadn't quite reached her yet. She had regained consciousness and, galvanized by the prospect of an agonizing death, was struggling against the ropes holding her to the chair.

Hootie, as frightened of the flames as anybody else there, had tied hasty, sloppy knots. She had gotten one arm and one ankle free by the time Joel reached her.

"Joel! Help me!" she screamed.

The fire was upon them now, chewing hungrily at the ceiling above their heads. It left Joel no time to do anything but pick up the chair, with Jenny still tied to it, and stumble toward the open door. He tripped on the sill and they tumbled into the yard. Joel landed on top of Jenny.

The three night riders were so stunned by Joel's act of reckless courage that they could only stare blankly as he quickly untied her arm and ankle.

Hootie was the first to find his courage, such as it was. He moved quickly toward Joel and Jenny, lifting his T-shirt and pulling a .38 caliber revolver from his waistband.

Jenny rolled off to one side, trying her best to cover her nakedness. Joel seized the chair, swung it like a bat and caught Hootie full in the face. The little cracker went flat on his back. Joel grabbed the .38 and stuck it inside Hootie's still unzipped fly.

"Back off, assholes!" he roared.

The two beefy night riders hesitated, looking like they wanted to rush Joel, but stopped in their tracks by this sudden reversal of their fortunes.

"Back off, now, or I'll shoot it right off the son of a bitch!"

Hootie began to shake and wimper and tears came to his eyes.

"He goin' to shoot Junior," he sobbed.

"Please, God, don' let him shoot Junior."

They looked at each other, but didn't move. The night, quiet but for the growling of the flames, was broken by the sharp click of the .38 being cocked.

"You heard him! I'll turn Junior into hamburger meat."

Joel, with an evil glint in his eyes, smiled down at Hootie.

"You'll be peeing through a rubber tube for the rest of your life, shithead."

"Oh Jesus! Please! No! Not Junior!"

"I doubt the girls will think too much of it either," said Jenny. "It is Mississippi, though; so who knows."

"Don't shoot Junior," one of the shadows said. "We're go-in'."

The two fat night riders were as good as their word. Still, Joel kept the .38 pressed right up against Junior until he saw their tail lights vanishing down Hoskins' main street.

"Now, take your shirt off," he said to the mightily relieved Klansman.

Joel removed the pistol so Hootie could sit up and get out of his dirty white T-shirt. He took it and tossed it to Jenny. She slipped it over her head and Joel instantly saw, more appreciatively than might have been expected under the circumstances, that it wasn't nearly long enough.

"Now your jeans," he said.

"I cain't do that."

"Why the hell not? You were just dying to have us all admire Junior a minute ago. Get 'em off."

He did and a few seconds later Jenny was on her feet, wiggling into Hootie's jeans and grinning triumphantly as their owner sprinted down the street in his undershorts.

Joel and Jenny found a new office and apartment the very next day. They also took the time to drive into Hoskins to Hapgood's Feed and Grain to return Hootie's freshly washed and pressed clothing.

"I've heard you might know who owns these, Mister Hapgood," Joel said pleasantly to the fat, tired looking man behind the counter.

"Seems I might," Hapgood replied warily.

"Y'all can just leave that here."

"Thank you. The lady really appreciated the loan."

"Okay, but tell me sompin' Perfesser. I heard all about the goin's on at Bottom's last night. You stepped up right proud. But I thought you was a *non-violent* coordinatin' committee."

Joel leaned across the counter, until his nose was almost touching Hapgood's.

"...and you'd better make damned good and sure I stay that way, Mister Hapgood. Pass the word now, y'hear."

Hapgood did that very thing. He made sure that everyone in and around Hoskins knew that Joel and Jenny were not to be trifled with. There was plenty of grumbling about nigger-lovers and outside agitators but, in general, the voter registration drive passed without incident.

Joel kept Hootie's .38 and it resided in the night table beside the bed he shared with Jenny for the rest of the summer. It lay unused in the drawer, even when the terrible news came from Philadelphia, Mississippi of the murder of Schwerner, Chaney and Goodman, the three registration workers who had been held by the Neshoba County Sheriff until the local night riders could get together, shoot them dead, and bury their bodies beneath an earthen dam.

"I had no idea people could hate so much," Jenny mused as she sat beside Joel on the long ride back to Pennsylvania.

"Come on, Jenny. You grew up black in this country. You share a bed with a white man. You should know better by now."

"I know, but I guess I never really understood."

"I hated the Germans and the Japanese once," Joel said thoughtfully. "Sometimes I think we're a nation of people who have to hate, Jenny. Now that the Germans and the Japanese are good guys again, we're left with nobody to hate but each other."

"Maybe, but it's going to change," Jenny replied. "We really started something down here this summer. Blacks and whites have lived together for so long that they've established, not a bond, but a real relationship. It's closer than anything that exists back home."

"I can't imagine it's one that anybody really likes," he said.

"Of course not. But blacks are starting to gain power now. When you get black sheriffs, city councilmen, and county commissioners in Mississippi, Alabama, and Georgia, folks on both sides are going to realize it's not the end of the world and that they'll have to start pulling together."

"That makes a great deal of sense," Joel replied, and broke into an ironic chuckle. "But who will we hate then?"

"We'll think of somebody, Joel. Don't you worry."

*****

The fault line forecast by Jenny Keith did not materialize right away. The coalition that she and Joel helped to forge during the hot summer of 1964 had its first, and greatest, victory that November when Lyndon B. Johnson of Texas overwhelmed Barry Goldwater of Arizona in the presidential election.

Both men were destined to change the face of the United States. Johnson picked up the torch of the Civil Rights Act from the fallen Jack Kennedy, launched the War on Poverty and, darkly, began chaffing at his opponents' charges that he wasn't doing enough to stop Communism in Vietnam.

'Soft on Communism' was a potentially devastating political charge in the days after the Cuban Missile Crisis and the Korean War, and canny old LBJ wasn't about to let himself be bushwhacked.

Goldwater's otherwise hapless campaign planted a seed of mean-spirited conservatism that would not bear its bitter fruit for another thirty years.

These were the 1960s, what some advertising agency sloganeer had christened the 'now generation' and Joel was enjoying every bit of it.

There was a difference, though. The joyful, public exuberance that had begun in the cold of January 20, 1961 had begun to fade with the murder of Jack Kennedy. The nation had survived. Joel had faith that it always would, with its idealism intact, but the shine had worn off.

The civil rights movement continued, as did the War on Poverty, and the race to the moon and nearly all of the quests that Kennedy had laid out before his people, but they weren't pursued with the same youthful joy that gripped the United States before Lee Harvey Oswald fired his rifle. They were pursued, rather, with a grim, legalistic intensity.

And even that was being pushed aside by an inward turning, self-obsessed pursuit of instant self gratification.

"Hey, Prof, if it feels good, do it, man," the lank haired young man said as he offered Joel a raggedly rolled cigarette. "It really expands your mind, man."

So Joel, whose mind felt in need of expansion at the moment, lit up his first joint. He gasped, choked and generally felt as though someone were working over his throat with a heavy hand on really rough sandpaper.

"Ya gotta inhale, Prof, really suck it in."

So he sucked and was pleasantly surprised by the mellow, gentle haze that descended over him. The world seemed softer, kinder, and Jenny's cello sounded like the music of the angels themselves as it flowed seamlessly from the stereo.

As well it might, for God knows, Jenny Keith was an angel. She had been a great success with the Philadelphia Orchestra ever since her first season in 1964-65. More and more selections were capitalizing on her virtuosity. She was playing more solos and Columbia Masterworks was talking to her about an album.

Joel was constantly amazed at how easily Jenny could change from an imposing, majestic stage presence into a light-hearted young woman, very much in love, who took a romantically girlish delight in setting up her new apartment just off Rittenhouse Square.

And in bed... in bed... she was capable of feats no angel ever dreamed of. She opened herself and drew Joel inside with voraciousness, and Joel responded by going as deeply into her as he could and filling her to the brim.

*****

"She's beautiful, Dad, gorgeous."

Giovanni, tanned and well-muscled after years of football as well as his recent airborne training at Fort Campbell, Kentucky, smiled broadly when he finally met Jenny.

He'd dropped out after a year at UMass to join the Army. Students were beginning to protest against the war in Vietnam, and Giovanni felt an obligation to step up and do something. He wanted to be a hero like his father.

Joel was beginning to wonder about the wisdom of Vietnam himself, but he was proud of Giovanni just the same.

The young man filled every bit of his green Army uniform. His Herman jump boots glistened, as did the paratrooper wings over his left breast, and the "Airborne" tab above the Screaming Eagle shoulder patch of the 101st Airborne Division. He wore the patch as proudly as young Joel Finningan had worn it.

And to top it all off, the kid not only accepted Jenny but fell instantly in love with her, welcoming her into the family.

"Are you guys going to… to… you know?" the young sergeant asked bashfully.

"I've heard worse ideas, Johnny," Jenny replied with a grin. "How would you feel about that?"

"Terrific! I've never had a black stepmother before."

"Speaking of which," Joel said in an attempt to change the subject, "how is your mother?"

"She's, well… she's Mom," Giovanni said with a rueful grin.

"Trying like hell to be a proper Boston matron but falling flat on her face. She went bananas when she heard about you and Jenny; said you're dragging the family name through the mud."

"She would," replied Joel. "She was always embarrassed that I wasn't a 'real doctor.'"

He turned to Jenny.

"You know the type."

"Only too well," she said.

Joel turned back to his son.

"Did she chance to read *Silver Wings*? She always thought I was having such great fun with the European girls."

"Mom, read!" Giovanni scoffed.

"Come on, Dad. She hated the idea of my even bringing the book into the house."

"Or any other book, I suspect," said Joel, "just one more goddamned dust catcher for her to clean."

"Exactly, Dad! That's exactly what she said."

"How's Greg Leone working out?"

"He did his best for me, I have to give him that. He's doing fine. He travels a lot, and I think he has a girlfriend down on the Cape."

"I can't say I blame him," Joel chuckled.

The waiter came and cleared away the dishes. When he went off to fetch the coffee, it was Joel's turn to lean across the table toward Giovanni.

"Now about you… how's life in the modern Army?"

"Probably not a lot different than your day, Dad; up at zero-dark-thirty, run five miles, spit shine the jump boots…. you're one of the heroes at Fort Campbell, you know. There're several pictures of you in the Division museum… charging down the road at Carentan…"

"The most damn fool thing I've ever done."

"…taking command of Company B, drinking coffee with First Sergeant Ruth at Bastogne…"

"Christ!"

"They keep telling me how much I have to live up to."

"Don't you even think it, boy!" Joel snapped angrily. "It was the times. We did that because we had to, not because we wanted to play hero. You get your ass shot off that way."

Jenny, who had never heard such hard, soldier's talk from Joel, rocked back in her chair.

"I have no intention of letting that happen, Dad."

"What about Vietnam?" Joel asked.

"We have to stop the commies, Dad."

"Be careful son. The 101st always manages to find itself in the deepest shit."

*****

Joel was long since over the exoticness of Jenny's blackness, and she, of his whiteness. It didn't matter to either of them and all Joel could think of was that he was in the loving, erotic, and joyful company of the finest woman he had ever met. Except for one.

"I love you, Joel Finnigan," Jenny said on the rainy Sunday morning after their dinner with Giovanni. She lay curled up in his arms, looking tired and very, very happy after a night only partially devoted to sleep.

"I love you too, Jenny Keith," he replied. He meant it too but… there was just that last little bit of himself he could not give her because it belonged to Susanna Winslow, and if he could not give it to Susanna, he could give it to nobody, not even dear, loving Jenny.

"I think it's time we brought up the M-word," she said.

Marriage, the idea of it anyway, had been in their minds for a while now. Joel had avoided it after the horror show he had gone through with Connie. But Giovanni had mentioned it; so he wasn't surprised when Jenny brought it up that morning. He just didn't know how to respond.

"Married! Jenny, we…"

"What'll the neighbors say?" she asked playfully.

"Of course not. The people we really care about wouldn't give a damn, and the rest… to hell with them. Besides, I'm too old to care what the neighbors will say."

"Okay," she replied.

Jenny sat up in bed and looked down at Joel. He did not look away from her. He offered his usual appreciative smile, but that was all he had for her. Their lives were beginning to change.

She threw back the covers and swung her feet to the floor.

"I'm going out for breakfast," she said.

"Great! Where shall we go?"

"I want to go by myself this morning, Joel. I need the walk."

Jenny bent over and kissed Joel gently on the forehead. She got out of bed and put on a pair of jeans and a sweatshirt. She shrugged into her raincoat, clapped an old, nondescript hat over her blossoming Afro, and walked out of the apartment.

Joel watched her go. Then he got up, put on his oversized terrycloth bathrobe, and went to the front window just in time to see Jenny emerge onto the rain slicked sidewalk twenty floors below.

He noted how lovely she was, even in her shapeless raincoat. He hated himself for letting her go so easily. He should have insisted on going with her or, better yet, pulled her back under the covers and made love to her in the way they so urgently needed.

*****

Jenny reached the street just in time for the rain to dilute her tears and flush them down her cheeks. This wasn't the end for her and Joel. Neither of them wanted that to happen. But their relationship was different now; she had seen it in his eyes a few moments ago. An opaque screen had fallen between them, and it made her ineffably sad.

"What am I not giving him?" she wondered.

"My body, and the love that it transmits to him? No. We're incredible lovers, gentle, with amazing endurance with orgasms of seismic proportions."

But if it was just about orgasms, why hell, they could do that by themselves. No, their lovemaking was so much more than getting laid. It was a great sharing, with each giving as much as the other.

"My God, Joel would give his life for me," she thought. "He proved that down in Hoskins when he dragged me out of that burning building and sent those Ku Kluxers running into the night."

She couldn't repress a smile at the thought of Joel plunging the .38 into Hootie's crotch and threatening to turn his beloved

Junior into hamburger meat. He'd have done it too, which might have made at least some of the girls in Hoskins and environs quite unhappy; or not.

And they were just as good with their clothes on as they were with them off. Joel had missed only one of her concerts at the Academy of Music, and they spent hours wandering through the magical chambers of the Philadelphia Museum of Art or Fairmont Park, jabbering away like a pair of teenagers, or in easy silence, communicating deeply without speaking a word.

Nor had he been fatally scarred by what she gathered had been a hellish time with Connie. He had been, once, but Jenny found her greatest satisfaction in knowing that she had erased the last of it from his soul.

His Connie stories, from her prancing around in time with the Light Cavalry Overture to the last night when he walked in on her and Greg Leone, had become so funny that Jenny thought he should try his hand at writing a sex comedy.

But the opaque screen was still there, and Jenny couldn't see through it or even identify it. Walking alone in the rain around Rittenhouse Square she really couldn't put her finger on any single thing that was wrong with the life she shared with Joel Finnigan.

But it was different now. His sudden freeze-up at the mention of marriage had changed it. It was still very, very good and a thing worth keeping. She forced the vague sadness to the back of her mind, let a broad smile crease her dark, mahogany face and headed for home.

Jenny had been too immersed in her thoughts to stop anywhere for breakfast and she was starving by the time she got back to the apartment. Joel had anticipated that, and after a hot shower and cozy sweatsuit had banished the damp November chill from her soul, Jenny found herself seated before a stack of pancakes and a pot of hot coffee.

That man thinks of everything, she thought.

Absolutely everything.

CHAPTER TWENTY-SIX

ALL FALL DOWN

Jerry Granier really hadn't changed all that much since 1945. He had thickened somewhat around the middle, but who hadn't as the date for his fiftieth birthday drew nearer? Hell, Joel Finnigan didn't look like the rock hard, rangy paratrooper he had once been either.

But he was still the same old Jerry Granier that he had been when he and Joel first joined the Philadelphia Inquirer rewrite desk right after the war; grayer of head and slower of tread perhaps, but still with sharp blue eyes that had served him so well in his years as Executive Officer of the destroyer *U.S.S. O'Dowd* out in the Pacific. He wore glasses now, bifocals in fact, but that was of no great consequence, for he was no longer charged with picking out channel buoys on dark nights, or watching for the pencil-thin wake left by the periscope of the Japanese submarine that was lining itself up for a torpedo attack on the fat, clumsy troop transport ships that the *O'Dowd* and Lieutenant Commander Jerry Granier were charged with protecting.

The submarine went straight to the bottom of the Pacific, and Jerry went before no less than Admiral Chester Nimitiz to have a Navy Cross pinned onto his dress whites. Nimitz said that Jerry had saved the lives of nearly five thousand U.S. Marines that night. Since they were bound for the volcanic hell of Iwo Jima, Jerry sometimes wondered just how great a favor he had done them.

But, the war was the war, and the early days of 1968 found Jerry Granier standing watch on a different bridge, searching for different targets. While Joel went on to academia, Jerry developed an insatiable hunger for the adrenaline rush brought on by breaking news, and stayed at the *Inquirer* where he steered a staff of eager young reporters to two Pulitzer Prizes, and himself into the managing editor's office.

"Well, I'll be damned," he roared as the familiar figure appeared in his doorway, "Poor old Sergeant Finnigan!"

He had followed Joel's career since Joel left the *Inquirer* to teach college and write about the war. He had read his books and relied on him for perspective on more than a few stories. But he never expected to see him standing in the city room.

"Hi, Jerry. I'd have called for an appointment, but…"

"Appointment, my ass," Jerry said as he came out from behind his desk to take Joel's hand.

"… I had an idea… for a story."

"A real story, Joel? Not a history text or a monograph?"

"Interested?"

"Damn straight! Sit, sit. Talk, talk."

"I'm taking a sabbatical, the whole 1968 school year, and I want to spend it newspapering."

"Hell, Joel, I thought you'd found an honest trade. You're great at writing history."

"And I will continue to do that, if you'll take me on; the history of this year… the election."

Jerry Granier's native news sense clicked on and his eyes grew shrewd and sharp, as if he were standing a watch at sea.

"What do you have in mind, Joel? I've got a whole battalion of political reporters already assigned."

"I know. And they're all better at the day-to-day hard news stuff than I'll ever be."

"Then what can you do that they can't?"

"I can bring some perspective to it, Jerry. This is easily the most crucial period in our history, at least since you and I were in uniform. There's more hanging on the election of 1968 than any election since 1932."

Jerry shifted in his chair. The eyes that had picked out channel buoys and periscope wakes on dark nights seemed to be looking toward a distant shore.

"Yes. You definitely can add perspective, Joel. Daily newspapers don't put things into context."

"Hell!" he said with a sudden sharpness. "I wonder if there's anyone here who knows what context is, or can even spell it."

"Don't be too hard on your reporters, Jerry. They're smarter than we ever were. It's just that they haven't seen what we have, and they're concentrating just on what's in front of them."

"Just like we were during the war," Jerry replied. "But they have no idea of what we were doing back then."

"One of the dreams we had for after the war," Joel replied. "was about creating a better world. When JFK was elected in 1960 we thought we'd won. Guys like you and me, who had been in the war, were coming into power. We had paratroopers becoming history professors, destroyermen becoming editors, and a PT boat skipper was the President. We were going to put things right."

"They're not right, Joel. That's for damned sure. The civil rights movement has turned into Black Power, which scares the hell out of people; freedom has become the worst kind of irresponsibility, and this goddamned war that Johnson bumbled into has become... what the hell has it become?"

"Institutionalized. It's become a regular part of daily life."

"It was a regular part of daily life in 1942, Joel."

"It was. But even then we knew that war is an aberration, a temporary sickness that would end, sooner or later.

"But Vietnam has become like a division of a big corporation. Shit, Johnson even got Congress to pass a tax surcharge last year to pay for the goddamned thing. This war is changing everything. The government is becoming just another big corporate entity trying to get its hand in your pocket. The war is becoming a fault line across all of society and it may do us some serious damage down the road."

"Tell me something I don't know, Joel," Jerry replied with a newsman's cynical chuckle.

"Taxes don't go down.

"Johnson's doing the best he can, trying to keep Communism at bay and keeping JFK's New Frontier going at the same time."

"That's the point, Jerry. He can't do both. He's turning the country against him and turning a big part of the world against the country. He's got us in a war we can't win, and have no idea of what we'd win even if we could. The kids hate him for that. Hell, their protests have turned from anti-war to anti-American.

"And Joe Sixpack, the guys in the factories with Confederate flags on their pickups are mad as hell at the tax surcharge and what, to them, is the hijacking of the civil rights movement by thugs. They're scared to death of sending their kids off to college to screw themselves bowlegged and fry their brains on LSD.

"The country seems to be falling apart. It won't, of course, but big changes are on the way and some of them are pretty ugly. That's what the 1968 election is all about, Jerry, and it's why I need to get out of my ivory tower and cover it from ground level."

"Is there a book in this, Joel?"

"Probably. I'm compulsive. But I just need to get into the mud and cover it close up."

Jerry turned his chair around and stared out his office window.

"Special correspondent," he mused.

He swung back to face Joel.

"I can take you on as a special correspondent for the election. I'll have to clear it with the publisher, but I'm sure he'll go for it. I can't promise a lot of money, though."

"It's a paid sabbatical, Jerry."

"Okay, Joel. You've got a deal."

Jerry stood and extended his right hand.

"Welcome back to the trenches, Professor Finnigan."

*****

On February 15, 1968, just about two weeks after Joel Finnigan and Jerry Granier struck their bargain, another, much farther reaching deal was struck 3,000 miles away in Pasadena, California. It didn't seem like that big a deal on the surface. George Erhard found he had no use for the .22 caliber Iver Johnson pistol that a neighbor had given him; so he sold it to a guy named Joe for twenty-five dollars.

Joe was a worker at Nash's department store in Pasadena, whose name was actually Munir Sirhan. He had come to the United States from Palestine in 1956 with his family, which included a younger brother Sirhan.

This boy with two first names, or two last names, was just a little guy, the kind who might make it as a jockey as long as his heart was bigger than the rest of him. By the time big brother Munir bought the Iver Johnson from George Erhard, Sirhan Sirhan had put in several years around the race tracks of Southern California exercising the thoroughbreds, leading them on the cooling-down walks afterwards, but never quite making it into the ranks of the professional jockeys.

He was quiet, truly passionate only about the tension between Israel and its surrounding Arab neighbors.

In all, a quite unremarkable young man.

*****

Joel nearly broke out laughing out loud, right there in the Academy of Music. He hadn't heard the "Light Cavalry Overture" for more than fifteen years, but when the Philadelphia Orchestra performed it as an encore to their final performance of the 1967-1968 season, he simply could not help remembering Connie.

The spectacle of her prancing around the lawn of the president's residence at Washington College as though she were riding a horse herself was too hilarious not to smile. Looking up on the stage, he saw Jenny Keith behind her cello and also on the verge of laughter.

"I thought you'd get a giggle out of that," she said playfully as they walked down Broad Street toward a late, post-concert dinner at the Harvest House restaurant.

"Did you put them up to that, Jenny?"

"No… I swear. We rehearsed it, of course, but it was for this summer's tour. I was as surprised as anybody else when we played it tonight."

Jenny tugged on his arm and drew him closer.

"I hope it didn't stir up any bad memories."

"Good Lord, no! She's a source of great amusement now; a grown woman who never managed to get past the terrible twos."

They settled into their seats at the Harvest House and ordered a couple of corned beef and pastrami combo sandwiches.

"So, what's the summer schedule?" he asked.

"New York, in Central Park no less. Then London, Paris, Berlin, Rome, and Prague. We fly to California for concerts in Los Angeles and San Francisco on the way out to Sydney."

"The new Opera House?"

"Yes."

"I've heard it's got great acoustics."

"We're all looking forward to performing there."

"I've got a summer tour myself, Jenny. I just saw an old friend at the *Inquirer*. I'm going to cover the election during my sabbatical year."

"Professor Joel Finnigan… a newspaper reporter? You're way past that, Joel."

"Maybe, but this is going to be a very important election. And don't forget, journalism really is the first draft of history."

"A cliché," she sneered contemptuously.

"Things become clichés by being eminently true, Jen."

Jenny looked disappointed that she and Joel would not spend the summer traveling to and making love in some of the world's greatest cities. But he had the sense that she was not as disappointed as she thought she might be, or should have been.

Nor was he.

*****

Which campaign, which candidate to cover? It was a dilemma that Joel faced as winter edged tentatively toward spring. Everybody wanted to become President of the United States but, of course, only two would survive the long season of primaries and the national conventions in Miami and Chicago to face one another in November.

Richard Nixon had a lock on the Republican nomination. It was his to lose. Joel was certain that neither George Romney nor Nelson Rockefeller had the stuff to win it from him.

Americans were turning against Johnson, the president who had led them into a seemingly endless war, and Joel was developing a sick feeling deep in the pit of his stomach that Richard Nixon was going to win the election. The mood of the American body politic was turning mean and nasty, and Richard Milhous Nixon was just the right man for mean and nasty people.

And, perhaps most important for a writer on the make for a good story, Nixon and his people were impossibly dull. They were not trying to win, only to keep from losing, and Joel always liked being around and writing about people who were at least trying to win.

The best way to be elected president is to be the president already. Denying the nomination to an incumbent president was almost unheard of, but the Democratic Party was in a particularly dyspeptic mood in 1968 and the unthinkable was becoming increasingly thinkable.

Joel saw no choice but to attach himself to one of the Democratic contenders. Hubert Humphrey was a good man; perhaps the most decent man in American politics. But good, decent Hubert would never turn against his president. And even if he did, Joel was one of those who thought that, as Vice-President, Humphrey had been too loyal to Lyndon Johnson and his hated Vietnam war.

Eugene McCarthy? His campaign was fueled by the anti-war sentiment that was burning on college campuses across the United States. It was electrifying. Joel nearly caught the fever himself from his students at Temple, but he felt McCarthy was too cool and too intellectual to find within himself the fire and the taste for combat required of a presidential campaigner, much less a President.

Ultimately, it was Joel's fundamental irrepressibility and optimism that made his decision for him. The historical adventure toward a better society that had begun in the cold of January 20, 1961 had not yet been completed. Robert F. Kennedy, the brash, abrasive, bare-knuckled bulldog of his dead brother's American Camelot, was reaching toward a new level of thoughtfulness, even spirituality. If he found it, and Joel was sure he would, he would be the only politician capable of putting not just the Democratic Party but the entire United States back on its idealistic, upward leading highway.

So, Joel's decision led him to Nashville, Tennessee, where he sat in an auditorium at Vanderbilt University scribbling in a long, slim reporter's notebook, trying to write faster than he had since his first post-war days at the *Inquirer,* hoping that he was getting each of Kennedy's broadly accented words correctly:

"When we are told to forgo all dissent and discussion, we must ask; who is it that is truly dividing the country?

"It is not those who call for change. It is those who make present policy… who have removed themselves from the American tradition, from the enduring and generous impulses that are the soul of this nation."

Bobby sounded an angry lament for the faltering spirit of his brother's years by warning of the retreat from "the public commitment of a few years ago to lives of disengagement and despair, turning on with drugs and turning off America.

"This is a time to begin again and that is why I need your help and that is why I run for President."

That closing line always got Joel. It resonated with the Vanderbilt kids and, as the campaign went on, with people around the United States. They remembered the heady days of 1961. Reestablishing John Kennedy's New Frontier seemed within reach, and if the energy they poured out to Robert Kennedy could do it, a New Camelot was assured.

Robert Kennedy caught the pulse of their energy. Added to his personal dislike of the crude, shifty Texan, Lyndon Johnson, and his constantly growing disgust with the bloody fiasco that was Vietnam, this swell of energy and idealism was all he needed to push him into a full throated campaign for the presidency.

*****

Robert Kennedy's was a campaign that Joel Finnigan had to cover close up, from ground level. Kennedy's message, scribbled in the slim notebook that Joel was carrying, was all but indecipherable. He was flying back to confer with Jerry Granier and the senior editors of the *Inquirer*, to plow through the mail that had undoubtedly piled up in his first few weeks on the road, and to write his first major piece for the Inquirer's Sunday magazine.

The first tentative sentences had already spread themselves across Joel's yellow legal pad and he was drifting into a brief nap, completely unaware of the seismic upheaval that was building several thousand feet beneath and several hundred miles behind his eastbound Boeing 707.

Donald Wood was behind the counter of his father's gun shop, the Aeromarine Supply Company in Birmingham, Alabama. A man who signed his name Harvey Lowmyer walked in and bought a Winchester rifle and a box of ammunition.

The Winchester was a fine piece, but it was not exactly the right tool for its intended job. Lowmyer returned to Aeromarine the following day and exchanged it for a Remington 30.06 rifle equipped with a telescopic sight.

It seemed an insignificant transaction, even less so than Munir Sirhan's purchase of the Iver Johnson pistol in Pasadena only about two weeks before.

*****

There are few things as good as whiskey and the steady drone of a quartet of Pratt & Whitney JT8D-11s for inducing, if not sleep, then a dreamlike state that leaves the mind free to wander through the maze of its own recesses. Joel would have preferred a wee Jameson's but this was, after all, an American airline and scotch was as good as anything.

The scotch mingled with the pervasive sound of the jet engines to lull Joel into his inner mansion. He was dimly aware of the sounds which had faded away to a distant, restful hum, and of the occasional jolt as the plane bumped across the odd air pocket, but Joel was still able to wander from room to psychic room like a tourist in a museum.

He found the rooms full of people. Closest to the front door of his mind were the likes of Richard Nixon, Lyndon Johnson and Bobby Kennedy. Walking in farther, he found old paratrooping buddies. There was, of course, Jenny Keith, with a broad, loving smile creasing her dark mahogany face, Freya Schultz, with her sharp, penetrating intelligence, and finally Susanna, serene and quiet but with a hint of sadness in her eyes.

Oddly, for the first time in years, Connie was nowhere to be seen — banished, no doubt, to Joel's psychological outhouse.

But Susanna... Susanna... Susanna... she would never leave him. Not that he would have it any other way, for whatever he had shared with Freya, Jenny, and one or two others, his brief time with Susanna, the letters from the war years and, finally, that long, exquisite weekend on Sansom Street had changed his life. The way he felt about himself, his work and, most of all, about women, were never the same after Susanna.

She'd be in her mid-forties now, with the silver starting to appear in her hair and the first lines showing around her eyes and the corners of her mouth. He hoped, even prayed if the truth be known, that they were smile lines, the mark of a life well lived with Justin Welch, and that she was surrounded by her children and, God help us, maybe even a grandchild or two.

It was of Susanna that Yeats might have written:
How many have loved your moments of glad grace,
And loved your beauty with love false or true?
But one man has loved the pilgrim soul in you,
And loved the sorrows of your changing face.

Maude Gonne supposedly wrote once that "Willy is so silly," but, by God, he had it right about Susanna Winslow and the way Joel Finnigan felt her even after all these years. The Susanna that swirled before Joel in time with the jet engines bore the face of a twenty-two-year-old young woman radiating love and the most intense kind of passion. He knew he was never to see and love the sorrows of Susanna's changing face, and Justin Welch damned well better have appreciated the gift he had been given in exchange for his legs.

And Jenny Keith? He loved her well enough, and felt as thoroughly loved as he had been since 1945, but she wasn't Susanna

The 707 lowered its nose and the notes of its engines changed as it began descending toward Philadelphia International Airport. The airliner would land on the west bank of the Delaware, not far from where Joel had spent his pre-war years and felt the first stirrings of his imagination.

The plane shuddered as it lowered its flaps and landing gear and made the wide turn over Gloucester City, New Jersey before lining up for its final approach. Joel was jolted back into the real world, or what passed for a real world in this increasingly strange year of 1968, and he found himself wishing that the whole man/woman thing wasn't so goddamned complicated.

*****

"Hell! It's the same old crap," Jenny snorted from the far end of the sofa. She had just broiled as fine a pair of steaks as could have been found in Philadelphia. Joel had whipped up a nice, if not great, Caesar salad, and they enjoyed their first dinner at their apartment on Rittenhouse Square since he had gone out on the campaign trail and she had plunged into the maelstrom of preparing for the Philadelphia Orchestra's summer international concert tour.

Now they were finishing off dinner with a fine French brandy and Lyndon Johnson's latest speech. The President's speech of March 31, 1968 wasn't expected to be a particularly important one, but everything was important in this highly charged political year.

"The same old crap! Jenny, you're getting downright harsh," Joel said in response to her brief outburst.

He had been watching Johnson with only one eye and part of his mind while he proofread his piece for the Sunday *Inquirer* magazine. He had already gone over it with Jerry Granier and was making sure he wouldn't be undone by any unfortunate typos or misspellings.

"I am harsh, Joel, or getting that way… or something. It used to be so right. Now it's all… it's all gone so wrong."

"It's the war," he replied. "There are other things but, mostly it's Vietnam."

Johnson was speaking on the war. What else could he do? It had taken everyone's minds off the other problems that had been on the America agenda throughout the 1960s. The victories that had been won at such great cost.

Joel finished proofing his Sunday magazine piece and as he was gathering the pages and placing them on the coffee table, he noticed a grin on Jenny's face.

"You were so angry just a minute ago," he said calmly. "What's so funny now?"

"Nothing funny," she said. "I was just remembering you sticking the gun down that cracker's pants and threatening to blow Junior to pieces."

She moved closer to Joel and slipped her hand into his.

"Those were great days, Joel... terrible, but great. It was like a war. I never saw such violence in my life, or realized how much some people can hate, but we were in it together and fighting for something good. And see what it got us," she snapped, her anger returning.

"Listen to this... bullshit," she sneered contemptuously.

Lyndon Johnson was leaning forward into the television camera and, just as Jenny had predicted, gave out the same old crap.

He hinted that he might at least offer to stop bombing North Vietnam if the other side could see its way clear to begin productive negotiations aimed at restoring, if not peace, then at least an American withdrawal.

The President spoke too of 'substantial progress'.

"Yeah! Sure."

"...in creating a durable government in Saigon."

Joel lifted an eyebrow when Johnson said the South Vietnamese might soon be drafting eighteen year olds.

"Bobby Kennedy's been calling for that in some of his speeches."

"... better than our eighteen year olds," Jenny replied, "especially the poor black ones."

This was new from Jenny, and she stared at Joel's sideways glance.

"Well, it's true, Joel. Young black men are dying over there by the hundreds. Young white men are going to graduate school or getting their daddies to hide them away in the National Guard."

"My son's not hiding out."

"Giovanni's a good man. I pray he gets out of Vietnam alive."

"I believe now, no less than when the decade began," Johnson went on, "that this generation of Americans is willing to pay any price, bear any burden, meet any hardship, support any friend, oppose any foe to assure the survival and the success of liberty."

"Great words," Joel said cynically. "I heard them the first time."

"And we believed them, Joel. We believed them so much."

And they had, very deeply. Joel remembered all too well the thrill he felt when he heard John Kennedy originate the phrase on that bitterly cold January 20, 1961.

It all seemed so long ago.

*****

Lyndon Johnson's promise seemed to be fading. His upward political journey was faltering, and he was the only one who could do anything about it.

"With American sons in the field far away, with America's future under challenge here at home, with our hopes and the world's hopes for peace in the balance every day, I do not believe that I should devote an hour or a day of my time to any partisan political causes or to any duties other than the awesome duties of this office, the presidency of this country."

Wondering if he had evolved into a true statesman, or whether he was merely concerned about being humiliated by Eugene McCarthy or, even worse, Richard Nixon, or if the whole business was just too much for a man who had barely survived a heart attack just thirteen years earlier, Joel and Jenny stopped their wineglasses at their lips and leaned even more intently toward the TV, determined not to miss a word of what was becoming the most significant presidential speech of their time.

He announced that he would drastically reduce the bombing of North Vietnam and, once again, declare that nothing would be allowed to block his search for an end to the interminable, institutionalized war.

Then he dropped the biggest bomb of all.

"Accordingly I will not seek, and I will not accept, the nomination of my party for another term as your president."

"Well, I'll be damned, Joel whispered as he went to the liquor cabinet for something a lot stronger than Chardonnay.

*****

The world seemed to take a bit of a breather, pausing to absorb Johnson's astonishing announcement. All but Joel Finnigan. He tossed his Sunday magazine article into the trash can and set to work on a new piece, analyzing the dramatically altered political landscape.

When the most driven politician of his generation turns his back on the most coveted prize of his profession, it had to have a seismic impact. But what impact? Joel's first thought was that the field was now free for Eugene McCarthy, Robert Kennedy, or even Hubert Humphrey.

But while Joel, newly admitted to the ranks of punditry, was contemplating the Democratic brawl, a far more fundamentally seismic upheaval was building toward a climax in Tennessee.

Martin Luther King, Jr. had spent most of that troubled spring in Memphis giving active, vocal support to a municipal sanitation workers' strike. Since most of the sanitation workers were black men, a case could be made that it was part of the civil rights movement, but it seemed to have no bearing on the presidential campaign and so King dropped almost all the way off Joel's journalistic radar.

On April 3, a cold, wet night, King stood before the crowded Mason Temple and elevated what had been an ordinary city workers' strike to the level of a spiritual crusade. The strike had generated an inordinate level of racial tensions and death threats. But this was the South, where Martin Luther King, Jr. was the most hated of all men, and he was used to it.

"So I'm happy tonight," he proclaimed, leading up to his normally rousing southern preacher climax.

"I'm not worried about anything!"

"I'm not fearing any man!"

"Mine eyes have seen the glory of the coming of the Lord!"

They loved it. They loved him as they always had. But the one man King should have feared, the one man who brought the coming of the Lord much closer than he would have liked, was already in motion.

On the afternoon of April 3, several hours before King spoke at Mason Temple, a man drove up to the New Rebel Hotel in a white Ford Mustang. He signed the register as Eric S. Galt, giving not the slightest hint that he was also Harvey Lowmyer who bought the Remington 30.06 hunting rifle at the Aeromarine Supply Company in Birmingham, Alabama.

Not, of course, that Galt was really Harvey Lowmyer either.

Early the next morning, 'Galt' checked out of the New Rebel and set off in search of one last piece of equipment that he needed for his upcoming job. It was a pair of Bushnell binoculars that he bought from the York Arms Company for $41.50.

The white Mustang was next seen pulling up to a rooming house, little more than a flophouse, really, at 424 ½ South Main Street. He registered under yet a third name, John Willard, and went up to Room 5B.

He seemed to be having stomach problems, or perhaps a urinary tract ailment, because he was seen making numerous trips down the hall to the common bathroom. It was an ordinary enough bathroom and nobody but Lowmyer/Galt/Willard noticed, or even cared, that by standing in the bathtub one could enjoy a fine, unobstructed view of the Lorraine Motel at 420 South Main Street.

Martin Luther King, Jr. spent most of that afternoon in Room 306 of the Lorraine Motel. He was working out the details of a demonstration scheduled for Monday, April 9. The city had gone into federal court for an injunction against the demonstration because, the lawyers said, they feared for King's safety.

It was an afternoon devoted to brainstorming with nothing on King's schedule until 7:00 p.m. when he was due for dinner at the home of the Rev. Samuel Kyles. After the previous night's tumultuous reception at Mason Temple and what promised to be an even more tumultuous demonstration in the streets of Memphis just a few days later, a quiet dinner with a few friends would be just the thing.

From his perch in the bathroom, Willard watched a car and a few friends arrive to take King to dinner. He stood in the tub and laid the crosshairs of the Remington's telescopic sight squarely on the door to Room 306. At 5:57 p.m., the door slid open and Martin Luther King, Jr. stepped onto the balcony. He paused to greet his friends, which made Willard's set-up just about perfect.

Willard, or whatever his name was, was an expert rifleman. He squeezed the trigger, gently so he would not shift his crosshairs away from King's head.

The 30.06 round tore into King's face at 6:01 p.m. Central Standard Time, and the one man who had managed to capture the conscience of the United States was dead.

The Remington was later found in the doorway of the Canipe Amusement Company on South Main Street. Of the white Mustang and the rifleman there was not a trace.

*****

As the Mustang dashed out of Memphis — toward Canada as it turned out — it left a considerable wake. 'Willard's' 30.06 round tore not just through the brain of Martin Luther King, Jr., but through the entire fabric of the United States. It tore through Joel and Jenny, too.

Joel later wondered just how much there was to be torn through anyway. Jenny, without really knowing the whole story, had been trying to move into the space occupied by Susanna Winslow. But that space in Joel's heart was simply too crowded. They both had begun to realize that when Giovanni first brought up the M-word and so, perhaps, the events immediately following April 4, 1968 were inevitable.

Joel had not gone west to rejoin Robert Kennedy's campaign in Indiana. American blacks, once celebrating the liberating effects of the early 1960s, were so devastated by King's murder that some of their rage exploded into rioting, hating, and burning in cities from Washington, D.C. to Boston, westward to Oakland, California and more than a hundred other cities and towns in between.

This, Joel realized with his newly sharpened reporter's instincts, was an upheaval as great as anything else that could possibly have happened in 1968, or any other year. He had to cover it, and set off for Trenton, New Jersey where the trouble had already exploded.

*****

"You idiot! You fucking idiot!"

Jerry Granier was really pissed.

"I've got twenty-five-year-old street jocks to do this, Joel. You're not a twenty-one-year-old paratrooper any more, for Christ's sake."

"Yeah. Well, it seemed like a good idea," Joel replied from his bed in the local emergency room.

It certainly did not seem like a good idea at the moment, however. The bandage around his head, the cast on his right forearm and the sharp waves of pain from his broken ribs were not, he knew, very much in the way of battle scars considering what was happening around the rest of the country.

Still, and it really did hurt only when he laughed, his fellow Americans in Trenton had done him more damage than the German Army ever did.

"Less than half an hour on the street," he groaned. "I don't think I took a single note."

"Blundering in between the Black Panthers and the New Jersey State Police isn't really conducive to that," replied Jerry.

"Shit, Joel! You're damned lucky you're not blinking once for yes and twice for no. Let's get you the hell out of here."

Jerry and the ER nurse helped Joel up into a sitting position and turned him to his left until he was sitting on the edge of the bed. He didn't feel nearly as dizzy as he thought he should.

"I can make it back to Philadelphia," he said. "I can make it home. I've got my car up here, someplace."

"The hell you do," Jerry replied. "It made a lovely bonfire I'm told."

"Burned...?"

"... to the proverbial crisp, old fella. I'm taking you back to Philly."

Joel slumped against the seat of Jerry's green El Camino. He closed his eyes and drifted into a fog that stopped just short of sleep. Maybe he was more wiped out than he realized; so he luxuriated in letting Jerry drive.

"I never saw it coming, Jer'; never saw it."

"It was night... confused as hell. You're just lucky that Trenton fireman saw you lying in the street."

"No; not that, damnit!" Joel snapped.

"... the hate. I never saw the hate."

"None of us did, Joel. We should have. It was always there."

*****

The sun was just starting to come up and so was Finnigan. He was by no means fully awake, but he was dozing away the last of the painkillers and the bad night in Trenton when Jenny finally came home. She glanced briefly at him and walked straight into his study without saying a word. Her eyes were not cold, exactly, but neither were they filled with the gentleness and love he had become accustomed to during their years together.

Even through his foggy and throbbing head, Joel heard Jenny rattling around in the study, on the upper shelf of the storage closet to be specific. He knew she was reaching for the black, battered metal box near the back of the shelf. He recognized the distinctive sound that its catch made when it snapped open, and that recognition filled his heart with fear.

He roused himself from the sofa and sort of half walked, half stumbled into the kitchen to tackle the complexities of making a pot of coffee.

"Where have you been?" he asked casually.

"Out," she replied, sounding somewhat curt.

"… out in North Philadelphia trying to keep those kids from killing each other."

"Did you really need the .38 for that? It can have the opposite effect, you know."

Joel hadn't thought much about the .38 caliber Smith & Wesson since he and Jenny brought it back from Mississippi in 1964. He kept it locked up, and of course there was no ammunition, but he had never really thought about the gun.

Except that right now he wished to hell he had gotten rid of the damned thing.

"I just took it in case you came after us," she said.

"Me? Just in case 'I' came after you, Jenny?"

"Not you specifically, Joel; your cops, your army, your corporations… Stokely said 'we have to be armed and ready when they come for us.'"

"What do you mean 'when they come for us,' Jenny? Nobody's coming for anybody."

"Well, they came for Martin, and they got him!" she snapped. "You remember what Stokely said the next day? '… when white America killed Doctor King last night, she declared war on black America and there could be no alternative to retribution. Black people have to survive and the only way they will survive is by getting guns.'"

"Look at the cops on North Broad Street, Joel… the National Guard ruling the streets of Washington! There's even a machine gun nest on the steps of the Capitol, for God's sake! They sure didn't come for any white boys."

"If white boys were rioting, burning and beating people, the cops would be coming for them, Jenny. As for King, that was most likely some misguided nut case. The FBI is looking under every rock for him."

"Oh, he's a nut case, all right, but he's sure as hell not misguided. The man who fired that rifle was guided. He was guided by big money — big, white money."

"Jenny! My God, what's happened to you?"

"I've had my eyes opened, Joel."

"Your eyes were always open, Jenny. You always knew where you were headed. You're on the verge of becoming a star."

"In your world, Joel; at the Academy of Music."

"It's our world. At least I thought it was."

"Maybe once. Now I don't know. Everything's different and I just don't know anymore."

CHAPTER TWENTY-SEVEN

HAPPY BIRTHDAY TO ME

Thirty! I can't believe it. I'm going to be thirty. I'm too young to be middle-aged.

In my mom's day, they said, 'don't trust anybody over thirty.'

I prefer to stick with Peter Pan's motto, 'I won't grow up', or, better yet, the one I saw on a T-shirt at the Moorestown Mall, 'I may grow older, but I won't grow up.' Maybe I'll buy it for myself as a birthday present. I've always believed a girl should buy herself birthday presents. That way you're sure to get something you like.

I wonder what Mark will get me. It's my first birthday with him, an important one — although I'd just as soon forget it.

Mom will certainly remember. It will probably be as traumatic for her as it is for me. God, I can't imagine having a thirty-year-old kid — although at the rate I'm going, I'll be a really old woman when that happens. So maybe it won't bother me that much.

It will probably make Mom nostalgic for the good old sixties. Her hippie days in San Francisco and all that went with them. But then, of course, when I came along, she did give all that up to become a responsible Haddonfield matron. I wonder if she would have stayed in California if she hadn't had me. I wonder if she would have gotten caught up in all the protests. 1968 was quite a year.

CHAPTER TWENTY-EIGHT

BOBBY

Gradually, through the rest of April and well into May, the distance between Joel and Jenny widened until they just couldn't reach across it any longer. There was no big blow up, like the time he came home to find Connie on her knees with Greg Leone's dick in her mouth — a scene that brought Joel more amusement than anything else.

They grew further apart until, one day in the middle of May, Jenny wasn't there anymore. Joel had come in late that afternoon after spending the day at the *Inquirer's* white tower on North Broad Street. He was reworking a piece for an upcoming Sunday magazine and conferring with Jerry Granier about his plans to rejoin Robert Kennedy's campaign in California.

Kennedy's earlier ambivalence about seeking the Democratic Presidential nomination had vanished since the death of Martin Luther King. The dreams engendered by John Kennedy were fading fast and Bobby was the last best chance to revive them. Joel, who had never presented himself as a completely objective reporter, if there ever was such a thing, knew it and was determined to see it all, right through to the younger Kennedy's inauguration.

The apartment was empty when Joel came in. That in itself was not unusual because Jenny would still be down at the Academy of Music rehearsing.

But the place was preternaturally silent. Spaces that had once echoed to the joyous cries of their lovemaking and the animations of their spirited conversations were cloaked in the haunting silence of a tomb. Slowly, as if he were an archaeologist exploring a tomb, Joel went from room to room, closet to closet, searching for any sign of Jenny Keith.

He found none. Jenny's clothes, her books, and her volumes of sheet music were gone. Conventional drama would have had a letter, or at least a note, on the dining room table or taped to the refrigerator, telling him that she had left and why.

But there wasn't even that. It was as though Jenny Keith had died, or worse, had never lived.

A sadness settled on Joel's shoulders. He and Jenny had been together since 1964 after all; ever since the day he had signed up for Freedom Summer. It was hard to let go of those years with all their worries and joys.

Joel was falling into a reverie, but not so deeply that he wasn't hoping that the telephone would shatter it with its insistent clamor. It would be Jenny, of course, calling to tell him why she had left.

But the telephone never rang. She was gone, and he knew it was for the best.

On the surface, it seemed like a micro-manifestation of the divide between black and white America that had been exposed in all its ugliness by the murder of Martin Luther King, Jr. There had been hints of that between them on that day.

But it wasn't because of their racial difference that Joel lost Jenny. They were smart enough and, at the beginning, in love enough not to let that happen. The world was full of interracial couples and becoming ever more so.

The real reason, and Joel knew this from the start, was that for all Jenny's warmth and love, there was always a part of him that felt alone, even in their most intimate moments. She was not Susanna. It was that simple. It was terribly unfair to Jenny, who really did see a future with Joel at one time, but it was inevitable that this day would come.

Despite his sadness and sense of loss, Joel was starting to feel a vague sense of calm and resignation as he began making plans to go to California.

He was coming to realize that he probably would spend the rest of his life alone. But he was proud of his life. He had come through the war with honor, indeed with distinction, played a small part in building the ideal America, and produced a substantial body of work about the most turbulent years of his century. And, most importantly, he was Giovanni's father — if not biologically, in all the ways that really mattered.

Not bad, not too bad at all as he thought on it. He had loved and been loved by Susanna Winslow, no matter how briefly, and that was pretty damned good for any man.

Irrepressibility was at the core of Joel's being, and he could feel it rising a couple of weeks after Jenny's departure as he packed for his flight to San Francisco where Bobby Kennedy was going to debate Eugene McCarthy.

*****

As Joel's 707 was passing over the Black Hills of South Dakota, a swarthy, bushy-haired young man asked the sales clerk at the Lock, Stock and Barrel gun shop in San Gabriel for a box of .357 Magnum armor piercing ammunition.

The shop didn't carry it. It was far too powerful for sport shooting; so the young man had to settle for four boxes of .22 caliber rounds — just the thing for his Iver Johnson revolver.

They cost him less than four dollars.

*****

"We want Gene!"
"We want Gene!"
"We want Gene!"

McCarthy's supporters were out in full strength, and voice, in front of KGFO-TV. It was shortly after six o'clock Pacific time on June 1, and McCarthy was to face Robert Kennedy thirty minutes later. It would be 9:30 p.m. on the east coast, where the voters, still trying to make up their minds between the two senators, would have finished dinner and settled in before their TV sets.

They were two Irishmen, of completely different, yet characteristic, stripes. McCarthy was cool, composed, thoughtful, even poetic. He expected voters to reason their way to his support.

Bobby Kennedy, a political craftsman who had learned his trade in Boston politics and sharpened his tools managing his brother's victorious presidential campaign, was a fighter. He came to San Francisco determined to attack McCarthy and pounce on every opening.

And Bobby Kennedy had been in the fight. As his brother's Attorney-General, he had enforced the civil rights laws. As Jack's closest friend and advisor, he had helped navigate the Cuban Missile Crisis and steer the United States and the Soviet Union away from the deadly rocks of war.

Joel elbowed his way into one of the tiny cell-like rooms that had been set aside for the traveling press corps. This was one of the early television campaigns, and the inky-fingered wretches of the old newspaper brigades were being shown their place in the new order by being channeled into quarters that would give a Trappist monk claustrophobia.

Still, there was enough room to wield a pen and his notebook. Joel reasoned, in barely legible script that he would decipher later, that of the two senators, Kennedy had the stuff to be President.

Not only that, but Bobby really wanted it now. A profound change had come over him in the eight weeks since the King assassination and he was determined to become President of the United States.

And Joel would be there to get it all. He had already been in touch with his book agent back in New York. His reputation, especially after the success of his World War II histories, particularly *Silver Wings,* was enough to secure an agreement for him to write a book on the campaign.

*****

It ought to make a pretty good book too, Joel thought as he boarded a flight from Los Angeles to San Francisco for a noontime motorcade through Chinatown on June 3, the last day of the campaign. When they arrived, Joel managed to find a seat near the front of the press bus right behind the open convertible carrying Bobby and Ethel Kennedy.

Suddenly, about three blocks into the motorcade, six sharp explosions cracked open the early afternoon and threw most of the reporters on the bus into a panic.

"Oh my God," cried the *Los Angeles Times*.

"What the hell was that?" growled the *San Francisco Chronicle*.

"Jesus! They got Ethel," sobbed the *Sacramento Bee*.

That last remark really got Joel's attention. He looked forward and saw that Ethel Kennedy was indeed no longer standing by her husband and waving at the lunchtime crowd. Given the Kennedy family's recent history and the events of just two months earlier, Joel tensed up as a terrible fear went through him.

"Christ! Not again."

Ethel was not hurt and there had been no gunshots. Joel, who had already heard too many bullets snap over his head, finally realized what had caused the commotion.

"It's firecrackers," he said, loudly enough to be heard throughout the bus and, he hoped, to calm everyone's fears.

From Chinatown the campaign flew south to Long Beach for yet another motorcade and then to San Diego for a late afternoon rally. Then it was back to Los Angeles where Kennedy was to spend the night at a filmmaker friend's ocean side house in Malibu while everyone else, including Joel, retired to the Ambassador for an evening of celebrating the end of the California primary campaign.

*****

As Kennedy and his entourage raced through the campaign's final day, the dark, bushy-haired young man was shooting off nearly all the ammunition he had bought at the Lock, Stock and Barrel Gun Shop.

He must have fired three or four hundred rounds of .22 caliber ammunition on the range of the San Gabriel Valley Gun Club in Duarte. His fire was so rapid that it violated the club policy requiring shooters to pause between shots.

But, no matter. The little Iver Johnson felt steady in his hand and never wavered from its target.

*****

Joel could feel the pulse of excitement growing within the Embassy Room, the Ambassador's main ballroom. The first results had started to come in and they didn't look all that good for Robert Kennedy. They were from outside Los Angeles County and showed McCarthy in the lead.

Joel took a seat at one of the long press tables, watching the numbers going up on the big scoreboard at the back of the ballroom stage, and typing out a rough lead saying that Eugene McCarthy had won the California primary.

"Don't send that out just yet, Joel," said a voice from over his right shoulder.

It was Jack Donnall of the *Sacramento Bee*, easily the most astute political observer in California journalism.

"I'm not sending anything, Jack... and stop looking over my shoulder."

Jack sat down beside Joel and placed a Styrofoam cup full of fresh coffee before him.

"Sorry," said Jack. "The devil made me do it. But you can't say anything definitive until all the results are in from Los Angeles County."

"Well, it is the biggest county in the state," Joel replied.

"And thirty eight percent of all Democrats registered in California are registered in Los Angeles County," said Jack.

"Kennedy should have it by the balls. If he wins L.A. County, he wins the whole state."

"How strong are McCarthy and Humphrey, Jack?"

"Strong, but I think Bobby brought the undecideds over to his side in the San Francisco debate Sunday. It happened up in Oregon, and the Democratic polls are saying that two out of three came over in California."

*****

Joel was mulling over Jack Donnall's assessment as he stood just outside the door of the Colonial Room, the official press room, enjoying his first beer of the evening. He was relaxed, having two different leads fixed in his mind — one announcing a Kennedy victory and another — just in case.

An increasingly happy crowd swirled in front of him. Then, almost like a bar of soap squeezed between two wet hands, a short, dark young man popped out of the scrum and into the Colonial Room doorway next to Joel.

"What a madhouse," the young man said in accented English.

"They smell a win," Joel replied.

"Or blood — a fresh kill in the political jungle," the young man said with a grin.

He nodded at the beer in Joel's hand.

"Where can I find something cold to drink? It's getting warm in here."

"It's going to get a lot warmer," replied Joel.

"... probably will," said the young man.

"Wait here. I'll get you a beer."

"Pepsi, please."

Joel stepped back into the Colonial Room and went to one of the big coolers stacked against the wall. He opened one, took out an ice cold Pepsi, popped it open and took it back to the dark stranger.

"Thanks," the young man said.

"Tell me," he said, almost as an afterthought, "are you a Democrat?"

Joel grinned.

"Officially, I'm here as a reporter. I'm supposed to be neutral. But yes, I'm a Democrat… a Kennedyite more exactly."

The young man broke into a broad smile and held out his right hand.

"Well, friend, shake hands with another Democrat."

They shook, and the young man drifted off, carried away by the gyrating tides and currents of humanity that flooded through the Ambassador. Joel saw him several more times that evening, but he was busy and he hardly noticed.

He didn't see him slip into the kitchen off the Embassy Room, much less hear him ask a busboy if Robert Kennedy was going to pass by on the way to his expected triumph.

The busboy said he didn't know; so the young man simply waited in the kitchen.

*****

Final results from Los Angeles County were slow in coming but confidence rose steadily in the Kennedy camp as the television networks' projections were announced. Robert Kennedy and most of his staff were already thinking about the New York primary in two weeks. He was trying hard not to make a premature victory declaration, which could be embarrassing to say the very least, but as midnight drew closer he felt he could no longer wait to go downstairs to the Embassy Room and celebrate with his supporters.

He came in through the kitchen. The young man, who had fought his way through the crowd in the Embassy Room and corridors of the Ambassador, had guessed he would do exactly that. Joel, the stalking instincts of a daily newspaper reporter growing ever stronger in him, was in the kitchen too, quite literally trying to get behind the scenes of one of the most dramatic political campaigns in American history.

Joel was struck by how much Bobby Kennedy acted like a winner. He looked smart in his dark blue suit and striped tie. He was relaxed and confident, buoyed by his increasingly apparent victory, as he made his way toward the Embassy Room, stopping every few yards to shake hands with kitchen workers — loyal Democrats all —who were frantically stoking the fires of the celebration.

Joel stuck out his right hand as Kennedy drew near.

"Congratulations, Senator. It looks like California is all yours."

"Thanks, Professor," Kennedy replied with his infectious grin.

"Look, Joel, we're having a party later at The Factory disco. Come on down and make a little more history."

"You're making enough of it right now," Joel replied.

Kennedy waved in the direction of the Embassy Room.

"No," he said thoughtfully, "they're making it. Let's make sure we talk about that on the flight back to New York."

Before Joel could reply, Kennedy's aides propelled him from the kitchen toward the door to the Embassy Room.

The newer, better world that Joel had fought for in Europe, in Mississippi, in the classrooms at Temple and at his writing desk, seemed to be on the verge of salvation after too many years of assassinations and a needless war. The years of tragedy were fading away as the clock edged June 4 closer to June 5.

Hardly anyone took notice of the young man for whom Joel had snatched a Pepsi from one of the press room coolers, following just a few steps behind the candidate. But Joel saw a campaign poster rolled up in one hand and the young man's eyes skipping over the entire room, as though he was searching for one particular spot.

It was 11:45 p.m., Pacific Daylight Time.

*****

Kennedy took his place behind the bouquet of microphones on the ballroom stage. He started out playfully, as was his style, but he quickly seized on the momentous political change that the day's victories in California and South Dakota had confirmed. He spoke of the new popular politics born in those states on that day in June and earlier in the year, in New Hampshire, where Eugene McCarthy's surprising primary victory had led Lyndon Johnson to abandon the race and made a great many cynical people realize that, yes, their votes did count.

He invited McCarthy's supporters to join him to work for a nation united among blacks and whites, rich and poor, old and young, to make America truly worthy of its history and its people and, above all, to end the Vietnam War.

Bobby thanked them all, and urged them "on to Chicago, and let's win there."

*****

Kennedy was supposed to have left the stage and made his way out through the crowd. But the hour was late. It was already nearly midnight — 3:00 a.m. in Philadelphia where Jerry Granier had already chewed his way through four thick, dark copy pencils waiting for Joel's lead — and the Embassy Room crowd was pressing toward the stage in a mad, inexorable tide of joyful political humanity.

It was decided to take Kennedy back through the kitchen and across to the Colonial Room so the East Coast reporters could talk with him in time to make their deadlines.

Joel was one of the first to reach the kitchen. For the first time he was ahead of Robert Kennedy. He was in a hurry to reach the press room and he missed the dark young man who was standing on a tray stacker near the huge ice making machine. Not that he would have thought there was anything strange about the young man in that maelstrom of happy people. He didn't notice anything at all until he turned his head to see just how far he was ahead of Kennedy.

It was then that he saw the young man raising his right arm above the heads of the crowd. He was pointing toward the back of Robert Kennedy's head with a hand that Joel saw too late held a small revolver.

Pop!

It sounded like one of Chinatown's firecrackers. But Joel knew right away that it was not.

There was a brief pause, and then a rapid volley of shots.

Six people went down in fusillade: Paul Schrade of the United Auto Workers union, William Weisel of the ABC News Washington bureau, Ira Goldstein of the Continental News Service, and Elizabeth Evans and Irwin Stroll, both Kennedy supporters from California.

The sixth was Robert Kennedy himself. Joel rushed back to see him on his back. His eyes were open; his feet were spread apart and he was bleeding profusely from a grievous wound in the back of his head.

Two powerfully muscled black men, Rafer Johnson, a hero of the 1960 Olympics, and Roosevelt Grier, late of the Los Angeles Rams defensive line, had seized the young man. Rosie Grier held him in a headlock while Johnson wrenched the revolver from his hand. The two athletes kept a tight grip on the young man. They were holding him for the police, of course, but they were also protecting him from the murderously angry crowd of Kennedy loyalists.

There would be no replay of Jack Ruby and Lee Harvey Oswald's deadly game in Los Angeles that night.

Joel stood rooted beside the ice making machine, scribbling notes that were as indecipherable as his memory of the horrible scene was clear. He was there when ambulance attendants came to take Kennedy to the Los Angeles Central Receiving Hospital, only about four blocks from the Ambassador , and when the Los Angeles police arrived to take the dark young man off Johnson's and Grier's hands.

*****

"Holy shit!" Jerry exclaimed when Joel called to tell him that a new and horribly unexpected lead would be coming to him in a few minutes.

"Save the color and eyewitness stuff for second edition," said Jerry. "You saw the guy do it, right?"

"Saw him? Hell, Jerry, I got the son of a bitch a drink."

CHAPTER TWENTY-NINE

THE END OF THE DREAM

The last place in the world that Joel wanted to be on a fine Sunday in June was Saint Patrick's Cathedral in New York. But he knew there was no other place for him and that he had to be there. When he rode out on the campaign trail behind Robert Kennedy, Joel knew that it would be a ride into history. And now, even though it had come to such a sudden, brutal end, he had to stay.

While he was in Los Angeles, Joel had stuck with the mundane basics of his temporary daily reporting sabbatical. He listened to Mayor Sam Yorty, a politician perpetually on the make for television face time, announce that the dark, bushy haired young man whom Joel had seen prowling around the Ambassador Hotel and then firing his revolver into the back of Kennedy's head, was named Sirhan Bishara Sirhan.

Sirhan was twenty-four years old at the time he shattered America's last hope of realizing its greatness. He was a Jerusalem born Jordanian whose family had lived in Southern California since 1956. He was angry about the outcome of the 1967 Arab-Israeli war and, somehow, his bizarre logic placed the blame on Robert Francis Kennedy.

"RFK must die… RFK must be killed," he had scrawled in the notebook of his lunatic ramblings "Robert F. Kennedy must be assassinated before 5 June 1968."

That was the first anniversary of the end of the 1967 war, and Sirhan almost made his self-imposed deadline. He had shot Kennedy in the first minutes of June 5, but did not achieve his desired result until the following morning.

Kennedy died at Good Samaritan Hospital at 1:44 a.m. on June 6 at the age of 42.

Now, Joel was at Saint Patrick's Cathedral watching Senator Edward M. Kennedy of Massachusetts mount the great altar to eulogize his brother.

"My brother need not be idealized, or enlarged, in death beyond what he was in life," Ted Kennedy said.

Bobby required only "to be remembered as a good and decent man, who saw wrong and tried to right it, saw suffering and tried to heal it, saw war and tried to stop it."

He finished up with a line that had become an almost trite set piece of Bobby's stump speech:

"Some men see things as they are and say 'Why?' I dream things that never were and say 'Why not?'"

Joel knew, as the funeral service ended, that one of the few politicians who dared to ask 'Why not?' was being laid to his rest beside his brother at the Arlington National Cemetery. The warmth that was first ignited by John Kennedy in 1960 and then so nearly fanned back to life by his younger brother was dying, and being replaced by the mean and ugly side of the American spirit.

*****

That mean, ugly side became increasingly more evident as the tragic spring of 1968 moved on toward the summer's heat. The sly, shifty looking Richard Nixon seemed to be rumbling inexorably toward the Republican presidential nomination while Hubert Humphrey, decent, good-hearted but fatally chained to the Johnson Administration, was certain to take the Democratic nomination in that shattered, bleeding party's disgraceful national convention in Chicago.

"On to Chicago, and let's win there," had been Robert Kennedy's last public words.

On to Chicago it had been, but nobody seemed to be winning much of anything.

From the graveside services at Arlington, he took the train back to Philadelphia, to the big, quiet apartment he had shared with Jenny Keith. It was time to begin preparing for his return to Temple's classrooms in September and start work on the book he was committed to write on the last campaign of Robert Francis Kennedy.

He pulled the first of what would eventually be dozens of long yellow legal pads toward him, took one of the Dixon Ticonderoga Soft Number 2 pencils, all sharpened and neatly lined up according to length, and wrote his working title at the top of the page.

The Last Campaign: With Kennedy to the End.

It was the melancholy truth but, even as he wrote it, Joel was dissatisfied with it. It sounded too ordinary, and if he was not careful he could end up writing just another campaign history. Theodore H. White's *The Making of the President* books had that territory well staked out since 1960, and any attempt to fumble along in Teddy's tracks would result in just a pale imitation.

Something else was needed to make the story of the last campaign, and death of Robert Kennedy mean anything, and to make Joel's book more than just another campaign history, or worse, another chapter in the legend of what was coming to be called the Kennedy Curse.

*****

While he was trying to nap on the train following Kennedy's service, Joel could not help listening to his fellow passengers buzzing not only about Kennedy but another dramatic event more than 3,000 miles to the east. As Kennedy was being laid to his rest, detectives from Scotland Yard descended on Heathrow Airport and arrested a small-time American criminal just as he was about to board a plane to Brussels. He had traveled as Harvey Lowmyer, Eric Galt and John Willard, but he was booked at Scotland Yard under his real name, James Earl Ray.

A United States Justice Department lawyer was in London within two days requesting, and receiving, a warrant for Ray's extradition back to the United States to stand trial for the murder of Martin Luther King, Jr.

The murders of Martin Luther King, Jr. and Robert Francis Kennedy were more than just a pair of horrific, but isolated, events in a year of national insanity. Both victims had been activists for the only two causes that truly gripped the United States in the 1960s.

King was the foremost figure in the civil rights movement that had been building since the mid-1950s. It didn't really matter if you were a white-sheeted knight of the Ku Klux Klan or a hymn singing liberal member of the Southern Christian Leadership Conference, King was the most visible symbol of a vast social movement that was either welcomed or feared.

The same was true of Robert Kennedy. While he too hoped to bring about equal rights and social harmony within the United States, he was perceived primarily as the anti-war candidate — which indeed he was. So, regardless of whether one was a peace-at-any-price pacifist, a nuke-'em-back-to-the-stone-age hawk, the draft-dodging son of a Very Big Man, or a corporate predator fattening up on the Vietnam War, Kennedy's candidacy and death meant something very important.

Joel clipped Arthur Schlesinger, Jr.'s piece out of *The Washington Post* and pinned it to the cork board above his writing desk. He underlined the one paragraph that he saw as the foundation not just of Schlesinger's piece but of his own developing view of 1968.

"With the murder of Robert Kennedy, following on the murder of John Kennedy and the murder of Martin Luther King, Jr., we have killed the three great embodiments of our national idealism in this generation. Each murder has brought us one step further on the downward spiral of moral degradation and social disintegration."

Joel had been an admirer of Arthur Schlesinger since his first day as a student of history. But this time, with his op-ed piece in the *WashPost*, the old boy had really nailed it.

God, how Joel wished he had written that! But, not everybody can be Schlesinger and Joel comforted himself with the knowledge that he was coming to the same conclusion, even if he had not yet put it into words.

Yes, it really did feel as if the country, if not the world, was bound merrily for hell in the proverbial hand basket. If Joel had known this back in 1942, he'd have squashed his idealism and avoided the 506th Parachute Infantry Regiment for a clerk's job at the naval aircraft parts depot in northeast Philadelphia, where he could have paid more attention to Susanna Winslow.

Things could probably be worse, but Joel wasn't sure exactly how.

CHAPTER THIRTY

JOHNNY AND CHARLIE

Night was coming on and Sergeant Giovanni "Johnny" Finnigan was damned glad of it. Keeping the Mi Dingh fire base up and running was not always an easy thing. The 2nd Battaltion, 327th Infantry of the 101st Airborne seemed to be continuously fighting off North Vietnamese attacks and keeping the place open both as a base for the artillery that commanded the area for miles around and as a landing pad for the helicopters that brought in supplies and evacuated the wounded.

"What the fuck do we need this shit hole for, Sarge?"

The question came from Private Gordon Waymon, a dark, chocolate-colored kid from Los Angeles.

"… cause The Man wants us to hold it, Gord. We can control everything from here. If Charlie takes us out, he can raise hell with the whole division."

"What the fuck; let Charlie have it. No Charlie ever called me a nigger, Sarge."

"I know, Gord. But it's not like you're not getting paid for it."

Waymon had to laugh at that. Johnny Finnigan had a way of breaking the tension. But before he could come up with an equally witty retort, a first lieutenant from company headquarters, a short black lawyer called up from the Army Reserve for a year's active duty, slipped in through the canvas flap that covered the entrance to their hootch.

"Sergeant Finnigan," the lieutenant said into the late afternoon gloom.

"Here, sir," Giovanni answered.

"The captain needs to see you."

"Another dirty job, Sarge," Waymon said cynically.

"That's the only kind around here, Gord. Have everybody check their weapons."

Giovanni followed Lieutenant Arnold Carson out of the hootch and across the hot, dusty fire base to the Echo Company Command Post where Captain Roy Comerford was waiting for him.

Roy Comerford was known as "Captain Ipana" around the 327th because of the big, toothy grin he wore whenever he was about to dump a load of shit on somebody's head. Giovanni found him sitting behind his folding field desk, wearing his big grin.

On the desk, at his right hand, was a dirty, thumb worn paperback copy of Joel Finnigan's *Silver Wings*.

"We may be in for a long night, Sergeant Finnigan."

"They're all long nights, sir."

"Yeah, well, this one may be even longer. Battalion G2 thinks we're about to be attacked. In battalion strength at least."

"Charlie or NVA, Captain?"

The North Vietnamese Army or the Viet Cong, didn't really matter one way or the other to Giovanni. It was just that the Viet Cong guerillas, Charlie, were more devious than the more formally organized NVA and Giovanni liked to know what he'd be facing.

"That they don't know, Sergeant. It's what I want you to find out."

"Okay, sir. I'm taking out a recon patrol then, I guess."

"You guessed right, Sergeant… a sneaky peeky job for only a few guys. Head out to the west, no more than a thousand meters.

"If you find them, radio word, and the target coordinates, back to the artillery battery and then get the hell out of there.

"You are not, repeat not, to engage. We'll let the artillery and the mortars take care of the bastards.

"If everything goes right, I expect your patrol to come back in with weapons unfired."

"Yes, sir. I'll take five of my best guys and head out to the west." There was a brief pause before he added, "I sure hope they attack from the east."

"Or not at all."

"Yes, sir, but I guess that's too much to ask."

Comerford picked up his copy of *Silver Wings*.

"I've been reading your father's book, Sergeant. He was all soldier... a credit to the 101st."

"Yes, sir. But he was ass deep in snow most of the time."

"Well, keep up the family tradition, Sergeant. Maybe we can all return home as gloriously as he did."

"I hope so, Captain. I'd better go and get my guys saddled up."

Giovanni slung his M16 over his right shoulder and turned to leave the Command Post.

"Good luck, Johnny," Comerford said quietly as Giovanni slipped out into the fading light.

*****

Yeah, right. Good luck.

"Good luck my G. I. ass," Giovanni muttered as he headed back to the squad's hootch to give his guys the bad news.

He thought of his father, jumping into Normandy and taking command of his rifle company in the snow at Bastogne.

But, hell, the old man had a war to win. What was there to win in Vietnam... and how would we know if we won it?

No. Victory here meant finishing your year in one piece. There would be no grand victory parade up Fifth Avenue, only a plane ticket back to Boston where a soldier returning from 'Nam could count only on being spat upon by the draft-proof legions of graduate students.

There was no glory to be had in Vietnam, or any other war, really. There was nothing for it but to lead his patrol into the night, keep them all alive, and hope to hell they'd all see another sunrise.

"Okay, guys," he said as he entered the hootch.

"We've got us a job tonight."

*****

Night had descended and it was as black as the very pit of hell itself when Giovanni led his patrol out through the concertina wire and machine gun positions that protected the western perimeter of the 327th fire base.

He struggled to find the words to describe the blackness — as black as a sergeant's heart... black as a ...

Hell, I'm a sergeant and I'm not particularly black-hearted. It was black enough, though, and he could barely make out Gordon Waymon just a few feet ahead of him.

Waymon had the point. He would be the first to see the enemy, if they were out there to be seen. Giovanni was second in line with Paul Olson, his radio operator, close by his right side. Hector Velez and Jamie Quinn, both Privates First Class and in Vietnam for less than a month, brought up the rear.

Their faces were blackened; any piece of gear that might rattle and give them away was muffled with electrical tape, and their thumbs tickled the safeties of their M16 rifles, ready to flick them off and open fire in an instant. In that darkness, and the thick, confining foliage of the forest, an instant would be about all they could expect between the time they spotted an enemy and one or the other of them lay dead.

Captain Ipana had told Giovanni not to engage the enemy, just report and fade back to the safety of the base perimeter. But they could assume that nobody told Charlie, and Giovanni doubted that he would have listened in any case. So, he and his patrol mates thumbed their safeties and pressed forward.

The patrol had gone less than 200 meters when Waymon stopped, raised his right hand as a signal for the others to do the same, and dropped down to his right knee. Giovanni, careful not to make a sound, was beside Waymon in an instant.

"What is it, Gord?" he whispered urgently.

"I couldn't swear, Sarge, but I think I heard something… about another hundred meters ahead of us."

"Charlie?"

"Dunno, but it sounds like people. I haven't heard any voices; so I can't tell if it's Charlie or not."

Giovanni motioned for Valez and Quinn to come up with Waymon. Then he stepped back to Olson and took the radio handset.

"Boomer Six, Boomer Six, this is Dancer," he whispered into the microphone.

"This is Boomer Six," the artillery battery commander himself replied from inside the fire base.

"Dancer; we've got some activity out in front of us. We're guessing it's Charlie and he's coming your way."

"Understand, Dancer… got anything for me to shoot at?"

"Not yet, Boomer. We're at grid square Red Five. I think Charlie's near the western edge, maybe into Red Six.

"I've got to get closer for a better look."

"Okay, Dancer… not too close. We'll need room to shoot our big stuff."

"Fear not, Boomer. Once we get you a good target, we're outta here.

"Dancer out."

Giovanni gave the handset back to Olson and they both went forward to rejoin the rest of the patrol.

"Okay, Boomer's just dying to shoot somebody…," he said.

"As long as it ain't us," Waymon said sardonically.

"… so we'll keep moving forward until we have something solid. Then we'll call it in and split.

"And, remember guys," he added, "Captain Ipana wants to see us come back with unfired weapons."

Sergeant Finnigan's tiny patrol inched forward, hoping to find the advancing enemy, but terrified of what could happen if they did. Each them wanted fervently to grant the Captain his wish, but doubted that it would be possible.

*****

It was Charlie, all right; a combined force of North Vietnamese regulars with Viet Cong scouts and special attack units ahead of them. Waymon saw them first, and then Giovanni, as the American patrol came to a break in the forest. From their positions just behind the tree line, they saw the clearing before them was not a particularly large one, but big enough for at least a thousand NVA soldiers to assemble into their formations for their final approach and attack on the American fire base.

The intelligence sources had been accurate. Charlie was out in at least battalion strength. It could be a regiment or more if there were more forces in the forest beyond the clearing but, even if there were not, it was obvious that they could hit the base perimeter damned hard and maybe break through into the base itself.

"Boomer Six, Boomer Six, this is Dancer."

"Boomer Six, Dancer. What's up out there?"

"Dancer; many enemy, many. They're forming up for their attack right now."

"Roger that, Dancer. Location?"

"They're in the clearing just west of Red Five. It should be on your map."

There was a brief pause while the battery commander checked his map and the firing coordinates he'd use to aim his 105 millimeter howitzers and 82 millimeter mortars.

"Boomer Six — you've done your job, Dancer. Now get the hell out of there. I'm opening fire in one minute."

"Roger that, Boomer.

"Dancer out."

"Back to the barn, guys!" Giovanni barked — just as a chorus of automatic weapons opened up on their right.

Shit!

"On me!" Giovanni shouted, as he flipped off his safety and fired into the forest.

Not that he really needed to shout, for Waymon, Velez and Quinn had already come to him and Olson so no one would be alone as they fought their way out of Charlie's snare.

Giovanni raised his M16 and fired at a group of black clad figures charging forward through the forest. He never knew how many of them there were, or how many went down, but at least the charge stopped and the pressure was off for a few seconds.

Then the minute was up and Boomer Six opened fire. Joel Finnigan had told his son that there were damned few things as terrifying as being under an artillery barrage. Now, as the cannon and mortar fire shook the ground, splintered the trees and dismembered the bodies, Giovanni realized just how right the old guy had been.

Boomer Six, confident that Giovanni's patrol was beating feet back toward the safety of the perimeter, shifted his fire slightly eastward to account for the enemy's advance. He succeeded in bringing his hellish rain of high explosive shells right down on top of the American patrol.

"They call this friendly fire," Giovanni said as they began running east, hoping to get out of the barrage.

"Some fuckin' friends," Velez shouted back. "We got friends like this… what the hell we need Charlie to kill us for?"

Hector Velez died cursing his friends and their big guns, but it was a small gun, a rifle, that took off the top of his head and killed him as dead as Kelsey's nuts.

Paul Olson was flattened by the impact of a bursting American artillery shell. He wasn't hurt, but the radio he carried on his back was smashed and there was no way for the patrol to tell anyone that they were being consumed by their own fire.

Giovanni told Olson, Waymon, and Quinn to go on ahead. He'd stay behind to cover their retreat. He knelt behind a tree and began picking off enemy soldiers who were also running eastward, both to press their attack and because they too wanted to get out from under the lethal wrath of Boomer Six.

He heard the crackling fire of another M16 close on his left side. He looked over and saw Gordon Waymon grinning fiendishly and firing into the shadows.

"You always want to hog all the fun, Sarge."

*****

Olson and Quinn, exhausted, filthy, and scared to death, staggered into the perimeter just ahead of Charlie's attack. But there was no rest for them and no question of reporting back to Captain Ipana. They took fresh bandoleers of M16 ammunition and faced back west to meet the attack. The fighting continued until just before dawn. When the last enemy had been killed or driven back, they led a platoon from Echo Company back to survey the night's work and to find Giovanni and Gordon Waymon.

The forest was littered with the bodies of the dead and their assorted body parts.

Paul Olson was the first to reach Waymon's side, He found him propped up under a tree. His right leg and left forearm were gone but he had been prevented from bleeding to death by the tourniquet and field dressings that Giovanni had applied in the last moments of his life.

"Where's Sergeant Finnigan, Gordon?" Roy Comerford asked. He had left his Captain Ipana grin back inside the perimeter.

Waymon could but nod in the direction of a G. I. green covered mass piled just a few feet away.

"He patched me up, Cap'n… ," Waymon gasped, "… kept me from bleedin' to death. Then he held the bastards off for the rest of the night."

Comerford counted fifteen enemy bodies about twenty yards out in front of Waymon, then went over to check the American body. There wasn't much to check really; no arms, no head, only the tattered G. I. shirt bearing the name tag of its late owner: Finnigan.

CHAPTER THIRTY-ONE

THE GREAT AMERICAN WALKABOUT

You had to say this much for Connie Leone; she always managed to look whatever part she chose to play at any particular moment. In this case, on a late August Thursday in 1969, it was the role of a stylishly grieving mother, a martyr, almost as if it were she and not Giovanni reposing in the tightly sealed coffin at Donatella's Funeral Home in Framingham, Massachusetts.

It was just as well that the coffin was sealed because the body that was to be buried later that afternoon at the Gate of Heaven Cemetery was not a fit object for public veneration; the North Vietnamese and American artillery fire had seen to that. Seeing what scraps were left of her only begotten son would have forced Connie to face reality, and that would have been a complete violation of her life's code.

Joel saw her immediately when he walked into Donatella's. Nobody could have missed the black designer dress — made especially for the occasion — the hat with just enough veil to cover her eyes and, of course, the dazzling diamond necklace and assorted rings. Black was supposed to have a slimming effect on its wearer, or so Joel recalled reading somewhere or other, but in this case it didn't come close to concealing the extra bulk that Connie had put on since the last time he had seen her ten years earlier in the little house on Sharp Street in Rock Hall.

Of course she had been on her knees between Greg Leone's gleefully twitching legs at the time, and so Joel thought he might have missed a few extra pounds.

Connie was, in short, a real lard ass; fashionably dressed and bejeweled to be sure, but a lard ass notwithstanding.

Greg Leone stood beside her, something like a faithful old dog Joel thought, holding her left arm while she used her right, the one with all the rings and bracelets, to reach up beneath her veil to dab at her eyes with her monogrammed white lace handkerchief. Greg looked tired and worn after ten years with his perpetual two year old and Joel remembered his parting blessing when they walked out of the house in Rock Hall.

"You poor son of a bitch," Joel had muttered back in 1959 and ten years later he knew he had really meant it.

Joel could only hope that Greg had a big enough boat and a lusty enough tootsie to keep his sanity.

Connie flashed her best faux Marie Antoinette regal smile as the receiving line brought Joel before her.

"How good of you to come, Joel," she intoned, extending her right hand, palm down as if expecting it to be kissed.

"Of course I'd come to my son's funeral," he replied coldly.

She opened her mouth to speak. He recalled all too well that she was always opening her mouth to speak, but he was in no mood to hear that he was not Giovanni's real father and that the boy might still be alive, and herself spared all the trouble of his death, if not for his goddamned books that made World War II seem like such great fun.

"I'm sure this has been very difficult for you, Connie," he said, putting the focus right back on her, as God had always meant it to be.

"Yes," she replied softly," it was, terribly."

It was a hell of a lot harder for Giovanni.

"The hardest thing a mother can face is losing a child, especially an only child," Connie said with a sob that might have been genuine.

"Now I'll never have grandchildren."

"They'll never know what they missed, Connie."

"Oh, Finney; I don't know how I'll go on."

Joel looked over at Greg, who was dutifully patting Connie's shoulder.

"Better you than me, old buddy," he thought as he moved on and knelt beside Giovanni's sealed coffin.

*****

Joel didn't flinch at the sound of the rifles. God knows, between Normandy in 1944 and the kitchen of the Ambassador Hotel just last year he was used to the sound of gunfire; so the rifle salute over Giovanni's grave was not unnerving by any means.

But strangely, considering all that was taking place at the Gate of Heaven cemetery, it was the rifles themselves, the look of the things that caught Joel's attention He thought, for a moment, that he was as much an escapist as Connie, but inconsequentials were often useful things at times like this.

The honor guard from the Massachusetts National Guard saluted his fallen son with the new M16 rifle. Joel knew it was a vastly superior rifle to the M1 he had lugged all over Europe; lighter, with a faster rate of fire and an ammunition capacity large enough to be sure it wouldn't run out at a crucial moment. It was a brisk, hard edged machine that looked exactly like... well, like a machine.

The softly gleaming wooden stock that Joel remembered from the old days had been replaced by modern alloys and some kind of high impact plastic and Joel could not imagine forming a relationship with the weapon the way he had with the trusty, life-saving M1 that he used to fight his way back to Susanna in what was becoming known as the last good war.

The last good war!

Shit; the last cruel, savage joke.

*****

It wasn't until the last notes of Taps died mournfully away that Joel was swamped by an overwhelming sense of loss. He kept his passionless paratrooper face on, however. Joel Finnigan was not a man to show his emotions, especially not in front of Connie and the crowd at the Gate of Heaven. Susanna would have seen them, of course, but Susanna had been gone from his life for twenty-four years now — God, nearly a quarter of a century — and so he kept it inside and just camped with it.

Connie was right. There is nothing as painful as losing a child.

Would Giovanni still be here, in graduate school, or even cavorting on green fields for the Detroit Lions if Joel hadn't fought so well with the 506th and written such successful histories of the airborne war in Europe? Suppose he had been a complete fuck-up in the Army and spent the war, as Georgie Patton once put it, shoveling shit in Louisiana?

Would Giovanni Finnigan have wanted to follow in his father's footsteps then?

"What if they had a war and nobody came?" was one of the better anti-war slogans that had appeared on bumper stickers and wall posters ever since Vietnam had turned into a disaster. Suppose Giovanni and the other youngsters had refused to follow in their father's footsteps and had simply not shown up for the unending passion play of Vietnam?

A lot of kids were doing just that as the 1960s, begun in such hope and optimism, slouched miserably toward their sorry end. They were on the television all the time, picketing, burning their draft cards and getting naked in the reflecting pool on the Washington Mall. Joel had seen them at Temple and he himself carried a small scar on his right hand from the savage Democratic National Convention in Chicago the year before Giovanni's funeral.

Joel knew as he walked away from the grave that he would have to see these kids, join them in their wandering and their questioning. He would have to take the same journey himself.

*****

Ivor Carlson, his dean back at Temple, was not all that happy when Joel telephoned him from the Westborough Plaza rest stop on the Massachusetts Turnpike to say he was taking off just as the Fall semester was about to begin. But he knew that Joel had been hit hard by Giovanni's death and, as a senior faculty member, he was entitled to a little more leeway. So, as his immediate boss, Ivor agreed to juggle the teaching schedule and, as his friend, to make sure his apartment was secured for a long absence.

His telephone call to Dean Carlson wasn't as difficult as Joel thought it would be.

"He must think I'm crazy," he thought as he guided his red Volkswagen back onto the Mass Pike. "Hell, I would too; or maybe the whole damned country's crazy."

Who the hell knew anymore?

Maybe the dream still existed. Maybe it was hovering just out there ahead of him. The Volkswagen wheezed anemically along the turnpike, through Connecticut, across the Tappan Zee Bridge and down the Garden State Parkway where he joined Interstate Route 80 and began heading west in earnest.

Interstate 80 was the new, modern land route between the Atlantic and Pacific Oceans. Joel would be able to drive all the way to California without once stopping for a red light. It was faster and easier, but he wondered if part of what he was searching for had been misplaced when the transcontinental traffic abandoned the old Route 66.

Would there be songs, stories and even a television program about travels on I-80? Probably not. Travelers might be able to cover a lot more ground in a lot less time on this new, antiseptic highway but they'd be going too fast to hear the music of their land and its people.

It might be considered progress of some sort, but Joel thought there was a sadness to it and he filed the thought away in the back of his mind for future reference.

*****

"Delaware Water Gap."

The late summer afternoon was fading into night by the time the sign appeared in the Volkswagen's headlights. Joel was beginning to think the Interstate Highway System might not have been such a bad idea. It was Dwight Eisenhower's idea, after all, and Joel still thought enough of his old general and president, now nearing the end of his life at the Walter Reed Army Hospital in Washington, to believe that he almost always had good ideas.

He mused for a little bit on the speed of modern travel made possible by the bland, soulless new highway, but not for long because he began to realize just how tired he was. It wasn't just the drive from Framingham to the Pennsylvania border. It was the emotional drain of the day that was finally catching up with him. He pulled into the first rest stop he could find, locked the car doors, reclined the driver's seat as far as it would go, stuffed his jacket behind his head and fell into a dreamless sleep.

When Joel awoke, it was still dark enough for him to crawl out of the car and take a leak without scandal. So, he did, and then continued west across the bridge between the towering, green-sheathed cliffs on each side of the Delaware. He decided to begin his personal exploration of modern mobile America as soon as he crossed into Pennsylvania. His stomach was actually the decider, growling as it was in protest of its yawning emptiness and, since he had always heard that the best food was to be found at truck stops, he pulled up at the first sizeable collection of tractor-trailers and automobile transporters.

The food was good; hot, greasy, and lots of it. Joel wolfed down a huge platter of scrambled eggs, bacon and home fries.

When his stomach was full, Joel realized that he was beginning to smell like a goat.

The truck stop offered so much more than gasoline and hot, tasty grease. There was a vast assortment of everything a professional traveler might need, from extra tail lights to aluminum covered clipboards and trucker's logbooks, and a greater variety of bungee cords than he ever dreamed existed, to the very essentials of life itself. He dipped into this cornucopia for a toothbrush, toothpaste, three packs of underwear, two pairs of jeans, a Pittsburgh Steelers sweatshirt, a blue ball cap and another T-shirt that tickled his sense of humor.

Taking his purchases into the men's room, Joel absorbed all the learned, detailed assessments of the waitresses' anatomical attributes while he washed and emerged looking reasonably well groomed in new jeans and emblazoned new T-shirt.

"Old truckers never die," it proclaimed proudly.

"They just get a new Peterbilt."

He ignored the smirks and chuckles of the real truckers as they watched the graying easterner fold himself into his red Volkswagen and head off toward Ohio and points west.

Joel found himself thinking of the people who had journeyed west before him and saw himself nibbling around the edges of a great American tradition. There were the early settlers, of course, the bold men and women who had set forth from these same low hills of Pennsylvania and Ohio in their ox-drawn wagons, peopling a land, building a nation and slaughtering Indians as they went. He had read Jack Kerouac's *On The Road* some years before and had a copy of John Steinbeck's *Travels With Charley* buried somewhere in the Volkswagen's depths.

He was fully aware of just how much of the history of his own time he had lived since the mid-1930s — the last years of the Great Depression, World War II, the pleasant, booming Eisenhower years, the bright promise of the New Frontier and its death in the bloodbath of 1968 and now the darkly scowling Richard Nixon and the even more darkly scowling people who had elected him. But regardless of how much he had written about the war and the last campaign of Robert Kennedy, he had never done the inquisitive intellectual roaming of Jack Kerouac or John Steinbeck.

Now he was embarked on the same journey and, as he stopped just outside Columbus, Ohio for a black and white marbled Mead composition book, Joel Finnigan was beginning to think that he might be able to leave an account at least as compelling as the other two. He pulled into a rest stop just across the Indiana border to scrawl the first entry in his new notebook.

The Great American Walkabout extended across the top of the first page. It would be the working title of whatever it was he would spin out over the white, blue-lined pages. Joel had no plans to write a book when he set out from the Gate of Heaven, but he was a compulsive chronicler of his times, so who knew what might grow from his notebook?

The pages filled, as Joel knew they would, as he continued across the United States. They caught the anger of the truckers and farmers — flag waving, commie hating, Nixon lovers all — in Illinois and Missouri; the sad confusion of housewives and Vietnam war widows in the laundromat in Kansas, and the ancient grievances and mysteries of the Navajo in Flagstaff, Arizona. He marveled at the stark beauty of the Nevada High Desert, the long descent down the western slopes of the Sierra Nevada Mountains and, finally, the strange mixture of wistfulness and anger that enveloped San Francisco.

Joel hadn't seen San Francisco in more than a year; ever since that last frightening day of Bobby Kennedy's California Primary campaign, but it was still a city that captivated him.

He did not have that fabled, fog-shrouded bay city in mind when he left Framingham the week before. Or perhaps he had, really, for San Francisco had always been the destination for adventurers and questers from the east and midwest.

And now, as the expansive 1960s gave way to the inward looking 1970s, soon to be christened the "Me Generation," San Francisco had become a portal into the evolving soul of America. The "Summer of Love" was two years dead, lost in the violence and desperation of the drug scene by the time Joel arrived, but it was clearly the starting point for many of the trends that would sweep the country and change it, sometimes for the better.

Foremost was the anger directed against the war in Vietnam, which was shifting from protest marches, poetry readings, and teach-ins to violence on the streets and on the picket lines. A kid had already been killed when he threw himself in front of a train carrying ammunition and supplies to the Oakland docks to be loaded on a ship bound for Vietnam.

Joel came across his first serious anti-war protest shortly after he crossed the Bay Bridge into the city. The *Iowa* class battleship *U.S.S. New Jersey*, Halsey's and Spruance's flag ship during World War II, which had been brought back into service to pound the Vietnamese coast with her huge sixteen inch guns, had come into the Mare Island Naval Shipyard for repairs and a port visit that touched off a torrent of rage that, quite frankly, astonished the newly arrived Joel Finnigan.

The protesters seemed to want not just to protest the war but to attack the battleship herself. The Marine guards at Mare Island were not about to let that happen; so the next best thing was to try and stop *New Jersey's* captain from going into San Francisco to speak at a Chamber of Commerce luncheon.

Curses, taunts, and occasional bottles were hurled at the nondescript Navy sedan, a gray 1965 Chevrolet, as it inched along California Street toward the Mark Hopkins Hotel. It was a frightening outburst of fury and Joel feared, briefly, that the crowd wanted to drag the captain from the car and hang him from the nearest lamp post. Joel had written a few pieces on the idiotic, bloody futility of the war, but this was different; a visceral hatred toward the United States and all its works that made him wonder if these vociferous, violent people were against the war or for the enemy.

A flash of sudden movement caught Joel's eye as he drew near the Mark Hopkins. A young man in long hair, wispy beard, tattered jeans, and sandals had burst from the main body of protesters and was sprinting toward the captain who had gotten out of the car and was walking across the sidewalk toward the hotel's massive front door. Five big policemen descended on the young protester like NFL linebackers joining up for a gang tackle.

The captain, if he noticed the incident at all, showed no sign of it and continued, untouched, into the hotel. The policemen dragged the youngster across the street, directly in front of Joel's patiently waiting Volkswagen, toward their police van. He struggled furiously and Joel could hear him screaming about the fucking pigs, Navy babykillers, and the world peace manifesto he wanted to give the *New Jersey's* captain.

He twisted, or was twisted, until he was looking straight at the Volkswagen and right into Joel's eyes. Their eyes locked and it seemed for a moment as though some degree of communication passed between them. He smiled beatifically at Joel and flashed the two finger peace sign, the modern version of Winston Churchill's old Victory sign, in the brief moment before he was hustled on his way and vanished into the police van.

*****

"Christ-like," Joel wrote in his notebook that night, "almost as if he was carrying a message to the world."

Joel had often thought that a lot of bearded young men, especially those of the 60s and 70s, had a Christ complex, as if they knew "The Truth," whatever the hell that was, and were bound and determined to hand it down to the nonbelievers, whether they wanted it or not.

That wasn't unusual in itself. Joel recalled having a Christ complex himself after the passion and crucifixion of Normandy and Bastogne, but it passed as he realized with age that he possessed no more truth or wisdom than anybody else, and probably a good deal less. Still, there was something in the young man's eyes. Joel knew it was what he had come west to find but that he would not find it on the first day.

*****

Joel knew the instant he set foot in the California Residence Club that it would be the perfect base for his quest. The rambling old Victorian structure on California Street, several blocks from the Mark Hopkins, was what most of Joel's contemporaries would call a boarding house — maybe even a flophouse.

In the big common living room a bearded young man with long red hair sat in an overstuffed chair strumming an acoustic guitar. He looked about twenty, and seemed oblivious to everything around him.

A young woman about the same age joined him. She had straight blond hair that hung midway down her back and she wore a paisley headband. Both she and the boy wore jeans and tie-dye T-shirts — the uniform of the late 1960s individualist.

The desk clerk told Joel the only vacancy was a shared room and he pointed to the red-haired young man who was slinging his guitar over his shoulder and heading out the door with the blond.

Joel frowned. He really wanted privacy to think about Giovanni and his life and his quest.

"He probably doesn't want an old man for a roommate," Joel commented.

The red-head, Danny Connors, looked up, eyed Joel up and down, and said, "that's cool, man," and walked out.

Joel was scribbling in his notebook when Danny returned to the room they now shared.

"Dinner's at six, man," he told Joel. "Then we usually come back here and play music and get high. We can go to Carrie's room if you want to be alone."

"No," said Joel. "It's fine with me if you don't mind me being here."

Danny lit a joint, put it to his lips, inhaled deeply and held his breath while he passed it to Joel who took it and did the same.

After dinner, five other kids joined Danny and Joel in their room. Two of them brought guitars and they spent the evening playing, singing, and getting high.

Joel soon learned the people in the California Residence Club were mostly kids who had come to San Francisco in search of their dream but who were slowly learning that you don't leave your problems behind when you move on; you just take them with you.

The others were young people who had recently left their husbands or wives and had nowhere else to go.

Joel — in his mid-forties among a group who espoused the philosophy "Don't trust anyone over thirty" — seemed a misfit. He wasn't sure why Danny and his friends accepted him.

"You got good vibes, man," Danny told him. "You're sad. Something's eatin' away at you — maybe a lost love — but you're cool. You fit in, man. Age is just a number."

So Joel became twenty again — at least in spirit. He felt no different than these kids who had run away to San Francisco to find themselves. After all, isn't that what he had done?

So during the day, he wandered the streets of San Francisco, filling the pages in his notebooks with everything he observed, from the help wanted signs in stores' windows proclaiming that "only Capricorns, Aquarians and Libras need apply," to the drag queens in the Tenderloin, to the topless dancers in North Beach, to the war protesters with their signs and chants.

One day, when Danny happened to be with him, he saw the young protester who had locked eyes with him the day he had arrived in San Francisco.

"Danny," Joel said. "Do you know who that is? I saw him being arrested in front of the Mark Hopkins."

Danny looked hard at the tall, over-coated figure.

"I think his name's Picasso," he said.

"Picasso?"

"It's not his real name, but he's an artist. I think he's from some fairly prominent family across the bridge, in Marin County.

"He had a pretty good future, at least according to some of the art critics… a couple of exhibitions in San Francisco too, I think."

"What do you mean he 'had' a good future?"

"He gave it all up to protest the war. I mean, I'm against it too, but Picasso's given up everything because of it. I'm told he's gone way over the top."

Over the top… around the bend… this damned war was making everybody crazy, regardless of whether they were for it or against it.

A lot of people were wondering if the United States would survive the Vietnam years, or would fly apart into viciously warring factions like so many other nations around the world. Joel, from his historian's perspective, had faith that it would not. The United States had suffered its own Civil War only a bit more than a hundred years before, the Depression of the 1930s, and traumas of his own generation and still, it held together.

But Joel thought that Vietnam would scar the nation for a good many years. Thankfully there were good men and women, some of them right here at the California Residence Club, whose hard work and good sense would keep the nation together and meet challenges he couldn't even begin to imagine

Joel knew that if he could do anything at all, it would be to contribute his to the understanding of this time. He jotted down his thoughts in his ever-present notebook. He had long since filled the composition book he had picked up in Ohio and another purchased in San Francisco. Now he was using wire-bound reporter's notebooks that could be tucked unobtrusively into a back pocket as he made the rounds of coffee shops, libraries and peace demonstrations that were making San Francisco such a yeasty mixture of ideas and confabulations.

*****

That night — like most of the others since he had arrived — started with a group in his and Danny's room singing songs about peace and love and getting stoned.

The old movie *House of Wax*, starring Vincent Price, was playing in 3-D in Sausalito and somebody thought it would be really cool to see it stoned.

Since Joel was the only one with a car, they all piled into his VW.

"Why are you going so slow?" Carrie asked as they headed across the Golden Gate Bridge.

"If I go any faster, I'll get pulled over, which wouldn't be such a good idea with that grass you have in your bag," Joel replied. Then he looked at the speedometer to see that he was going all of twenty-five miles an hour. Cautiously Joel pushed his foot down on the throttle and got up to a roaring forty. He counted himself lucky to get to the movie theater without incident and swore he would never again smoke and drive.

That was the beginning of the end of Joel's mid-life crisis. He wasn't twenty. He was forty-five. These kids he was hanging out with were young enough to be his children. He should be setting a better example for them.

"Wanna drop some acid, man?" Danny popped a sugar cube into his mouth and held one out to Joel, who looked at it and hesitated.

"No. Thanks, Danny."

The next day Joel packed his bag, paid his bill, and headed south. A high speed parade of fire engines, police cars and ambulances held him up for a couple of minutes on his way out of town but he made it to the Pacific Coast Highway and, as the sun rose, he was well ahead of the morning's traffic.

The decision to leave San Francisco and head back to Philadelphia seemed sudden, but it really had been more than just the realization that he was not a twenty-year-old flower child.

His notebooks were beginning to pile up, and he felt the need to settle down at home in his study overlooking the Art Museum and get to the work of molding his thoughts into a cohesive manuscript; *The Great American Walkabout*. The time for observing and making inspired notes was past and, like a carpenter at his workbench, he had to start the difficult, painstaking craftsmanship involved in carving, shaping, and finishing his rough planks into a fine, gleaming piece of work. There was no better place for a craftsman to work than in his own shop.

And, he found himself missing Philadelphia itself — the Academy of Music, Fairmount Park, the Art Museum, and even, dare he admit, the Phillies and the occasional Saturday morning at the Melrose Diner. Most of all, he missed Temple University, teaching youngsters and distilling all that he had learned in California, first with Bobby Kennedy in 1968 and then at the California Residence Club the following year and passing it on to his students and, he hoped, his readers. Getting back into the gritty atmosphere of North Philadelphia would help temper the heady air of San Francisco and shape the final outcome of *The Great American Walkabout*.

As he headed toward Los Angeles, Joel decided that he was going to go back home on a road that touched the lives of his fellow Americans. He would have a good long look at the Grand Canyon, the long road up Pikes Peak, and perhaps swing south for a taste of New Orleans.

The car radio was a constant reminder that the craziness, the deeply felt discontent of San Francisco, was continuing without him. He had not quite reached Carmel when an announcer broke right into the middle of a Barry Manilow song to say that that morning's fire back in the city had been the fire-bombing of a Navy recruiting office.

One of the bombers had been killed.

"Giovanni and... who the hell knows?" Joel wrote in his reporter's notebook during a roadside coffee break, "A perverted version of the Unknown Soldier; somebody's son or daughter dead, like my own son, at opposite ends of the same war."

He put the notebook aside while he concentrated on his coffee, a glazed cinnamon roll he knew he shouldn't be indulging in, and his thoughts on where that last entry would lead him. He did not notice the gangly, dark haired young man who sat down beside him and began glancing furtively at the still open notebook.

"Oh. Man. That's really some heavy stuff," the young man said quietly.

"What?" said Joel.

"Here, let me get that out of your way," he said, closing the slim notebook and slipping into his back pocket.

"Oh, no problem," the kid replied.

"Are you some kind of a reporter?"

The right side of his mouth turned up into a crooked grin. "I mean, you look too old to be a hippie."

Joel managed to get his mouthful of coffee swallowed just before his outburst of laughter sprayed it all across the counter.

"Too damned old," he said. "I found that out on the Golden Gate Bridge. Pot's okay for you kids, but not for us old guys."

"Yeah. I didn't like it either. I can't write with all that shit in my head."

"What do you write?"

"Songs; sometimes it's just poetry until I can get the music right."

"Really? What's your name? Maybe I've heard some of your songs."

Now it was the young man's turn to laugh.

"Tom Buckman, and you haven't heard anything of mine; not unless you've been hanging out at some of the road houses and honky tonks around Memphis. I was a country and western singer. That's still my basic style but I'm trying to broaden it out."

"How? Country and western's a fine style, not to mention a good market."

"Yeah. Hank Williams and the rest made some great stuff, but then I read Walt Whitman and heard Woodie Guthrie's old records and I was gone.

"I'm trying to write songs about the country."

"Songs of Ourselves, eh?"

"Yeah; just like Whitman said."

"It looks like you've been searching hard."

"I left Tennessee and came west, Boise, Seattle, San Francisco... all places like that. Now I'm headed for Los Angeles to hole up, write songs, and maybe make a demo record."

Tom looked wistfully out the window at the golden brown California hills.

"New York's the place, though. I should end up there."

"I'm headed that way, Tom," Joel said.

"New York?"

"Philadelphia, but that's close enough. It's got a good recording industry itself."

Joel looked at his watch and swallowed the last of his coffee.

"Come on, young Tom; let's get on down the road."

*****

Tom Buckman's guitar and back pack, stuffed with song lyrics and scraps of notes, made Joel's Volkswagen feel even more crowded. But Tom was a smart, talented kid, which made him good company and helped the miles slide by more easily. Memories of June 1968, especially that last terrible night at the Ambassador Hotel, made Joel want to bypass Los Angeles. Tom, having decided to seek his fortune in New York, was amenable, and so the searchers, separated by age but united in their same basic quest for the soul of America, drove right through Los Angeles without stopping and pressed on south toward San Diego.

When he took his guitar from its travel worn case, a case so battered that it seemed held together only by copious applications of the silver duct tape that Joel was coming to regard as a true modern marvel, and hauled it up into the passenger's seat, the Volkswagen became even more crowded. But when he began strumming, searching for just the right notes and chords, it made the miles even easier. Joel began to sense he was on the road with the Woodie Guthrie, or even the Walt Whitman, of this troubled age and that the sounds being developed in the cramped, raggedly breathing little car would soon be heard throughout the land and might even help transform it.

They stopped briefly in San Diego and then turned eastward into the San Bernardino Mountains which treated them to a few late May snow squalls, and then on toward Yuma, Arizona. The detour to Tombstone was their first side trip. Naturally Joel had to see the OK Corral, the site of the gunfight that was more famous in the legend than the actual history of the American West.

"I thought it would be... bigger," said Tom. "You know... more dramatic."

"That's how it goes," Joel replied. "Nothing's as grand or glamorous as the picture in your mind."

All but Susanna, that is. Joel was astonished at how the memory of her remained, even in this dust scourged corner of southern Arizona. It filled him with sadness to know that she was gone forever.

But, if the OK Corral was a minor disappointment, Arizona more than made up for it with the Grand Canyon. A fellow traveler had warned them at a rest stop that, at first, they might not believe the canyon was real.

"Jesus Christ," Tom whispered in awe as they walked to the edge of a viewing area on the south rim of the Canyon.

The multicolored geological strata of the northern wall was spread before them, shimmering in the heat rising from the canyon floor and stretching, on both sides, beyond the range of their vision.

"Jesus H. Christ," he said again.

"A really grand canyon," Joel interjected.

"Yeah; the grandest damned canyon I've ever seen."

Tom's expression changed from awe to thoughtfulness.

"There must be a million songs and stories down there," he said.

"Jesus H. Christ."

*****

Yes, there were a lot of songs and stories to be found in the Grand Canyon and the country all around in Arizona, New Mexico, Utah and, indeed, all of the American Southwest. It was almost enough to make Joel wish he had become an anthropologist or archaeologist delving into the mystery of the long vanished Anasazi people, the deep spirituality of the Navajo, and even the still unresolved story of how two airliners had come together over the canyon itself back in 1956 and killed everyone aboard.

Had one pilot changed course, even by a degree or two, to give his passengers a better view of the canyon, only to give nearly two hundred people a permanent view of eternity?

That seemed the most likely explanation, but it was more than ten years in the past and Joel had to complete his exploration of his native land and report on its present condition. His raw information was tucked away in an old suitcase full of notebooks and newspaper clippings and he had to get back to Philadelphia and weld it into shape.

Anasazi, Navajo, and the unfortunate airline passengers would have to be left to younger researchers and scholars.

But not for Tom Buckman. He felt anchored to the Grand Canyon, if only temporarily, and decided that he had to stay.

There's a gold mine out here for me," he said over dinner in Flagstaff.

"A gold mine? I hope it's about more than money, Tom," Joel replied.

"Yeah; the songs and the stories I was talking about."

"Down in the Grand Canyon?"

"Down in the canyon, in the hills… out in the desert. This is a special place… mystical, like."

And so Tom, his guitar, pages of music, and his one or two changes of underwear, took root in Flagstaff.

"I'll miss you, Tom," Joel said a couple of mornings later. He was seated in the Volkswagen, its engine running, and ready to head toward the rising sun.

"You've been good company."

"You too, Joel."

"Be sure and stop off in Philadelphia on your way to New York."

"Don't worry; you'll hear from me."

"I know I will, Tom. I know I will."

The way east from Arizona was not difficult. Unlike his trip west, Joel avoided Interstate Route 80 like the very plague itself. He had been in a hurry to get to California but now, anxious though he was to return to his study in Philadelphia, he felt the need to take the classic Route 66, both to take the pulse of his nation and to decompress after his time on the Pacific Coast.

He found the pulse steady and strong and when Route 66 ended in Illinois, he continued down side roads until he finally hooked up with the Pennsylvania Turnpike and headed back to Philadelphia. The United States was not going to collapse in the wake of Vietnam and the savage traumas of 1968, but he did sense a meanness of spirit seeping into the national soul.

"We'll survive that too," he thought as he slowed for the Fort Washington exit from the Pennsylvania Turnpike. He slid on down along the Schuylkill Expressway toward Philadelphia. The low green hills of Bucks County and the glass sheathed, faceless corporate tombs that were starting to infect the northern and western suburbs of Philadelphia gave way to the old working class homes and workshops of Manayunk that seemed unchanged from his earliest days.

The powerful bulk of the Philadelphia Art Museum towered over Fairmount Park and the sweating young lads, and ever more lassies, flexed their muscles and rowing skills in front of Boathouse Row on the Schuylkill River. The trains to New York and Boston glided to and fro from the 30th Street Station, one of the few really grand, old-time railroad stations left in America, and then it was time to take the exit into Center City.

His time on the road was over. Now would be his job to tie the events of the past two years together in *The Great American Walkabout*. As to where it would all lead; that, he thought, would be the work of younger historians, young men and women with world views formed in the 1950s and 1960s instead of the crucible of the 1940s, but he would at least have to take a stab at it.

Joel slipped back into his old apartment and his place on Temple's teaching roster hopeful about the long term future of his nation but disturbed by what he foresaw in the short term. The dark, scowling Richard Nixon, his ideologically thuggish young acolytes and the yowling fundamentalist hillbilly voices he heard in the south, as long ago as the Civil Rights Summer of 1964, did not bode well for the remainder not just of the 1970s but for the closing years of the 20th Century and the opening of the 21st.

He began to write. It was all he could do.

The Great American Walkabout reached the bookstores in 1974, just before Nixon resigned in disgrace. The book was praised and damned in equal measure; praised for its hard, penetrating examination of two of America's most pivotal years and damned for celebrating the free love, free drug hippie counter culture that was the ruination of the world.

*****

Weird though they unquestionably were, Joel slid into the 1970s and tried to participate in the decade's evolving trends. He was particularly interested in the talk he had been hearing all around Temple and Philadelphia about the new age of self discovery and personal freedom.

Taking control of his own life was something Joel Finnigan had never quite been able to accomplish. Instead, events — both great and small — had shaped his life.

When his parents died, he went to live with Aunt Kate.

World War II turned him into a paratrooper and took Susanna from him when Justin lost his legs.

The civil rights movement had brought him Jenny.

Vietnam took Giovanni and led him on 'The Great American Walkabout'.

He had played an active role in many of the pivotal events of the times. He had even had some small influence upon them and would always be proud of that

In his personal life, however, he had been carried too often by the tide. That made the 'do your own thing' ethos of the 1970s very attractive.

It did not take a great deal of effort for Caroline Nasham to talk Joel into attending a BYBS guest seminar with her at one of the big motor lodges that were sprouting up in the New Jersey suburbs. BYBS was the acronym for Be Your Best Self, one of the trendy new self actualization seminars.

Caroline had a friend who swore BYBS had changed her life and she had been pressuring Caroline to come and see for herself.

"It's about getting *It*," Caroline said. "Sally is a totally different person since she went to BYBS. She keeps telling me there's more than one way to look at things. It couldn't hurt, Joel."

"Why not?" Joel thought.

He got his answer as he sat in the big conference room listening to the fat, arrogant, grinning moderator tell him and the hundred plus others in the room that their lives sucked and BYBS could make it all better — for a small fee, of course.

The fat man told them they couldn't wear watches or take any breaks — even to go to the bathroom. But he never told them why. Instead, he launched into a litany of insults that would have made a drill sergeant blush.

"Your life doesn't work," he yelled.

"You have no integrity."

That was only the beginning.

His assistants — all wearing the same goofy grins — took every available opportunity to ask the guests, "Do you see value for yourself in doing this program?"

"Hell, no," Joel thought, squirming uncomfortably in his seat. "I see value in going to take a leak."

Caroline was hanging on the moderator's every word, waiting to learn how she could get the indefinable *It*.

As Joel rose from his chair to unobtrusively find the men's room, he felt a hand clamp down on his shoulder.

"Where are you going, friend?"

Joel smiled pleasantly.

"I'm going to find the men's room."

"Sorry. We don't take breaks."

"I do," Joel said, trying to maintain his dignified, professorial manner.

"But that's not part of the program," the assistant said. "Do you see value for yourself in the program?"

"I see value for myself in taking a leak," an exasperated Joel replied.

"You won't be able to come back."

"I'll take that risk."

"Stop that man," Fats yelled from the front of the room.

The BYBSters, including Caroline, stared in shock as Joel strode defiantly toward the double doors leading to the hotel lobby.

The doors were locked and as Joel approached, a second assistant, wearing the same goofy grin, intercepted him.

"Do you see value for yourself in doing this program?" he asked, sounding like a clone of the previous assistant.

Joel took a step back and stared at the stocky young man. "There was a day," he thought, "when I could put this obnoxious little shit on his ass." That day was long past.

He saw a Rubbermaid trash can in the corner and, for a moment, was sorely tempted to unzip his fly and go then and there, but he *was* a distinguished member of the Temple University faculty, and, besides, he was too much of a gentleman to embarrass Caroline.

So he stared straight into the face of the grinning automaton.

"I see absolutely no value for myself in this inane program. Now open the door and get out of my way."

The assistant was stunned. People just didn't say no.

The automaton opened the door in the proverbial flash and Joel walked through it with a regal flourish. He continued across the carpeted lobby to the men's room where he enjoyed a thoroughly luxurious pee.

The doors to the conference room were locked when he returned and two of the larger BYBS assistants stood firmly before them, looking as if they were guarding the papal apartment itself.

And that was the beginning of the end of Joel Finnigan's venture into the never-never land of the 1970s self-help movement. It was the end, too, of Joel's brief time with Caroline Nasham. He had reached the time in his life when, he told himself with increasingly bitter humor, what he used to do all night now took him all night to do, and Caroline, an exceptionally lusty middle-aged discoverer of the joys of sex, was growing increasingly interested in the purely carnal aspect of their relationship.

Caroline had been, like most of Joel's other lovers, beautiful, intelligent, and talented.

But she was truly on a voyage of discovery and, in the end, did not want to continue her life as an appendage even to the best of men.

So, Caroline found a new guru and a new self-realization regimen and moved on. Joel couldn't help wondering what sort of self discovery pathway Susanna was on and hoped that she had found someone as supportive as he had tried to be with Caroline and Jenny Keith.

*****

Joel was disappointed but not really surprised at Watergate and the fall of Richard Nixon. He, like the vast majority of his countrymen, did not want to believe that their President was just another political hack, but with the focus of political life shifting from governing to simply raising money and getting elected, the whole disgraceful affair was inevitable.

Nixon and his ludicrous "I am not a crook" outburst replaced Martin Luther King Jr.'s "I have a dream" optimism of the 1960s, Vietnam and all, and Caroline Nasham was replaced by Symphony.

Symphony, long legged, long haired Symphony, had a last name once upon a time, but all Joel ever learned was that she had once been known as Evelyn from Voorhees, New Jersey. Joel found her interesting, but hardly fascinating and knew that if he wasn't careful he could turn into an old fool.

This realization came one Saturday night when he accompanied Symphony to a place in southern New Jersey that she had seductively referred to as 'the sex farm.' The farm was a big, sprawling old farmhouse out in the Pines near Ong's Hat.

He knew that Ong had been an old fool, perhaps the definitive old fool, who tossed his hat into a tree in some strange show of devotion for a farm girl young enough to be his daughter. Poor old Ong was too embarrassed, or too old, to climb the tree to retrieve his hat; so it remained hanging from the tree branch until its fabric finally rotted away. So, Joel called it a sociology study to avoid joining Ong in the pantheon of foolish old farts and went with Symphony to the sex farm.

As they entered, Symphony told him the sex farm was a 'lifestyle enhancement facility.'

Exactly how lifestyle enhancing he realized less than a minute later when a bearded, anemic young man young man walked up to them and took Symphony's right breast in his hand.

"Nice," he said as he lifted and appraised it.

"… bouncy… nice and firm… good nippies, too."

"Why, thank you," Symphony said, slipping her hand down between his legs for a digital inspection of her own.

"It's just like the old cigarette ad… so round, so firm…"

"So fully packed," he replied.

"Would you like to go upstairs and try some?"

"Sure; let me find a friend for Joel first. Why go upstairs, though?" she said as she nodded in the direction of a broad futon spread on the floor in a corner of the room where one couple was driving hard toward the completion of their evening's first encounter.

"They'll be off that pretty soon."

"Cool," the kid replied as he reached out for Symphony's left breast.

"See you in five."

Joel was long past being amazed at the peculiarities of his fellow human beings, but this encounter between Symphony and her odd young admirer did give him pause.

He looked at her.

"I presume you know each other."

"Oh, Joel, you're so naïve. Here grabbing someone's boobs is the equivalent of shaking hands."

"You find someone… check out her boobs. We'll make room for you next to us on the futon."

As open as he was, or at least felt he was, Joel had had enough of the sex farm. Pounding away between the legs of a complete stranger while his "date" did the same just a few feet away did not seem like the way for a distinguished member of the Temple faculty to spend a Saturday night. He made his way toward the front door, confident that Symphony could find a ride home. He drove his now tired old Volkswagen back to Philadelphia and went to a movie.

*****

Things continued to change; they always did. Joel was glad that they did, too, for he had always hoped that the younger people were coming along to clean up the mess left by the old men and women of his generation.

Now he was beginning to wonder. The age of "ask not what your country can do for you; ask what you can do for your country" had given way to the decade of "I'm okay, you're okay," but when it gave way to Ronald Reagan and the decade of "I'm okay, fuck you," Joel began to wonder if it was time to pack it in. He was no longer connecting with the students. The idealism and sense of adventure that students had once brought to his classrooms and lecture halls was being replaced by a striving for corporate conformity and well-lined pockets.

But, Joel being Joel, his irrepressible optimism kept him going for another decade.

The breaking point — if it could be said that there was one particular breaking point — came in class one day when he openly derided the takeover of the world by what he called 'corporate weenies.'

"That's offensive and hurtful!" a nineteen-year-old business major exploded, almost sputtering in her rage.

"I *want* to be a corporate weenie! It's the only reason for going to college."

"I see," Joel replied, "and to just what kind of weenieship do you aspire?"

"Insurance!" she proudly proclaimed.

"Insurance?"

"Yes! Filling out insurance forms is the most exciting thing I've ever done."

It was, too, but when that same young lady told him, in a tone that would brook no contradiction, that Winston Churchill was the first black President of the United States, he knew it was time to start looking back.

He put in his retirement papers and, in his new Emeritus status, found himself spending more and more time in libraries, Temple's and the magnificent Philadelphia Free Library on Logan Circle. As usual, he always had a notebook with him and found, as he looked through it at a Starbucks on Rittenhouse

Square, that it was filling up with jottings on the life and times of Dolley Madison.

CHAPTER THIRTY-TWO

TO ALTHEA

I met Finnigan today. He was signing his book at Barnes & Noble in Marlton and I was getting a start on my Christmas shopping. I didn't know he was going to be there — or I forgot. Or maybe I forgot on purpose. I don't know.

I was looking through the new fiction section when I saw him sitting there signing copies of *The Belle of Haddonfield.*

There he was — looking just like the picture on the dust jacket. My mouth dropped open. I picked up a copy of his book and joined the line of people waiting for him to autograph their copies. I moved without thinking — as though I were a puppet and my subconscious was pulling the strings.

Suddenly, I was face-to-face with him. I couldn't move. I just stood there.

"Did you want me to sign that?" he asked.

"Uh, yeah," I mumbled, handing him the book.

"What's your name?" he asked.

"Althea Burnside."

He started writing, "To Althea…"

"I wrote a book about Dolley Madison, too."

Where that came from, I don't know. I just blurted it out. He was the first person I'd told about my *Queen of the Indian King.* I hadn't had the nerve to shop it around after his book hit the street.

Maybe it was just my way of letting him know that he had ruined my whole goddamned life.

He looked up. "You did? What's the title?"

"*Queen of the Indian King.*"

"I'll have to read it."

"You won't get a chance. Your book came out before I had a chance to find an agent."

I don't know how I sounded when I said it. But he looked at me as though I'd told him he'd killed my best friend which, I guess, if you think about it, he did. Then he said, simply, "I'm sorry."

Do you believe it? And he was so sincere that I nearly screamed.

"You're sorry! I spent three years of my life on that book. How do you think I feel? I was tempted to burn the damned thing. Why I didn't, I'll never know."

He just sat and stared. What else could he do?

"Just because my book came out first doesn't mean you shouldn't try to get yours published. I've often seen reviews of two books on the same subject."

He resumed writing, then handed the book to me.

He was so reasonable I wanted to strangle him.

"Yeah right," I said. Then I looked at the inscription.

To Althea: Keep writing. There's more than one way to tell a story. Wishing you success, Joel Finnigan.

I thrust the book back at him.

"Keep writing! Hah! I haven't been able to write a word since I read your damn book. Keep it. I sure don't need two copies. One was more than enough." I stormed out of the store, stomped to my car and cried like a fool.

I hadn't expected him to be so... so sensitive. It made me feel worse than I did when I read the review of *The Belle of Haddonfield*. Well, maybe not that bad... but damn... he's done it to me twice now. Once by writing such a damned good book and getting it published first, and now by making me feel guilty for feeling bad about it. What a guy! My ex couldn't have done a better job if we'd stayed together and he made me miserable all these years.

If only he'd written something like, *Tough luck, Toots. Get over it,* I wouldn't feel so bad. Well I'd still feel bad, but I wouldn't feel ashamed. I really did make an ass of myself.

CHAPTER THIRTY-THREE

FINNIGAN'S LAMENT...

AND ALTHEA'S, TOO

J oel poured himself a glass of red wine. The doctors said it was good for his heart. Tonight it would be good for more than just that. There he was basking in his success at Barnes & Noble, signing books and feeling great that *The Belle of Haddonfield* was selling so well.

Then along came this young woman. She couldn't have been more than twenty-six or twenty-seven. Tall and thin, kind of pretty, and with the bluest eyes he'd seen since Susanna. She gave him her book to sign, then told him she had spent three years writing a book about Dolley Madison. After she read his book, she was tempted to burn her manuscript. She didn't but she hasn't been able to write a word since.

Joel knew that problem all too well.

In the fifties, he had to make sense of what had happened in the forties. *Operation Market-Garden* and *Silver Wings* were histories of his part of those terrible, tumultuous years. They were stories that needed to be told, and he thought he did a fairly decent job of telling them.

The book on Bobby Kennedy's last campaign was a modest success. But after the horrors of 1968 and Giovanni's death in 1969, he just didn't want to write any more on recent history or current events.

After *The Great American Walkabout*, he felt there was nothing more left for him to write. That's when he suffered from the same writer's malady as Althea — although for different reasons.

Writing is a compulsive thing, at least it was with Joel, and when he packed it in at Temple a few years ago he went out and bought a new package of yellow legal pads, lined up his Number 2 pencils according to length, and started again.

He felt like an old linebacker putting on the pads for one more game. His only requirement was that since he would be devoting a lot of time to researching and writing, the subject should be someone he'd enjoy spending time with.

Perhaps he was getting trendy and thought that writers of history had given prominent women short shrift in our national story. But he was attracted to lively, spirited Dolley Madison. She looked like she'd have been great fun to be around and he'd liked to have known her.

Perhaps he was thinking ahead to his meeting with the as yet unknown Althea Burnside, or maybe it was the influence of Truman Capote's *In Cold Blood* — a reaction delayed since 1966 — but he had an instinctive feeling that the novelist's tools were what was needed to bring forth a true picture of Dolley Madison.

He wasn't exactly sure what those tools were, or how he should use them. He defaced many a legal pad and vandalized many a pencil but finally cobbled something together.

So, there he was, sitting in the Barnes & Noble bookstore in Marlton, New Jersey just a few days before Christmas, signing books, passing pleasantries and trying to pull young Althea Burnside back from the brink of despair.

He felt terrible. All the optimism of his renewed life was going down the drain. He'd spent his whole life trying to inspire young people and now this one comes along and says she's given up on writing because of him.

He kept seeing that look of defeat on her face. It almost made him wish he'd never written *The Belle of Haddonfield* or, at least, that it hadn't been published until Althea had a chance to get hers out. What difference should it make to him if the *Times* calls him brilliant? "I only have a few more years anyway. She has her whole life ahead of her," he thought.

Joel felt obligated to say something; so he wrote what he thought was an encouraging inscription. But Althea just screamed at him, tossed his book back in his face and ran away.

He wished he could find her and talk some sense into her. But she was long gone. So he took another sip of wine and retreated to the place that had given him solace for more than 50 years — the memory of Susanna Winslow.

*****

Finnigan is going to be at Borders in center city next week. I'm going to see him and apologize. I acted like an idiot. I keep seeing those sparkling blue eyes staring up at me in shock after my tirade.

It really isn't his fault. It's not like he set out to ruin my life. He did, but it wasn't intentional.

*****

Joel never expected to see Althea again. Then she showed up at his book signing at Borders and apologized for her outburst in New Jersey. She even offered to buy him a cup of coffee or a drink so she could explain why she had behaved so badly.

Joel felt like he could use a drink but decided coffee was safer. He wasn't sure how she'd be with a few drinks in her and he didn't want to find out.

There was a Starbucks in the book store, but Althea thought they might be interrupted since Joel had just finished a signing. He didn't have the energy to go anywhere else. So she gave in, and they talked until the store closed. First about their mutual interest in Dolley Madison, then about her reaction to discovering Joel had written a book on the same subject.

When it was time to go, it seemed as though they still had a great deal to say to each other, and since Joel was feeling more comfortable with her by then, he suggested stopping at a nearby bar for drink.

It was then that he began to suspect how fragile and complex Althea was. She seemed so lost. She told Joel she lived with someone, but he suspected it wasn't a match made in heaven.

"I'd like to read your manuscript," he said when they settled in with their glasses of wine. He meant it, too. He was beginning to catch a hint of something in this young woman and wanted to see what she could do.

"Okay," she replied, "I'll put it in the mail tomorrow. You'll be the first one to read it... well, the first one who really knows anything. Maybe it's not too late to get it published."

"Maybe, but let me read it first."

He didn't want to get her hopes up since it might not be as good as he suspected. But it did sound like she took an entirely different tack than he did, and he didn't see why there couldn't be two different novels based on the same historical character.

"In the meantime, Althea, I think you should get started on another project," he told her.

"God, Professor Finnigan..."

"Joel, please."

"... Joel. I don't think I have another one in me."

"I suspect you do, Althea. They're all out there, just waiting for a channel to open up and let them into the world. I think you might be such a channel."

"Really?"

"Really."

She seemed to grow thoughtful then; as if she were searching for something, or opening herself to let something find her.

He'd only known Althea for a short time — a matter of hours, really — but he detected changes taking place within her.

It was the best feeling he'd had in a long time.

*****

Finnigan is quite different than I imagined. He's really very nice. He offered to read *Queen of the Indian King*, and I think he might even try to help me get it published if he likes it. He didn't say so, but he seems like that kind of guy. Wouldn't that be ironic? I get my book published *because* his was published first.

I know I shouldn't go counting my chickens, but I really have a good feeling about this.

I stayed up all night rereading it, and, if I say so myself, it's pretty damn good. Still, I want to rework a couple things before I send it to him.

Mark is annoyed because I'm so wrapped up in this. I can't believe that after all I've been through with this book, he wants me to sit and watch *ER* reruns with him instead of getting Dolley ready to send to Finnigan. I can just imagine what he'll be like if I ever start a new project. I can be a real mad woman when I'm writing. I tend to bulldoze anything that gets in my way. Oh, well, I'll be extra lovey after I get the book in the mail.

*****

Joel read Althea's book as soon as it arrived.

Her Dolley was a totally different person than the one he wrote about. His was about a woman who was a role model for all the first ladies who followed her. He had tried as much as possible to stick to the historical facts and, at the same time, make her into a real flesh and blood woman.

Althea, on the other hand, had made Dolley Madison into the main character in a romance novel. She put her in an historical setting, but she spent much more time on Dolley's fantasy life than she did on anything else. Joel just didn't see a proper young Quaker woman imagining in such graphic detail what it would be like to make love in the White House.

"My God! I just can't imagine Lady Bird Johnson or Pat Nixon cavorting naked in the Lincoln Bedroom," he thought. "It does make an interesting mental picture, however.

"Queen Beatrix of The Netherlands is supposed to have seen Lincoln's ghost there while she was visiting FDR during the war. If old Abe was still hanging around in the 60s or early 70's... good grief!"

Maybe Althea made Dolley too much like herself... the "self" character that pops out of even the most disciplined writer. Or maybe Joel was looking at it too much like an historian, though he couldn't really fault himself for that. It's what he was.

In any case, there was something engaging about Althea Burnside and her book, even if the Lincoln Bedroom wasn't called that back in Dolley's day. Joel just didn't know how he could help her. She left three messages on his voice mail, and he felt guilty about not calling her back. Maybe if he read the book again, he'd think of something.

CHAPTER THIRTY-FOUR

LIFE SUCKS

I think Finnigan is putting me off. He probably hates my book and doesn't want to tell me. My whole life is going down the toilet. Nothing is working out the way I thought it would.

Mark is really getting on my nerves. I swear sometimes I think he's trying to make an art out of being annoying. It's nothing big — really. Just a lot of little things, like constantly flipping the channels when I'm watching TV, and never putting the toilet seat down, and leaving dirty dishes on the living room table. You'd think he could at least put them in the sink.

And now Finnigan won't even return my calls. Life really sucks.

Well, he's not going to get off the hook so easily.

CHAPTER THIRTY-FIVE

THE NATURE OF THINGS

It was one of the strangest nights of Joel's life; which is saying quite a lot.

Like many strange nights it began with a phone call.

"I need to come over and talk, Joel; just talk."

"That would be nice, Althea, but…"

"I'll whip up your favorite dinner for you."

A beautiful, smart young woman offering to come over and cook his favorite dinner? He thought he was past all that, with his gray hair, what the Brits call a gamy knee and the recent news that he had Type II diabetes. But how could he refuse?

"I really haven't finished reading your manuscript yet," Joel said, lamely.

"I don't want to talk about my book. I just want to talk about writing in general — with a real writer."

"A real writer? You flatter me too much, Althea."

"Oh," she said with a touch of disappointment in her voice.

"… but, by all means, come on over.

"And don't even think about cooking. I'll get some take out from Mickey Wu's."

"Great."

She sounded relieved. Joel thought it was more because she got out of cooking than because he had agreed to see her.

So, on a cold Wednesday night early in the New Year, Althea Burnside knocked on the front door of the small but comfortable townhouse on Spring Garden Street where Joel lived.

*****

Joel wasn't sure how to broach the subject of her book — which he knew was the real reason she wanted to see him.

They nibbled around the edges, at first, talking about the craft of writing versus the art of the thing. It was new territory for him. He had never considered himself a writer. He was simply an historian who wanted to tell his stories. Althea, on the other hand, was a storyteller looking for inspiration.

Joel knew they were avoiding the main topic and the subject of her manuscript suddenly burst from the depths.

"You hated it. Didn't you?" she finally blurted out in a voice that was really pleading for him to disagree.

"I'm not really in a position to judge your work, Althea. I'm not a novelist," he told her. "I'm just an historian who decided to try something different. But I do wonder how you, who worked almost your entire adult life as a journalist, could stray so far from the known facts about Dolley Madison?"

"But I didn't stray from them," she countered. "I just gave her an interior life — made her a flesh and blood woman. What's wrong with that?"

"I just never saw her that way," he said.

"I wanted people to relate to her in a way that's familiar," she continued. "It's fiction, not history. What does it matter? Journalists like to say they're publishing 'The Truth,' as if anybody knows what that is. I certainly believed it, but then I came to realize that all I was reporting were facts. It's the novelist who writes the truth, regardless of the facts."

She had a point and besides, Joel didn't want to argue. Before he could say a word, Althea went into a long dissertation about the nature of truth. She became the teacher and he, the student.

"If I'd wanted to write about what Dolley did, I'd have written a biography," she told him. "I wanted to explore who Dolley was or who she could have been. A young Quaker girl whose uncle ran a tavern where revolutionaries met and discussed the future of the colonies became the wife of a president. Your view of who she was is different than mine. It doesn't really matter if she was like either of them. She could have been.

"Everything we see in life we interpret through our own experiences. I personally can't imagine any woman who marries a politician not wondering what it would be like to make love in the White House. I certainly would.

"Fiction is meant to raise questions, not necessarily to answer them. It's meant to stir the imagination, not dictate to it.

"If a woman reading *Queen of the Indian King* or *The Belle of Haddonfield* can see herself in the Dolley you've written about or the Dolley I've written about, she may look at both herself and our history in a different way."

"I never thought of it that way," he told her.

"But you knew it," she said. "You must have or you couldn't have written such a damned good book. You must have used bits and pieces of your own life and your own experiences with women to create the woman you wrote about. There's so much more to the Dolley Madison in *The Belle of Haddonfield* than there was in any of the historical books and documents I researched. You must have asked yourself what kind of woman she would have to be to do the things she did."

Then Althea asked him something that stopped him cold.

"Do you feel like your own life has been true?"

"What do you mean?" he asked.

"Have you lived your life the way you think you were meant to live it? Have you been true to what you believed? Have you listened to your inner voice and followed it? Is the Joel Finnigan you've been the real Joel Finnigan?"

"Those are good questions," he said. "I'll have to give them some thought. What about you, Althea? Has your life been true? Are you the real Althea Burnside, the one you were meant to be?"

"Damned if I know. I guess that's why I'm asking you."

Before he realized it, Joel was talking to her about his life. It seemed the most natural thing in the world. He couldn't remember when he'd been so open with someone. It reminded him of the way he and Susanna talked the day they met.

He told Althea about Susanna and how his life collapsed when she abandoned everything they had built up back in 1942 to stick with Justin Welch; about how he envied Justin even though he'd lost both his legs and Joel still had his, about how he met Connie and married her, about how bitterly ironic he thought it was that his only son died trying to be like him, about Jenny whose free spirit he loved until it soared off without him.

He didn't tell her too much about his war years, the hellish, glorious time in the 506th. There was too much to tell and, besides, to a young woman her age, Normandy, Market-Garden and Bastogne would be ancient history.

In the end, it came back to Susanna. He couldn't help wondering what his life would have been like if he had insisted that she stay with him. He wondered whether she had been happy with her decision to follow her sense of duty and go with Justin. He felt a deep sadness for all that could have been.

Althea seemed to sense his pain and became the most empathetic soul he'd ever met. He opened his heart to her in a way he never had to anyone since Susanna. Over a half century of emotion crashed through the invisible dam he'd built as he told this young woman about another woman, now old enough to be her grandmother — if she was even still alive — and whose loss still left a vast emptiness deep in him.

Althea put her arms around Joel and comforted him like a mother; this incredibly sexy woman who was young enough to be his granddaughter. Then she kissed his cheek and left.

Joel stayed awake the whole night thinking about Susanna and about Althea.

CHAPTER THIRTY-SIX

WHO ARE YOU, ALTHEA?

I'm dead tired today. I didn't sleep a wink. I went to see Finnigan to get some feedback on my book and it turned into something I never expected. He bared his soul to me. I can't remember when anyone has been so totally open and honest.

I've never had a true love, nothing like Joel had with his Susanna, or thought he had, anyway. But when I see what's possible — for me too, I hope — I can imagine the pain that Joel feels at having lost it.

And Connie. How Joel could ever have wound up with a fat, self-centered bimbo who never read a book, and probably still hasn't, is completely beyond me.

To lose his only son in Vietnam… that had to be the most horrible of all.

And Jenny Keith. I've seen her perform and have a few of her CDs. She's good, and very beautiful, even today. But a black and white couple must have had tremendous strains on their relationship back in 1968.

Of course if their relationship couldn't withstand those strains, it probably wasn't strong enough anyway.

Susanna must have really been something if she still haunts him after all these years.

Joel is a prince in a world — hell, a universe — full of frogs. I'm sure he gave a great deal to the women in his life, probably more than most men, but his best, his very essence, was for Susanna alone, and any woman who really loved him would know that.

All that got me thinking about my own life. Who am I reserving my essence for? Will he ever come to claim it?

Whoever he is, he isn't Mark. I could hardly stand to be in bed beside him last night. I wanted to curl into a ball, pull the covers over my head and pray he wouldn't touch me.

I'm not sure what I'm feeling, but whatever it is, it's damned uncomfortable.

I have a great urge to call Finnigan to see if he'll let me talk to him the way he talked to me. I feel so lost — as though my whole life has been cut into a jigsaw puzzle and tossed into the air, leaving pieces everywhere and me with no clue how they fit together.

Who are you, Althea Burnside? What do you want? What is your purpose in this life?

CHAPTER THIRTY-SEVEN

QUESTIONS

Althea had asked Joel some hard questions, and it shocked him to realize he didn't have any answers for her. Did he live a life true to what he believed — or thought he believed? He always thought he was honest with himself. But she got him wondering. Why did he simply accept Susanna telling him she couldn't leave her Justin? What if he had tried to talk her out of it? What if he'd gone home instead of to O'Flynn's Bar? What if he hadn't gone to that motel with Connie?

He wondered whether Susanna had a good life with Justin. Was he a good lover? Did they have any kids? Did she ever think about him? Did she ever regret making him leave? He knew he'd never get answers to those questions. If only he could know that she was happy.

CHAPTER THIRTY-EIGHT

MY FRIEND FINNIGAN?

Mark and I can't stay together. I guess we could and it might even be okay.

Being bed partners with Mark isn't all that bad. It's not great, but how many people get great? We'll never be soulmates. I know that 'soulmates' sounds very 70s, but there's more to being lovers than just getting naked, and Mark and I will never be real lovers.

We never communicate like Finnigan and I did last night. He has no idea who I am. Not that Finnigan does either. I didn't reveal myself to him. But the way he talked to me — with complete faith that I would understand — showed me what real communication can be between people. I will never have that with Mark.

Maybe Finnigan and I can do it because there's nothing sexual between us.

Sex ruins too many really good friendships.

Joel Finnigan is old enough to be my grandfather. Still, he touched me more deeply than I've ever been touched before.

Would what I share with Finnigan be possible with a lover?

It has to be. I know it. It's what I've always wanted but never thought I'd have.

And now that I do know it, nothing will ever be the same for me again.

So where does that leave me? Alone again. But maybe I won't be so lonely if Finnigan will be my friend.

CHAPTER THIRTY-NINE

A TRUE LIFE?

Susanna married Justin Welch the same day Connie and Joel got married. He couldn't help but see the irony in that.

He hadn't made any effort to track her down since he walked out of the apartment on Sansom Street. What was past was past, he figured.

But after his talk with Althea, he knew he couldn't hide from the past any longer. It was all part of discovering whether he'd lived the life he was supposed to live. So, he took a long walk to the library and immersed himself in the old *Inquirer* and *Evening Bulletin* archives.

And there it was: the wedding announcement. No picture, though. How he wished there had been.

He had no idea where to go from here. He had been haunted by Susanna's memory since the day they had parted, but he couldn't see her face clearly. How could he have loved someone so much and not even remember what she looked like? It had been well over fifty years, but why should that matter? How he wished he still had the picture she gave him and her letters. Those letters kept him going when bullets were flying all around him. Those letters were faded and streaked with mud because he read them so many times in foxholes, under GI canvas or in the back of C47s.

He had memorized each one. How he'd love to read them just once more. But Connie burned them.

Good old Connie. He wondered how she was faring. "She's probably making Greg Leone as miserable as she made me," he thought. "That really isn't fair, but who cares? What did fair ever get me anyway? It lost me Susanna. Maybe she didn't love me as much as she said she did. How could she have let me go? I wish I could see her beautiful face. I wish we could have had children together.

"Giovanni would have been born anyway, though I never would have known him. Who knows? He might have grown up wanting to be a baseball player instead of a paratrooper and maybe he would be alive today.

"God, how I loved that boy. I was a soldier for such a short part of my life and if I was to be his role model I wish he could have focused on the part that came after the war.

"But that's over now. Giovanni lies in Gate of Heaven Cemetery in Framingham, and his Congressional Medal of Honor is on display among Connie's collectables in Boston. And here I sit in Philadelphia, an old man now, wondering if my life has really amounted to anything."

He thought about Althea's question again. Many of his students had gone on to great things and he wanted to think he had inspired them, or helped, anyway. Everyone seemed to think *The Belle of Haddonfield* was very good, even Althea; so he guessed that had been a success as well.

Seen from the outside, then, he supposed he could say that he had lived the life he was meant to live. But his inner life, down deep where it really counted, what about that?

A large part of him had been empty since he and Susanna turned away from each other all those years ago. He had worked hard to fill that empty space and overcome the loneliness.

But how true was it, really? Nothing, nobody had ever meant as much to him as Susanna Winslow.

CHAPTER FORTY

ALTHEA'S DILEMMA

I don't know how to tell Mark I don't want to be with him anymore. And I don't know where I'd go if I leave him. I can't really afford another place. I hate to hurt him. He really didn't do anything. I know I complain about him, but he really is a good man. If anything, he's been too good. He's everything I said I wanted. Maybe if I push for more, he'll back away. But what if he doesn't? What if he wants to get married and have kids? That's what I always said I wanted.

Get a grip, Althea! You'll figure out something. You always do.

CHAPTER FORTY-ONE

WHITHER ALTHEA?

Althea was on Joel's mind nearly as much as Susanna these days. There was something about her that was endearing. If Giovanni hadn't been killed in that damned war, he might have had a daughter like Althea.

Maybe Joel felt that way because Althea seemed to think he could offer some wisdom about what she should do with her life. They had met for coffee several times and Joel had told her that she couldn't continue to live with a man who is so wrong for her. She's got to find another place. Or ask him to. She agreed it's the only thing to do, but she seemed paralyzed by the logistics of it all.

Joel wondered whether he should offer to let her stay with him temporarily. After all, he had more room than he needed. She could sleep in the den. It would be nice to have the company — if she didn't drive him crazy.

CHAPTER FORTY-TWO

BREAKING UP

What was the name of that old song: "Breaking Up Is Hard To Do?"

Yeah, that's the one and, boy, was it right on.

I've always hated playing games, but I was a week working up to my final break with Mark.

Honesty is the best policy, or so I've always been told; so my first thought was to come right out with it.

"Mark, I think we've made a mistake," I said one rainy spring evening.

He was ensconced in his Lazy Boy recliner, so deep into the statistics textbook he was studying as part of his MBA program that I don't think he'd have noticed if I spontaneously ignited right there in the living room.

"Hmmm — what, dear?"

What, dear? Jesus H. Christ on a Harley! Archie and Edith had nothing on us.

"We're really not right for each other," I said.

"We're really not... what?"

"Forget it."

I thought he'd be shocked, maybe even angry, just a little.

"Are you making some popcorn?"

So I went and made popcorn.

Mark seemed so perfectly content, and I felt so... lonely... so not understood, and when you get right down to it, even the sex was boring. I thought I would explode from frustration.

Finally, I decided to pick a fight and get him good and mad at me; so mad he'd be delighted when I said I was leaving. Or maybe, just maybe, he'd stalk out on his own.

But the whole thing backfired. Boy, was that a shocker. Mark has always been so predictable. That was one of the things that drew me to him in the first place and one of the things I've found most maddening ever since.

I decided I'd spend the entire evening writing, or pretending to, since I'm still totally uninspired. Mark would wait patiently for a while, then knock on the door and ask when we were going to have dinner. I'd tell him I was in the middle of something and would be out soon. An hour or so would go by and he'd do the same thing.

Finally, the third time, I'd scream at him, "Can't you see I'm in the middle of something? You know how I've struggled and now I'm on a roll and you want me to quit and play the happy homemaker and make dinner for you! Make your own damn dinner. If you can't see how important this is, maybe I should find another place to write. Hell, maybe I should just find another place, period!"

Good plan. Right?

Wrong.

He knocked on the door once and that was it. An hour later, when nothing happened, I went into the kitchen on the pretext of wanting a glass of juice to tide me over till I was ready to stop for dinner. He was sitting in front of the TV, eating soup and crackers. I could see my whole plan had gone to hell; so I improvised.

"Couldn't you have waited for me? I said I'd be finished in a few minutes."

"I was hungry, and I didn't want to bother you. You seemed so involved with what you were doing."

"Well, aren't you the thoughtful one?" I said sarcastically.

He just smiled.

I was flabbergasted. Now what?

"There's more soup in the pot," he said.

I wanted to fight with him, but I really was hungry; so I ate instead.

In the end, after three days of trying to pick a fight, I was forced to fall back on the old honesty trick.

"Mark," I said, "I'm really not happy in this relationship. I have to get out of it. I think it would be good for you too."

"What?"

He was shocked, really shocked. I had his attention at last.

"We're splitting up, Mark."

"Why didn't you say anything?"

"I've been trying to tell you all week. You haven't been listening, or you haven't heard me."

God, the man is utterly clueless — a Valley Girl with balls. How come I never noticed that before?

Maybe I did.

"I heard you, Althea. I just didn't believe you. I still don't. I think you're just having another one of your artistic hissy fits."

I wanted to show him what a real hissy fit was, but I made myself stay calm.

"It's over, Mark. We've had fun, but we can't move up to the next level."

"But where will you go? What will I do?"

I thought of Clark Gable telling Vivian Leigh, "Frankly, my dear, I don't give a damn."

A great line, that, but I held back the urge to throw it to him.

"I'll go over to Philadelphia," I said. "Joel Finnigan has an extra room he said I could use temporarily."

And Mark thought I was having a hissy fit!

He went ballistic, almost completely 'round the bend, and it was the only time I ever saw him express any real emotion.

"Finnigan!" he roared. He actually roared.

"I should have known! You know, Althea, I really fell for it when you said he was helping you with that goddamned book! He was helping you all right... helping you get your weekly quota of cock."

"Which is a lot more than you've been doing!" I shouted back. I couldn't resist, I just couldn't.

"Professor Finnigan? That old fart. I'll bet you have to get on top."

I couldn't believe it. He was accusing me of sleeping with Finningan. Then he called me a whore. Me! Did he really think that would make me want to stay with him?

Finally, he stormed out of the room and I could hear the front door slam as he left.

I didn't know whether to laugh or cry.

How could he even think I was sleeping with Finnigan? Maybe he thinks Finnigan is a rich old coot and I'm after his fortune.

I'd never seen Mark act that way. I wasn't sure what he'd do when he came back; so I decided I better pack a few things and get to Finnigan's while the getting was good.

CHAPTER FORTY-THREE

LOST WAIF

Joel never thought of Althea as a waif, but that's just what she looked like when she showed up on his doorstep. It was around 11:30. Jim Gardner and the Channel Six Action News was just signing off after the nightly serving of gang banging and lost puppies.

There he was, with a lost puppy of his own; her hair a mess, a Temple University sweatshirt and jeans, both of which had seen far better days, and a backpack stuffed with the few female essentials she had managed to grab on her westward flight from New Jersey.

"It's over," she said with a forlorn grin that somehow still managed to look hopeful.

"Mark and I had a big blow up. I walked out."

"I guess you damn well did, Althea," he replied.

"… a really big blow up. I'd have waited until morning before I left but I'm afraid to be anywhere near him tonight. Can I crash here, Joel?"

"Of course you can. Come right in. I'll put on some soup."

"And a Guinness?"

"Definitely a Guinness… maybe two. I suspect you have quite a tale to tell."

"Oh boy, do I! Can I take a quick shower while the soup's heating?"

He nodded and she was off to the bathroom. She shut the door behind her, but not before he caught a glimpse of the sweatshirt being pulled over her head and the thin white bra strap across her back.

Joel started the soup and tried to think of what to say to a beautiful young woman as he listened to the evening's tension being swept away by the hot water in his own shower.

He smiled as he thought about what the neighbors might say about the gray haired old prof with a nubile young tootsie spending the night.

Althea came out of the shower a much different girl than she was when she went in. Her face was fresh and still glowing from the hot water and she was dressed in a red sweat suit and a ridiculous pair of fluffy bunny slippers.

Her face reddened even more with laughter, as did Joel's, when she told him about her final confrontation with Mark. It was traumatic but she was right to leave him before he smothered her in his ever thickening blanket of corporate conformity.

Perhaps because he too had once been in a similar situation, Joel found himself feeling somewhat sorry for Mark. What a damned fool he had been to let Althea get away. She had everything, wit, talent, courage and the capacity for incredible love for a man worthy of it.

Of course Joel had been a damned fool himself and was paying for it to this very day. He hadn't met anyone like Susanna until young Althea came into his life — maddening, but terribly refreshing and invigorating.

He knew he was a fool for not putting up more of a fight back in 1945, for not at least trying to make Susanna see that they had far more than she'd ever have with Justin Welch.

But none of that altered the fact that Mark was a damned fool.

CHAPTER FORTY-FOUR

ALTHEA REBORN

Althea got her wish at last. She opened her heart to Joel in the way she had never been able to with anyone else. She told him about her failed marriage, her unfailing attraction to the wrong men, and her conscious decision to finally be smart and choose a solid man like Mark.

"Love is not a conscious choice, Althea," Joel told her. "If it were, I'd have put Susanna out of my heart long ago. That is, unless I'd been smart enough not to let her get away in the first place. God, my life would have been so different."

"Would it really have?" Althea asked. "You still would have been a teacher. Wouldn't you?"

Joel stroked his beard that had long since turned white.

"Probably, but I would have been a much happier teacher."

"And you still would have gone to Mississippi in '64. You'd still have written about Bobby Kennedy in '68"

"I don't know," Joel said. "If Susanna and I had kids at home, I might have stayed put. I might not have been so restless."

"Is that why you did it... because you were restless?"

Joel wasn't sure how to answer. They were all things he had to do because, if for no other reason, the times demanded it. But would he have felt the need to be so active, to be right in the thick of things, if he had been with Susanna?

"Well you certainly would have written *The Belle of Haddonfield.*

"Maybe."

"Wow!" she said. "If you didn't write it, my life would have been different too."

With that, she yawned and Joel pointed her to his bedroom, then grabbed some sheets and a pillow and made up the couch for himself.

As they went to sleep in their separate rooms, he couldn't help puzzling over the life that might have been if he hadn't let Susanna send him away.

He imagined a life of harmony with a woman who loved him as much as he loved her. Susanna wouldn't have argued about the move to Chestertown. She would have encouraged him and she would have thrived there. She would have taken some courses at the college, maybe even become a teacher herself. And they would have had beautiful, well-balanced children.

They might be on the Eastern Shore to this day; still in the house in Rock Hall, sailing and living the Chesapeake Bay lifestyle.

He thought of Giovanni. He could never have wished away the time they'd had together, but he would never have known Giovanni. Instead, he would have known the children he had with Susanna. A beautiful little girl — a miniature of the woman he loved so much — and a son he would have loved as much as he had loved Giovanni, a son in whose life he would have had more influence, a son who might still be alive.

Would he have gone to Mississippi? Would he have written about Bobby Kennedy? He'd told Althea he wasn't sure. But inside he knew he would have. As for *The Belle of Haddonfield*, well, he probably would have done that too.

But one thing would have been different. He wouldn't be sharing his bachelor quarters with a confused would-be writer less than half his age. He would be cuddled in bed with Susanna planning a fishing trip with their grandson.

*****

Finnigan and I had a really good talk tonight, the kind of talk I wish Mark and I could have had.

So many more things seem possible now. I had dreamed of being the acclaimed new novelist of the year — maybe even the decade — whose book on Dolley Madison brought rave reviews, a guest spot on Oprah and, of course, wealth. I saw myself signing books at Barnes & Noble, telling young Althea Burnside wannabes to keep the faith. *Queen of the Indian King* would be number one on the New York Times bestseller list, and I would be on my way up the literary ladder.

Or maybe not.

Finnigan's book was too good not to have been written. He'd have done it whether he was with Susanna or not. I am sure of that, even if he isn't.

But my talk with Finnigan gives me hope that there's another book in me and, even more important, that I can have a relationship like the one he had with Susanna.

Finally I fell into a deep, comforting, and restorative sleep, but through it all the image of a stalwart paratrooper and a tall, slim young woman with ash blond hair slipped silently through the mists of my mind.

*****

The sun was up and bathing the townhouse in its slowly strengthening light by the time I woke up. The idea that had been dancing through my mind all night was fully formed, or nearly so, and I was anxious to tell Finnigan.

It was daring, perhaps brilliant even if I do say so myself, but there was nothing to do but wait until Finnigan was awake to hear it. So I lay quietly in Finnigan's bed waiting for the soft thump of the refrigerator door opening and closing or the hollow rattle of the coffee maker being coaxed back to life.

I was really patient — something new for me — but after thirty minutes had gone by, I decided I had waited long enough.

The smell of the brewing coffee brought Finnigan to life. He trundled into the kitchen, barefoot and wrapped in a huge terry cloth robe.

"I know what to do," I blurted out as he poured himself a cup of coffee and joined me at the table.

"And what might that be?" he said groggily.

"We're going to find Susanna and find out what happened in her life."

"I've been thinking about that a lot lately," Joel said. "In fact, I checked the marriage license records and the *Inquirer's* society pages. She got married the same day I did. How about that one? I've been puzzling about what to do next, but if I did find her, I wouldn't want to disrupt her life. Maybe I should just let it go."

"Maybe she's a lonely widow who's been pining for you for years. Maybe you could still get together and be happy."

"Yeah, sure."

"Come on, Finnigan. You don't strike me as the cynical type."

"I don't think it's such a good idea."

"Finnigan…"

"If you want to find her, Althea, be my guest," Joel said.

Joel saw a new Althea Burnside born right there at the breakfast table. From the confused, angry, frustrated young girl he had first met at Barnes & Noble, she had completely reinvented herself, in a matter of hours it seemed. She was a woman with a mission.

Once Althea retrieved her computer and other belongings from the place she had shared with Mark Steinfeld in Haddonfield, she attacked the keyboard like a woman possessed. She spent countless hours crouched before the glowing screen, racing through Google, Dogpile, and every search engine and newspaper archive she could get into, searching for the mythic, but oh-so-real, Susanna Winslow, or Susanna Winslow Welch, or Susanna Welch or… whatever.

There was a new look in her eye as she began the search for Susanna. Joel had seen that look before; in the eyes of other friends as they flew into Normandy and Holland, or froze their asses in trucks on the icy road to Bastogne.

If Susanna was out there to be found, Althea Burnside was certain to find her.

And then what?

CHAPTER FORTY-FIVE

OPERATION SUSANNA

"Finnigan!" Althea yelled. "Finnigan, I think I found her!"

Joel was deep into Doris Kearns Goodwin's *No Ordinary Time* and wishing to hell he had written something that good when Althea's excited announcement broke in upon him.

She had taken over his bedroom. He had gone out and bought a folding bed for his office and ventured into his own room only to fish out the day's fresh clothes. It wasn't a bad arrangement. She expected to be out in no more than a couple of weeks, but until she was, his bedroom was the command post for Operation Susanna.

"Finnigan," The voice was louder now. More insistent. Joel stuck a bookmark in the page he was reading and went to see what Althea was so excited about.

It looked as though she had, indeed, tracked down Susanna — or someone with the same name who was the same age. A Susanna Welch Morrison was living in a retirement community in Whiting, New Jersey, deep in the Pinelands, about an hour and a half drive from Philadelphia. Perhaps Justin Welch had died and Susanna remarried. It was a possibility.

It was news Joel had been waiting to hear since 1945. But that was mainly because he was sure he would never hear it and now that the irrepressible Althea Burnside may have located Susanna less than fifty miles away, he became more nervous than he ever thought possible.

"Now what?" he asked.

"You'll go see her, of course."

"But what if…"

"What if!" she exploded

"What if your aunt had balls, Finnigan?"

He didn't answer. He was seeing a new, saltier side of Althea and he wasn't quite sure just what to make of it.

"She'd be your uncle, silly. If you don't go see her, you'll always wonder. And I'll never give you a minute's peace."

"But I can't just pop in and say 'here I am, Susanna.'"

"I don't see why not. She was the love of your life. Wasn't she? If nothing else, she'll be flattered that you wanted to find her after all these years."

Joel was skeptical.

"You're afraid. You're still in love with her, and you're afraid you'll get hurt all over again. Maybe I was wrong. Maybe I shouldn't have forced the issue. Maybe it's better for you to keep the dream you have of her."

She looked intently at him.

"But is it, Joel? Do you really want to forget the whole thing?"

"No. But, I… what if she isn't my Susanna?"

"What if she is?"

"How about if I go see her first? Check out the situation. Then you can take it from there."

"What would you do?"

"I'll come up with a good excuse," she said. "I'm a writer. That's what I do. Make up stories."

She sat back, cupped her hand under her chin thoughtfully, then raised her arm in triumph.

"I know!" she said. "I'll go see her and tell her I was adopted and I'm trying to track down my birth mother who had the same last name she has. I'll ask about her family and when it's clear I'm not a long-lost granddaughter, I'll make friends with her, tell her I've always wanted a grandmother like her. I'll ask if I can come back and see her. She won't be able to refuse.

"Then when you know the story, you can decide what to do."

"Althea, you really have quite an imagination."

"And…?"

"And I couldn't stop you if I tried."

Althea smiled.

"So don't try."

CHAPTER FORTY-SIX

PINEWOOD MANOR

It was hard for me to believe that I was on the trail of an old lady who lived in a retirement home. Susanna was old, in her seventies like Finnigan, but she was, for all that, the fastest moving target in South Jersey.

On my first visit to Whiting in hopes of finding the elusive, but perhaps so near, Susanna, the receptionist told me she had gone to New York to catch the violinist Midori at Lincoln Center.

That first visit to Pinewood Manor had been a surprise, if not a shock. I had expected to find a nursing home full of frail old people, confined to beds or wheelchairs or clinging to their walkers playing bingo or watching television with blank, hopeless eyes.

Instead I found a surprisingly cheerful place that was more like a resort, complete with an indoor swimming pool, library, crafts room, and a dining room as elegant as anything in Philadelphia — or Cherry Hill anyway. Residents who could fend for themselves had their own apartments in the independent living section; there was an assisted living section for those who needed a bit more help to get through their days and, in a separate building, a nursing section for those who required hospital level care.

I expected to find Susanna, elderly, frail, and pathetically eager for companionship, but healthy enough to reconnect with Finnigan, They would spend their last days in matching rocking chairs, holding hands and blessing me for bringing them back together after all those years.

Instead, Susanna was in New York.

On my second visit, Susanna was in Atlantic City for some gambling, a nice dinner, and then Liza Minelli.

The third time would be the charm, or so I hoped as I drove my beloved old Volkswagen down Route 70 from the Benjamin Franklin Bridge ever deeper into the Pinelands.

I was beginning to regret my "what if" taunt to Finnigan. I had plenty of "what ifs" of my own.

What if I wasn't going to bring two old lovers back together for a joyful reunion?

What if I only reopened old wounds?

What if Justin Welch really had been Susanna's one true love and she was alone in the South Jersey Pine Barrens missing him and not Joel Finnigan?

What if it wasn't even Joel's Susanna?

And what if I had just minded my own damned business?

The answer to that last "what if" was clear enough. I knew that if I hadn't gone in pursuit of Susanna, Joel would never learn what had happened since 1945. One of the things that drew Finnigan and me together was our need to at least try to search for the truth, or for the facts anyway. If I hadn't tried to find Susanna, I know Joel and I would wonder forever "what if."

*****

"Am I in luck today?" I asked the fat, jolly woman at the receptionist's desk in the lobby.

"Did I catch her or is she off taking flying lessons?"

"Oh no," the receptionist replied with a laugh.

"Today's bridge day. Susanna never misses that. I wouldn't be the least bit surprised at flying lessons, though."

The receptionist directed me down the main corridor leading into the independent living section. The recreation room was on the left. The square tables were occupied by men and women completely immersed in their cards.

I must've stood in the doorway for a good five minutes.

A kindly woman with sparkling blue eyes interrupted my speculation about which of the bridge playing women was the one I had come to find.

"Can I help you, honey?" the woman asked.

"I'm looking for Susanna Morrison," I said.

"That's her," the woman said, pointing to an elegant, silver-haired woman at the far end of the room.

CHAPTER FORTY-SEVEN

SUSANNA

I started across the room, buoyed by the confidence from my successful computer search. Then I started feeling like Marie Antoinette on her way to the guillotine.

What if it wasn't Susanna? Or what if it was and the memory of Joel Finnigan was not as fond as I supposed? Either way, lying face down beneath the French National Razor might very well feel more comfortable.

But I had come this far and there was nothing to do but press on. I kept going until I found myself standing next to the woman I had come to see.

"Excuse me…"

"Yes?" Susanna replied.

She put down her cards and looked up at me with eyes filled with merriment and great kindness.

"Well… um… my name is Althea Burnside and I…"

"… and you think I may be your long lost grandmother. Wouldn't that be exciting?"

It was a line that could have been delivered with sarcasm, cruelty even, but it was not and it put me instantly at ease.

"I'm not sure but… how did you know?"

"Joy, the receptionist told me. You've been here twice already."

"Yes. I didn't want to bother you until I was sure, or almost sure anyway."

"Nonsense, my dear. This would have been a lovely meeting regardless. Let me finish this hand. Then we'll go back to my apartment and talk about it over a cup of coffee."

This had to be Finnigan's Susanna. She was tall, thin, perfectly groomed and elegant — just the kind of woman I could picture haunting Finnigan all these years.

The hand — and game — were over surprisingly quickly. Susanna bid her bridge friends good-bye and led the way down the main corridor to her one bedroom apartment in the independent living wing. It was small, as befits an older woman with no further use for the grand homes she had lived in over the years. Her shelves held the works of William Shakespeare, Beryl Markham and, to my amazement, Joel Finnigan.

The well read copies of *Silver Wings* and *The Last Campaign* were not tucked away on the book shelves, however. They were out on the coffee table where they could be reached easily. I was beginning to feel certain that I had found the right Susanna.

Any remaining doubts were erased when Susanna went into the small kitchenette to make the coffee, leaving me free to scan the old, framed photographs on the wall. There was a perfectly barbered and blue-suited business type — a bit too pompous looking for my taste — an older man in a sweater whose eyes twinkled over his salt and pepper beard and a tall young officer in the uniform of the U.S. Army, specifically the 101st Airborne Division. I knew that could only be First Lieutenant Joel Finnigan.

I found her! By God, I found her! I was close to tears but I was stopped by Susanna's entrance with the coffee and some petite fours on delicate bone china.

"Now, what makes you think I might be your grandmother?"

Actually, nothing made me think Susanna might be my grandmother. It was the only excuse I could think of to get inside Pinewood Manor.

"My mother's name was Morrison, or it was back in her San Francisco days."

"Ah, San Francisco," Susanna sighed with a wistful smile."I remember it well... much too well.

"But Morrison is quite a common name, Althea. And I never had a daughter, only a son and his name wasn't Morrison. It was Welch. He was my son from my first marriage. My husband gave him his name, but he went back to using Welch as an act of rebellion against us."

"It sounds as though you and your son aren't on the best of terms."

I could tell I had brought up something that saddened Susanna, and I was sorry for it.

"My son died many years ago."

"I'm sorry."

"So am I. We might have put things right. I know we would have, but we never had a chance to do that. He was so angry the last time I saw him..."

Susanna's voice grew husky and I could see her eyes starting to mist up.

"Can you tell me what happened... if you want to?"

Susanna paused, using the quiet moment to compose herself. She refilled our coffee cups.

"You'd think after all these years that it would hurt less. But I don't think you can ever get over the death of your child, especially if you were never able to let him know how much you really loved him. Listen to me! I'm rambling on like a foolish old lady.

"Are you sure you really want to hear all this, Althea?"

Althea put down her cup and gripped both of Susanna's hands.

"Yes. Yes I do, Susanna."

"Did you ever fall in love with the boy next door, Althea? I know it sounds trite, but it does happen."

"Tommy. He was the boy next door. I did fall in love with him... in lust anyway," I said. "What a bastard."

"That happens too, dear," Susanna replied with a chuckle. "I fell in love with the boy next door — well, two doors away. His name was Justin Welch."

My pulse quickened.

"It was a case of family expectations, friendship, and a certain degree of affection. We got engaged when Justin joined the Marines. If you knew him, you'd understand why. I got a job in Philadelphia and settled in to wait for his heroic return. And then Joel Finnigan walked into my life."

I picked up the copy of *Silver Wings*. "*This* Joel Finnigan?"

"Yes, dear, *that* Joel Finnigan. I was working at the jewelry counter when he came in to buy a present for his aunt. He was in the 506th Parachute Infantry and was on a ten-day furlough."

She placed a hand on the book. "*Silver Wings* is about the 506th."

My pulse quickened even more. "Is that his picture on the wall?"

Susanna got up from the couch and took Joel's picture from the wall. She looked at it lovingly and handed it to me.

"This was taken at their camp in France, right after they came back from that Market-Garden fiasco. It was love at first sight. He was what I always wanted, but never thought I'd have, and we decided we wanted to get married as soon as the war was over. Then he went back to Georgia and on to Europe.

"He was in the worst of the fighting — Normandy, Market-Garden, Bastogne. He wrote me that the German army was the only thing standing between us and, boy, were they ever going to regret it."

"You wrote a lot, then?"

"Yes. Most girls wrote lot of letters then. I did almost every day. We shared everything in those letters, our hopes, our dreams, everything. Those were some really steamy letters too, Althea. I never wrote anything like them before, or after. I never wanted to.

"Joel told me his dreams, about the war, the fighting, the challenge of becoming an officer and taking care of his boys… boys! Most of them were about his age, and some of the sergeants were old enough to be his father."

"And what about Justin Welch? Did you write to him too? Did you tell him about Joel?"

"I wrote to Justin, not quite as often, but I wrote. I never told him about Joel, though. I just couldn't send a 'Dear John' into a combat zone. I thought I'd tell him when he got back.

"My tone must have changed, but Justin never seemed to notice. I hoped he'd tell me he was in love with some South Pacific island girl. Of course he was leading a platoon of Marines through some of the worst fighting in the Pacific and I guess he didn't have much time for reflection."

"Did you marry Justin or Joel? What happened?"

A hard grin crossed Susanna's face and for the first time, I saw her looking cynical.

"Justin lost his legs — both of them — on Peleliu. It was one of the last great battles of the war in the Pacific. It didn't accomplish a thing, a total, horrible waste. Joel got home about that time."

Susanna moved closer to me, as if to share a particularly deep secret.

"You should have seen him, Althea. He was tall and fine looking in his uniform… polished jump boots, First Lieutenant's bars on his shoulders, airborne wings, Silver Star and that blue Combat Infantry Badge on his chest. And that night… oh, that night. I couldn't wait to get my dress off. We made love all night."

"Susanna. You don't…"

I was shocked; delighted, but shocked notwithstanding.

"I'm surprised at you, Althea. Do you really think gray haired old grannies don't remember things like that… what it was like?"

"I guess so, but…"

"Well, I do! I remember every second of that weekend with Joel."

"But… Justin?"

"Ah, Justin. Monday morning, when Joel and I were supposed to go down to City Hall for a wedding license, I got a telephone call from Justin's sister. He was in the naval hospital in San Diego. His legs were gone, and he was being transferred to the Naval Hospital in Philadelphia. He'd told her he didn't want me to see him like that, but she was sure he was hoping I'd be there.

"I was still in a wonderful daze from that long weekend of lovemaking with Joel. But that telephone call, that damn telephone call!"

She shook her head, in ancient sadness and wonderment.

"I knew I was in love with Joel, but Justin... our years growing up... our families and everything they expected. I had a duty to stand by Justin, no matter how I felt about Joel. I thought I did, anyway — like a damned fool. If you see me as a foolish old lady now, Althea, you should have seen me when I was a girl. Now that was real foolishness."

"I don't think you're foolish... and you broke the news to Joel when he came for you... to get the wedding license?"

"Yes. He ranted and raved a little bit, and then he stormed out. I was so mad at him for not putting up more of a fight. I don't think it would have taken much to convince me to change my mind. But, I guess I was madder at myself for letting him go... still am."

"So you married Justin?"

"Yes."

"Did life settle down then?"

"Sort of, for about a year. I got pregnant right away. I always thought the baby was Joel's, but I had no way of knowing for sure. Justin went to rehab, and I got a job after the baby was born. My mother helped with him.

"I was a good wife to Justin. I really was, but I must admit that I kept Joel in a special place in my heart. Everything was going along fine until our first anniversary."

"What happened then?"

"Justin left me."

"Now that's a real bastard. I'm so sorry, Susanna."

"I thought the same thing for a while, but now I know it turned out for the best. I wanted to make a big deal out of our anniversary that night. I was going to cook his favorite meal, whatever that was. I set the table with all our best china and silverware, all the stuff you collect as wedding presents… and candlelight, don't forget the candlelight."

"I took little Joel over to my mother's house, and then drove down to Cottman Avenue to pick up Justin at the rehab center. That's when I found out.

"I found him in the lobby, talking with his nurse. They were holding hands and discussing something that was obviously very important. The way they looked at me you'd have thought I'd caught them naked. Another few minutes and I guess I might have.

"'You remember Ramona,' he said to me. I didn't, but it was obvious she had been developing her own special nursing techniques. 'It's not easy to say this, Susanna,' he said. 'Ramona and I are in love. I'm going home with her tonight. I'll be by tomorrow to pick up my things.'

"She pushed his wheelchair out the door and that was that."

"Wow! That must have been rough," I said. "But at least it left you free to go after Joel."

"I did look for him," Susanna said, "but I found out he was married and had a son of his own. I saw him going into the *Inquirer* building on North Broad Street. I almost went up to him, to talk to him, but after Ramona, I couldn't do that to another woman."

"Still playing by the rules, eh?"

"I guess so. I don't think Joel ever found out that I was looking for him. He may have read about the divorce in the legal notices, but I just don't know. I had saved up a little money and Justin had given me a bit more, a goodbye present, I suppose. So I took little Joel and headed west, to San Francisco, as far from Joel Finnigan as I could get.

"I got a job in the loan department of the Wells Fargo bank and married Brad Morrison — Bradford Ingersoll Morrison, if you please — a vice-president. We had a nice house in

Marin County, a beautiful spot, but do you know what I remember best?"

"No."

"It was sitting on the deck, looking out over the Pacific Ocean, and reading *Silver Wings*."

"Joel again?"

"Joel always. I think that's the reason Brad and I never really connected. Don't misunderstand me, Althea, Brad was a good man. He was in love with me. I loved him too, but not enough, not like Joel.

"He did love little Joel. He adopted him and cared for him as though he were his own little boy, tried to do his best for Joel. We sent him to the best schools and he was admitted to Stanford."

"Not bad."

"No. Not bad at all. He started out studying business and finance. Brad always hoped he'd follow him into the banking business, into Wells Fargo itself as a matter of fact."

"It sounds like he was off to a good start."

"Perhaps, but it was the 60s. You aren't old enough to remember the 1960s, dear."

"No, but my mother was part of the San Francisco scene then."

"That was a strange time, Althea. The country had finally emerged from the trauma of World War II and President Eisenhower's 'return to normalcy.' The newer, better world we all hoped for seemed like it was finally at hand. Everyone had their own ideas about what this new world should be like and, naturally, it led to some real conflict. Kids, particularly, were rebelling against their parents all over the country, and we were no exception.

"Joel dropped out of Stanford to become an artist. He was pretty good, too. He had a bit of a following in the San Francisco art scene. He even had a few exhibitions. But, naturally, he wasn't making much money and so Brad thought it was all a waste of time. He was always threatening to cut Joel off if he didn't return to Stanford — to business and finance."

"He didn't, I assume."

"Of course not. Pretty soon Brad and I learned we were at the heart of the international capitalist conspiracy. If there were more artists and fewer businessmen, the ideal world would be ours, Joel said, very frequently and very loudly too.

"He traveled for a while and eventually ended up back in San Francisco in a commune. We lost touch but I know he became part of an anti-war group whose demonstrations became more and more violent.

"He died firebombing a Navy recruiting office. Brad and I saw it on television. I had to go down to the morgue to identify his body — or rather what was left of it. It was horrible.

"After that, Brad and I drifted apart. I think we blamed each other for Joel's death; me for being too indulgent, him for being too unyielding.

"It just wasn't working anymore. I left. Brad gave me a really generous settlement. It was his idea. I didn't sue or anything, and I came back east."

"To Philadelphia?"

"No, to New York. I enrolled at City College. I studied hard, worked in various social service agencies and the next thing I knew, I had a Ph.D in psychology."

"Very good. You're Doctor Morrison, then."

"Only to airline ticket clerks."

"Why them?"

"Have you ever noticed that when you buy a plane ticket, they always ask, 'Miss or Mrs.?'"

"Yeah. It's infuriating."

"Not for me. I just say 'it's Doctor Morrison', and they shut right up. Anyway, I set myself up as a family counselor. Since I've managed to make a mess of all my own relationships, I thought I'd work on other peoples for a change."

"I finally got it right. My practice was going well, and then I met Eric Reilly.

"Eric was a retired psychologist and an adjunct professor at NYU. His wife had died a few years earlier. Since he had been so happily married, he knew what a good relationship was supposed to be. He didn't put me on a pedestal the way Joel had. He didn't need me for a crutch the way Justin did, and he didn't feel any great need to protect me the way Brad had. He loved me, warts and all."

She chuckled mischievously and leaned closer to me.

"Do you know what he used to say to me?"

"No. What?"

"If you were perfect, you'd be a real pain in the ass."

"How can you not love a man like that?" I managed to wheeze out between her laughter.

"You can't, of course. Because Eric was so much older than I was, we decided not to waste a minute. I sold my practice; he sold his house and we hit the road — Europe, the Orient, and Australia. It was a wonderful seven years, until our second trip to Australia."

"What happened?"

"He died, during an intermission at the Sydney Opera House. He was like a British soldier; years before he'd insisted on being buried where he fell. So, we had his funeral in Sydney and I came back to the States.

"You'd think that as you get older, you'd get used to loss, to having the people you love slip away, one by one. But you don't, Althea. Losing my two Joels and then Eric was almost too much for me. I didn't think I could go on living, or even that I wanted to."

"But there's so much life in you, Susanna."

"There is. It was lying dormant after Eric, but it was there. I was moping around, not being very much fun, when a friend told me about Pinewood Manor a few years ago. The idea of being around people and doing things was like the proverbial tonic — a gin and tonic to be precise." She looked at me and smiled wistfully.

"At your age, we must look like we're just sitting around here waiting to die — in God's waiting room so to speak. Perhaps we are, but while we're waiting we're really living so that when it does come, it catches us by surprise."

A soft bell chimed in the distance.

"Speaking of surprises, dinner is about ready. Would you please be my guest tonight?"

"Yes, I'd love to. If you're not sick of me, that is."

Susanna turned off the light in the apartment and motioned for me to precede her into the corridor. We headed for the dining room, arm in arm, the young woman and the old, having shared more than most sisters would have dreamed.

"After all that, Althea, I couldn't possibly be your grandmother. I never could have told my granddaughter about such things."

"No, I guess not. But it feels like I've known you for such a long time. Would it be all right if I stopped in for a visit now and then?"

"Of course. Any time."

We reached the dining room entrance.

"You're a lovely young woman, Althea. I really wish I could have been your grandmother."

CHAPTER FORTY-EIGHT

NOW WHAT?

I had found Susanna. Now what?

I made a delightful new friend. Susanna Winslow Welch Morrison led a fascinating life. She has a lively, truly beautiful spirit, filled with the grace and wisdom that comes with age. I'm looking forward to spending more time with her and acquiring some of that wisdom myself.

But what will I tell Joel?

That if he had done things just a little differently, made just a few corrections in the course of his life, he might have won Susanna and been with her for the past fifty years?

How should I tell him the story of Susanna's life?

How would he react to the tale of Eric Reilly, the one man she loved nearly as much as him?

And what about little Joel — Joel Welch Morrison — a young man who might well have been his son; a young man who had led a pampered, turbulent life and who, ultimately, died an idealistic, horrific death?

I know what Finnigan went through with Giovanni. How would he handle the possibility that he may have lost another son — the son of the woman he had never stopped loving?

I'd promised the full story — the truth, whatever it was. I owe him that. But how will he take it? Knowing that if he had waited, he could have been with Susanna all those years?

As for me, I have a feeling that in learning about Susanna's life, I've also learned something potentially momentous about my own. But I'll have to pull a Scarlettt O'Hara. I'll think about that tomorrow.

CHAPTER FORTY-NINE

ALTHEA'S REPORT

J oel was as excited as a schoolboy. That didn't surprise
me. He had been a professional schoolboy all his life.
He had simply gotten older. He stalked around the
apartment in a mad rush that reminded me of old Alastair Sim's
Christmas morning romp in the classic film *Scrooge*.

"Tell me all of it. I'm dying to hear," he pleaded.

I could swear I heard Scrooge's ditty of self realization:

"I don't know anything.

"I never did know anything.

"But now I know that I don't know,

"All on a Christmas morning."

Come on, Althea. Serious up, I chided myself.

"Out with it, Althea. Every bit of it."

"I'm not certain that I know every bit, Joel. She's beautiful."

"Come on, Althea. She's over seventy."

"She's beautiful... and elegant... my God, Joel!"

"Her life? How was her life? Was it good?"

"It had its good spots, quite a few of them in fact. But
there was a lot of sadness too, and tragedy."

"She was miserable with that Welch. Wasn't she?"

"She wasn't with him that long. Only about a year."

"What happened?"

"He dumped her for a nurse he met at the rehab center."

"The bastard!"

"My thoughts exactly. Susanna's too. He left her with a baby, a little boy."

"The bastard," Joel repeated, snarling this time.

The moment was now. Having come this far, I knew I could not retreat. "The baby could have been yours, Joel, from that weekend on Sansom Street."

"My God! She told you about that?"

"You'd be surprised at the things she told me, Joel."

"Yes. I guess I damn well would."

"She always thought you were the father, but she had no way of being sure."

He shook his head bitterly. "No wonder Welch left her."

I laughed and it sounded very cynical.

"He didn't leave her over the baby, Joel. He had the hots for his nurse; the little head took over for the big head."

"Tell me what she said about the boy," he said somberly.

"She named him Joel. He was an artist in San Francisco."

I took a breath. "He died, Joel."

"Died? What happened?"

"It was some kind of antiwar action back in 1969."

Joel shook his head despairingly and, for the first time, I thought he looked really old.

"I was in California in 1969," he said.

Joel looked off into the distance. I could only imagine what he was thinking.

"What happened after Welch left?" he asked.

"She went looking for you, hoping to put it all back together again."

Joel looked at me in complete amazement. "I never knew... if I had...."

"She did find you. She saw you on North Broad Street once, walking into the *Inquirer* building."

"And she never said anything?"

"She found out you were married, and she didn't want to be a home wrecker."

A look of disappointment and anger came over Joel.

"I am a goddamned idiot, Althea, a first class, gold plated idiot."

"Stop it, Joel! Remember what I said about your aunt."

"I know. I know. If she had balls, she'd be my uncle, but… dammit-all, Althea. If only I'd had the balls to stand my ground and convince her.…"

"You couldn't have convinced her. And you can't go on beating yourself up over what happened. We live the life God intended us to live and we can't complain about it. What were you supposed to do? Pine away for Susanna forever?"

"What the hell do you think I've been doing since 1945?" he snapped.

He shook his head, as if rattling the old ghosts out of their hiding places.

"I'm a foolish old man, Althea, but what's done is done. What happened after she decided not to come back to me?"

I told him everything, from Susanna's marriage to Brad Morrison and their breakup to her success in New York and her all too brief time with Eric Reilly.

I didn't tell him everything about Eric, though. I told of their travels, adventures, Eric's sudden death in Australia and why he was buried there. I couldn't tell him that Eric was the only other man Susanna had really loved.

In my heart, I knew that it had always been Joel, and still was. This was a secret that only Susanna could tell him.

And what of my own emerging question?

Young Joel, who might well be Finnigan's son, was a long dead hippie artist from San Francisco, and my own father, whatever his name was, was also a hippie artist from San Francisco.

Good Lord, Althea, where are you going now?

There was no point mentioning that to Finnigan. I wasn't even sure why it had come to my mind.

"So, Joel, when do you want to meet her?"

"Meet her?"

"Of course. Isn't that what this was all about… so you could find Susanna and reconnect with her?"

"Yes, it's what I've wanted since 1945, but now... now that Susanna is less than a hundred miles away in the New Jersey Pinelands... it scares me half to death. Should I go down to Pinewood Manor and try to see her, or should I just leave everything the hell alone?"

CHAPTER FIFTY

SLEEPLESS

Most people managed to get a decent sleep that night. Tired after a long day at the desk or work bench, delightfully dissipated after an evening of lovemaking or simply worn out by the struggle to get through another day, they collapsed into their beds, pulled up the covers and set themselves adrift on the sea of sleep.

But Joel Finnigan was not among them. There was too much churning around inside his head and there would not be rest until he made some sense of it.

Joel's mind and spirit, restless at the best of times, had been working overtime ever since Althea had burst in through his front door with the news that she found Susanna. He lay in bed, staring at the ceiling and recalling a comment from one of his Army efficiency reports: "This officer displays great skill and initiative in getting out of situations he should never have gotten into."

Could he find the same 40s era skill and initiative to get out of the situation Althea had gotten him into?

Damn Althea anyway! Her with her determination to track a story to the very end and the ability to Google and Dogpile the known world until it yielded its secrets! She clacked and clattered her way across the keyboard until she found the ghost that had been haunting Joel since 1945. But Susanna was not a ghost. She had always been alive deep within him and now she was coming to the fore again.

And who had gotten him into that situation? Certainly not Susanna herself. She had lived her life in Philadelphia, California, New York, and now Pinewood Manor. She had done nothing to maintain him in the state of low-level mourning that he had been in for more than fifty years now.

No. It was him, Joel Finnigan, who was responsible for his present emotional situation, and a sleep period that seemed more irretrievably lost with each passing minute. His sleeplessness was the fruit of his joyous, frightening, trembling school-boy knowledge that his love was close at hand and his fear about what might happen if he reached out for her.

He cursed himself for his foolishness as he twisted his body back and forth in bed. To the rest of the world, Joel Finnigan was the man who parachuted into the snapping fangs of the German Wehrmacht, fended off murderous rednecks in Mississippi, and wrote the history of his people with a vision and style that many — most — reviewers said put him in the same league with Tuchman, Ambrose, and even the great Schlesinger himself.

But they, whoever they were, didn't know the real Joel Finnigan. Looking inside himself during that long night, he saw not the hero of Carentan and Bastogne or the inspiring teacher of Temple University. He saw only a weak, frightened old man, afraid of his own feelings, afraid to challenge Susanna over the most crucial decision of their young lives.

If only he hadn't been too great a coward to stand his ground that morning on Sansom Street.

For him, there would have been no Connie, no Freya Schultz, and no Jenny Keith. Except for Connie, those women had all touched his life, even if only to remind him that, as smart, talented, loving and erotic as they were, they were no Susanna and never could have been.

Connie, with her cold water in the warm shower, her constant demand for attention and her perpetual Terrible Twos, could burn in hell as far as Joel was concerned. She had been out of his life since 1959, and, while his memories of her were now most often amusing, she still had the capacity to stoke his anger.

Freya and Jenny were a different matter, however. They were real keepers, but they weren't Susanna.

"What a damned fool you've been, Finnigan," he cursed silently. He had lost count of the times he had told himself that since 1945, but it had to have been at least once a day.

Now, thanks to Althea Burnside, Susanna was practically within his reach. If she didn't despise him for his emotional cowardice, if... if... if....

If my aunt....

If Joel let her go this time.... if he didn't reach out to see what remained of 1945 and Sansom Street....

Then he really would be a damned fool, with no ifs about it.

That simple realization allowed him to relax and, finally, fall asleep.

*****

Susanna wasn't sleeping all that well either. She couldn't get Joel Finnigan out of her mind and, truth to tell, she didn't really want to.

The fact was Joel had always been with her — ever since that December day when he came to Lits to buy his aunt a Christmas present.

Susanna had fancied herself in love with Justin Welch. She had allowed the expectations of the Welch and Winslow families to convince her that he was the only boy for her.

They had always been good friends, and she remembered more than one occasion when a relative remarked how cute they were together.

And the girls in school all told her how lucky she was to have the captain of the football team gaga over her.

A girl would have to be crazy not to love Justin Welch.

Then along came Finnigan and he rocked Susanna's safe little world. How could she fall so deeply in love in such a short time?

She had already said yes to Justin. She would marry him when he came home from the war. She couldn't send him a Dear John. God knows what might happen. If he was killed, she would blame herself.

Besides, it was kind of romantic to have two gallant men on opposite sides of the globe fighting their way back to her with rifles, bayonets, and their bare hands. She had felt a little guilty reveling in the thought.

But she knew that when Joel returned, she would have no choice but to end her engagement to Justin. She loved Joel too much and Justin would have no trouble getting another girl. Yes, he would probably be hurt and Susanna really hated to think about that, but Joel was Joel. He was everything she had always dreamed of but never thought existed.

His homecoming had been even more than she could have imagined. They had been as close as any two people could be — not just their bodies but their hearts and their souls.

Then came the phone call from Justin's sister that shattered her life and her dreams.

How could she leave poor Justin after he had already lost so much? What kind of person would do such a thing? She would not be able to live with herself. And Joel would never be able to love such a heartless woman.

"What a damn fool I was," she thought. "If only I'd known the real Justin — the heartless bastard who could leave me with a baby — and on our anniversary.

"Why didn't Joel convince me that it would have been a far greater wrong to give up our love? Part of me wanted him to convince me or to take me back to bed and make love to me until I had no will left.

"I can't blame him. He probably loved me too much to want me to spend my life feeling guilty. It would have taken the joy from our life together.

"But couldn't he at least have pined for me for a while? He must have married the first woman who came along.

"And young Joel. Would things have been different? Was he Joel's son? In my heart, I think so. There was always something in him that reminded me of Joel. Would Joel's son have gotten himself killed the way he did if Joel had been there for him?"

What if she could go back and live it over?

What if she hadn't told Joel to leave?

What if she had been honest with Justin? His life probably would have been much the same as it was. He still would have met Ramona.

Susanna and Joel would have had children. Probably young Joel would be among them.

She wouldn't have met and married Brad Morrison, but — good man that he was — she would have no regrets there.

Eric Reilly was another matter. She truly did love him, but if Joel Finnigan had been there, she never would have missed Eric. Joel would have been her life and he would have been enough... more than enough.

She knew something of Joel's life because she had followed his career.

What she didn't know was whether he had been happy. She hoped he had.

If only she had the courage to find him — just as a long lost old friend — but she didn't know how he would react, and besides, she wouldn't know the first thing about how to go about it.

She thought again of their weekend together — the glorious weekend that had warmed her for more than fifty years.

With that thought, her eyes grew heavy and she drifted to sleep.

*****

It was, of all things, the voice and image of Stan Laurel that was keeping me awake. Joel had told me how much he had enjoyed the Laurel and Hardy movies when he was a boy, and after having seen a few of them on AMC, I found myself liking them too.

"A fine mess you've gotten us into now, Ollie," was the theme of my search for Morpheus and all his charms. Stan Laurel wasn't exactly torturing me, but he wasn't giving me much rest either.

The fine mess wasn't entirely about Joel and Susanna. They had wanted to find each other to see what had survived since 1945. It could never be anything like it had been, but I knew that something remained, quite a bit in fact. I had done all I could and it was now up to Joel and Susanna themselves to figure out how to meet and discover what fire there was to be breathed back into their fifty-plus year romance.

No. This time the fine mess was all about me. I couldn't get the story of Susanna's son out of my mind.

Young Joel had been a rebellious hippie artist on the strange scene that was late 1960s San Francisco — just like my father.

My own father! That had been a joke throughout my life and not always a very good one. He abandoned me and my mother and simply vanished into the peace and love, do your own thing, if it feels good do it ethos of that bizarre, self-indulgent time.

Just as Joel and Justin had been forced to live up to their time, my father, whoever he was, had lived up to his.

I had never learned his name. My mother never told me, or she had forgotten. Perhaps Mom had never known his name either. After all, it was the 1960s.

Sometimes — in fact, usually — I blamed my vanished father for the mess I had made of my life. The fiasco of a marriage to Tommy, the ridiculous live-in arrangement with Mark, and the far too many men passing through my revolving door.

"Could it be," I wondered in the darkness of the long night, "that every time a man took me to bed, I was really searching for my father and trying desperately to make him love me in the only way I knew?"

I read that somewhere and wondered what a shrink would make of it.

Sid Burnside loves me and, God knows, I love Sid right back. But as fine a man as he is, as well as he has taken care of me and my mother, Sid Burnside wasn't the one man I really needed to know.

After all these years, I remember the day Mom and Sid sat me down and explained, as best they could, that he wasn't my real father. The absurdity of middle aged parents trying to explain such a complex thing, and such complex times, to a five-year-old girl seemed never to have occurred to Mom and Sid.

It occurred to me, however. I had screamed, "Nononononono," over and over. It seemed a perfectly rational response, even now, and I gave some serious thought to trying it again.

When I was older, Mom tried to talk to me about my father again. She started by talking about her own life in San Francisco where she lived in a commune with a handsome young artist.

They had a baby together. He loved the little girl and thought she was the most wonderful thing in the world, but he wasn't grown up enough to take care of her. So my mother left her baby with other friends in the commune and went to work dancing to get money to take care of them. But she missed the baby too much and finally went home to New Jersey where she met a special man — Sid Burnside. They got married and he adopted the little girl. That little girl was me.

"Why didn't my real daddy want me? Why did you let you take me away?" I had asked.

Mom tried to explain but I just didn't understand. All I knew was that my real father didn't want me and if he didn't want me, I didn't want to know anything more about him. If he had abandoned me, I would abandon him too. Sid Burnside was my father. My only father. He loved me. I didn't need anybody else.

As I lay awake wondering whether Susanna's son could have been my father, I was angry all over again.

Why did I even care?

Maybe because if my father had died so young, he never had a chance to find her.

Maybe if he had lived, he would have looked for me.

"Althea you're being ridiculous," I told myself. "Susanna's son can't be your father. It would be just too weird. If you made up a story like that, nobody would believe it. There were lots of hippie artists in 1960s San Francisco. Most likely, he wasn't the same person."

But I still had to get to the bottom of it. And there was only one way to do that.

I would have to talk to Mom.

CHAPTER FIFTY-ONE

FUDGE RIPPLE MOMENT

Iwas always amused by the spirit of harmony and peace that defined my home town of Haddonfield. Harvard and Princeton graduates promenaded past one another on Kings Highway with cordial nods and, sometimes even smiles. There were even places where Volvos and BMWs could be found parked side by side in perfect contentment.

The town had tried to hang onto its Norman Rockwell movie set style despite the flood of yuppies with their McMansions and grotesque SUVs.

Not that long ago, there were even useful stores along Kings Highway. For many years, I challenged myself to having mall-free Christmases, where I did all of my shopping in town. But those days were fading. Even the book store where I had envisioned seeing *Queen of the Indian King* in the window was gone. I felt a little sad as I drove slowly past the row of tea rooms and gift shops.

There are parts of the United States that have never gotten over the Civil War. Haddonfield, however, was still caught up in the Revolutionary War. The British Union Jacks fluttering before one of the tea rooms, and even one of the Kings Highway McMansions, seemed to indicate a wistful hope that the 42nd Highland Regiment, the Black Watch, would march into town, pipes skirling and kilts flapping in the breeze, to restore graciousness and decency to at least this small corner of New Jersey.

But for all of its pretentiousness, Haddonfield was home. I had grown up in Sid Burnside's big house on Chews Landing

Road and now spent a lot of time hoping to live in a place as full of love and happiness again.

As I turned left onto Chews Landing Road and pulled into the driveway of my parents' home, the source of that happiness was coming out of the house. His step was a little slower than it had been the last time I saw him and there was a lot less hair. But he was at least seventy-five percent the Sid Burnside of old — big, smiling, and tanned as he carried his golf bag out to his Mercedes.

He was bound for a round of golf at the Tavistock Country Club before heading down to Somers Point to get his big Hatteras sport fishing boat ready for a day of marlin fishing.

Sid had all the toys, but God knows he earned every one of them.

"Hi, Punkin," Sid boomed as I got out of my Volkswagen.

"Hi, Daddy," I replied, throwing my arms around his neck and stretching way up on tiptoes to kiss his left cheek.

"I'm going to catch a little golf and then go get the boat ready for tomorrow. Can you join us? It's the big marlin tournament."

"Probably not. I have a couple of chores stacked up."

"Well, if you change your mind…" Sid said as he tossed his heavy bag into the car.

"I'd better clear out before you girls get started."

I watched Sid's Mercedes as it went down the driveway, then I turned and went through the side door directly into the kitchen.

*****

Mom was just finishing loading the dishwasher when I came in. She looked as fit and trim as ever. She walked or rode her bicycle every day. She was as good with deep sea fishing tackle as Sid himself and had a big blue marlin mounted over the fireplace to prove it. I could only hope to look as good as my mother when I reached her age.

"Hi, honey. Let me put on a fresh pot of coffee," Mom said as I stepped into the kitchen.

She switched smoothly from dishwasher to coffee maker. One of the things I always admired about Mom is the way she can shift seamlessly from one task to the next. Going from dirty dishes to clean coffee cups was no big deal, but to me, it symbolized the way my mother had gone through life, switching from Plan A to Plan B without missing a step.

"So," Mom said as we sat down at the kitchen table to wait for the coffee maker to do its stuff, "bring me up to date. What have you been up to?"

"I.. uuh.. broke up with Mark."

"Oh, honey," Mom said sympathetically. "That's too bad... I think. I always liked Mark."

"He was okay, Mom. but only okay."

"In that case, it's probably for the best," Mom said, reaching across the table to take both of my hands.

"Do you want to talk about it? Or is there something else on your mind?"

"My father, Mom. I'd really like to hear about my father."

"Your father? You don't mean Sid, do you?"

"No. My real father — from San Francisco."

"Let me get the coffee. I think this is going to be a long conversation," Mom said as she rose and went to the coffee machine.

She came back from the kitchen counter bearing not just two mugs of coffee but a wistful look and a dreamy girlish smile.

Susanna must have been right. A woman does remember down through the years.

"Your father... your father..."

I marveled at how much my mother, gray hair and all, seemed like a starry-eyed school girl searching for the words to describe her first love.

"He was the cutest boy I'd ever seen. And sexy!"

" Sounds a lot like Tommy and me."

"Yes. I suppose it does."

"And look where that got me."

"Yes, I thought about that when you were getting married to him. But I hoped it would work out for you anyway."

"So, my father was cute and sexy?"

"Yes."

"Tell me everything, Mom," I said. "I should have asked a long time ago."

"I always wondered why you never did. You seemed so angry all the time."

"He didn't want me. Of course I was angry."

"Oh, Althea. It wasn't that he didn't want you. He thought you were the most beautiful, wonderful thing that ever happened."

"I always thought he hated me."

"No! He was just too self-absorbed to know how to be a father, and I think he was afraid to try and learn. And things were a little crazy back then, anyway.

"I used to get mad at him. But he wasn't a person you could stay mad at. He was a real charmer, had a smile that could melt an iceberg."

"Do you have any pictures of him?" I asked.

"Yes. I saved one in case you ever wanted to see it."

She got up and started toward the door to the front hall.

"Come with me, daughter dear."

*****

I gave the cups a hurried rinse and followed my mother up the stairs to the attic.

It was a classic attic and, like any child, I had always loved to play up there. The dust made me sneeze every now and again and in the summer it was terribly hot. But I thought it a small price to pay for the treasures I unearthed there.

And now, so many years since I had last plumbed the inner recesses of my parent's attic, I was thrilled to find that it looked just the same. My childhood, my history, or at least a part of it, remained intact — even if it was only because Sid and Mom had yet to get around to getting rid of all that junk.

Mom navigated around the storage boxes, Christmas decorations and my old baby furniture until she came at the last to the row of suitcases — every one they had ever owned, it seemed.

"Aha! There it is!" she cried triumphantly.

"It's right where I put it back in the seventies," she said with a sheepish grin.

"It" was a battered, obviously well-traveled old piece of really cheap luggage. I recognized it too, which is not surprising since I had moved it any number of times during my childhood archeological digs. It was the luggage a young person of the 1960s would have carried on their first trip into the wider world. It had served Mom on her westward pilgrimage and later when she came back east with me.

It served her still, as a time capsule, a repository of the artifacts of a pivotal time in the great American drama.

Mom sank to her knees, opened the old suitcase, and pawed through the jumble of mini-skirts, a leather fringed jacket, and notebooks full of poetry. In the center of it all was a big manila envelope stuffed with old photographs.

She spread the pictures out on the floor, searching for one in particular. She found it and held it in both hands, studying it in almost reverential silence before handing it to me.

I looked at the photo of my father and understood immediately what Mom meant about not being able to stay mad at him. He did, indeed, have a smile that would melt a heart far harder than mine. Even though the photographic paper had yellowed and faded, I could feel the magnetism that had so completely charmed Mom.

All the anger I had felt toward this impossibly handsome, charmingly roguish stranger faded. He could not possibly have hated his little girl. He just didn't have a clue about how to be her father — something at which good, conventional, loving Sid Burnside excelled.

I examined his face to see whether I looked like him. I'd always thought I looked like Mom, but now I could see that my eyes were the same as my father's — except that his had a mischievous quality that mine don't.

"Tell me about him," I said.

Mom took a deep breath. She held it for a few seconds and then slowly exhaled as the import of the moment descended on her.

"This sounds like a fudge ripple moment, Althea. I just got some; so let's go back down to the kitchen and really enjoy it."

Mom started to rise, abandoned the attempt and looked up at me.

"Would you help me up, please dear. I can't hop around like I used to."

I tucked the picture of my father into my shirt pocket and held both hands out to Mom. She rose, gracefully despite the protestations of advancing decrepitude, and led the way back to the attic stairs.

We descended, not just for the relative comfort of the kitchen nor for a couple of dishes of ice cream, but for a female tribal ritual that had been a vital part of our bond over the years.

Whenever I felt confused by the often tumultuous transition from childhood to girlhood to womanhood — the ever increasing bra sizes and meeting or rejecting boyfriends, sometimes two or three times in the same week — we would sit down and discuss it over ice cream, usually fudge ripple.

I missed the fudge ripple moments with my mother. I was surprised at how comforting the old ritual was as we carried our dishes to the kitchen table. This time, however, our positions were reversed. It was Mom opening her soul to me.

"I see what you meant about his smile, Mom."

"I think you'd call him a hottie today."

"How did you meet?"

"I had just graduated from Rutgers, and I wanted to see the country — the world. I had just enough money to buy an old 1959 Volkswagen Beetle and get it repainted — in hot pink."

"Wow! Hot pink?"

"I thought it suited me at the time. I took off, headed… I don't know where."

"Did anyone back then?"

"No, I don't think we did. We were a whole nation of restless, sometimes angry, young people. We were rejecting our parents' world and striking out on our own — to make a new one, I suppose.

"I spent two months roaming around the country and ended up in California.

"I stopped in San Diego for a while, waitressing at a restaurant in Old San Diego. Then I headed north along the Pacific Coast Highway. That's the most fantastic driving trip in the United States. You should do it.

"Anyway, that's where I met your father. He was hitchhiking along the highway, somewhere between Oxnard and Ventura, I think it was."

"Mother! You always told me not to pick up hitchhikers."

"And with good reason, too. My mother told me the same thing. And I did listen — at first anyway. But by the time I got to California, I was feeling more daring.

"In any case, there stood your father — your father to be — by the side of the road with his sleeping bag and an old Army duffel bag.

"I think I fell in love with him as soon as he got into the car. He was headed for a commune in San Francisco. Since I didn't have any particular plans and I'd always heard that San Francisco was where things were happening, I said I'd take him the whole way.

"They invited me to stay and I decided to — for a little while at least."

"It was a lot more than a little while, wasn't it, Mom?"

"Yes," Mom replied.

We were silent for a bit. I watched my mother's eyes as she relived those long gone days.

"You never told me his name," I said at last.

She looked amazed.

"I never knew his name."

"You never knew his name?

"You had me, his baby, and you never knew his name?"

"He never knew mine either. I don't think anybody knew anybody's real name then. Our parents had named us and we had rejected those names because we were the herald angels of a whole new age... or so we thought.

"I was Wandering Flower, I guess because I'd wandered around the country. Your father was an artist, so naturally, he called himself Picasso. You were Pumpkin because you were so round and jolly."

"Jesus! What did you put on my birth certificate?"

"It says 'Mother: Sara Evans; Father: Picasso O'Rourke.'"

"Picasso O'Rourke? How did you come up with that?"

"I was pretty groggy when I came out of labor — wiped out as a matter of fact. I hadn't planned on having you in a hospital, but the pains were so intense that I was afraid something would happen to you if I didn't. Picasso was sick and couldn't take me."

"Maybe he was scared," I mused.

"After you were born, they asked me your name for the birth certificate. The nurse, a tiny black woman, had been so nice to me that I asked her what her name was.

"'Althea' she said. And I told them, 'Then that's her name too.' When they asked your father's name, all I could think of was 'Picasso.' O'Rourke just popped out. I have no idea where that came from."

Mom looked at me. Her eyes widened and she seemed to be looking for the understanding that I had so often sought from her.

"God, you must think I was a real flake? I guess I was back then."

"You did say it was a crazy time. Why did you leave?"

"I finally realized this wasn't the kind of life I wanted for you. Your father had become really obsessed with the war in Vietnam. We were all against it, but he was going over the top. All he did was paint and protest against the war.

"I left you with other people and danced topless at a bar in North Beach nearly every night. I told myself there wasn't anything wrong with it. The human body is beautiful, and the money I made helped us live a free life. But you already know about that.

"One night — and this is the God's honest truth — a sailor asked me that old cliché question, 'What's a nice girl like you doing in a place like this?' I didn't know what to say.

"I told the manager I'd had enough and that I wouldn't be back. He just looked at me and said, 'I don't blame you, kid.' Then he gave me an extra hundred dollars, right out of his own pocket.

"When I got home, Picasso was stoned as usual. You were sleeping so peacefully. You looked like a little angel. I had a vision of you growing up calling me Wandering Flower and thinking I was no more to you than any of the people I left you with — and maybe less because they spent more time with you.

"I took all my money out of the bank. I had managed to put about a thousand dollars away and this was what it was for."

"And Picasso didn't know about that money?"

"Lord no! He'd have gone through it in a shot. I did give most of the money I earned to the group. It was a commune, after all. But I knew I had to keep something for you and me. I guess I always knew, at some level, that we'd have to make a break for it sooner or later."

"Were you going to tell Picasso or take him with us?"

Mom thought long and hard before answering that one.

"Althea," she said. "When I told him you and I were headed back to New Jersey and that we wanted him to come, he just went nuts. I said he was obsessed by the war. He wasn't just against it. He was consumed by it, and if you weren't as committed as he was, you were part of the problem, part of the imperialist American war machine. There was no talking to him."

"Did you ever see him again?"

"No. But I think he's dead."

"Dead?"

"We had stopped at a motel. We both needed the rest and I was determined to keep you clean and properly fed the whole way. I put you to bed and had just come out of the shower when the TV news reported that a Navy recruiting office in San Francisco had been firebombed in an anti-war action. One of the people was killed."

A chill went through me as I heard a story that was, at least in part, so similar to Susanna's.

"I always thought it was him," Mom said. "I don't know why. I don't think I wanted to know for sure. I just kept heading east. I moved back into my parents' house in Collingswood, signed up for law school at Rutgers in Camden, met Sid Burnside and now, here I am. Mrs. Haddonfield Rich Bitch."

CHAPTER FIFTY-TWO

GRANDPARENTS?

Not knowing where to go next had never stopped me from plowing forward. This particular situation, however, had me stumped.

The story my mother told me about my father was strikingly similar to the one Susanna had told about her son.

Joel Welch had died firebombing a Navy recruiting office in San Francisco back in 1969. Mom believed that Picasso, my biological father, had died in that blast. If Mom was right, then Picasso O'Rourke and Joel Welch were one and the same.

That would mean Susanna really is my grandmother.

There is no way to be sure, of course. But if she was, then Joel Finnigan could very well be my grandfather.

Should I tell Finnigan?

How would he react? Would it make him more or less likely to go see Susanna? What had I gotten myself into this time?

Despite all the angst, it wasn't long before I realized that it would be impossible not to tell Finnigan.

*****

"Are you out of your mind, Althea?"

Finnigan was glad at that moment that he had not fathered a girl. They can, indeed, drive a man crazy.

"What in God's name gives you the lunatic idea that I'm your grandfather?"

"Might be, Joel, might be."

"Okay, might be. It's still a lunatic idea."

"Is it? My father was an artist who may well have been killed firebombing a Navy recruiting office in San Francisco. Susanna's son, who might very well be your son, was an artist who definitely was killed firebombing a Navy recruiting office in San Francisco. Doesn't that at least hint at something, Joel?"

"So? Do you know how many artists there were in San Francisco in 1969? You said your mother only thought it was your father who died in that firebombing. Even if it was him, Susanna doesn't know for sure I was her son's father."

"But don't you want to find out as much as you can? Don't you want to at least explore the possibility?"

Joel could see Althea grasping frantically at the first straw that floated past in her new torrent of emotion.

"Maybe it's why we're together like this, Joel. Maybe it's why we each wrote about Dolley Madison. Maybe it's why we both like to track things down to the end. Maybe it's in our genes."

Joel had to laugh at that one. His anger, if anger it had really been, faded away. He leaned forward in his chair and took Althea's face in his hands.

"Althea, Althea, Althea," he intoned.

"You've taken this as far as it can go. You've found Susanna. I know what happened in her life. That's enough for me. As to this other business, the nonsense about me being your grandfather, I think it is highly unlikely. The similarities between Susanna's son and your father are probably just coincidences — coincidences embellished by your very fertile writer's imagination."

"This can't be the end of it, Joel. You have to see it through."

He drew his hands back.

"It'll have to be enough."

She nodded solemnly.

"Okay, Joel. It's enough."

She said it, but he didn't believe her.

CHAPTER FIFTY-THREE

COLD FEET

J oel woke with assorted aches and pains. He wished someone had told him just how difficult getting old could be. Simply getting old was no great trick in itself. All one had to do was keep from dying too soon.

Joel had mastered that part of it. But he had come to the time where he was wearing out bit by bit as the Type II diabetes, the fluttering heartbeat, fading eyesight, aching joints, and other minor annoyances closed in on him, reminding him that he was a good bit closer to the end than the beginning.

But what bothered him the most, far worse than the knowledge that any one of several vital organs might be about to stop working, was the fear coming over him. He had reached the point in his life where he should know no fear. He had been through the greatest and most terrible moments of his time, and now he was getting closer to embarking on the most mysterious journey of all.

He wasn't afraid of dying. He wasn't really looking forward to it, but he had to admit that he was curious to see what would happen next.

What frightened Joel was in the here and now, or at least at Pinewood Manor.

Althea was right. He was hiding from the truth. He had done a lot of that since she had ventured into cyberspace in search of Susanna. He had realized during that first sleepless night after Althea told him the Susanna at Pinewood Manor was really his Susanna, that he would be a fool to let her go again. But now, in the light of day, when he had to commit to actually going to see her, the fear of what might happen if he did was stronger than the fear of letting her go again.

And now that Althea had established the parallels between the dead Joel Welch and the quixotic and possibly also dead Picasso O'Rourke, the implications were even more terrifying.

He had loved the son he knew wasn't really his. It had never mattered that he was not Giovanni's biological father. But to think he may have had a son with the woman he had loved his entire life, and to consider the possibility of a granddaughter who was also one of the best friends he had ever had, it was all too much.

Joel felt that he should be angry at somebody, but at whom?

Not even a good night's sleep, the time when the mind was supposed to be free to find its natural equilibrium, helped. When the sound of Althea rattling around the kitchen and the smell of fresh coffee finally roused him, he felt pretty good but still somewhat confused, especially by the new set of questions that she set before him the previous evening.

He found her at the kitchen table in her red Temple sweat suit. A half-filled coffee mug and the remains of an English muffin were at her left elbow and the *Camden County Record* classifieds were spread open before her.

"Good morning," he said as he went in search of his own coffee and English muffin.

"Anything interesting in the classifieds?"

"Yeah. There's an apartment over in Haddon Heights that looks good. I think it's time for me to find my own place. I'll probably go see it this afternoon."

"You should. You don't need a dried up old school master for a roommate."

Althea's face softened as she looked up at him.

"Oh, Joel. You've been a life saver. When I walked out on Mark you gave me the space to find myself — ourselves, maybe."

"Now don't start all that grandpa stuff again."

"But don't you want to know for certain?"

"No. I don't, Althea. Susanna… all that… it's in the past. I can't go see her."

"Why not? You've been in love with her for more than fifty years, most of your life. Now you know she lives less than fifty miles away. It's a forty-five minute drive, Joel."

"No. Dammit. I don't want to see her. I… I can't."

"Joel, you feel about Susanna the same way I felt about my father. You're rejecting her because you thought she rejected you. Only she didn't. She tried to reach out to you while you were still working at the *Inquirer*. She spent the rest of her life missing you."

"Don't you act so smug with me, young lady," he snapped. "I have every right to feel the way I do."

"You do, but can't you see that…"

"Can't I see what? You don't even know if she wants to see me."

"She does. She told me so."

"What's the point of all this, Althea?"

"You wanted to know what happened to Susanna. You've wanted to know since 1945 and it's been an obsession. You really have to hear her story."

Joel slammed his mug down on the table.

"No. I damned well do not. You had to find her, Althea. You've used your computer and investigative reporter tricks as some kind of torture technique. Is this your way of paying me back for getting my Dolley Madison book published first? Is that what this is all about?"

Joel knew Althea was stunned. This morning he was a very different man than the one she had come to know over the past few months. She had seen him annoyed, even angry, but she had never seen him erupt like this. It seemed that all of the disappointments of his life could no longer be contained within his increasingly frail body.

Althea got up and took their breakfast dishes to the kitchen.

"I'd better get a shower," she said. "I want to go over and see that place in Haddon Heights."

She left the kitchen and soon Joel heard the shower running. He poured himself a second cup of coffee and went into the study, sunk into his favorite reading chair and stared out the window at the traffic making its way up Spring Garden Street toward the Art Museum.

There was a Renoir exhibit at the Art Museum that he wanted to see. He'd probably go this weekend.

But there were more important things on his mind.

He was still sitting and looking out the window, the coffee having long since gone cold, half an hour later when Althea slipped quietly into the study.

She looked young and vital in her jeans and polo shirt and she was wearing a ridiculous red Phillies baseball cap.

"I'm sorry, Althea. Please come in for a moment before you go."

Finnigan stood and they wrapped their arms around each other.

"I shouldn't have blown up like that. I'm sorry."

"No. I'm sorry," she replied. "I pushed too hard. I guess I should have minded my own business."

"No. You were right. I'll never be free if I don't learn the truth, whatever it turns out to be. If my life is ever going to mean anything, I'll have to find out if I've been lying to myself all these years. Will you go down to the Pines with me, Althea? Next Wednesday? That's her bridge day. Isn't it?"

CHAPTER FIFTY-FOUR

THE VISIT

"There was an old paratrooper named Sergeant Finnigan..."

Althea was in a playful mood as she and Joel drove along Route 70 ever deeper into the New Jersey Pinelands. Her attempt to sing the little ditty both annoyed and mystified Finnigan.

"Where did you learn that bit of nonsense?" he asked.

"In your book, *Silver Wings*."

"You read that?"

"I've read all your books, Joel."

"You must have had damn little to do, reading about an old fart babbling about his glory days. I'm surprised at you."

She smiled, and they both fell silent until they passed a sign welcoming them to Whiting. From there, it was just a few hundred yards farther down the road until they turned into the Pinewood Manor parking lot. Althea smoothly slipped Finnigan's old Mercedes into a slot between a Cadillac and an outlandishly huge Ford Expedition.

"Stand in the door, Sergeant Finnigan," she commanded. "I'm the jumpmaster now."

Joel's right leg had stiffened up on the long drive from Philadelphia and it took him a few seconds to swing around so he could put his feet out through the car door and plant them on the pavement. He stood and closed the car door. His leg had loosened up and he was feeling a bit younger, not like he had been in his Army days, but like a boy of sixty, at least.

Althea came around from the driver's side, took Joel's left arm and guided him toward the front door.

He hesitated.

"Come on, Joel," she said. "We've come this far. We can't turn back now."

They went in, identified themselves at the front desk, then walked into the long hallway leading to the independent living recreation room.

"Look to the right... at the front of the room," Althea told Finnigan.

He looked beyond a sea of white fringed heads, adjusted his glasses and looked again.

Then he saw her.

Susanna was immersed in her bridge game.

Joel let his eyes settle on her for the first time since 1945.

God, she was beautiful, even after all these years. Or maybe because of them. Everything faded away — Althea, the roomful of bridge players, even the walls of Pinewood Manor themselves — as he focused on the most lovely woman he had ever seen.

He did the only thing he could. Joel Finnigan ran like hell. He was striding across the parking lot nearly as briskly as he had once strode across France, Holland, and Germany.

"Joel! Stop!" Althea gasped.

Joel reached his Mercedes, turned and leaned back against the trunk. He folded his arms across his chest and stared fixedly down at the pavement.

Althea put her right hand on his left arm.

"What's gotten into you, Joel?" she asked gently. "I thought you were ready for this."

"I was... I thought I was, anyway. But after all these years, I didn't know what to say. I... I felt like a tongue-tied schoolboy."

"That's exactly what you're acting like. But you're not a boy. You're the man who jumped out of airplanes and took on the whole German army, for God's sake."

"How smart did I have to be to do that?"

"Smart enough not to let the love of your life get away again. Let's go back in."

Joel took a deep breath.

"Okay. Let's try again."

Joel heaved himself off the car trunk and straightened up.

*****

Susanna sensed something, and turned her head to look around the room. She thought she saw a familiar face near the back of the room near the double doors.

Her heartbeat barely had time to quicken when her partner summoned her attention back to the game.

"Your play, Suz"

"What? Oh sorry."

Susanna played her card and looked back towards the doorway.

It was empty.

Susanna remained focused tightly on her bridge game. She looked back toward the doorway a couple of times, but saw no one there.

"Maybe you really are old enough to be having a senior moment," she chided herself. It was strange, though. Her heartbeat felt faster than usual.

Then it began to hurt. Just a small pain in the middle of her chest, at first. Then it grew into a searing, crushing feeling that radiated upwards and outwards into her shoulders and then her arms. She tried to rise, but her knees felt all rubbery and she slumped back down in her chair. Her head lolled forward until her chin nearly touched her chest and her arms flopped listlessly to her side.

She could hear the weekly Pinewood Manor bridge tournament come to an instant halt. The room filled with gasps and horrified cries. She saw nurses and attendants rush through the double doors and race toward the front of the room. But they gained not a step on Joel Finnigan who was running toward his

stricken Susanna every bit as fast as he had run down that deadly road into Carentan.

CHAPTER FIFTY-FIVE

BYPASS

Joel had never felt quite as helpless as he did while he was standing in the Pinewood Manor recreation room watching the attendants and the resident nurse working furiously on Susanna. They eased her out of her chair, stretched her out on the floor, and went to work to save her life. Arnie Nielsen, a brawny attendant, administered CPR with such enthusiasm that Joel thought he was going to break one of Susanna's ribs.

Better a broken rib than a stopped heart. Still, he felt a distinct sense of relief when the nurse, Marion O'Dowd, rushed up with a portable defibrillator. Marion's nimble, well trained fingers deftly unbuttoned Susanna's blouse and placed the electric paddles on her chest. "Clear!" she shouted as she sent a jolt of electricity coursing through Susanna.

"Come on Susanna, don't leave us now, dammit," Arnie shouted as Marion listened through her stethoscope.

"Don't shout, Arnold," Susanna said weakly.

"We've got her!" Marion said triumphantly.

"Heartbeat's normal... breathing's normal."

She looked down at Susanna with a gentle smile.

"You're not going anywhere just yet, young lady," she said.

"I certainly hope not. My game's not finished yet."

"Where are you sending her?" Joel asked Marion.

"Community Hospital in Toms River," she replied.

The paramedics from the Whiting Volunteer Ambulance Squad wheeled a gurney into the hall, carefully put Susanna on it and wheeled her out the door and into the waiting ambulance.

*****

Joel and Althea arrived at Community Hospital just as Dr. Len Adcock was ordering Susanna taken upstairs from the Emergency Room. He was filling out his admissions report when Joel found him at the nurse's station.

"How is she, Doctor?" he asked

"Are you family?"

"... the closest she's got."

"She needs emergency bypass surgery. A cardiac surgeon from Deborah Heart and Lung is on her way. She's the best."

"How long?"

"The surgery can take several hours. Then she'll be in intensive care for a while. Only immediate family can visit her in the ICU."

"I said she had no family. I just don't want her to wake up alone."

"What's your name?"

"Joel Finnigan. We've been friends for years."

"I'll tell her as soon as she wakes up, Mr. Finnigan. If she say's it's okay, you'll be able to go in."

*****

"What do you want to do?" Althea asked. "Do you want to wait? Do you want to go get something to eat and come back? Do you want to go home and call later to see how she is?"

An avalanche of feelings cascaded over Finnigan.

Althea must have sensed that he felt totally lost.

"We'll wait until we hear something," she told him.

"You go get something to eat. I need some time alone," Joel said in an unusually subdued voice.

"Are you sure?"

"Yes. I left her once. I can't leave her now."

He handed Althea the keys to the Mercedes. She took them, stretched up to kiss his cheek and left him to his thoughts.

As Joel sunk into one of the overstuffed waiting room chairs, it seemed that relaxing the strain on his body left his mind free to wander through a thick, confusing forest of feelings.

At first, he could not help but to roam backward. It was simply in the nature of old men. A smile crossed his lips as he relived their first meeting at the Lit Brothers jewelry counter and the too long, but oh so short, lunch hour at Logan Circle.

Of the war, he recalled nothing but their letters. The long, hard training at Camp Toccoca, jump school, the horrors of Normandy, Hells Highway, and the cold of Bastogne were all supplanted by the memories of their letters planning in exquisite detail the new life they were to begin together when he returned.

He stopped at the memory of that warm August night in 1945 when he and Susanna made love over and over again. It remained as fresh and green as it had ever been. It was to have been the beginning of the wondrous life he and Susanna had planned.

What would be their future now? What was ahead for Joel and Susanna? He was a good many years past the tall, dashing airborne officer of 1945, and she was no longer the long legged, trim, erotic girl he once knew.

They still had a great deal to share, including the stories of two long, eventful lives in which they hovered in one another's background. They had quite a bit to share, as a matter of fact — if Susanna wanted and if her heart allowed it.

The memories and hopes for the future faded as Joel slipped into a proper sleep. It was not a particularly comfortable sleep thanks to the odd contortions encouraged by the waiting room chairs and the nagging fear of losing Susanna again.

He drifted along until a distinctive, delicious smell began nudging him back toward the surface.

"Beef barley," he mumbled.

"Right. I got it from the restaurant down the road." Althea said, handing him a hot cup of soup. "You haven't had anything since breakfast."

Joel felt the weakness in his knees and the beads of sweat forming on his forehead.

"Thanks," he said. "I think my blood sugar is starting to crash. I shouldn't have gone so long without eating something, but…"

"I'll get you some orange juice. You get started on the soup."

Orange juice and beef barley soup is nobody's idea of a gourmet meal, but it was just what Joel needed at the moment.

*****

Joel was out of the chair and practically standing at attention in the proverbial flash as soon as Doctors Len Adcock and Inga Cummings came into the waiting room wearing the tired but triumphant expressions of a pair of athletes coming off the field after a tough game.

They had won. The surgery had gone not just well, but perfectly. Susanna would be asleep for a long time yet. When she awoke, she would feel as though the Philadelphia Eagles had been scrimmaging on her chest. And Joel would be there.

CHAPTER FIFTY-SIX

REUNION

Dr. Adcock let Joel see Susanna for just a brief moment when she woke in the ICU. She had opened her eyes, looked lovingly into his eyes, then gone back to sleep.

Joel would happily have slept in the waiting room all night, but Dr. Adcock insisted he go home.

"We'll be moving her to regular room tomorrow. You can spend more time with her then," he said.

*****

Susanna was asleep when Joel and Althea arrived the next day.

Joel sat quietly beside the bed staring lovingly at her. Althea sat in a chair at the foot of the bed reading Lisa Scottoline's latest mystery.

Susanna slowly opened her eyes. She looked directly at Finnigan, probing as tentatively as a child at the beach testing the water with her toes.

"Joel?" she asked. "I thought I was dreaming. You really are here?"

He took her hand. "Yes, my love. I'm here."

She started to raise her head. Finnigan stopped her.

"Rest," he said.

Susanna blinked her eyes, still not quite accustomed to the light.

"They took my glasses. Isn't that a terrible thing to do to an old lady? Who's that at the foot of the bed?"

"It's me," Althea said, standing and taking Susanna's glasses from the bedside table. "Althea Burnside. Here are your glasses, Susanna."

"Thank you, dear," Susanna said, taking the glasses and putting them on. "That's much better. It's good to see you again, Althea," she said, turning back to look at Joel again.

"Joel, how did you...?"

Althea interrupted.

"Excuse me. I've got a couple of errands to run. I'm sure you two have lots to talk about. I'll be back in an hour or so."

She left her book on the chair and slipped out of the room. Joel and Susanna barely noticed her departure.

"Joel, you're really here? You're not a dream?"

"I'm not a dream, Susanna. I just hope I'm not a nightmare."

"My dear Joel. Seeing you could never be a nightmare."

"I'm amazed you recognized me after all these years," he said.

"Nobody ever looked at me the way you do, Joel. I thought I saw you at Pinewood... when?"

"Yesterday, at the bridge tournament."

"Was it only yesterday? I thought I saw you just before I went down. Then I...."

"You had other priorities."

"You could say that, I suppose," she chuckled, then grimaced. "Don't make me laugh, Joel. It hurts... After all these years, how did you find me?"

"It's a long story and you need your rest."

"There will be plenty of time for resting," she said as she sat up. "Get your arms around me before you dot another i, Joel Finnigan."

And he did, taking great care not to press too hard against her sorely abused chest.

It had been a lifetime since Joel and Susanna had last had their arms around each other.

It didn't matter anymore. They had survived those years, and now here they were in a room at Community Hospital acting like a pair of love besotted teenagers. The sagging skin, wrinkled faces and silver hair had vanished. Joel saw, and felt, the beautiful young woman he had met at the Lit Brothers jewelry counter back when he was a tall, fit young paratrooper who had gone to buy a gift for his Aunt Kate.

There was no past. There was no future. There was only a present in which two souls knew each other and loved each other and were blind to anything but the truth of the spirits that were locked in their increasingly frail bodies. It was one of those rare times of perfect understanding.

"Joel, we have so much to share," Susanna said, finally pulling away. "Would you raise the bed up a bit?"

Joel did as she asked and she settled back and took his hand.

"I've read all of your books…"

"What," he replied with surprise that was only partly feigned, "you actually waded through all that stuff?"

"All of it. They were brilliant, Joel. Everything you wrote — the war, the civil rights years, Bobby Kennedy, even your book about Dolley Madison — made the years much easier. But what I really I want to know, my love, is what wasn't in your books."

"Now that I'm with you, those years are a blank," he said.

"Were you happy, Joel? I always prayed that you were."

"I suppose I was as happy as I could be without you in my life. I'll tell you about it when you're feeling stronger. Althea did tell me something about your life."

"Althea, what a lovely girl, Joel! I told her how lovely it would have been if I'd been her grandmother."

Joel shook his head. "She seems to think you might be."

Joel told Susanna about Althea's father and about her mother's belief that he'd been killed firebombing a recruiting office in San Francisco back in 1969.

"Hmm," Susanna said, "That would be quite a coincidence, but I suppose it could be. Does she have a picture of her father?"

"I don't know. We can ask her when she gets back."

"Wouldn't it be wonderful if does turn out to be true, Joel? I always felt in my heart that you gave me a baby that first time we made love. I always believed Joel was your son, and if by some remote chance, he happened to be Althea's father... well, I'd be very happy to think she is the result of our time together and our contribution to the world."

"Is that what you want to believe, Susanna?"

"It would be nice, Joel, nicer than anything I can think of."

"Then believe it, my love; believe it."

"I'm awfully tired," Susanna said, "and my chest feels like a truck ran over it. Will you stay with me Joel... please?"

"Of course, I'll be right here when you wake up."

He pushed his chair closer to the bed. Then he lowered his angular frame into it and closed his eyes without once letting go of her hand.

A smile crept across Susanna's face as she gradually let go of the world.

CHAPTER FIFTY-SEVEN

HOME AT LAST

Susanna's recovery was long and slow, which was what they expected. She had had a heart attack and that, combined with her open heart surgery left her with the distinct feeling that a very large gentleman was tap dancing on her chest.

"I don't really mind," she said. "An enforced rest will give us a chance to get caught up."

'There's a lot to get caught up on," replied Joel, "1945 till now."

"Don't worry about the old days, Joel. I lived through them too…. don't forget, I've read all your books… and your letters."

His weathered face reddened with a hint of embarrassment.

"So Althea said. Did you really have to tell her about… Sansom Street?"

"I did; and as soon as I get out of here, I want to start on all the days ahead of us."

They were together and — as strange as it was and as different as their lives had been since 1945 — it seemed as though they had never been apart. They were as at ease with each other as though they had spent the last fifty years together. They seemed more like a couple who had grown old together than one who had just found each other.

Joel moved in with Susanna in Pinewood Manor while she recovered. It was easier because all of her things were there and she was closer to her doctors.

Their first night together — the first since that erotic weekend on Sansom Street more than fifty years ago — was even more filled with love. There was no passionate sex. Susanna was far too weak and Joel was already feeling the effects of his years and his Type II diabetes.

"What I used to do all night now takes me all night to do," he said ruefully.

But it didn't matter. Susanna lay with her head against his chest in the crook of his arm. They held each other tenderly and the love that flowed between them filled them with the same warmth they had felt in the afterglow of their most passionate sex. They talked and kissed and loved and talked some more.

When Susanna was recovered enough, she moved to Joel's apartment in Philadelphia. Althea had found her own place but had cleaned and put out a bottle of Jamesons, two snifters, a box of Godiva chocolates, and freshly cut flowers to welcome them home.

"This is lovely, Joel," Susanna exclaimed when she entered the apartment and saw what Althea had left for them.

"Althea really is a lovely girl."

"Yeah; she's a good kid," he replied.

"Do you really think she might be our granddaughter?"

"I don't know. I'm an historian, don't forget. I can only deal with the provable record. Only novelists can go into the land of 'what if.'"

"Well, I can, Joel Finnigan and I'd like to think she is."

It had been a long drive up from the Pinelands. Traffic along Route 70 had been impossible, which left Susanna worn out by the time they reached their destination. Joel got her settled into his old, comfortable chair by the front window, then walked over to the table where Althea had set out the Jamesons and chocolates.

"How about a nice Jamie?" he asked.

"I don't know, Joel. Doctor Adcock didn't really say anything about drinking."

He poured out one Jameson's for himself.

"Well, they say if Ike had had his usual brandy back there in '55, he might not have had his heart attack."

He paused, the dark green bottle poised over the glass.

"I am the historian here, you know."

Same old Joel, she thought… thank God.

"If there's an historical precedent, then."

He poured Susanna a drink and carried it to her. She took the glass with a smile and continued her contemplation of the view down Spring Garden Street.

"Remember where we were planning to go that last morning in '45?" Joel said softly.

"Yes," she replied with a grin. "City Hall."

He took her hand.

"So, how about tomorrow we pick up where we left off?"

*****

They were married at St. Tom's in Chester, as they had planned in 1945. The wedding was smaller than it would have been back then. There was no family left on either side, unless you count Althea who was convinced Joel and Susanna were her grandparents because they all wanted it that way.

Althea wouldn't show Susanna any pictures of her father, Picasso O'Rourke, and she refused to take any DNA tests.

"Let's just take it on faith," she said.

CHAPTER FIFTY-EIGHT

FELIX REDUX

Joel couldn't help but break into a grin when he was finally able to take his eyes off Susanna and look around the dining room. The room was aglow with soft electric lights, and even some candles, glittering off the exquisite glassware and dinner settings. Perfectly tuxedoed waiters scuttled back and forth bearing magnums, tureens, exotic looking dinners, and sterling silver coffee pots that gleamed of their own accord. There was a great and constant to-ing and fro-ing from what looked like the most modern, high-tech kitchen on earth.

"Felix's sure is a lot more elegant than it was in 1944," he said. "The waiters were all wearing sweaters and most of the food seemed like it had been scrounged from British or American supply dumps. God knows the French didn't have much then."

"Where were you sitting when you wrote me that letter?" Susanna asked.

He looked around the room, bewildered by the extensive remodeling it had undergone since December of 1944.

"Damned if I know. It's all been changed around."

His eyes focused on a spot just to the right of the wide double door to the kitchen.

"Over there, somewhere, I think. I'd just ordered some kind of mystery meat sandwich when this big MP Sergeant came over with orders for me to get back to the unit."

"That must have been a surprise," she said.

"It ruined my whole Christmas."

"Were you as surprised as that marriage license clerk at City Hall; or that nice Father McGinn at St. Tom's?"

Joel reached across the table to take her hand.

"You'd think they'd never married a couple of old farts before, Mrs. Finnigan."

"Senior citizens. Joel, senior citizens. We are at the most elegant restaurant in Paris, remember. The same one that you wanted us to come back to after the war."

"Not this long after the war," he replied. "We really are a couple old farts now."

Phillippe, the waiter who had just arrived with their dinners, understood enough English to feign shock at Joel's observation.

"But I always knew it would happen, sooner or later."

She squeezed his hand. Her eyes glittered. "Did you really?"

"Of course. Why do you think I fought the war? Remember those fotomat pictures we took?"

"Oh, God, I must have looked ridiculous."

"You looked beautiful. I carried that picture all the way from Normandy, through Holland and Bastogne, all the way to Germany."

"All the way to Germany," she mused. "I carried my copy of it all the way through… Philadelphia during the war. We never lost sight of it. Did we?" she asked, almost plaintively.

"… not through everything that happened?"

"No," Joel replied. "We might have gotten distracted, but deep down, at the core, I think we both knew that sooner or later it had to come to this."

CHAPTER FIFTY-NINE

BASTOGNE AGAIN

T he sun illuminated Susanna's face in a warm, golden glow as Joel guided their rented Mercedes eastward along the A34. They had reached Rheims after their first, easy day from Paris and were pushing on to Bastogne.

Susanna leaned back in the comfortable leather seat and closed her eyes against the glare. She looked more relaxed and contented than she had in a while

Joel sat behind the big plastic steering wheel so beloved of German car makers with his eyes flickering over the highway and the countryside on either side.

"This is a lot better than the last time I came this way," he observed. "That Jeep was freezing cold; most of the trip was at night so we couldn't see anything.

"Then, when the sun did come up, I wished it had stayed dark. I'd helped create carnage like that — in Normandy, up Hell's Highway, lots of places. But when we came up here to Bastogne, I really got to see the bombed out towns, the destroyed fields, the dead cows and horses, all bloated up with their legs sticking straight out…"

"What do you think we'll find in Bastogne?" Susanna asked.

"I don't know. I hope there'll be some sign they remember us."

"Haven't you been back since the war?"

"Not to Bastogne. I've been over to a couple of history conferences in the UK and France. In fact, it was when I came from a Market-Garden conference that I found Connie practicing her… sword swallowing."

"Sword swallowing," Susanna replied in an amused tone. "Did they really call it that?"

"They still do, love," Joel replied, "You never heard it called 'sword swallowing'?"

"Of course not! Nice girls never even heard of such things, Joel Finnigan!"

Ahead, the first sign welcoming them to Bastogne appeared.

"Place McAuliffe," she said as they drove into the central town square that had been named after the 101st Airborne Division commander during the Battle of the Bulge.

"It looks like they remembered you."

"They remembered General McAuliffe, anyway," Joel replied with a grin. "There aren't any Place Finnigans around here."

"Is that one of the tanks that rescued you?" Susanna asked as they drove past an M4 Sherman tank on a pedestal in the middle of town. It was neat and clean in fresh looking olive drab paint and looked, generally, like it was ready to go another round or two.

"Could be," Joel said. "What does it say in the tourist guide?"

"That one's from the 11th Armored Division," Susanna said. "According to the book, it got into town just in time for the Germans to knock it out of action somewhere near Reaumont and capture the crew."

"The ones that saved us were from the 4th Armored Division," said Joel. "I wonder if those guys survived the war?"

"Tanks are ugly looking things, Joel," Susanna said, "but I guess they made great Christmas presents that year."

"They were beautiful. I… Jesus H. Christ on a pogo stick! I don't believe this."

Joel's mouth dropped open in shock. He couldn't utter a sound, but pointed a shaky finger to a sign above the elegant doorway leading into a decidedly upscale looking café.

La Brasserie Jaworski

"That doesn't look like a Belgian name," she said. "Not French sounding enough."

"No. It isn't," Joel said. "We've got to check this out."

He pulled the Mercedes into a parking spot not far from the commemorative tank. He climbed out, more slowly and painfully than he would have had he been exiting his Jeep in 1944. He helped Susanna out of the car and together they picked their way across the cobblestoned square toward Le Brasserie Jaworski.

If the outside sign wasn't enough of a shock, the display in the entrance lobby certainly was.

"Bastogne's Best Coffee," proclaimed a banner on the wall to the right of the door. Over it was an enlarged photograph of three American soldiers, cold, unwashed but trying to summon up smiles, standing ankle deep in snow, holding GI canteen cups full of a steaming brew.

Joel bent forward to study the picture. He ran his fingers lightly over each one.

"That's Ed Ruth, my First Sergeant, on the left," he said. "On the right is Major Arnold, our old CO and the battalion Operations Officer."

Susanna stood on her tip toes and squinted.

"And that's you in the middle, Joel. The tall one with the rifle."

"Yes, it damned sure is," he replied.

"May I help you, Monsieur — Madame?" the maître'd inquired. He was a tall, dark haired young man whose English, while French accented, was excellent.

"Yes, young man" replied Joel. "You can tell me about that picture. That's me in the middle, between the other two soldiers."

The maître'd was astonished, recoiling with shock.

"You....," he mumbled. "You are Lieutenant Finnigan... the great Finnigan?"

"Nobody's called me that in a long time, kid."

The maître'd recovered his senses and his poise.

"Come. Let me show you to your table. Then I must fetch grand-pere. He'll be thrilled."

Joel and Susanna took their seats. A waiter brought their menus and the handsome maître'd scuttled off as he had not scuttled since he was a waiter. Joel and Susanna ordered two coffees and perused the menu while grand-pere was sought.

Grand-pere relied upon a cane when he finally came slowly into the dining room. Except for that, and his tri-focals, he seemed fit and alert. His aging could not disguise his identity as he came across the dining room, stopped and tried to raise his right arm in a salute.

"Lieutenant Finnigan," he said. "Welcome to La Brasserie Jaworski, sir."

Joel rose, and with a huge smile, wrapped his arms around Paulie Jaworski.

"Cut that 'sir' crap, Paulie; that was more than fifty years ago."

"Not around here, sir….sorry, Joel. You were right when you said folks would remember what we did here for the next hundred years. There's ten year old kids here who talk about the Battle of the Bulge like it was last week."

It was that historic memory that stood Paulie Jaworski in such good stead and resulted in what looked like a damned good living if not an outright fortune.

"I remember you becoming somewhat famous for the coffee you were making up at our CP. Don't tell me that led to all this."

In fact it had, he told them. Not long after the siege of Bastogne was lifted and the 506th moved toward the east, Paulie found promotions coming his way with increasing rapidity — Corporal, Sergeant and, by the time the war ended, Staff Sergeant. Major, later Colonel, Arnold, always told him that the promotions were because of his mastery of the Army's paperwork.

Paulie, however, always suspected that the coffee he made at the Company B Command Post had more than something to do with it. He had 'liberated' it from Claude LeClerc's small coffee shop when the paratroopers first marched into Bastogne and he always felt somewhat guilty that his success had been built on what the less charitable members of the U.S. Army might think was a theft.

So, a few years after the war, Paulie took a vacation from his office job in Pittsburgh and came back to Bastogne to at least thank Claude for the 'gift' of his coffee.

Claude, as it turned out, had a lovely daughter named Brigitte, whom he hoped would take over the business. One thing led to another in the usual boy-girl run of things. Brigitte LeClerc ended up as Mrs. Jaworski and matriarch of a steadily multiplying band of Belgian Jaworskis and, with her husband Paulie, operator of the small restaurant and coffee shop that simply had to be named Le Brasserie Jaworski.

"But the picture, where the hell did you find that?" asked Joel.

"Don't you remember, sir? When the 4ᵗʰ Armored finally got here and it looked like we'd get to live a little longer, I put on a pot of special coffee to celebrate. Then Major Arnold came up to get a report and he had to have a cup too. There was a war correspondent with him. He took the picture and gave me a print."

"And now it's a poster," Joel said with a grin.

"I guess so," replied Paulie." It'll always mean something in this town, though. Like I said, you were right; what we did here will last forever."

"He's right, you know," Susanna said later that night on the drive back to Paris.

"I've read all the stories, but I never really felt it until today; the tank in the Place McAufliffe, the Mardasson Monument.... all of it."

Joel felt his face soften as he drove into the setting sun.

"Just think, we lived through so much of it. We made so much of it happen."

She reached out and placed her hand on his leg.

"Yes we did, love. Yes we did."

CHAPTER SIXTY

CONTENTMENT

Joel marveled that life with Susanna was as wonderful as he always knew it would be.

Sometimes he still felt sad about how long it had taken them to finally get together. He thought about the long, beautiful life that he and Susanna could have had together — the years of living with someone who really understood and loved him in spite of his long catalogue of faults.

But all that would be over now anyway and they would still be where they were — sharing their old age together. He'd have still lost a son, not Giovanni, but the son he had with Susanna, young Joel.

"I've had a good life," he wrote in his journal. "I fought for things I believed in, and I hope I've had a positive influence on my readers and my students.

"And, of course, there was *The Belle of Haddonfield*. It brought me a degree of fame, but even more it brought me Althea Burnside. She opened the way to everything else.

"We still visit often and she's taken to calling Susanna Grams and me, Gramps — which I both love and hate. Gramps always makes me think of a toothless old codger, but coming from Althea, it's a joy to hear. She gave me back Susanna. And she helped me understand what my life has meant."

CHAPTER SIXTY-ONE

ALTHEA'S DIAMOND

Seeing Joel and Susanna together has shown me what a real relationship should be. It's what I've yearned for my whole life. I'm not going to settle anymore or talk myself into believing I'm in love because I want to be.

Everything seems so clear to me now. It's as though I was living my life behind a veil and by helping Finnigan discover his truth, I ripped it away and saw my own.

Gee, Althea, that's deep. You're so insightful. But what does it all mean? Is your life suddenly going to become perfect?

Yeah. Right.

There I go, being sarcastic again. I really do feel different. Like there is a sense of peace deep in my gut. Like I can go on and move forward instead of running around in a maze of my own creation.

Imagine Althea Burnside going with the flow instead of trying to control everything. I kind of like it.

I'm working at the paper again. This morning I got an idea for a new book. Not really an idea, more a kernel of an idea. I was reading an article in the *Times* about people being made into diamonds after they die. No kidding. They stop the cremation and extract the carbon and send it to this place where it's purified. Then they ship it to a diamond press in Russia. The final product is certified at a gem lab in New York. One couple said they were going to have themselves made into quarter carat diamonds for each of their five kids.

Can you say weird?

Anyway, I see horror or mystery novel written all over it.

Suppose a woman had her husband made into a diamond necklace and he strangled her when she was fooling around with another man?

Or suppose a funeral director was killing people to get the carbon in their bodies to make into diamonds? The possibilities are endless.

CHAPTER SIXTY-TWO

HARRY

B oy, the life of a girl reporter. That's what some lecherous old editor called me back in the day. I like 'girl reporter' a lot more now than I did then.

But the thing I like best about newspapering is that there's never a dull moment. I always get out of bed in the morning without the faintest idea of what the day will bring.

Take today, for instance.

Today, Harry Rutledge told me he loves me.

The same Harry from my party where I trapped Mark Steinfeld.

Harry marched across the *Record* newsroom straight to my desk. I was pounding away on the old keyboard, putting the finishing touches on the story about a Camden County Grand Jury's indictment of the mayor of Lindenwold. Harry banged his fist down on top of my old computer and made my poor pixels skip a beat.

"Life is too damned short to leave things unsaid," he proclaimed.

Harry learned his trade when reporters were taught to get straight to the point. He did exactly that and all I could do was stare at him and try to look like I knew what the hell was going on.

"You're right," I replied, hoping I didn't sound too stupid.

"I've been in love with you from the first day I walked into the *Record*," he said.

My mouth dropped open and then slammed shut at least three times, but not a word slipped out.

I always liked Harry. In fact, when he first started at the *Record* we teamed up on a story about police departments living off the proceeds of property confiscated in narcotics cases, even if the subject was found innocent. It won a New Jersey Press Association award for us and it got me more than just a little interested in Harry.

He was sexy. He was smart. He was everything a girl could ask for. But he also was married.

"Married," I finally mumbled. "You're married."

"Not for long," he said, "at least not to Marissa. I'm going to marry you, by Jesus."

"What! I… I…."

"And the least you can do is have dinner with me so we can talk about it."

"Where? I mean, yes. Of course… for dinner."

"The Villa Barone in Collingswood," he said.

So the Villa Barone it was. I left my car at the Record and we drove over in Harry's old MGB.

His story was simple enough, but I've also learned enough about relationships and emotional entanglements to know that they are never really simple.

Short, plump, foul-mouthed Marissa Rutledge was — how best to say it — a cow, and a singularly ill-tempered cow at that. She hated blacks, hated Jews, hated gays, and had never read a book. These qualities might have made her a first rate far right political candidate out in Kansas but they definitely made her the wrong partner for Harry.

"Why did we stay together all those years?" Harry asked rhetorically.

"When I first got to South Jersey, I was going to school almost full time. I had a lot of academic ground to make up. And I was working pretty hard at journalism. I basically shut Marissa out of my life. I mean, there was nothing we could talk about."

"Not school? Not your work?"

"Are you kidding?"

Harry and I were off and running. Just when I'd finally decided that I didn't need to find Mr. Right after all, when I'm settled into my place in Haddon Heights and my diamond thriller is progressing and generating some interest from a couple of publishers, here comes Harry.

He's been right in front of me all along and now he tells me he's been in love with me for years.

Like I said, the life of a girl reporter is never boring.

CHAPTER SIXTY-THREE

A PERFECT PAIR

Joel and Susanna were delighted when Althea introduced them to Harry Rutledge and told them they were going to be married.

Joel liked him instantly, and they had a lot in common. Harry loved history, too.

Most of all, Joel liked that Harry thought Althea walked on water.

"They complement each other perfectly," he told Susanna. "And they kind of remind me of us."

CHAPTER SIXTY-FOUR

LIFE WITH HARRY

Harry moved in with me last week and I'm happier than I've ever been. It's funny. I never wondered whether I'm in love with him, and I never doubted that he loves me. It's just something that's there and we both know it and we don't have to say it. But, of course, we do say it because neither of us can believe how lucky we are to have found each other.

And what's even stranger is Harry does the same annoying things Mark did — like leaving the toilet seat up and constantly changing channels when we're watching TV. But they're not annoying when he does them. In fact, they're kind of endearing. If he were perfect, he'd be a real pain in the ass.

For the first time in my life, I feel completely understood, although I must admit Harry sees me as better than I am. He sees me the way I wish I could be. Who knows? Maybe I'll live up to what he expects. I just don't want to come crashing down from the pedestal he's put me on. He says not to worry, that won't ever happen. I believe him.

I've never felt this right about anything in my life. Our only regret is that we waited so long to get together.

If he'd only said something sooner, we wouldn't have wasted all those years. And, I would have avoided that whole fiasco with Mark Steinfeld.

Sometimes we talk about what might have happened if I'd invited him in for a drink when he dropped me off after the day we spent in Trenton interviewing the attorney general.

He says he should have asked to use my bathroom. Then I would have offered him a drink and we would have ended up in bed.

On the other hand, maybe we wouldn't have because I really have this thing about not getting involved with married men.

Of course, Harry turned out to be different.

It does seem a shame that we lost all those years together. But maybe we needed to grow separately first. There were probably things we needed to do before we got together.

And, I wouldn't have found Finnigan.

CHAPTER SIXTY-FIVE

ALTHEA'S WEDDING

When Joel went to Althea's wedding, he thought she was the most radiant bride he'd ever seen — besides Susanna, of course.

"She looks a bit like you did when we first met," he told Susanna. "Or am I imagining it? Maybe I'm just being a sentimental old fool. But so what? At my age, I think I'm entitled."

Joel enjoyed watching Althea become the woman she could be. And he liked to think he had a little to do with helping her along.

CHAPTER SIXTY-SIX

HOWDY, HOOTIE

Joel Finnigan is, above all things, irrepressible, and not even the stroke that weakened his right leg could bring him to a complete halt.

Fortunately, only his leg was damaged. His mind is as sharp as ever and he really only lost about two weeks of work. He has assumed the mantle of Professor Emeritus, which he insists is just Latin for 'old fart', and he limped back to his desk the same day he came home from the hospital.

He's working on a new book titled, I swear, the *Geezer's Guide to the 20ᵗʰ Century*. He says he wants to make sure the people of his age fully realize all they lived through: the Great Depression, World War II, the civil rights movement, the assassinations and, finally, the hillbilly's 'Contract on America.'

"There are too damned many of us who don't realize what we accomplished. Too busy, I guess," he said.

Joel is never one to just sit at his desk and make pronouncements. He needs to be out, as close to the action as he can get, and that's just where I found him.

I hadn't seen him in a couple of months. We've kept in touch by telephone and e-mail, but I was settling into my new life as an old married lady and Joel was busy with Susanna and his *Geezer's Guide*; so neither of us ever really found the time to cross the Delaware River.

But one night, I had to go over to the Airport Sheraton to cover a speech by Hootie Harlan, a congressman from Mississippi who was campaigning for one of the far right candidates in the Republican primary.

I found Joel as soon as I entered the ballroom. He was sitting at one of the press tables with his aluminum cane hung on the back of his chair and a coffee cup in his hand. He was swapping yarns with some of the younger reporters and a couple of college students.

He looked so much older than he had when we first met and began our search for Susanna. His hair was whiter and sparser than I remembered. He had lost just enough weight to appear frail and, when he stood to say hello, he leaned heavily on his cane and didn't seem quite as tall.

"Gramps, what brings you out tonight?" I asked.

"I wanted to hear this character," he said.

"You wanted to hear him? I'm getting paid to listen to him."

"Well ol' Hootie is supposed to be pretty tight with the President. It's good to know who the leader of the last superpower is listening to these days. Besides I seem to remember meeting someone named Hootie a few years ago, and I'm wondering if it's the same one."

The advance man for Hootie Harlan and Peter Starr, the Pennsylvania candidate Hootie had come to help, had been getting the crowd warmed up by the time the congressman from Mississippi was introduced. I was surprised at what a little guy he was, and for someone who spent most of his time speaking to crowds, he had a nasal, high, whiney voice.

"Good evenin,' my friends, my fellow supporters of Pete Starr to be a congressional representative from the great Commonwealth of Pennsylvania."

That alone nearly brought down the house and it was just his opening. Ol' Hootie had more.

"You know, my friends, after I leave here tonight, I have to go to a dinner over in New Jersey. Woodbury, I think it is. But it's going to take me a bit longer than it might. And do you know why, my good friends? Do you know why?"

"Why, Hootie?" someone bellowed from the back of the room.

"I'll tell you why, my good friends. It's because I'll be crossing over to New Jersey by way of the Benjamin Franklin Bridge instead of the Walt Whitman, which is more direct. Why do you think that is, my friends?"

"Why, Hootie?"

"I'll tell you why. It's because Hootie Harlan of Mississippi is not going to cross any bridge named after a flagrant, degenerate *homosexual*!"

"You tell 'em, Hootie!"

"God Bless Peter Starr!"

"In fact, my good friend Peter has assured me, given me his solemn oath, that when you send him to Washington, he's going to tear the Federal Highway Commission apart until he finds whoever it was who advanced the Homosexual Agenda by naming that beautiful bridge after that notorious faggot, Walt Whitman."

Not health care, I wondered. Not social security? But some faceless bureaucrat, now long retired or even dead, who passed on the naming of a bridge almost half a century ago.

"And do you know, my friends, when I cross the Ben Franklin Bridge, I'm going to have to say a prayer as we go past the Camden County Courthouse. Do you know why?"

"Why, Hootie?"

"Because right in the lobby of the Camden County Courthouse they have the gall to have a bust of this fag Whitman. We can't have the Ten Commandments in the courthouse, but we can have a statue of a notorious queer. Why they even have an arts center named after... who?"

"Whitman the fag," the true believers roared.

Hootie shook his head.

"My good friends, the liberal Democrats that encourage this kind of thing, that's the enemy that Pete Starr's is going to fight when you good people put him on the President's team, God's team, in Washington."

They loved it. As a member of God's team, Peter Starr would help Hootie and the President keep a lid on education spending (there's only one book anyone needs to know anyway) and on health care (to help folks get to heaven that much quicker).

"You think you know this guy?" I whispered to Joel.

"Yeah. I'm almost certain of it now. Come with me."

Joel was off, slowly and a little painfully toward the head of the room where Hootie and Peter Starr were greeting the faithful. We stood in line and by the time Joel came face to face with Hootie, he was wearing a grin of malicious glee.

"I thought I recognized you, Hootie," he said.

"Well it's sure nice to meet you, sir. Have we met before?"

"Yes. Hoskins, Mississippi… July, 1964."

"July 1964? I don't seem to recall."

Joel leaned right into Hootie's face and his voice dropped to a whisper.

"How's Junior, Hootie… and the twins.?"

Joel aimed his right index finger at a point just below Hootie's belt buckle.

"Bang. bang," he said.

"You… you… nigger-lovin' liberal," Hootie screamed as he flung his hands down to protect Junior.

The damage was done. For all their talk about compassionate conservatism and faith based initiatives, there were certain core beliefs that people like Hootie Harlan and Peter Starr could be made to expose as blatantly as any Broad Street flasher.

"I thought I recognized that little son of a bitch," Joel told me as I drove him home on my way back to the Record in Cherry Hill to write, in detail, the story of Congressman Hootie Harlan's evening in Philadelphia.

CHAPTER SIXTY-SEVEN

SEPTEMBER 10, 2001

It's been three weeks since Susanna died in her sleep, and two nights ago Joel followed. Today I was asked to give Joel's eulogy.

This is only the second time in my life that I've been at a loss for words — the first being when Harry stormed my desk and told me he loved me.

I felt both an overwhelming sense of loss and an overwhelming sense of abundance.

Loss because I'll never see those twinkling blue eyes again, or hear Finnigan's voice or share his friendship and his wisdom.

Abundance because I know Joel's irrepressibility and wisdom remain with me. I can only hope that someday I'll be able to pass them on, just as Joel did to me. They are gifts far too valuable to be allowed to die out with any one person.

I've never had a friend like Finnigan before, and I never will again.

Sure, Harry and I have something really special — more than I ever had with Finnigan in many ways. Harry is my husband, the one great love of my life and a true soul-mate. But I can't help thinking that if Joel Finnigan hadn't come into my life, I wouldn't have this wonderful relationship with Harry.

When I first met Finnigan, I asked him if he had lived a life that was true. He didn't know how to answer me then, but as I got to know Finnigan, I realized that as much as he questioned his life and doubted himself, he was the truest soul I'd ever met.

He didn't always do the things he wanted to do. But he always did the things he had to do. He always knew why he had gone through that hell in Europe, but he never fully understood why he let Susanna send him away until he saw her more than half a century later.

He wondered, too, why he'd married Connie and why he had put up with her until she left him.

The answer lay beneath a stone in a cemetery in Massachusetts.

Like most of us, maybe all of us, Joel wondered about the choices he made in life. But he never lied to himself about who he was.

He never talked himself into believing something because he wanted it to be true, the way I talked myself into believing I loved Mark and tricked him into moving in with me.

Before Finnigan, I tried desperately to control the course of my life.

Finnigan showed me how to discover who I really am. That knowledge set me free to discover what Harry and I have together, and to let the stories I'm supposed to write find me.

By becoming like Finnigan, I've been able to become myself.

But to try to describe Finnigan is doing him an injustice.

He was my friend. He was my mentor. He was my grandfather.

But mostly, he was just Finnigan.

Acknowledgements

Writing a novel can often seem like a solitary pursuit — especially when the writer is staring at a blank piece of paper. But, in reality, the birth of a book is a collaborative work.

When the book deals with historical events, as *Becoming Finnigan* does, writers and historians who have gone before us are invaluable in helping us create a world that, while fictional, still provides the essence of the reality of the times. We read a lot of the history of the times we wrote about and are grateful to all those whose research helped us set the scenes of Joel Finnigan's life. We are particularly indebted to Jules Witcover, author of *The Year the Dream Died*, a history of the traumatic year of 1968, and Stephen Ambrose who wrote *Band of Brothers*, the story of the 506th Parachute Infantry Regiment in World War II. Their exhaustive research was invaluable in writing about the events Joel Finnigan lived.

Then there is the publisher who believes in the book and says "yes" and the editor who helps make it better. We thank the fine folks at High Tide Publications.

Special thanks to Carl and Jeanne Johansen and to Narielle Living who we were fortunate to have as our editor. Jeanne and Narielle, both talented novelists themselves, provided helpful insights. Jeanne's cover design captured the essence of the story, and Narielle's skilled eye made *Becoming Finnigan* better than when we put it into her capable hands. Thank you also, Narielle, for being our mentor in the world of publishing.

Thank you to relatives and friends who read our work and encouraged us. We are so fortunate to have you in our lives.

And we want to acknowledge each other. It wouldn't be the same book if either of us had written it alone.

ABOUT THE AUTHORS

Karen and Tony Muldoon have been writing partners for many years. They are award-winning journalists who have worked on the staffs of several daily newspapers.   Tony also has written for numerous magazines, including Sail, Cruising World, Good Old Boat, Professional Mariner, Chesapeake Bay Magazine and Spinsheet. Karen is an award-winning poet and an accomplished photographer and artist.

   In addition to *Becoming Finnigan*, Karen and Tony are at work on two more novels.

   They live in Hampton, Virginia.

   Their website address is www.readmuldoon.com

www.ingramcontent.com/pod-product-compliance
Lightning Source LLC
Chambersburg PA
CBHW071523260626
47170CB00002B/477